doctors

and

other

casualties

doctors
and
other
casualties

STEWART
MASSAD

WARNER BOOKS

A Time Warner Company

Warner Books, Inc., 1271 Avenue of the Americas, New York, NY 10020
W A Time Warner Company

Printed in the United States of America
First Printing: March 1993
10 9 8 7 6 5 4 3 2 1

Library of Congress Cataloging-in-Publication Data
Massad, Stewart.
    Doctors and other casualties / by Stewart Massad.
    p.   cm.
    ISBN 0-446-51683-X
    1. Physicians—Fiction.   I. Title.
PS3563.A7996D6   1993
813'.54—dc20   92-54095
                                                    CIP

Book design by Giorgetta Bell McRee

To Peggy

Like me, a casualty.

doctors
and
other
casualties

dreams of a doctor's wife

*W*hen I was young, I dreamed that love was free. It was a soft, plush garment I luxuriated in. It left me peaceful and warm but had no other consequences.

Then my friend Louise had an abortion. "Had an abortion"—a clean phrase, so simple to say, so clinical, so deceptive. I remember the way that it really was: scenes with her boyfriend, scenes with her parents, gossip in the classrooms. I remember her lying on my bed, across the old worn quilt that smelled of little girl's perfume, as I watched her sobs shake apart our sheltered world. Louise taught me that babies are blowouts on the fast lane of life.

I developed a horror of pregnancy. The sight of deformed women in maternity clothes filled me with panic. I got fitted for a diaphragm, bought condoms, and went on the pill. Sex took on the extra thrill of high-stakes gambling.

Years after, I met a man I loved so much he frightened me. When I saw him on the street, I lost my way. I clung to his body like it was my own salvation. I asked him about babies. We made great plans about the children we'd have, thought up names for them, told stories about them. But those babies were safe fantasies, dreams dismissed and recalled at whim. They weren't real; they were my metaphor for commitment. He embraced them and married me.

Those dreams we deferred. John was in medical school, and I had to work so we could eat and pay the landlord. Then John was in an obstetrics residency; he made a little money, but when his student loans came due we had less than before. Home from work, John used to tell me of junkies and whores who had babies, but we could never afford one. Our neighbors had children, but we could never find the time. I collected months of wasted fertility like losing lottery tickets. I grew convinced that I was barren, even while I kept taking the happy little colored pills that kept me sterile. I ate them out of habit, hopelessly, day after day after month after year.

In the last winter of my husband's residency, I quit the contraceptives. I made love to him religiously. I wrapped myself around his body and tried to draw my sustenance from him. I lay in the dark with my hips tipped up while he slept, holding his seed inside me and dreaming of my pregnant future.

But he was away too often for me to succeed: away on call, away looking for a practice, away at conferences, just away. Even when he was home, I was alone; I lost him to sleep, or to his private world of women's diseases. And I found that part of me was grateful, for at the end of each month, the first stain was a sudden, welcome dispensation.

John signed on that spring with an upstate New York gynecology group. Looking for a place to live, we drove through all the suburbs of our new hometown—so friendly and green after the city. He fell in love with a house in the hills south of the hospital. After our fourth-floor Washington Heights walk-up, it was enormous, with separate rooms for dining and living, dressing, sleeping, and bathing, with walk-in closets and a two-car garage, with shrubs and a lawn and a redwood fence all around.

"What do you think?" he asked me as we drove back to Brooklyn.

"It's so big," I said.

He put his hand on my thigh and gave me a squeeze. "We'll fill it," he said. "You'll see."

I put a hand on his. Afraid that he was wrong, worried he might be right, I sat in silence and watched the Mohawk River scenery pass us by.

At the end of June, movers took our bed away. I kissed my husband good-bye and followed it up the Thruway. I filled up time cleaning and unpacking. I was too dirty to meet the neighbors, but they barged in anyway, so nice they made me cry.

After a week, I drove back to New York City. I picked up John at the ugly urban hospital he swore he'd never see again. We drove all night. On the Ocracoke ferry, the diesel's throb put him to sleep. I left him and went on deck to watch the little island spread out across the bow rail. Later, ashore, after oysters and Chablis, we made love on the lumpy mattress of the bed and breakfast by the lighthouse. Listening to the sighs of surf and wind and sex, I conceived.

From the age of thirteen, I had been as regular as a lunar clock. My cycles had become one of the rhythms of my life. Now, suddenly, the rhythms stopped, and like a woman who'd played musical chairs until her attention lapsed, I was left standing alone.

In my new home, in a strange city, I had no doctor and no desire to strip for one of my husband's partners. Instead I got a blood test from Planned Parenthood. Their waiting room was filled with nervous teenage girls snapping gum, haggard matrons of thirty-odd, screaming children, and a few sleazy-looking men. My test was positive.

"Now, as I'm sure you know," the counselor began, "you have several pregnancy options. Of course, you can keep the pregnancy and raise the child. However, should you be unable to, for whatever reason—"

"Actually," I interrupted, "it's good news."

"Oh?" she said. Her tired face brightened. "That's great. Congratulations."

"Thanks."

She frowned, professional again.

"Now, do you have an obstetrician?" she asked.

"Sort of," I said, joking with her, thinking of John. "I don't see him very often."

"Well, it's very important that you start your prenatal care right away and keep up with it faithfully." Her voice took on the exasperated patience of a grade-school teacher remonstrating with a refractory child. "We don't want any complications, now, do we?"

"No," I said. "I'll take care of it."

Her eyes were skeptical. "If there's anything we can do . . ." she offered perfunctorily.

"That's all right," I said. Her lips tightened. She wrote me off as one more hopeless case and called the next woman. I went out into the street.

Conception was inconvenient. I hadn't found a job, and suddenly it seemed pointless to look. I didn't get morning sickness, but I lost my appetite. I slept all the time. I'd get up to fix John breakfast and see him off to work, then go back to bed. Hours later I'd wake up feeling like someone's inflatable bedroom toy with the air let out. Still, if nothing else moved me, I had to get up to pee. My life became centered around sleep and urination. Of course, there were always things to do, and I got them done—God knows how. Dust settled in empty rooms as fast as I wiped it away. There were toilets to clean, meals to prepare, boxes to unpack and throw away. It was too late to start a garden, too hot to work the unkempt flower beds. Inside the cocoon of my home, I underwent a housewife's metamorphosis.

I spent hours writing letters to the friends I'd left behind in New York. They wrote back with pages of advice and droll stories. Some days I roused myself to walk next door and see my neighbors, but none of them were homegirls—none knew Bensonhurst from Bedford-Stuy. To them, my tales of city life were exotic, and their closed suburban rounds seemed insupportable to me.

For two months I kept my secret from my husband. An obstetrician's wife knows how tenuous early pregnancy is. She hears all the tales of hemorrhage and tears, and she knows that miscarriage is part of womanhood's routine. Fearful that my baby might reject me, I was afraid to raise false hopes in my husband. When I did tell him, he was surprised. He took me out to dinner. We ate rich food by candlelight. I almost fell asleep on my plate, but he was so sweet I just had to stay awake. Once home, I passed out on the bed in my underwear.

John's surprise amazed me, but looking back, I understand. Being junior partner in a busy practice meant that he was away from home as much as he had been during residency. Office hours ran on into his free evenings. During some call nights, he was able to slip away for dinner, but not often. It seemed that he was working all the time, either on call and up all night, or just off call and exhausted, or about to go back on call and sleeping in anticipation. We had no time to talk, no time to plan.

It was worse than residency, except for the money. Even after the mortgage company and the tax man took their bites, we had thousands left at the end of every month. John bought new suits, but I wasn't ready for maternity clothes. We bought new furniture and gave back the Salvation Army specials we'd lived with all through the years. We bought carpets and water-colors, a microwave, a food processor, a CD player, a VCR, a new TV. I sat around in the vacuum of my days, caring for a stranger's home.

Our house was in a development recently built, and like any newborn, the neighborhood had no personality. Inhabited by WASPs, lapsed Catholics, and assimilated Jews, it lacked ethnicity. The lots had been homogenized by bulldozers. The unweathered houses stood out awkwardly against the pastoral landscape. But down the old rural road at the foot of the hill were dairy farms, with cows and cornfields, blue silos and red barns. On sunny days in the early fall, as my strength returned, I wandered that way. I went alone, never far. Things I had learned in ecology camp during Catskill summers came back to me: the names of birds and trees, the quiet of an unmown meadow, the coolness of a shadowed forest. I stood in the sun for ages, leaning against aluminum pasture gates. The cattle and I watched each other ruminate. A path along a stream led through fields and into woods where hemlocks leaned low over waters that burbled down a stair-step cascade. I sat under maples on the ridgetop, listening to the wind sigh through the trees while squirrels chased each other through last year's leaves. I bought a guidebook to flowers and sat against roadside fence posts with bouquets in my lap. I filled my house with black-eyed Susans and Queen Anne's lace.

One evening, bathing after love, I ran my hands over my belly and first felt the swelling womb that held my child. It was no larger than a swollen bladder, just a fullness above the bone. I stood before the mirror but could not see it—neither it nor the swelling of my breasts that made them sore. With eyes closed, I passed my fingers down my body; though I was still myself, its changes were clear. I slid back into bed full of wonder and cuddled up against my sleeping husband. I fell asleep already dreaming.

It's strange how sterile an obstetrician's office is. Lost fish trolled about in a cold aquarium. On the walls hung impressionist cityscapes in steel frames and posters admonishing those of us who were with child not to smoke or drink alcohol or take drugs or ignore the innumerable warning signs of premature labor. There was a little notice by the receptionist's window advising everyone how simple life would be if all charges were paid in full at the time services were rendered. I filled out the intake forms. A nurse drew my blood. I peed into a cup. The obstetrician examined me. He was a gentle man in a white coat, a little older than my husband, with many more lines in his face. We reviewed the schedule of prenatal visits and set a due date for early April. He patted me on the knee and told me everything would be fine. I told him to save the bullshit for bubbleheads. He smiled in an infinitely tired way. After that we got along nicely.

Since I was downtown, I went window-shopping. Like all women, I had worn good clothes to the doctor's office, though he never saw me in them. At all the upscale boutiques I wandered through, the salespeople were quite polite, but they had nothing that suited me. I bought John a scarf because I had heard that the winters were had upstate. I found myself in a bookstore. Its basement was stacked with old volumes, the air there scented with mildew and old glue. I drove home and spent the afternoon reading in a sundress, my bare feet buried in my deep green lawn. I turned the sprinkler on and fell asleep as it played across my legs.

October brought the first frosts. The chill air revived me. I filled the house with plants: Swedish ivy in hanging baskets, herbs in kitchen planters, ficus trees in pots by the door. I dug up and reset the neglected bulbs along the foundation wall and pruned the hawthorns along the fence. I bought books by Julia Child and carried out French chemistry experiments in my kitchen. I made friends with the village librarian. We met for lunch at the diner where the railroad depot once had been. We talked for hours about women's books and the stories of our lives.

The hills doffed their drab summer dresses to put on pert skirts in the pointillistic colors of autumn: the ash's purple, the gold of a beechwood, swamp maples' scarlet, an orange sugarbush, and the evergreen of a Christmas tree plantation across the valley. The cornstalks faded to yellow, and combines turned the fields to stubble where southbound geese in ragged vees flew down to feed. In the pastures, Holsteins huddled in the lee of young pines. All through the nights, the north wind blew.

We were invited to dinner with John's partners. I wore a loose dress that almost hid my pregnancy. Before the meal, the men stood about drinking single-malt Scotch and talking about sick women. I sat with the wives and listened to stories of their pregnancies. Though John disapproved, I drank a glass of wine to hide my shyness. The unfamiliar alcohol made me giddy. The food was marvelous, the china exquisite, the conversation pleasantly dull. We sat up too late, and by the time we left I felt achy and ill. In the car, John put an arm around my shoulders, but I could not stand his touch. I made him stop the car. I threw up in the weeds and wiped my mouth on the sleeve of my gown. At home, I changed into a comfy old robe. John sat up, dosing me with weak tea until I dozed off. When I woke he had gone for the day, and I cried away my lonely morning.

There is nothing more useless than a sick pregnant woman. I had a cold all that week and lived through it in bed, bored to tears whenever I was well enough to think. I added antipyretics and decongestants to my hemorrhoid creams, my antacids, and those noxious prenatal vitamins whose extra iron kept me constipated. I grieved for the miscarriage I dreamed was coming. I imagined all the deformities my virus might cause the fetus I carried. When I told my husband my fears, he laughed them away.

I got into maternity clothes by degrees. At first I just kept my shirttails out and my jeans unsnapped. Then the time came when I could no longer zip my trousers, so I wore my husband's sweat pants until I had grown as formless as they. At the end I bought a bulbous dress and pants whose broad elastic band pressed furrows into the flesh and fat where my waist once had been.

On Thanksgiving I stuffed a turkey. With my little belly pouching out, I felt equally distended.

For the sake of the baby's baptism, I went to church each Sunday. I went alone; even when not on call, John saw his postoperative patients every morning and never came home before noon. Inside, the church was the dark color of old wood, dim with stained glass. I used to chat with the pastor on Sunday mornings when the weather was fine. From the church door, we looked down on the old country village that the suburbs were engulfing. We looked out over bare trees, gas station signs, clapboard houses, and the limestone Town Hall.

Advent was a season of sleet and cold. The sky seemed always gray, and the stripped black boles of trees stood out wet and stark against the fallen leaves. Cardinals and damp chickadees gathered at the feeder I hung outside my kitchen window. One afternoon a bearded man dressed in wet wool backed into our drive with his pickup full of cordwood: my husband's surprise for me. John, my big Boy Scout, taught me to lay a fire, and on dark afternoons I used to sit before the flames, reading and dreaming my life away.

In those days John was away before sunup and never back before dark. He came home loaded down with stories of difficult surgical problems he and his partners had solved, stories of whining women, of obese and ugly women, of spoiled women who demanded the impossible and thought that threatening John with suits at law might extort miracles from God. Compared with his, my troubles were trivial, so I kept them to myself. He told me of pretty nurses with nice names. I wondered about the strength of his fidelity, but there was little I could do save tie his scarf around his neck each morning when I kissed him good-bye and rock him in my arms on those nights he managed to come home.

Just before Christmas, it moved. I was rinsing dishes for the washer when I realized that the sensation in my belly was more than shifting gas. I put my hand to my womb, but it was still. I came to know that the movements happened only at inconvenient times, the unborn child already demanding my attention.

Over the holidays John could not get time off, and he was on call all Christmas day. We could not get away to visit my parents, so they came to us, driving up from Jersey on highways packed with migrant relatives. Dad and John bought our first live tree. They dragged the smell of balsam into our living room, and we hung the boughs with decorations from my youth. Afterward we sat around reminiscing about my babyhood, and John heard all the stories of my first words, my first steps, my first falls. They seemed as fresh in my mother's memory as though I were still toddling about in the next room, not sitting up before her and listening, nearly six months gone with a child of my own.

After Epiphany, the real snows came. There had been squalls before, eight inches or a foot that kept the road crews busy overnight, then melted away after a week or so, leaving patches of white on the north slopes of hills and the shady sides of buildings. In January, though, the powder piled up. It grew too cold to walk, and I grew too big to keep my balance in the deep drifts along the road. I stayed at home and put on weight, with my baby tumbling about inside of me. The snow sifted down day by day. The dark sky lowered, and we brooded together.

Once each month I went to the obstetrician's office. Through the electric stethoscope I heard my baby's heartbeat race along, with my own slow, dull pulse for a background beat. One day the doctor wheeled in his portable ultrasound machine and went about the tedious business of counting arms and legs. They were all there, with no supernumerary babies alongside the one I was coming to know.

"Do you want to know whether it's a boy or a girl?" he asked me.

"No," I said. "I want it to be a surprise."

"You're sure?"

I nodded. "And don't tell John," I warned him. "The man couldn't keep a secret to save his life."

I was filled with pregnant dreams, and every day my dreams changed. I made up lives for my child—dull lives, eventful lives, tragic and glorious lives. I imagined how it would look, how it would grow. I imagined how I would carry it, how it would suckle, how it would cry. I wondered if it could ever love me.

By the first of February I felt ready to burst. My ankles were puffy, my back always sore. I waddled about like an obese penguin and laughed at my own reflection whenever I passed by big mirrors in our dressing room. The more awkward I grew at love, the more I came to need it. I kept my husband up nights when we should have been sleeping, I made love on my knees with my butt in the air, my baby beneath me and my exhausted husband draped across my broad back.

March brought shopping and baby showers. The wives of John's partners gave me all sorts of gifts for the kid: designer clothes, mobiles from the Met, rattles, and fashionable little teething toys I mistook for rawhide dog bones. My mother made the rounds of my downstate cousins and mailed me

cartons of utilitarian hand-me-downs. We bought a state-of-the-
art stroller and a gross of diapers. John rearranged his study to
hold a crib and bassinet.

One afternoon, when all the bookshelves were dusted and
all the vacuuming done, I sat watching the wan sun on the snow
with my hand on my belly. At first I thought it was just the
baby flexing to kick my bladder once again. But the baby was
still; I was moving. Like a long, leisurely yawn, my womb rose
and tightened, grew firm, and relaxed. I broke into a sweat and
couldn't move, convinced that I was about to break into labor
weeks before my time. I had visions of my baby crucified in an
incubator, taped to a respirator, tangled up in intravenous
tubing. I sat and sat, but no more contractions came that day. I
walked on eggs all week, afraid to disturb my sleeping womb.
But after a while contractions got old, just another annoyance,
like leaky boobs and trick ankles.

I asked my husband about a name.

"Well," he said, "is it a boy or a girl?"

"Which do you want?" I asked him.

"A boy," he said. It was the wrong answer. I wanted sugar
and spice, not snails and puppydog's tails.

"You would," I said.

"What's that supposed to mean?"

"Still," I went on, "I guess we could use a man around this
house."

"Oh, so that's how it is. You loaf around and gestate all
day while I work like a slave, and you have the nerve to say
that."

"You couldn't gestate if you tried," I told him.

After a while he realized that I was teasing him. He can be
so slow sometimes. He came and sat beside me. He kissed me
once, and we were okay again.

Near the end, I lost control. Whenever I happened to drop a
plate, or read about human rights abuses, or remember my dead
grandparents, I fell to weeping. One sleety night John called me
to tell me he was coming home. Hours went by, and he didn't
show up. I saw him dead in his car, saw him all alone in some

emergency room. When he came in and started to explain about a stat cesarean section, I exploded. I cursed his thoughtlessness so long that I drove him back out into the storm. After he had driven back to his damn hospital, I cried myself to sleep. That next night he came home with roses, and I sobbed on his chest till he took me to bed.

The tempo of my obstetric office visits picked up: bi-monthly, then weekly. I got bigger and bigger, but nothing else changed. My feet swelled, my face grew fat, my breasts became enormous. I used my belly to push my way through crowds; everyone gave way for such a huge cow.

The waxing sun melted salt into the winter wounds of the frost-cracked country roads. Crocus bulbs I'd set along the drive sprouted up through dead leaves and crusted snow. Mated cardinals chased around the yard. Sap buckets sprouted from roadside trees. The ground was sodden, and seeping water ran in rivulets and rills over all the land. The south wind smelled of manure and the gravid earth.

After John got into a shouting fight with the instructor over the importance of monitoring, I went to childbirth classes alone. It was hard being my own coach, trying to rub my own back and yell "Breathe! Breathe!" while blowing my lungs out. All the other couples pitied me, the absent obstetrician's wife, but I didn't give a damn. I knew things they'd never know. We toured the delivery rooms. Our guide showed us a pair of forceps.

"What are those for?" the woman beside me whispered.

"They're to pull the baby out," I told her.

"The doctor puts those things *inside* you?" she asked. Her eyes were bugging out.

"Sure," I said. "And by the time he does, honey, believe me, you'll be grateful."

My due date came and went. My mother, who'd come to stay with me while John kept working, was not surprised. I'd been born a week late myself, she told everyone, and I'd never caught up.

Nothing lasts forever, though. One night soon after, sometime between midnight and dawn—God knows just when—I started cramping. I got up without waking my husband, since the poor dear had been up all the night before. I went downstairs to fix a cup of tea and walk off my aching. The contractions eased, and I napped awhile on the sofa. I woke up in pain.

"They're getting bad," I told my husband.

"Huh?"

"The contractions. They're getting pretty strong."

"How often are they?" he asked.

"I don't know," I said. "But they hurt more than they ever did before."

"Yeah, but that can go on for days."

"Shit."

"Are you leaking any fluid?"

"No," I admitted.

He sat up and handed me his watch from the bedside table. Then he flopped back and pulled a pillow over his head.

"Wake me up again when they're every four minutes or when your water breaks," he said. "Till then, keep walking."

So I walked until my feet hurt. The contractions got closer and closer. I concentrated on my breathing—slow in, blow out: puff, puff, puff. Each contraction was a big wave that swept down into my pelvis. It built and peaked and held and ebbed away. I sat down on the floor with my head between my knees to get to know them.

I was still sitting there like that at five when John came down.

"What the hell are you doing?" he asked.

"Four and a half minutes," I said, holding out his watch and rocking myself with the pain.

"Jesus Christ," he said, "what a nut you are."

He woke my mother and carried me out to the car. We drove in to the hospital with the new sunrise. All the darkness faded out of the beautiful spring sky. I didn't notice a damn thing.

John left me with a nurse and went off to see a few patients before his operating room opened. My mother went off to call my dad. I struggled out of my clothes and put on a flimsy cotton thing. I was sweating pretty hard. Thelma, my nurse, was a big black lady in blue scrubs. She strapped me to a monitor and checked my cervix.

"Girl," she said, "you done good. You're more than halfway there."

She left me to call the obstetrician. I was left alone with the sound of my baby's heartbeat booming out of an amplifier till a technician came in to draw my blood and start an intravenous line.

My doctor was in a delivery room with another woman. When he came out, I was pretty far gone. The distinct little waves of my contractions had become a maelstrom. I curled up on my side and let them sweep me away. It was all I could do to come up for air. The obstetrician checked my cervix several times. I didn't care if he did—I just fell on my back with my gown up around my breasts, my knees up, and my ass bare. He broke my bag of waters, and all the waves I'd been riding spewed out of me.

By the time I was clean again, it was time to push. My mother had a washcloth, and she bathed my face between contractions. I was working hard, the baby driving down as if to cleave me from inside. I was ready to quit, but I just couldn't refuse my poor mother each time she cradled me up for another big heave.

John came by between hysterectomies. "How are you doing?" he asked.

"You son of a bitch," I gasped. "How do you think I'm doing?"

We conversed in that vein for a while, so people would know we were married. Then he had to go off to his next case.

The rest of us proceeded soon after to the delivery room. I was the only one who got to ride, though I'd just as soon have skipped the whole thing. My mother looked hilarious in her oversize cap and mask, but somehow I just couldn't manage to laugh.

These days it seems every child has the honor of its father's presence at its birth, except for bastards and obstetricians' babies. I realized that John would not be there and began to cry.

"There, honey," said my nurse, "those pains'll all be over soon. You just bear up a little longer."

I couldn't explain my tears to her. I just reached out. My mother took my hand and held me.

Then I went back to work, pushing and grunting and squealing and sweating like a hog. Everyone was shouting instructions I couldn't understand. I was insane, I was lost, I was dying. In fact, I wasn't even there: all this madness was happening to someone else's body far away from me.

"Oh, my God," I gasped as I felt myself split in two. I collapsed onto the hard table pad. I looked up. The doctor's eyes were smiling at me over his mask.

"The head's out," he said. "One more push and we're done."

I took a slow breath in and bore down. Very slowly, very gently, my body turned itself inside out, and my world turned to crystal.

The baby was pink, smeared with blood and shiny with fluid. It wrinkled up its nose and cried.

I dropped back again, exhausted.

"I'll be God damned," said a voice by my ear. "That kid's so ugly it's got to be mine." I twisted around. "Yeah," he said, in answer to the question on my face, "it's me. Late again, but better that than never."

"Damn you," I whispered, and kissed my husband's hand. "Is it all right?" I asked him.

"She's a girl. Otherwise she looks fine."

I stared into his face.

"You knew," I said. He only smiled and kissed my mouth hard.

My daughter kept on crying while the nurse swaddled her. My mother was teary. I was blubbering.

"Women," John said proudly to the obstetrician while we all waited for the placenta. "What am I going to do with another one on my hands?"

"You hush," said Thelma. "Everybody here knows you're in trouble. We all know you never could handle what you've got at home as it is."

The afterbirth flopped out like a wet jellyfish. After that we had only twenty minutes of suturing—only that and twenty years till I found out which of my pregnant dreams would finally come true.

change

Change comes, even to eastern North Carolina. Old patterns, old structures that I came to know, growing up in Tartan, are lost now. It seems everyone I know is divorced, and the children leave town as soon as they can afford the down payment on a secondhand car. Soybeans drove cotton from our fields years ago, and the marijuana that grows back in the pocosin woods brings in more money than tobacco ever could. The Southern Line pulled up tracks the year I finished residency. The mills have all closed; the mortar in their brickwork crumbles away under a pitiless sun. Convenience stores have replaced general stores. Racism is a thing of the past, too: black folk here keep to themselves, and we do the same; no more demonstrations, no more lynchings.

Tartan Hospital hasn't changed much. The words *colored* and *white* are still legible under the paint on the bathroom doors, and the wards are still segregated, if only by the price of the private rooms. But for fifteen years there's been a federally subsidized clinic at the Davis Crossroads that serves black and white the same. It needs a gynecologist badly these days, but I turned forty-eight last spring, too old for the changes that kind of practice brings. The clinic limps along with two family practitioners and a resident who drives there from the university medical center in Greenville once a week. I used to visit the clinic often, to see a doctor who once worked there, so I know how it is. In the overfilled waiting room, rows of pregnant women sit on folding chairs under a single ceiling fan. In the little exam rooms the lamps are broken, the specula rusted, the vinyl pads on the exam tables stained and torn. The nurses are inept, or maybe just exhausted. The air is full of the wails of bored, hungry children and the smell of hair straightener and unwashed clothes. No, I'm too old to dream that I could ever make a difference there.

The clinic did have a doctor once who had that dream. Not that she wanted to be there—at least not at first. The National Health Service sent her to Tartan, to serve out the four years she owed for the medical school tuition the government had paid. She'd wanted to work up north, she told me later, Maine, maybe, or Montana. But her application had been lost in files in Washington, and between the strains of residency night call and the end of her marriage, she forgot the matter until her assignment to Tartan came, irrevocable.

She arrived early one July in a new green Volvo wagon, straight from Boston. She moved into Mrs. Tripp's converted carriage house, the closest thing to an apartment in the only part of Tartan where a white woman could live alone.

Her name was Rachel Polonowicz, a Yankee name that no one around here could ever pronounce or spell, so that from the first she was always just "the lady doctor." It was a simple title that was clear enough, since she was the only one in three counties.

I heard about her first day at work from the clinic's head nurse, Rita McComb, who'd been two years behind me at Tartan High, back in the days when white kids still went there. Rachel came to work in a long white coat with her hair down over her shoulders. By noon the midsummer heat had stripped her to sundress and sandals. She had her hair up in borrowed bobby pins, with sweat spread in a long stain down her spine.

She worked till past six, struggling with the dialect, learning from the black nurse's aides in their blue pinafores the meaning of words like "ministrate" and the differences between sprangling pains and drawing ones.

The diseases she saw were familiar enough, though, from her work in the Boston ghetto; premature labor, drug abuse, gonorrhea, obesity, toxemia, obscure hurts, the marks of beatings, neglected tumors, neglected lives. She met Leitha Mae Jeffers, a fat mother of eight in her thirty-fourth week of pregnancy. The woman sat on the end of an exam table with her torn panties in her hand while Rachel thumbed through her chart.

"You haven't been here since May," Rachel said.

"No, ma'am," Leitha May admitted, her eyes downcast.

"Why not? Don't you know you should be coming in every week when you're this pregnant and forty-one years old?"

"Yes, ma'am, I knows," said Leitha Mae.

"Well then? Don't you care about your baby?"

"Yes, ma'am. It's just I been doing for my other babies. I ain't had no ride till today."

"Isn't there anybody to help?"

"No, ma'am."

"Nobody? What about your husband?"

"He in Raleigh."

"Raleigh? Why isn't he here? Doesn't he know you need help?"

"Yes, ma'am. He know."

"Then why doesn't he help you?"

Leitha Mae just stared at her puffed ankles till the nurse's aide spoke up.

"Ma'am," she murmured. "He's in prison, ma'am."

I met Rachel during that first week. I was in the little delivery suite at Tartan Hospital, where I spend most of my time when I'm not in the office across the street or in surgery downstairs. I'd been called in to check on Jody Corbett, who was, as it turned out, starting the last night of her first pregnancy. I wandered back to the delivery room, looking for a nurse. There was Rachel, with blood on her gown and a newborn baby in the crook of her arm. She clamped and cut the umbilical cord. When the blood spurted, she turned her face away and saw me watching from the doorway.

Her black hair was tucked up inside her surgical cap, with wisps of her curls twining out around her face. Her eyes were dark, with long dark lashes; above her mask, they smiled at me.

She turned back to the child, sucking the fluid from its mouth with a blue rubber bulb while it squirmed and cried. She held it up to its mother, but the woman—exhausted, wet, and shivering, her legs up in stirrups and her privates exposed—kept her arms over her eyes, cursing softly. I turned away.

Later, when Rachel was out of the delivery room, I introduced myself. She was cleaned up, save for little gouts of blood on the cuffs of her scrub pants.

"I've heard about you," I said, introducing myself. "You don't know how glad I am to see you."

"I'll bet," she said. She knew that I'd been backing up the clinic's family physicians since her predecessor had left.

I showed her into the doctors' lounge, which was also the men's locker room; Rachel had to change with the nurses. I turned on the television, while Rachel filled out her patient's chart. She started asking me questions about the hospital. I warned her about our radiologist and one of our two general surgeons, about the weak points of our emergency room and lab, and about the things her family practitioners had never learned about obstetrics. I didn't realize how frank I was being until she put down her chart, drew her knees up under her chin, and asked me why I stayed.

I might have told her about my grandfather's farm—my farm now, even though it's all rented out to men with gumption and fertilizer, all except my piece of yard, with twin live oaks and a white house with quiet and a verandah all around. Or I might have tried to explain the comfort I take from the cadences of our language and the tough fabric of our interwoven families. As a doctor, maybe she'd have understood the sense of belonging that comes from delivering the babies of women born into my father's hands and from solacing the many women who have trusted me down the years with their sins and secret sorrows. But pride of place, however strong, a Southern man learns early on to keep to himself.

"I guess," was all I could say, "that Tartan's the kind of town only a son could ever love. Besides, I'm too old to move."

"You're not so old," she said.

"Sister," I warned her, stretching a little and turning back to the television, "old is a state of mind. You'll learn that here."

"We'll see about that," she said, smiling to herself. She had her mouth open to say more, but then a nurse put her head in the door, asking Rachel for her patient's postpartum orders. Rachel went out, and I went back to check on Jody Corbett again. By the time I'd finished talking to the father-to-be and the mother-in-law, Rachel had gone. I stayed on, napping in front of the television until Jody was delivered of a pink little girl. I was home by three, wide awake, the blood and bright lights of the delivery room still in my eyes. A short glass of neat bourbon put me right. I caught four hours of sleep in the empty, overcooled house before the new day broke in on my dreams.

My place is on the state road between Tartan and the clinic, the road the dust blows across after the plowing in the spring, the road trucks scatter with white feathers as they haul from the chicken houses to the Perdue packing plant. Rachel took to stopping by, evenings after work when the labor suite was quiet. I'd cook steak or ribs on the backyard brick barbecue, while she sat with her feet up and her hair down. After the meal we'd sip drinks and talk till past dark. I tried to teach her to fry the catfish a patient's husband once brought by, but the sight of the fat, dark fish lying dead by the sink, its eyes still bright and its whiskers still wet, drove her onto the porch.

She asked a lot of questions and didn't talk much herself. I expect she did enough talking at the clinic, interviewing patients and cajoling nurses. She asked me about the history of our town, built at the first shoal water upriver from the Albemarle, and I told her the little there was to tell; nobody famous ever dared be born in Tartan. She asked how Tartan had figured in the War Between the Sates, and I had to admit that it never did, except that too many Tartan boys went off to die fighting it, same as they did in every war since.

She had all the Yankee preconceptions about race relations. She didn't believe me when I told her it wasn't conspiracy that kept all the aldermen and the county commissioners in Tartan white. Around Tartan, even when black folk aren't too busy or too tired, too high, or too hopeless to vote, they don't seem to hang together any better than we do. And besides, there are more of us—that's why they're called a minority.

In October I invited her to a pig picking that the First Baptists put on every year to benefit their choir. The day was fine, warm but no longer as oppressive as the summer had been. The church people set up long tables on the lawn and spread them with pots and paper plates. There were slabs of pork and piles of hush puppies, turnip greens, cabbage, fried okra, butter beans, bowls of slaw, and deep dishes of sweet-potato pie. Rachel was fascinated by the sight of the carcass butchered out beside the roasting pit, as though she'd never seen a dead hog before.

We wandered. I introduced her to cousins and their kids, old friends, my patients and their husbands. Rachel flattered all the cooks with compliments for foods she'd never tasted before.

"How many calories in all this?" she asked me, her mouth full of pecan pie.

"Enough for a full day's fieldwork," I told her.

"And how many of these nice people work in the fields?"

"Not many," I admitted, "not anymore. Used to be most of them did, women and young ones, too. But not many now."

She shook her head. "I wish it didn't taste so good," she said, "I can feel my arteries hardening already."

We strolled past the cars parked on the grass, new Buicks and Oldsmobiles, a couple of big Lincolns, the Japanese cars that the kids drove home from college. Out on the softball field, those young men and women stood about, sweating in the sun.

"Where are the blacks?" Rachel asked.

"In the kitchen," I said without thinking. When I saw her face, I bit my tongue.

We walked onto the bare sand under a sweet gum tree. I introduced Rachel to some of the church matrons talking in the shade. They all gushed over her, our lady doctor.

"How do you say your name?" asked Mrs. Peabody. Rachel sighed, used to the question, and repeated it slowly.

"How've you been getting along in Tartan so far, doctor?" Mrs. Jenks asked her.

"Pretty well, thanks," Rachel said. "It's quite a change, though."

"Dr. Polonowicz is from Boston," I told them.

"Oh, my," said Mrs. Jenks. She glanced at her friends with big eyes. "You must find us just terribly dull."

"No," said Rachel. "The work keeps me very busy, actually. I saw more than sixty women in clinic on Friday."

"Goodness," said Mrs. Hairston.

"I had no idea," said Mrs. Jenks, "although I must say that whenever I drive by on my way to visit my brother in Winton that parking lot is always full. Still, you can't be seeing as much real sickness out here in the country as you did in a big city like Boston."

"Oh, but Mrs. Jenks, you couldn't be more wrong," Rachel told her. "In Boston, people go to a doctor when they first get sick. Here I've already seen women with huge tumors, with bleeding that's gone on till they're almost too weak to walk. The infant mortality rate here is worse than Costa Rica's, and the teenage pregnancy rate is a scandal. Syphilis here is out of control, and all this week it's seemed like every woman I've examined has had a roaring dose of the clap to go along with whatever else brought her in to see me."

I could see Mrs. Jenks start to cloud over and Mrs. Hairston turn away to hide her blushes. I put a hand on Rachel's arm as she launched into a story about a gorgeous young man who'd celebrated his release from the Marine Corps by spreading herpes across half the county.

"I know things aren't what they should be in Tartan

County," I interrupted, "but I'm sure that now we've got helping hands like yours with us, things will start to change. Mrs. Jenks, Mrs. Hairston, Mrs. Peabody; it's been fine talking with you all, but the doctor hasn't tasted the ice cream I hear is being cranked in the vestibule. Won't you excuse us?"

They did, graciously and with smiles, but as we walked toward the church, over the brown Bermuda grass, the muttering started.

"Rachel," I cautioned her, "you have to be careful how you talk to folks around here."

"But it's the damned complacency that lets poor people around here get so sick," she said. "And besides, what did I say that wasn't true?"

"Sometimes you have to go along to get along. Just because something's true doesn't mean a lady has to say it."

"Shit," said Rachel. "I haven't been a lady for a long time."

"Well, if you want to be accepted in this town, you may have to go back to it. People expect it. It can't be so hard."

She turned on me.

"It's about as easy as becoming a virgin again," she snapped. She turned back toward the church and started walking away. "And about as much fun," she grumbled. "But then, I suppose these people expect that of me, too."

In November elections came and went: nothing new. Rachel talked to me about the campaign, surprised that I felt too busy to be involved, even in the local races. I learned from a patient—my attorney's wife—that Rachel had started sitting in on meetings of the county commission.

All through that winter Rachel and I scrubbed on surgery together. She put together a collection of terribly difficult cases, the kind I usually referred to Greenville or to Duke, the kind that take so long that there's no money in them. But Rachel was still young and proud, and she asked me to help. She reacquainted me with the chill fear of failure I'd long forgotten, pushing me to take risks a prudent man would surely have forgone. She made me remember skills I hadn't used in years, and I taught them to her. She taught me about new stapling techniques, new sutures, new procedures for old diseases. She had good hands, too, surprisingly good for a woman so young, but she was impatient, always so impatient.

Coming from Boston, Rachel was used to quality in medical care. I suppose she was right to have spoken up at the medical staff meetings of Tartan Hospital, though decorum and deference were expected of her. She started off by suggesting we ban smoking in the rooms of pregnant women, a droll idea that no one took seriously. Then she started criticizing the timidity of our monthly morbidity review. Of course, it was true that Dan Rainey, one of our older general practitioners, should never have sent home that pregnant girl with headaches and high blood pressure who came back convulsing and in a permanent coma. But to suggest that we revoke his obstetric privileges because of that incident and a few others, after poor Dan, with his sick wife to care for, had lost his savings in Texas real estate investments—well, that made Rachel enemies she didn't need. And in retrospect Ram Swamareshi should have checked a pregnancy test on little Keisha Buttler when she came to the emergency room with cramps. But Keisha's always been a whiner, and Rachel had her in the operating room with her ruptured tubal pregnancy out hours before the internal bleeding would have killed her. Those things happen, even in Boston, and if Rachel had been more smart than smart-ass, she'd have known that there are names a Southern man never forgets being called by a woman and a Yankee.

That was a wet winter. The floors at the clinic where Rachel worked were always slick with mud, the air full of dampness and the sound of children coughing. Every night she left after dark, always the last to go, too tired to see me as often as I might have liked.

And yet she never seemed discouraged. When I stopped by the clinic, she always could manage a smile. She listened patiently to the rambling stories that ragged illiterate women told her. She held classes for the clinic nurses, gave tutorials for her family practitioners, bought books from her pitiful little salary. She praised the posters Rita picked up from a public health nurse in Raleigh and pasted up in all the rooms. She admired aides' pictures of children in uniform and grandchildren in toddler's clothes. She rewrote the chart forms for gynecologic visits. Her enthusiasm even infected that slothful bureaucrat who was the clinic's director; he spent a week in Washington learning new guidelines for federal funding and grantsmanship, then reworked the clinic's fee structure so that the place almost paid its way that year.

Most of all, though, Rachel spent her time fighting teenage pregnancy. She traveled about the county preaching to ministers and lecturing high school sophomores about it. She was quoted in the Tartan *Tattler* and sat through an interminable interview on public radio one Saturday evening. She even lobbied the county commissioners, nagging them until they gave her a hearing.

A group of people came together around her. They met every first Wednesday in the convention room of the A.M.E. Church. They were mostly black, since white girls in Tartan by and large could afford marriage or abortion. They worked all through the winter and spring, their campaign opening out into the community as the dogwood blossomed. In May the county voted a few thousand dollars for a pilot program that paid for a Tartan County public health nurse to dispense nonprescription contraceptives and the fear of God at the high school. Rachel was very proud that night. I don't think she realized that the commissioners' vote wasn't all altruism: in Tartan there's always money to keep more pickaninnies from being born onto the welfare rolls.

I was at the commission meeting for that vote. I spoke up for Rachel, an easy enough favor, since she was right. It had been easy enough, too—though Rachel never knew—to spend my Sundays that spring calling on the commissioners, sharing their whiskey, inquiring after their children, admiring their azaleas, and persuading them to promise their votes for Rachel's cause. And when Rachel, all aglow, asked me to cover for her till morning so that she could celebrate the funding of her program with her friends, I saw no harm in it. I had to be in the hospital anyway, having been paged right before the meeting's end because one of my patients had broken her bag of water.

Rachel and her friends went to Elijah Watson's place, flushed with the congratulations of the town. I should have seen what would follow, I suppose, but I thought that Elijah had sense as well as brains, even if sometimes Rachel didn't. I'd known Elijah for years; he was from Tartan, too, and we were of an age, though he was black. Like me, he'd left Tartan in the sixties, but instead of going off to college he'd enlisted. When I left medical school for internship, he went to Vietnam. He came back after two years, drifted awhile, then joined up with radicals. He moved around the South, organizing and agitating. During holidays spent at home, I heard stories about him. He got a law degree from Howard, moved to Philadelphia, spent a year in Senegal and another in Los Angeles, married, and was divorced. Eventually, like me, he came home. He found a job in Ahoskie, and every weekday he drove his sun-blistered Cutlass there, to serve the clients of the Legal Services of the Coastal Plain.

Rachel may have believed that no one would notice, though how she could think that her Volvo was inconspicuous in Elijah's driveway at sunup, in front of the old shotgun house with its peeling paint and weedy yard, I cannot comprehend. She may never have considered the consequences, though I'm sure Elijah did. They may have thought that no one would care, that the South had changed so much. If they thought that, they were wrong. I expect that they just neither one gave a damn.

Gossips here hold that there's only one reason a white woman sleeps with a black man, but I know that she loved him. She talked about him all the time, about where he'd been and what he dreamed. Her love showed in her work, in the way that she spoke to her patients, who became for her victims, comrades, sisters. She dressed more brightly. She even let one of his nieces cornrow her hair.

Her speech softened and slowed. She learned to say "ain't," to let a handshake trail off. She learned to ask about family before business, to work up to her questions, not throw them in a body's face. She learned to call blacks "mister" and "miz" because other white folk never did.

She learned other things, too, hard things. Mrs. Tripp, her landlady, took to locking the door to the kitchen where they used to sit and chat. In surgery Rachel's cases always started late. The nurses assigned to her were the least trained, always black, and never much interested in waiting on a white girl. The special instruments she wanted were always unavailable. My mechanic, the only one in Tartan, wouldn't look at her car the day it died. He made her get it towed to the dealer in Rocky Mount, who found nothing wrong with it but an air filter clogged with the dust of the back roads she'd taken to driving with Elijah.

Still, they were happy together. He took her fishing on the Albemarle; she burned a deep brown, and the sun bleached her hair. He introduced her to people: a poetess, a woman trying to unionize poultry workers, the couple who founded the only day care cooperative in Tartan after their daughter, lost on New York drugs, sent them their grandchild by Greyhound. He took her to the state prison to meet his old friends and hear their stories. He took her to visit the toxics dump and the Haliwa reservation. They went to the museums in Halifax, Bath, and Edenton, where his people were ghosts in the panoramas, unacknowledged, omnipresent. He took her into the country, the real country, into the dark woods and swamps and scrublands, where old folk told her of segregation and stoop labor in a dialect she could scarcely understand. He took her to meetings, where he tried with patient questions to shift focus from children's pregnancies to children's hopes and opportunities, forcing the admission that Tartan held none, trying to elicit ideas for change. Coming up empty, they still persevered.

Her visits to see me tapered off; I wasn't part of their solution. Still, one night in September, like old times, her car pulled into my drive. I was on the porch, drinking bourbon on ice with no lights on. I got her a drink. She sat with me, listening to the crickets shrilling in darkness, thinking her own thoughts. I had my feet up and was rocking the night away in my grandmother's chair.

"Why did your wife leave?" she asked me, after we'd been through the pleasantries.

I thought about that awhile. God knows, I'd thought about it enough by then.

"You'd have to ask her," I said, but I knew that wasn't true. "She was bored here," I ventured, but that was wrong, too. "She was stifling here. She was born in Asheville, you know."

"I didn't know," Rachel said with her new gentleness, leaning forward to listen.

"She was used to that kind of society. She liked music and art, and there isn't much of that here. She like formal parties, and galas, and debuts, and nobody here does that. Then, too, she was from the mountains; she couldn't stand the summers."

"I can understand that," Rachel said with a wry smile.

"Sure. Well, she was fine in Chapel Hill, where I met her, and she was happy in Germany, when the army sent us there. She was marvelous in New Haven, but she was stifling here in Tartan."

"When were you in New Haven?"

"After residency. I spent a year in pathology at Yale. Back then, you know, Southern universities weren't what they are today."

"I never knew you were at Yale."

I shrugged. "Actually, they asked me to stay on."

"And you didn't?"

"I didn't belong there."

"You belonged here instead."

"My father died. We came back for the funeral. My brother and sisters had married by then and moved on—to Charlotte, Houston, and Mobile. Nobody else wanted the house. I couldn't let it go. Besides, there was no one to pick up his practice."

"He was a gynecologist, too?"

I nodded. "We weren't here long before my wife wanted us to leave. I couldn't. She couldn't stay."

We talked on into the night. The moon rose. Its light shimmered on the deep green leaves of the camellias around the porch and frosted the dusty chinaberries along the drive. I lit a citronella candle for Rachel. We listened to moths thud against the screens. After a long time and a second bourbon, she opened up. We talked about the delusions of love. I had to lie a lot to cheer her up. It grew very late. I stood up and stretched. She stood, too, stepped close, and took my hand. Her upturned face studied mine. Ever a gentleman and a fool, I could only kiss her forehead and send her home.

As the fall cooled to winter, the preachers turned on Rachel. They never called her name from the pulpit, but in a town the size of Tartan, they never had to. At first it was only one man, one of our white fundamentalists, who condemned her for promoting contraception over abstinence—though down the years his crying parishioners have confessed to me from cold exam tables that abstinence has never been his way. Then Rachel drove the high school valedictorian to Greenville for an abortion. When word of that got around, the denunciations crossed lines of race and denomination. There was nothing Elijah or I could do to help her, though we tried; here in Tartan, the wages of sin are babies, and that will never change. People stopped listening to her. Members of her little group drifted away. After the leaves fell, her pilot project came up before the commissioners for review and renewal. It never made their agenda.

Hurt, Rachel moved out to Elijah's place, scandalizing black and white together. He cooked for her, kept house for her, hung her laundry on the backyard line, under the leafless pecan tree. Her skirts flapped in the north wind that blew wood smoke over the rusty roof.

In February a pregnant speedball addict came to the hospital. She had grown too big for prostitution, and since she was broke, she was in withdrawal. Since she was withdrawing, she was in labor. When the nurses undressed her, the baby's feet were already out, and by the time Rachel arrived the child was dead, its body born but its head still entrapped. The nurses called me in. Together Rachel and I wrestled with forceps while the woman screamed and called out to Jesus. We delivered the baby, but the afterbirth refused to follow, and the patient began to hemorrhage. Rachel tried all the right manipulations and every proper drug, but the bleeding kept on. The anesthesiologist was delayed. The woman lost consciousness. In the end, her hysterectomy took three hours, for the viscera were matted together by the scars of old infections and three previous cesarean sections.

Afterward, exhausted but confident that the woman would not die that night, we sat around the nursing station. I was drinking another cup of coffee. Rachel sat on a stool, her scrubs black with sweat, her hair loose in its pins, staring at nothing. I took the chart from her.

"I'll take care of the paperwork," I said. "You go on home."

She blinked, as if just waking from a bad dream. "What?" she said.

"Go home. I'll take care of the charting. You look beat."

"God," she said. "God, I was scared."

"You did good," I said. She just kept shaking her head, lost in the maze of her fatigue.

"Is there any family to talk to?" I asked Rachel.

She shrugged. We looked to the secretary, who made a face.

"You don't want to see him," she said. "He's drunk."

I had to help Rachel to her feet. She went down the hall to talk to the patient's companion: husband, lover, pimp—no one knew. I was finishing the paperwork beside the unconscious woman in the recovery room when I heard a man shouting outside the nursing station. He was a skinny black man with gray in his uncombed afro and cigarette burns in his jeans. He stank of alcohol, and his voice was taut with cocaine. He was shouting at Rachel, slapping her shoulder with the flat of one hand as he cursed her.

He was too angry to see me coming. I took him by the upper arm and put him against the wall.

"Hey now, boy," I whispered in his ear. "None of that here. We don't want none of that here, do we, boy?"

I expect no white man had called him "boy" in years. It caught his attention. He looked at me up close, cold angry.

"You," he said, as if we knew each other. "You ain't got no right to do a man this way." He pointed to Rachel. "That bitch," he said, "she kilt my baby. She went and kilt him, just like that. You damn whitefolks think a nigger ain't nothing. You think you can kill my baby and just walk away. Well, I ain't bowing down to you, white man, not to you or nobody else. I know my rights, and you going to be sorry you ever messed with me."

"Boy," I said, bumping him against the pale green wall tiles, "you got the right to leave this hospital now, and you got the right to set your sorry ass in jail for one very long time. Which right you planning to exercise? You got no other rights at all. You understand that?"

"Motherfucker," he said to me, getting spittle on my face.

"Janine," I said to the ward secretary, "call up the sheriff's dispatcher for me."

"Glad to, honey," said Janine. She picked up the phone. The man against the wall went limp.

"No," he said. "It's all right. I'm cool. I'm walking."

I let him go. He backed toward the door, his hands up, palms out.

"You're welcome back here when you're straight and you can act decent," I told him.

He paused. "I want to see Leora," he said.

"You can't see her now," I said. "She's not awake yet. She had a bad time. She like to have died, except for the lady doctor here. You're lucky you didn't lose her and the baby both. Now, you go on home. You come back in the morning. You can see her then."

"Shit," he said, but he went out. I turned back to Rachel.

"He'll leave you be from now on," I said. Then I saw the hatred in her eyes, angry and deep.

"I can't believe you did that to him," she said.

"He's a junkie and a drunk," I said. "He'll get over it. He could have hurt you."

"He's a human being, you racist Southern bastard."

I hesitated, looked at her, and glanced at the nurse, who rolled her eyes.

"Whatever," I said. I turned away to hide my pain.

"What is wrong with you people?" Rachel screamed. I didn't answer, didn't turn around. I just went on to the little call room, lay down on the narrow bed, and killed the light.

After that night none of the obstetrics nurses would speak to Rachel, except on business. They made her life unendurable, calling her in the small hours of every night, again and again, about little things that they once had taken care of themselves.

Leora's case was selected for medical staff review. If my name hadn't been on the chart with Rachel's, the other doctors would have pilloried her. As it was, Rachel's patients came up month after month. Every decision she made was questioned. Her competence to practice was impugned. She grew hostile, bitter, withdrawn. She began to make mistakes.

By spring Rachel was burned out. Only Elijah and her NHS contract kept her from leaving. One evening, at dusk, she and Elijah were out walking, holding hands. In his easy baritone, he tried to smooth over her latest wounds. She took the soft shoulder of the road while he walked on the edge of the asphalt. In the woods the redbuds were in bloom. The air was charged with the day's afterglow. She told me later how she heard the truck coming up behind, heard the engine's noise and the tires' growl growing louder. There was a glare of lights, the surprising sound of impact, Elijah's grunt, and then only twilight and the red taillights shrinking into the distance. Elijah was thrown against her. They fell together, and by the time she got to her knees, the pickup was too far away for her to make out anything but the Confederate battle flag on its bumper.

There's no ambulance in Tartan. Rachel had to run a quarter of a mile back to Elijah's house to call a neighbor. By the time they had Elijah in the back of the station wagon, he was unconscious, and by the time they reached the hospital, he was dead. All the way there, Rachel tried to keep him alive with mouth-to-mouth and CPR, blood and sand clotting together on their clothes. Whenever she looked up, she saw the reproachful face of the old black man at the wheel staring at her in the rearview mirror.

They never caught the hit-and-run-driver. There are hundreds of pickups around Tartan, and most of them wear a Southern Cross. Rachel, city girl that she was, didn't know if the truck that killed Elijah was a Ford, Dodge, or Chevy, didn't know if it was blue, black, or dark green, couldn't even estimate the model year. She alienated the sheriff's detective who interviewed her by insisting that it was a racial killing, when he thought it might only have been one more good old boy too drunk to keep the road. And then, too, Rachel never could understand that to too much of Tartan, a dead nigger has always been just a dead nigger, no matter where he'd been to school or how much of this wide world he'd seen.

Rachel went to the funeral. Except for me, she was the only white person in the chapel. She stood out in that congregation like a lone blossom among magnolia leaves. It was his mother's church, a real holiness temple, a steepleless church of whitewashed cinder blocks under second-growth pines, where everyone wore black and fans with King's portrait were the only cooling system the congregation had when the preacher warmed to his work. The eulogy was given to the backbeat of an electric bass guitar, and the pianist's syncopations drove her listeners to an ecstasy of tears.

As we filed out, the mourners were cordial to us, but no more than that: just as white folk in Tartan had ostracized Rachel for loving a black man, so the blacks shunned her because her loving had killed him.

After the others had gone, I stood by the car while Rachel stood at the grave, alone with the stone, her memories, her anger, and her grief, a beautiful woman amid trampled sand, tufts of grass, and faded plastic flowers scattered by the wind.

Rachel is in Arizona now, finishing her service obligation

on a reservation. She sent me a postcard. It came today. It says she's happy now.

Life goes on in Tartan, the way it always has, the way it always will. Cycles of birthing and dying are imperturbable; a doctor but attends their revolution.

Tonight, with the Indian on Rachel's card grinning up at me from the cold brick floor, I sit in the still heat on my back porch, too old to be drinking alone in the dusk like this, too old to change. In the shadows under the trees, mourning doves cry.

healers

$\mathcal{T}$he abortion was nothing, a simple procedure no different from any of the other three that morning. As always, the bleeding at first had been terrible and unreal. But as I emptied the womb, the routine returned: reaching blindly into the pink flesh of the open cervix with the cold steel instruments, pulling down a limb or a length of spine, counting pieces and laying out the bony fragments until my little puzzle was complete. After the head was out, the bleeding stopped. I tossed the instruments onto a tray with the remains. While the anesthetist woke the woman, I slouched on a stool by the door and wrote postop orders.

I walked beside the gurney to the recovery room with my hand on my patient's arm, daydreaming of sunshine in deep woods. When she was settled, I changed from my spattered scrubs into a new suit. I went downstairs to lunch.

After the stillness of the operating room, the noise of so many voices in the chaos of the crowded cafeteria disoriented me. I sat at an empty table against the wall. I took out a crushed pack of smokes and lit a cigarette. I sat alone, staring at gaggles of women in white uniforms and long lab coats as they chattered over their food, gabby girls too young and ignorant to be unhappy. I worked my cigarette with long drags, holding in the smoke, trickling it out through my nostrils, enjoying the burn and the nicotine rush. Then the taste went bad. I stubbed out the butt and picked up my fork. By then the food was cold. I bolted it and went out.

My clinic is a solitary brick building under old oaks. As I turned toward it off the main road, I waved to the old woman on the corner. She hunched her shoulders up inside her sandwich board and looked away. She had a new sign every week, but the message was always the same, a plea to end the killing.

There were no demonstrators at the clinic. It was late fall, and too chill for that. The demonstrations had gone on all summer. Mothers had chained themselves to the doors and been arrested while their children watched. The sign under the trees had been vandalized: obscene words in red paint across the name my father gave me. The windshield of my truck had been smashed. I had walked to work through mobs that cursed and spat on me while television cameras ran. Now, in November, the demonstrators had stopped, but pregnant women kept coming. They could not afford to quit just because the weather had changed.

Inside the clinic, women with rigid faces sat about the waiting room. I smiled at one. She turned her eyes away, ashamed. I went into my office and changed into my white coat. I sat alone to smoke another cigarette, then went out.

Shirleen, my office nurse, was waiting for me in the hallway.

"Hello," she said brightly. "How was lunch?"

I shrugged. "What's the tally for the afternoon?" I asked.

She made a face. "Thirty-five," she said.

We were finished by half-past four. I sat by myself in my office, filling out charts while Shirleen cleaned instruments in the room outside. Of the thirty-five women, only five had been suctions; eight had been in for follow-up after prior procedures, nine were new, and thirteen were in to refill their birth control prescriptions. I did their paperwork methodically. Shirleen came in to say good night. I thanked her absentmindedly and waved over my shoulder, then went back to the charts. When those were done, I went through the mail. There were the usual vituperative notes, handwritten and awkward. I reviewed the pathology reports ("products of conception," "products of conception," " products of. . .") and the Pap smear readings, initialing the forms, taking notes. I thumbed through a journal, trashed letters marked "Personal and Confidential" to seduce me into reading about lucrative practices in Atlanta, Charlotte, Memphis, Miami—the South's big cities that were Southern no more. I smoked another cigarette, killed the butt, and went out by the back door. The last things I saw were the clotted specimens in plastic jars by the sink.

At home, the dog was waiting. He bounded off the step and ran around my pickup until I got out. The dog was a mongrel, abandoned on the highway the year before. I reached out and caught him under the body and shook him. We wrestled on the yellow grass beside the drive.

"You old bastard," I whispered into his floppy ears. "Where you been all day, you worthless dog, you?"

The dog squirmed about, trying to lick my face, slobbering on my suit instead. I threw him down and scratched his belly.

At the door, I fumbled for the lamp while the dog ran over the carpet and into the kitchen where his dinner bowl was. In the high-ceilinged room the light was feeble. I put my briefcase by the door, shucked my suit coat onto a chair, and went to feed the dog. While he ate, I put a steak under the broiler and dumped a package of frozen broccoli in the microwave. I put three fingers of bourbon into a tumbler and went onto the screened back porch. Between pulls on my drink I smoked and played with the dog's ears. Overhead, the wind rushed through the dark loblollies on its way down the river to Cape Fear.

I ate with the television on in the other room for company, listening to invisible people. I read a Bobbie Ann Mason story through the soft haze of the alcohol. I let the dog out for the night, pulled the telephone out of the jack, checked my beeper, and went to sleep.

The next day was like all my days. I started the morning in the hospital, stopping to check on a woman I'd admitted with postabortal sepsis; she was better but still hurt too much to walk beyond the bathroom. Then I had two second-trimester evacuations and a full afternoon clinic. It was like any day, except that it was Friday.

After work I went home and played with the dog in the dark yard under the trees. When we both were winded, I showered and changed and drove to the hotel out near the airport and the interstate. Marie was waiting for me at the bar. She had on a cream-colored suit with padded shoulders, a tight, short skirt, and heels. She was studying her drink. I came up behind her and kissed her ear. Her hair smelled of honeysuckle, a sweet, ripe, country-girl smell.

"Hey," she said softly, turning in my arms and smiling, "how you been doing?"

"Older but no wiser. You?"

"Same old same old. When am I going to quit thinking you'll ever be on time?"

"Not till you get smart enough to quit seeing me, girl."

"Were you working or just at home getting it on with that damn dog of yours?"

"Both. You hungry?"

"Honey," she said, kissing my throat, "you know me: being around you always gives me an appetite. What you serving tonight?"

"Bullshit," I answered. "Like always."

"Ain't that just my luck," she said with a pout and a twinkle in her eye.

We laughed and went to a corner booth with a single candle. I ordered prime rib; she had snapper. The waiter called us by name. A dance band was playing oldies in the lounge outside the open double doors. I sipped two Manhattans while she played with her drink. We talked about nothing for the longest time.

"You know . . ." she began, but then she bit her tongue and ran her little finger around the rim of her glass.

"What?" I said.

"No," she said. She shook her head. "No. I can't ask. It's none of my business."

"What? Go on, honey. You can ask me. We're friends. We got no secrets."

"Well, I've been wanting to ask you . . ."

"Yeah?"

"Well, why do you do what you do?"

"You mean abortions?"

"Yes. I mean, it's kind of an unusual job. You know?"

"It is." I took a drink from my glass and swished it around awhile before I swallowed. I leaned over the table to speak to her.

"Listen," I said. "I haven't told you this, but that brooch looks real nice on you."

"Oh, God," she said. She put a hand over her face and peeked at me from behind her fingers. "Now I've done it. You're mad at me, aren't you?"

"No," I said. "What is it, a wolf?"

"What's what?"

"The brooch."

"No, dummy. It's a fox. You're not mad at me?"

"That's no fox. I know foxes. You're a fox."

"All right. It's a wolf, then. I get your message. I didn't mean anything. I was only asking."

"You finished eating?"

"Yes."

"Care to dance?" I asked.

"Not here," she said, so we drove in separate cars north across the river and through town to the strip where the Eighty-second Airborne liked to party. There were bars and surplus stores and tattoo parlors, hock shops and gas emporiums, strip joints and Chinese takeout places all along the highway. The signs were lit, arrows flashing, little bulbs winking and swirling. In jacked-up cars, young men with no hair and young women with big hair honked and revved and posed under the traffic signals. We went into a cozy place, where old noncoms liked to hang out and tell lies about Grenada and Panama and the desert to painted ladies who'd heard all their stories too many times. It was a place with a bandstand, where old black men with scarred faces played rhythm and blues in smoky voices that made the sergeants and their women get up and dance.

Marie and I sat through the first set and the first round of drinks. Then the conversation trailed off, and when the music started again, I took her hand and led her out on the floor. She danced with her eyes closed.

Like me, Marie's the wrong side of forty. Like me, Marie is divorced. That night, under the bad lights, she looked very good. Maybe her brows were penciled too sharply. Maybe her lipstick was too bright. The lines around her eyes were deep and unforgiving. Her figure, though, was still good: like me, she believes in discipline and little else. She pressed that good figure against me, and she took me home.

When the time came, after the last drink, the soft music, the gentle lighting that let us pretend that we were still young, I fucked her. For a gynecologist, there's no mystery to sex. It's just practical anatomy and physiology, and I've always been proud of the way I practice what I learned in medical school. I lay on top of her and watched the orgasms shake the painted indifference off her face. When she was finished, I got up and took off my condom and washed, then went onto the porch to smoke in the dark. She followed.

"What is it?" she asked. She put her forearms against my temples and held my head between her breasts. I turned my head to kiss a nipple.

"Just thinking about work," I lied.

"What about it?"

I shook my head and sucked on my cigarette. "The hell with it," I said, and blew smoke across the room.

"You won't tell me?" she asked.

"You wouldn't know what I was talking about," I told her.

We went back to bed. I watched her cuddle up against her dreams and wished to God I could do the same.

In the morning I woke before dawn out of habit. Half-asleep in the half-light beside one naked women, I though about other women who had been my patients over the years. I had flashbacks to bad operations. I was dragging fetal parts from a womb I could not empty while the bleeding went on and on. I drowned in my fatigue with the screams of a thousand babies ringing in my ears. When it began to get light, I woke again, slipped out of bed, and dressed. When I turned around, she was looking at me.

"Where you going, lover?" she asked dreamily.

"Home."

"Stay with me."

"I'll be back."

"But I need you."

I looked down at the fingers knotting my tie. "You'll live till I get back."

"It's that damn dog, ain't it?" she said. I did not reply. "Shit. You and him are tighter than man and wife. He's a smart old hound dog. Let him take care of himself."

"I'll be seeing you," I said. I bent to kiss her, but she flinched.

"What's he got that I ain't got, damn it?" she asked.

"Fleas," I said, grinning. She laughed and threw a pillow at me, but I was already gone.

The dog ran alongside the truck down the length of the drive. While the dog ate, I had a cigarette and a cup of coffee and a pair of country ham biscuits I'd picked up at the hospital after seeing my patient there. When the dog had finished, he sat beside my chair and put his head on my thigh. I went to finger a gash down his snout, but he pulled away.

"What's this, boy?" I asked, taking his head in both my hands and gentling him with my voice. "You been fighting over some bitch again?" I shook his head playfully. "How many times I got to tell you they ain't worth it?" I took a bite of biscuit and a slug of coffee. "You're just a damn fool, ain't you. Yeah, you're just like me: can't help yourself. Shit, yes. Old dogs like us, we never learn."

I changed my clothes, and we went out into the yard. I threw a stick for him to fetch till we both were bored with it. Then we went into the woods behind the house.

The leaves were down from the red oaks and the sweet gum trees, but the poison ivy leaves on the trunks were still scarlet. The air was misty, the distance an infinite tracery of twigs black against gray ground fog. The dog romped through the dead, wet leaves, sniffing out the interwoven trails of nameless animals. We wound about for an hour or so and came out near the twin ruts of the drive.

The house was still, save for the clock ticking on the mantel. No one ever called on weekends. There were never any emergency abortions. I sat with the dog at my feet in a chair by the front bay window and read while a hardwood fire spat and crackled to break the silence.

I picked up Marie around five. We ate at a steakhouse downtown, then hopped bars till the dance halls opened up. On the dance floor, she was all over me. We went home early.

On Sunday morning I sent my patient home from the hospital on oral antibiotics. Then I went to church. I sat in the back, apart, while the Baptist minister spoke to me of the wages of sin and the wrath of God. I knew my own God: a tired Galilean who'd tried to save the world and ended up too discouraged to save himself. I dropped a fifty-dollar bill in the collection basket. All the congregation knew how I earned it, but they never refused my offerings.

On Monday morning there was a black woman with a shower cap on over her lyejob shivering in a halter top on the sidewalk outside my clinic door. I stopped in front of her.

"What is it?" I asked.

"Go 'way," she said.

"Angie, ain't it?"

A scowl was her only answer.

"I thought I knew you," I said. "Why you sitting in the cold with no coat on, girl?"

"Bitch inside put me out, and my ride ain't coming back till three."

I put a hand on her bare black shoulder. "You come with me. We'll see can we straighten this out."

Inside, the receptionist sent us along to the new book-keeper. She was from Connecticut. Her husband was an ROTC second lieutenant at Bragg.

"Ms. Ranson," I said casuallike, "I was wanting to know why you put Angie here out on the sidewalk."

Ms. Ranson glanced at the woman.

"She's here for the second time in five months," the white woman said, "and she hasn't paid but forty dollars on her last bill. I told her to come back when she could pay."

"That right, Angie?" I asked.

"Ain't got the money," she said. She would not look either of us in the eye.

"How late are you?"

"I don't know. Five weeks, about."

"Doesn't she qualify for Medicaid?" I asked Ms. Ranson.

"Not hardly. She works at the turkey plant in Hoke. We figured it out: she makes close to eleven thousand a year."

"You got kids, Angie?" I asked.

"Two," she answered.

"They in school?"

"Not yet. They only two and five years old."

"Who takes care of them?"

"My momma."

"Who else works at your house?"

"Just me."

"Angie, Angie," I sighed. "I guess you just got careless."

She shook her head and shrugged, hopeless and bored.

"Well," I said, "you go wait out front with the rest. We'll work you in."

She frowned at me, suspicious. I waved a hand at her.

"Go on, now," I said, "before I change my mind." She went out fast. After she was gone, I leaned over Ms. Ranson's desk.

"How long you been South, Ms. Ranson?" I asked.

"Three months," she answered.

"Well, Ms. Ranson, you got a lot to learn. You ever tried to feed four people on eleven thousand a year?"

"No."

"Well, Ms. Ranson, it's hard, even in the heart of darkness here in Cumberland County, North Carolina. It's damn hard. And if I hear about you turning away any woman because she can't pay, it'll be you sitting on that sidewalk."

"I'm sorry," Ms. Ranson said sarcastically. "I didn't realize this was a charity clinic."

I turned in the doorway. "Honey," I said, "it's my clinic. As long as I'm paying you that's all you need to know, ain't it?"

"Yes, sir," she said.

Long ago, Shirleen, like Marie, had asked me: "Why do you do it?"

I'd stared at her for ages, then blinked, looked away, and shrugged. "It's good money," I'd said.

She'd chewed on that awhile and spat it out. "That ain't it," she'd said.

"Somebody's got to do it," I'd said, and she'd never got anything more out of me. I'd just kept on with my paperwork until she'd gone away. When she was gone, I'd put my elbows up on the desk and tried to rub the tiredness out of my eyes. It didn't work.

The truth is that I do abortions because I love women. Shirleen's right: it's not the money. Nobody could ever pay me enough to do this job. I know men who became abortionists because they're no damn good, but that ain't me. I don't do abortions out of pity, though God knows some of the women I see are pitiful enough. I don't do them from political conviction, either: no woman ever accused me of being a feminist. I don't do abortions the way some do, to snuff out the petty lives of a human race that they've seen too closely and come to despise. I've found somehow that when women in need come to see me, I can never refuse.

People hereabouts say that women who get knocked up have only themselves to blame, victims of their own lust and stupidity who have to bear the fruits of their carelessness. But lust and stupidity, like self-sacrifice and love, are part of the raw craziness of humanity that I admire. When women come to me, they leave artifice at home. They open up to me. They look inside themselves and see how they've messed up their lives. They drop their masks and their makeup and become human. Knowing I'm no better than the least of them, I help them.

No one ever thanks me. Before I became an abortionist, people were happy to meet me. Women whose children I'd delivered and whose names I'd forgotten would embarrass me by greeting me on the sidewalk or at the mall. I was introduced proudly by my acquaintances to individuals of importance. All that is in the past now. Old patients avert their eyes when I recognize them on the street. Pillars of the community look at me with faces full of hate when they bring their daughters to see me, as though I am to blame for youth's licentiousness. My colleagues are ashamed of me, and though they use me when their patients require my services, I am always left at the end of the table with no one to talk to at county medical society meetings. It's as though I've become deformed by my work, as if the smell of it emanates from me whenever I go into society. Only my dog accepts me.

Monday's mail brought a letter from my ex-wife. She makes a point of writing every month, to thank me for the child support. I'm sure that if I ever forgot, she'd write her lawyer just as punctually.

With the letter, there was a picture of my son. I hadn't seen the boy in three years. She had kicked when she learned I was teaching her baby to box on his visits to me, and when the idiot child told her in the fatuousness of his pride that Daddy was teaching him to handle a rifle, she'd cut me off. I was too tired then to fight her—had been too tired for years before she divorced me. She sent photographs of the boy to hurt me, I know: the kid at fifteen, with his baggy black clothes, his flattop haircut, and his kiss-my-ass grin, looked like the New York pimp she'd shacked up with. I trashed the letter and the photo and threw myself into my charts again.

On Friday night the dog didn't meet me. I sat in the truck while its heavy motor rumbled on and on, foolishly, like a bore at a party; I killed it and got out. I stood by the open door with a lit cigarette in my hand and listened to the wind sigh over the desolation of the empty world. I waited for the dog awhile, then dropped the cigarette into the dirt and stepped on it. I walked to the door through darkness that was viscous and cold, like the river in winter. The dog was on the step. His chest had been blown in by some fool's twelve-gauge. There was blood all over the concrete. I bent down and put my hand against the dog's head, then—realizing how futile the gesture was—I straightened, wiped my pants, and went inside.

A note scrawled on torn paper was stuck in the door. "You are next you bucher," it read with all the erudition and originality of a Southern public school graduate. I crumpled it in my fist and dropped it on the rug. I went to the cabinet against the far wall, unlocked it, and took out my .38. I pulled an armchair around to face the door and sat there with the gun in my lap.

I was still sitting there when the telephone rang, ages later. It was Marie.

"Goddamn it," she was shouting, "what kind of tramp do you think I am? If you think you can leave me standing up in some bar all night while you fuck around with your damn dog, boy, you better think again."

"I'm sorry," I said. She didn't even stop for breath.

"I used to think you were different, used to think you were somebody special. You sleaze-bag bastard. You're just like all the rest. You think I'm your personal slut. You think you can just whistle, and I'll crawl to you. Well, think again, asshole, Seventeen years of that was too many for this girl."

"I'm sorry," was all I could say. "I'm feeling pretty dragged."

"Well, for God's sake, why couldn't you have called me?" she asked. Her vehemence was cooling. "All you had to do was pick up the damn phone and dial. You know how to dial a telephone, don't you?"

"I forgot," I said. "I'm sorry."

"Yeah, I know: you said that. All right. I forgive you. What's wrong—you got a cold? I thought you sounded a little stuffed up. I can hear you sniffling." She paused, but I didn't answer. "I was sick a little, too, this week. Nothing much, just twenty-four hours of cramps and a touch of the trots—you know how that is."

I heard her send a smile down the wire, but I had nothing to give her in return. Her voice became concerned.

"What is it?" she asked. "What happened? Jesus—are you crying? Oh, baby, I'm sorry. I didn't mean to yell at you. I was just pissed at being stood up. I'm sorry. I didn't mean anything."

She was still going on like that, trying to get a word out of me, when I hung up the phone.

I sat in the dark, wrapped up in the silence, with the pistol on my lap. The moon, rising through the trees over the Cape Fear River, glared at me through one window. I sat very still, but my mind, like an engine without a governor, ran on faster and faster. Random thoughts flitted through my brain like demons, tormenting me. The futility of my days, of every doctor's work, oppressed me. The contradictions in me—a healer who makes a living destroying life to ease women's suffering—tortured me. I gave in to my despair.

Then I heard her car door slam. I heard the jangle of her keys and the click of her heels on the brick walk, tiny sounds in the muffling enormity of the night. I heard her pause at the door where the dead dog lay. She opened the door and flicked on the light. She squinted at me in the sudden brightness, then went up to me and held out her hand.

"Jesus," she said. "Give me that pistol."

I thumbed off the safety catch and put the gun on the coffee table. I stood and stretched.

"It's all right," I said. "I'm over it."

"The hell you are," she said.

She pushed me against the wall and took me in her arms. She had to pull my head down to kiss me. I stood there, numb and alone even as she pressed against me. After a while she stopped for breath and sat down on the couch. I sat at the other end, as far from her as I could get.

"What happened?" she asked.

"Somebody shot my dog," I said.

"Well, shit—I can see that. Who?"

"Somebody who doesn't like baby killers like me."

She jumped the length of the sofa and put her warm hand over my mouth. "Stop," she said. "You just stop it. You got no call to go saying things like that about yourself."

She took her hand away slowly, as if she were afraid I'd start again. She needn't have worried: I sat staring out the window, dead silent.

"It's not your fault," she ventured. I snapped my head around at her, suddenly furious.

"No?" I asked. "Whose fault was it, then? His? Hell, he was just a damn dog. He was my only friend, and he got killed for it."

"That's not right," she said. "It was nobody's fault. It's just the way the world is: there's crazies everywhere, and that's nobody's fault. Besides," she added in a voice suddenly small, "he wasn't your only friend."

"I should have expected it," I said, ignoring her answer just as she had ignored my apologies on the telephone. I went on talking just to clear my heart. "Whatever this town is, it ain't reticent. And it sure to God ain't shy about guns. Jesus, I wish I'd been here when it happened."

"I'm glad you weren't," she said.

"No?"

"You'd have killed whoever did it."

I slumped down on the cushions and ran my fingers through my hair, thinking. "That's so," I admitted. I closed my eyes, drifting away from her.

"You eat yet?" she asked, dragging me back to consciousness.

"No," I said. I rubbed my eyes awhile, exhausted, then opened them again. She was smiling at me.

"I'll fix something," she said, perking up.

Mine is a bachelor's icebox: plenty of beef, all of it frozen; a twelve-pack of beer, part gone; ketchup and mustard and odds and ends. She fried a mess of collards in bacon with a pair of eggs on the side. She apologized for it, told me it was shameful, the kind of meal her momma might have served the night before another cotton mill payday, but I ate it gratefully. When I finished she was leaning against the counter with her sleeves rolled up and her arms folded. I grinned.

"What?" she asked.

"You," I said. "You look like a damn housewife. All you need's an apron."

"Huh. All I need's a rolling pin. If I owned an apron, you'd be wearing it now."

"You're right," I said, feeling chastened again. I got up and started the dishes.

"You think they'll come back?" she asked.

"Not tonight. Maybe someday."

"You're pretty calm about it."

"No. I'm scared as hell. But what am I supposed to do—quit?"

"Maybe. What you going to do with the dog?"

"Bury him in the morning."

"You just going to leave him there on the front step all night?"

"He ain't going anywhere. And I'm not expecting any more callers tonight." Then I quit joking. "It's too dark now to bury him right. He deserves that much."

"You want a drink?" I asked later, racking the fry pan in the dish drainer.

"No," she said. "Just sit with me awhile."

I nestled up against her on the sofa. It was like getting to know her again from the beginning. I kissed her tentatively. She let me take my time. We warmed up slowly.

Later, upstairs, in the big bed with all the windows open, she made love to me. She put her arms around me and comforted me. She massaged all the tension out of my muscles. Drawing me inside herself, she reached deep inside me. I felt her touch me where I had been hurt so much, so long ago, so many times. And with that touch, I felt this sad old man—this doctor—begin to heal.

the veteran

*B*ehind my back, I know, they all despise me. Their geniality, their courtesy, their slick collegiality, only screen their scorn. When I come into a room, conversation stops, for I am the professor emeritus, the living textbook of experience, the respected elder physician, the senile embarrassment. The residents, the faculty, the nurses, even the laboratory technicians and ward secretaries, all despise me deferentially. They think that they can hide the mockery in their eyes, but they forget that I once was young, that human nature is still my favorite open book, self-delusion my favorite page.

Like every new generation, this one thinks itself wise. The young have no time for me, an old fool who wastes their time recounting the discoveries of long-dead men. They have no patience for the arts of palpation, percussion, and auscultation that they know have been superseded by scopes and scans. To them my skills are antique and irrelevant, my successes only flukes, my errors egregious. Interns change my orders without consulting me, prescribe faddish drugs whose interactions they do not understand, and transfer my dying patients to special units where their machines blow out life's last flame.

Nor have I time for them. Once residents' training was everything to me, and residents I once taught have become the chairmen of university departments. But today's young people are whiners, and I cannot stand their complaints. They are ignorant of the days when residents were just that, when we lived in the hospital, forbidden to marry, the privilege of learning our only remuneration. I served my internship in a New Guinea field hospital, treating dysentery and gangrene, gonorrhea, malaria, and madness; the Japanese bombed our tents whenever the rains subsided. These tyros' claims of hardship evoke no sympathy in me, and debt and loneliness are no excuse for slovenly dress or indulgence in incomprehensible jargon.

Still, we cannot escape each other. Like all old men, I am insomniac, and long after dark, long before dawn, I am on their wards. I check charts, discover medications not given, notes not written, treatment plans inadequately thought through. The residents resent me because I keep them awake, but lost in the tangle of their own fatigue, they respect a man who disdains sleep.

I drive home in a Cadillac. It is expected of me, and my wife demands it. I would rather drive a Jeep, but explaining why would cost me too much trouble. I buy a new car every year. This one is too light; in a good wind it cannot keep the road.

When I reach home the porch light is always on, the rest of the house always dark. If she is home, my wife gets up to heat my dinner. We sit at the kitchen table and recite to each other the details of our separate days. To me her stories of salesgirls and cleaning women, delivery men and bag boys, ministers, artists, and the chiefs of charity boards, are as tiresome as my litanies of disease must seem to her. Still, with nothing else to fill our old age, we talk. When we have wearied each other enough, she kisses my cheek and goes back to her room. I sip a highball or two in my study, reading medical journals and statements from my broker. Rarely, little naps nab me as I sit in the deep chair. Usually, though, I go upstairs and undress. I curl up in the bed that once was our daughter's. I lie awake, listening to the darkness until I recall something at the hospital left undone. Then I shower quietly and put on a fresh suit. Going out, I never slam the door.

After morning rounds I stop by the microbiology laboratory. Though I have ceded its formal directorship to Martin, I meet over coffee with the section supervisors each weekday to hear about unusual cultures that I follow up later. Ten years ago there was little to talk about. Today, AIDS fleshes out our agenda. Every morning we devise strategies for identification and discuss tactics for treatment. For most it is a dull routine, and finding a fresh Danish has become more of a challenge than determining a correct diagnosis.

After the others have drifted back upstairs, I sit in a corner of the cafeteria with Martin. He is a brilliant little man with a toothbrush mustache and the pallor of a dedicated laboratory scientist. He is the kind of collaborator I've always longed for: original, energetic, idealistic. He is an expert on the fungi that infect the human body, and he is developing new techniques for their culture. He has computerized our laboratory's reporting system, so that we can publish our institution's experience with rare organisms now, searching back thirty years. I have to edit all his papers and his grant proposals: he cannot compose a grammatical sentence. Then, too, he is a homosexual frightened into celibacy, and he has transferred his passion to his work. Having heard reports of the deaths of old lovers whose funerals he can no longer endure, Martin has no patience for the exigencies of proper prose. He works feverishly to forget. He succeeds no better than I.

At eight I meet with Sasha, the young woman who is our infectious diseases fellow. Two years out of residency, she has come to realize that her life will be spent caring for drug addicts and the promiscuous. She tries hard to hide her disillusionment from her students. She once complained to me, but I could not console her. She is a fine physician, and I love her like my own daughter, but I learned long ago that I can only treat the physical ills of those who come to me. I cannot even heal my own heartache.

We wander the wards, Sasha and I, checking on our patients, visiting the living men and women who are the sources of those strange organisms I heard about at breakfast. I shake their hands and touch their fevered bodies. The medical students hang back. Even Sasha, who should be hardened by now, is ginger. But an old man like me has nothing to fear from an infection that might kill him in five years.

I am sick, too. I know all the little annoyances of age—constipation, bad teeth, stiff joints—and I am intimate with angina. On most days drugs control it. By reputation I am imperturbable, but that is only my medicine, and prudence, for emotion precipitates pain. Sometimes just walking between wards sets off my symptoms. Usually there is only a heaviness that blunts my concentration, which I can fob off as senility. When the constriction in my chest grows too sharp, I duck into a men's room for nitroglycerin. I sit on a covered toilet to rest until the pain passes. I have convinced Sasha that the problem is only my prostate. My cardiologist told me to get a bypass, but I deflected his insistence with a quote from his own writings in the *Journal of Advanced Cardiology*. He argued that his editorial had been just a political gesture, while we were talking about my life. I thanked him and buttoned my shirt.

Three mornings a week I lecture to the medical students. The amphitheater has changed little over the years. The chairs are upholstered now, and portraits of the university president and the hospital CEO have replaced Osler and Halsted on the walls. The students are the same, too. Perhaps there are more women in the seats now, more blacks and a scattering of Asians, but they are all just as docile as the young white men have always been.

From the first, lecturing has been my pride. As I have aged, the amphitheater has been modified to accommodate me. Slides and a laser pointer obviate the need for scrambling about before a blackboard. The microphone compensates for pipe smoke's injury to my vocal projection. I stand at the podium, the lights go down, and I set my notes in order. I put my left hand in my vest pocket, leaving the other free for gestures. The content of my lectures evolves from year to year, but the flow of the rhetoric is unchanging. The logic is smooth, and elision conceals gaps in science's understanding that the students never notice. My slides are brilliant with special stains: carmine and violet, deep blue black, orange. The shapes of the bacteria are intricate and legion: the blunt lance of the pneumococcus, the sinuous coil of the spirochete, the squat pink couplets of the gonococcus, the curlicues of the vibrio, the stubby bacilli with their elegant flagella. The colored shapes are the trademarks of disease. My enthusiasm for them infects my audience. The students listen, rapt, as I explain techniques for isolation, criteria for diagnosis, the nuances of illness, and the options for therapy. Initiates of voyeurism, they are enthralled by the seductive beauty of death unclothed.

Of late, however, errors have insinuated themselves into my lectures. They pop up at odd moments, catch me by surprise, and leave me speechless. A train of thought trails off into blankness. Alien images, subtle as phagocytes, engulf my mind. I glance at the screen and realize—sometimes mistakenly— that I have fallen out of synchrony with the sequence of my slides. I clear my throat, search through my notes, fumble at the carousel control. A murmur begins in the lecture hall. A titter joins it. I grow flushed. I collect myself and resume, but haltingly, without confidence.

The hour ends. The lights come on. The students rise and straggle out. One or two come up to the podium to ask questions. Hiding my humiliation behind a mask of arrogance, I brush past them.

Luis has my slides out of the machine already. He has been an audiovisual assistant at the medical school for twenty years. He hands me the full carousel.

"You left out *Gardnerella* this year," he says.

"The taxonomy has changed again. You'll see its new name on Monday. I'll point it out to you."

Luis knows nothing of science and has never looked through

a microscope. He claims to have an equivalency diploma, but I do not believe him. Still, after years spent sitting in a tiny booth nursing sound and light systems, he can name the organisms responsible for common encephalitides, the appearance of osteomyelitis, the chief symptoms of pneumonia. He knows which lecturers can hold their audience, too, and these days he asks after my health frequently. His face is full of concern. I lie to reassure him.

At noon I lunch with Martin. My cardiologist has told me to watch my intake of saturated fats, but that advice is for patients. With no desire to live forever, I eat what I please. Nevertheless, even the foods I choose are tasteless. I pick at my plate. I'm losing weight, everywhere but in my ankles. My paunch still protrudes, but my shoulders are shrunken, my arms spindly, my neck scrawny. My clothes no longer fit me.

In the afternoons I attend to my office, a generous space decorated with bookshelves and a potted begonia too neglected to bloom. The windows look out over the undergraduate quadrangle, down paths once lined by old elms, to the Gothic chapel. On sunny days I pull the curtains, for the light is too much for my aging eyes.

The walls of the room are covered with frames. There are diplomas, licenses, certificates of membership in professional associations, a pair of honorary degrees, commendations—even somewhere a D.S.M. I find it all useful only for intimidating unwanted visitors.

They wander in through the afternoon, interrupting me as I try to draft papers and dictate correspondence. Once there was a steady flow of students, but this year, tired of expounding the same simple concepts to empty minds, I have assigned teaching assistants to evening study sessions. Now students barge in only to argue and complain. A young man in a pressed shirt and a college tie takes a seat opposite me.

"I didn't deserve a B," he insists after the usual cordialities.

I look up his name in the grading book and drop him to a C.

"You can't do that," he tells me. He is outraged.

"It's done," I say. "I'll write the registrar this afternoon."
He fumes in silence until I dismiss him. He stalks out. I
have no time for his kind. I studied for a year in Vienna,
between the Anschluss and the war, and I know that these are
not victims, however much they may pity themselves.

A lawyer has written, asking me to be an expert witness for
the plaintiff in a malpractice case. He hints at a large fee. I throw
his letter away. Also in the day's mail are glossy announcements
of pseudoscientific conferences at Vail, Paris, Nassau, Rio. I
discard them unopened. There is a packet of reprints from a
former resident, now a division chief in Richmond. I dictate a
reply, suitably grateful yet still superior. There is a letter from
my son.

In retrospect I know that I was too young to marry until I
was too old to have children. Jonathan and my daughter are
strangers to me, their lives incomprehensible. He stayed in
school only long enough to escape the draft, then drifted through
communes and monasteries for years. He lives in San Francisco
and works as an instructor in mystic religions. He writes to me
at odd times, sending me pamphlets, asking me for money. I
send him what he needs. I drop his pamphlets in the trash
unread. In this letter there is something new, something indirect
and disturbing. I cannot place it, though, and move on to other
work.

A salesman is ushered in. A drug peddler, he has reams of
literature extolling the benefits of his newest, most expensive
antibiotic, all of the research that supports its efficacy paid for
by his company. He launches into his spiel. Though he is
young—his pro forma mustache is still downy—he is polished. I
listen awhile. He grows tedious. I turn toward the window. An
early fall rain has begun. It hisses on the brown leaves of the ivy
on the wall. Through it, the shapes of nearby buildings are
blurred. I turn back to the salesman.

"Get out," I say, stopping him in the middle of a well-
rehearsed phrase.

"Pardon?"

"I don't have time for this. Leave your papers. I'll read them tonight, I'll discuss your request with our pharmacists."

"But I—"

"Get out!" I shout. I play the irascible old man. I slap the desk. "Get out, damn you. I have no time for you hucksters, and you have no right to ask for it."

He stands, reaching into his briefcase.

"Can I offer you...?" he begins, bringing forth a handful of pens, pen lights, plastic rulers, gewgaws all labeled with his brand names. My temper ebbs into disgust. I sit back, shaking my head.

"If you could bribe me," I tell him, "I wouldn't come that cheaply."

He hesitates, wondering if he has been propositioned. He smiles to himself.

"There are some protocols," he says, "that my company would be willing to fund generously, if you could supply the patients."

We stare at each other across the desk. I raise one eyebrow, to let him believe he's about to consummate his seduction. Then I turn back to my paperwork.

"Don't be a shithead," I tell him.

He flushes and leaves without a word. Ordinarily I detest vulgarity, but it has its uses.

At the end of the afternoon Sasha comes in to review the day's new cases with me. She has already rounded with Schnurrstein, the bombastic parasite who took over as head of the division of infectious diseases when I retired. He resents the time she spends talking with me, regarding it as a slight to his authority. Now and then I hear him carping next door to Biddle, a young man who showed great promise until he was granted tenure, when he gave up science for sycophancy.

When Sasha finishes I go out onto the wards alone, visiting all the patients I've heard about through the day. Over the years the hospital has grown labyrinthine. Two new wings have replaced the old open wards, now converted to accountants' offices and secretarial pools. All the new rooms are private, good for my patients with their contagious diseases but lonely for all the rest. I get lost among the identical ranks of closed doors.

I meet colleagues. We ask about each others' families, trade amusing stories, comment on the weather. They ask for my opinion on clinical problems, though less often now than they once did, much less often. I affect not to notice.

It is Friday night, and I dare not linger: we have reservations for dinner and tickets for the symphony.

At home I put on evening clothes, then sit and watch my wife make herself up. She sits in her slip before the vanity mirror, playing with her innumerable cosmetics jars. Although she has had her face lifted, her breasts augmented, her buttocks reduced, and her fat suctioned, the surgery has failed her. She has grown old and ugly in spite of this, and I can see the tiny scars that disfigure her. She paints her face, trying to plaster over her wrinkles. When she stands to dress and smiles for me, I cannot recognize her.

At the door she stands me up as though I were a little boy again. She adjusts my tie and takes a comb from her purse to rearrange my hair. But we are late, and besides, there is not enough hair to bother with anymore. I brush away her hands, cursing her in a voice almost too soft for her to hear. Her face crumples, but we have no time for false apologies.

In the restaurant, we order. The waiter is too chummy. I correct his French. He glares at me condescendingly. My wife is appalled. Then she brightens, chattering about her friends' scandals— divorces, ruined children, dissipated wealth. I ignore her. She sees that but blithely babbles on. I eavesdrop on the conversation at other tables; it is everywhere the same.

The symphony hall is crowded and overheated. In the dim light the program is illegible. The orchestra, tuning up, is raucous. I try to nap, but my wife elbows me. Finally the lights go down. The conductor comes onstage. The music is avant-garde. At first it is invigorating, but soon the irregular rhythms grow annoying. I whisper to my wife; she shushes me. At intermission we slip into the lobby. She meets a fellow Junior

Leaguer. I leave the two of them and wander into the street. The rain has stopped, but the sidewalks still shine. I walk into a bar and order a Budweiser. The patrons stare at my clothes. I sit at a table by the window and watch the passersby. When the beer is gone, I leave an excessive tip and return to the hall. On its portico I sit and pack my pipe, then find that I have forgotten my matches. I borrow some from an usher. He agrees that the music is dull; he prefers rap. After the performance I search out my wife in the lobby. Relieved to find me, she scolds me interminably. We drive home in silence.

After leaving her at home, I go back to the hospital. What once was dedication has become only habit, a way to evade overwhelming ennui. There is nothing on the wards for me to do. I unlock my office and sign letters.

Waiting for an elevator, I study the sixty-odd years of residents' graduation photographs that cover a wall outside the departmental offices. Faded and blurred, the faces stare at me, ranks of young men with short hair and big ears and such cocky smiles. So many of them are dead now, and all the rest so much changed. The elevator doors rumble open before I work up the courage to look at the stark black-and-white image of the young man I once was.

Pulling out of the parking garage, I clip a guard rail. The scream of steel rips me out of my reverie. Shaking with adrenaline, I arrive home too tense to sleep. I sit in the den and read Dickens until I realize that I have been reading the same page again and again. I look at my watch. It is two o'clock. I go into the kitchen and pour Scotch over ice, then go up to drink it in bed.

My wife and I sleep in separate rooms. Years ago I learned she had taken her first lover; I have never returned. Besides, I am an old man now. I am impotent—or, rather, nothing arouses me anymore.

Once again, the Scotch fails me. I lie awake and listen to the furnace exhale. The darkness clasps me, crushes me. My mind races into my past, rehearsing a litany of lost opportunities. Sleepless, I dream of days when I had a future. Now I have only a past; famous men congratulate me on it, but to me it is only dust and ashes.

In the room where I try to sleep linger mementos of my daughter's childhood: high school pastels, an embroidered pillow, worn stuffed animals, old dresses in unopened closet clothes bags, the smell of powder and a little girl's perfume. On the bookshelf beside the single bed are Jane Austen's novels, Emily Dickinson's poetry, and Nancy Drew mysteries.

I get up from the bed and turn on a light. Her doodles decorate the blue blotter on her old pine desk. Scattered pencils she once sharpened sit blunt and disused. I pick one up and turn it in my fingers. In the top drawer, with old chewing gum, bits of eraser, a nail file, and loose change, is blank paper. I take a sheet. At the top I write the date and her name. No words come, only memories. I sit. The minutes pass. Outside the window, the starlings wake. The darkness fades out of the room. I put the pencil down, put the paper away, and leave the room.

That afternoon I attend a departmental research meeting. One of the junior faculty, a young woman up for tenure next year, presents her work. Her slides are computer-designed. Her lecture is quite good. When she finishes Jamison stands to question her. His point of argument is valid: her study design is subject to hidden biases that may have affected her conclusions. But his assault is vicious, his voice charged with ridicule. Flustered, she falters in answering him. He names other flaws in her study design, each of them correct but all probably irrelevant to her conclusions. He cites a few old studies, most later discredited, that contradict her results. She tries to respond, but he cuts her off. Finally he sits down, glancing about and smirking. Two residents ask the lecturer to repeat points that they had missed, having fallen asleep when the lights went down. The hour comes to a close.

"If there are no further questions..." says the conference coordinator. I stand.

"I would point out," I interrupt, "that the study design used in this instance matches that used in 'The Importance of

Calcium Homeostasis in Acid-Base Disorders.' The conclusions are no more and certainly no less valid."

Heads turn. Jamison, the paper's author, twists in his seat to scowl at me.

'That paper," he notes, "was a lead article in the *Massachusetts Journal of Medicine*."

"Yes," I say. "But prestigious publication can never make bad science good, even when it renders a disreputable man a reputable scientist."

I sit as Jamison comes to his feet, coloring. From his podium, the conference coordinator closes the meeting.

In the hall, Martin comes up to me. "Touché," he says. "But of course you know that you're wrong."

We turn to walk toward my office.

"You don't believe that," I say.

"Wouldn't it be nice not to have to? But we both know that publication is everything. Science only matters when it serves that end."

"Get thee behind me," I say, but he is serious, and being Jewish, he misses my allusion. Besides, he is right. I am suddenly angry, and I see that he enjoys having provoked me. I close the door in his face to keep him from seeing mine. All the ideals that I once believed in have been vitiated or lost. I sit alone in the vacuum of my office, unable to focus, unable to mourn.

At the end of the day and the drive home, I park in front of my house, where large trees stand interspersed with utmost artifice upon an immaculate lawn. All the buildings in the neighborhood are monotonously unique. My house is in the contemporary style, all flat surfaces of rough-cut wood, with rows of small windows above eye level. Its roof is too flat to shed rain or snow, and in consequence the studs beneath have begun to rot. Still, it will outlast me, so I let the fungi do their work.

This evening there is a strange car in the driveway. I walk up the brick walk with the floral border that my wife's gardener keeps so clean. After last week's frost, his flowers died. Now the earth lies spaded and mulched, waiting for winter.

My daughter opens the door for me. The unexpected sight stuns me. Her face, which I have not seen for too many years, is suddenly old.

"Hello, Dad," she says. Then she drops her eyes as she steps aside for me.

I stare at her. Where in this austere woman is the pudgy baby I used to carry, or the child who used to run to the door, shouting "Daddy, Daddy!" and jump into my arms when I came home? Where is that shy, proud young woman not yet grown into her prom dress who posed for the photograph that I keep on my office desk, or the wide-eyed girl who loved to chat with the pink-smocked volunteers in the hospital gift shop on Sunday mornings while I ran through rounds?

My daughter grins at me.

"You're still late as ever," she says. "Come on: Mom's got dinner waiting."

The meal is subdued. The two women have a secret that they do not want to spoil the occasion. I ask no questions, and my daughter asks few. We tell her what little we know of her brother and bring her up to date on local events: what has been built and what torn down, what has become of the few of her childhood friends who never moved away. I mention all the people of my generation who she did not know had died. She grows pensive.

After we finish eating, she and her mother rinse the dishes and pack the dishwasher. I go to my study. Later, my daughter knocks and enters. She sits in the armchair by the desk, where she used to read her picture books to me while she sat in my lap. I turn toward her.

"So," she says, "how are you, really?"

"Fine. You?"

"Fine. You look good."

"So do you," I say, though she looks dry and drawn, and I know that I look like a man on the edge of death.

She stares at her hands, searching for words, but they hold none.

I could ask about her ex-husband, but she probably doesn't hear from him, and besides, my asking would sound too much like "I told you so." I could ask about her work, but I cannot remember what it is, or even if she still has any, so I keep silent to keep from seeming foolish. I could ask about her trip, but I no longer know where she lives.

She sighs, looks up, stands, turns away, paces, turns back, and sits again, facing me.

"I might as well just ask," she says. "God, I didn't think this would be so hard."

I tip back my chair and reach for a pipe and tobacco.

"I wish you wouldn't," she says, frowning. I put the things down, like a sheepish child.

"Shit," she says. "I'm sorry."

I wait.

"The reason I came," she finally begins, "is to ask you for a favor. I live in Washington now. I'm a lobbyist for a gay health advocacy group. I need your help."

"What is it?" I ask. I try to be gentle, but my words are gruff as I realize that she has come home only to use me. In spite of myself, I sound peevish. Then I rouse myself to courtesy and put a hand on her arm. The gesture is reflexive, my bedside manner breaking through, ingrained and insincere.

She takes a breath and plunges in. "I need your help," she begins. "A few of us have been trying to persuade the FDA to change its regulations for AIDS treatments. We've been trying to get experimental drugs released earlier, so that sick people can benefit from them while there is still time. We've been refused. I came to ask you—"

"No," I tell her, unwilling to listen. This woman, no longer mine, has become just another parasite. I settle back in my chair and cross my arms. "I can't help you."

"But I haven't even asked yet," she cries out. The pain in her eyes is naked. I can see the vulnerability she has taken on in venturing to visit me, but it fails to move me. I know I should reach out to comfort her, but I cannot. "All I'm asking," she goes on, "is for you to use your influence."

"I have no influence anymore."

"But that's not true." She looks away before going on. "Your name got me this job. It opens doors for me that no one else can get through. People will listen to you."

"You are wrong," I insist, closing the matter.

She sinks back into the chair, defeated. She studies her folded hands again. They are an old woman's hands, spotted, dry, and unnaturally tanned, though she is scarcely forty.

"The regulations are correct," I inform her. "These drugs have to be scientifically evaluated before they can be released. Their side effects can be worse than the disease."

"Nothing can be worse than this disease," she says bitterly. "All those deaths, those young men's deaths: it's all so meaningless."

"All deaths are meaningless," I tell her. "Young men's, old men's: they're all the same."

The second hand on the wall clock sweeps around and around.

"You are so hard," she whispers in her despair, "so damned hard."

I shrug. I am who I am, and what my life has made me.

She looks into my face. Her eyes are full of condemnation. In a moment, her looks soften. She leans forward, puts her hand out to touch me.

"I'm sorry," she says. There are tears in her eyes.

I smile knowingly and shake my head. "That won't work," I tell her.

She runs from the room, slamming the door behind her just as she used to when I told her to be home from a special date by nine. I pick up a copy of a manuscript that I have been asked to review for a small journal. The work displaces my daughter from my thoughts. When I finish reading and have set down all my comments, it is late. The house is dark. I walk to the stairs, then realize my daughter must be in her bedroom. I lie on the sofa and doze, lost between sleep and wakefulness. Hours before dawn I sit up suddenly, jerked back to consciousness by the ghost of a dream I cannot recall. I turn on the television. I am a connoisseur of forgotten films. Tonight, though, there are only music videos, plotless clips of garish young people acting out exaggerated reactions to their sexual repressions. I turn it off and listen to barely audible Bartók while I get fresh clothes from the basement laundry room and dress over a cup of stale coffee in the kitchen.

I go to work before sunrise. When I return, my wife is alone again. She has nothing to say to me. Her face is full of unspoken hatred.

I have been invited to address a conference in New York on the crisis of AIDS. It is no crisis, not any more than tuberculosis, pertussis, or polio were crises, or Hitler, or Stalin. Death remains only death, even when it comes to those who think themselves immortal.

My own death comes closer every day. It is very close now, perhaps six months away, perhaps a year. The edema in my legs grows worse week by week. I know my heart is failing, so I have little sympathy for those who, dying, beg for attention. They complain that they die with their youthful potential unrealized; I realize that mine has been wasted and know whose lot is worse.

On my way to the airport, the traffic is swift and dense and angry. Young men in jacked-up cars honk as they pass, gesturing out their windows at me. The highway's convolutions confuse me. I miss the airport exit and get tangled in one-way side streets at the next. I forget the name of my airline. Digging through my briefcase for the ticket, I forget to watch the road. Horns bring me back to attention. The terminal seems to have grown enormously since my last trip. All the garages are full. Cars are backed up at every curve. I begin to worry that I may miss my flight. In spite of all my medication, anxiety rises in me. I break into a sweat. Finally I find a parking place in an outlying lot. In my hurry I mistake the angle as I pull in and have to back out twice and try again, scratching the paint on the Honda in the space next to mine. The shuttle bus is delayed. I try to convince myself that my watch is fast. I arrive at the terminal too late to check my suitcase. I wander about the huge open space, searching display screens for my gate number. I scuttle through the halls. I grow breathless. My heart skips beats. I am the last passenger aboard. The uniformed woman at the gate purses her lips as she tears my ticket. On the plane, the other passengers glare as I try to stow my suitcase into the full baggage compartment. A stewardess, disgusted, takes it from me. I fall into my seat and must be reminded to fasten my belt so that we can leave the terminal.

I am drenched with sweat, and there is a weight on my chest, a dull pain I cannot shake off. As the jet wrenches itself from the earth, my nausea overflows. I vomit into the little bag in the seat flap while everyone stares at me. Only when the plane is fully airborne can a stewardess rise to help me clean myself. After four nitroglycerin tablets, the angina ebbs away.

At La Guardia a resident in whites is waiting for me. He pilots me through the crowd, carrying my bags.

In the hotel I am high above the city, encased in silence. I hang my clothes and unpack my little pharmacy. My eyes burn with exhaustion. I am too ill to eat, too tired to review the lecture packed away in my briefcase.

Outside the conference hall the next morning, demonstrators line the street. They wave crude placards and shout at me as I walk between their lines. In the hall, the employees of sponsoring drug companies in uniform navy blazers help me to register. I mingle among men in gray pinstripes who stand about outside the auditorium. At the proper time I am directed to a seat on the stage. My exhaustion plays with me: I cannot sleep, but I cannot stay awake. I stand and receive a plaque, then step to the podium, my unrehearsed speech in my hand. I stumble over the words. In the back of the great room, hushed conversations resume while I talk. People sidle out to see the exhibits. When I finish there is polite applause. Afterward I stand in the lobby surrounded by my former trainees, each now a gray-headed authority in his own right. No longer at ease together, we discuss our work, praising each other insincerely and denigrating those of us who could not attend.

An angry woman is haranguing a group of men in business suits. She is staring at me. She is my daughter. Her look warns me away.

At a dinner paid for by drug salesmen, we drink too much complimentary wine. Our self-congratulation exceeds all bounds. We convince ourselves that we will soon conquer the scourge of the new generation. The rhetoric, like a child's balloon, grows more rotund, more inflated, more distorted, as more bottles are brought, emptied, and taken away. Finally conversation collapses into belches, grunts, obscene stories, and drunken cursing. I alone stay sober: intoxication is for me an oblivion I can no longer attain. The party disgusts me. I slip away to my room. No one notices my departure.

I call my wife at home. There is no answer.

The next day I sit among the distinguished in reserved front rows. Behind us, half the audience is still drunk, the rest hung over. Earnest young researchers up on the stage try to present a year's work in seven minutes. There is no time for questions, but then no one is listening anyway.

The protesters outside grow frustrated as their demands for a hearing continue unmet. There is a scuffle on the sidewalk as I leave for dinner. Police hustle out of the lobby. Young people are led away in handcuffs, yelling slogans I do not understand. No one remarks on their presence, which has nothing to do with any of us.

My daughter is waiting for me in the lobby of my hotel. She has on a tweed suit. Her face is puffy, her makeup all awry.

"How are you?" I ask. The deference of famous men has made me affable. I want to embrace her, but she is too distraught.

She shakes her head. Her lips are thin, her face too pale. She hugs her purse to her chest. She is a portrait of rigid self-control.

"I hope you're satisfied now," she says to me. Her face twists up with bitterness.

I am baffled. I can recall no tragedies for which I am responsible.

"Satisfied about what?" I ask.

"Don't be coy," she spits out at me. Then my confusion convinces her of my ignorance. "You don't mean that you haven't heard?"

"Heard?"

"Jesus Christ. Jonathan was admitted to a hospital yesterday. Didn't Mom tell you?"

"No," I admit. Then I ask the clinician's question: "Why?"

She steps back and looks me up and down. Before her scornful gaze, I feel suddenly very small.

"You old fool. You old damn fool. Why do you *think* a man his age gets admitted to a San Francisco hospital?"

The implications sink in. I wait for the shock, the horror that never comes. I an inured to news of this disease.

"Does he need anything?" I ask her.

"It's too late," she spits at me. "It's been too late for a long time."

She collects herself, shakes her head once again, and walks away, wiping tears from her cheeks. I wait, watching her blend into the mass, but she never turns back.

The next afternoon I fly home. Since I left, the ground has frozen. There is a spit of snow on the wind. It swirls across streets and highways, gathering in lee places. It is a last, cold dust over my world.

My house is empty. There is no note, no number for me to call. I leave my bags by the door and drive back to the hospital.

survivors

*P*eople used to tell me that I reminded them of Harry Wilkerson. They were kidding, of course. Sure, we had the same Irish eyes, but from the beginning there was always something crazy in his. We had the same dark hair, but while he kept his combed back and slicked down, like the men in the magazines, I never gave a damn about the way mine fell into my face. We both spoke with New York accents, but his carried the sounds of Long Island money, and mine came off the side streets of Utica. Back then we both wore the same uniform: white coat, white pants. This story is about the different ways we wore that uniform, where the wearing got us, and the woman we both loved.

We'd been to the same medical school in Manhattan, too, but we'd never been close. Harry spent his free time at class parties, while I was working at a community clinic uptown. He learned to make connections, and I learned to take care of sick people. It takes knowing both to make the honor roll, and neither one of us did, so we ended up in Albany together.

At orientation that first day as interns, we sat together. He fell asleep during the lecture on the importance of the autopsy in the intern's education, stayed asleep through the discussion on malpractice, and didn't wake up until the presentation of dictaphone operation was done and it was time to break for lunch.

We walked together when the program director took us on tour. How provincial the place was, I thought as we walked the cluttered corridors. The library was tiny, the laboratories empty. The computers were obsolete. And all the patients were white.

"Christ," said Harry, "what a hole."

And it was. But my grandfather had died here. My high school physics teacher had come here for chemotherapy. As a kid, I'd walked the same wards to visit them, uncomprehending. For me, the place was only as foreign as home.

Harry was late the first day on duty. With me, he'd come in the afternoon before to run through charts, to fill index cards with patients' names and numbers, the names of diseases, the dates of admission, the results of studies. The old interns laughed at our earnestness. Harry left long before I did.

After rounds that first morning, after Harry finally came in, he came up to me.

"Man," he said, "I'm glad it's you on call tonight and not me."

"Yeah?" I said. Already I didn't like the way the guy worked. We walked toward the rows of open doors hung with clipboards that carried graphs of temperature and urine output.

"My head," he said, shaking it. "God, what a night! But what a great time!" He grinned conspiratorially. "I spent hours trying to find my apartment. I got up this morning, and I'd lost my car. Had to take a taxi in."

"You went out drinking last night?"

"Sure."

"The night before your internship?"

"What better reason, guy? Won't have much chance to do it again for a few days. Worth it, too. Met a very fine piece on the way. Lost her somewhere, too; I forget just where. Wish I could remember. I'd go back right now and try to pick up her scent again."

He had on a happy-go-lucky grin, full of orthodontist's

teeth. That was another way people could tell us apart: he was the smiling Irishman.

In the chart room I'd put up a schedule. It listed all the conferences we had each day: work rounds, attending rounds, chairman's conference, residents' seminar, radiology conference, pathology rounds, sign-out rounds. I'd worked it out the night before. Harry never read it. He cut all the departmental sessions that day and most days after that. He was out of the big house by four, his notes written, his patients seen. On his way out that first day, he gave me a list of his players.

"They're all fine," he swore to me when he saw me looking at my watch. "No problems from any of them all day."

That night I was like a raw dory man, shipping out into a great sea alone. All the preparation, the study, the sheltered apprenticeship, were done. I had cast off. There would be storms, I knew. I had seen others in heavy weather; some had gone down. But at last I had started out on my great voyage.

I foundered right away, and I spent the rest of the year keeping my nose above water.

A nurse—I've forgotten her name, but I remember she was Lithuanian, blond, and bluff and big-shouldered—asked if one of her patients might have a laxative. I went to see him, asked him questions, poked his belly. I looked up laxatives in a book at the nursing station. There were infinite choices: liquids, tablets, pills, suppositories, enemas—all in a bewildering variety of dosages. I called the resident.

"I need a laxative," I explained.

"What?" he said. "Already?"

"No," I told him. "It's for a patient."

"Oh."

"I don't know what to give him."

"What have you tried?"

"So far? Nothing. Any suggestions?"

"Jesus," he said.

I felt humiliated. I knew what to do for cardiac arrest, for acute hypertension, for medical crises, but when it came to laxatives I was lost. After a time we came up with something. I never found out if it worked. Life got busy. First I took a call from the emergency ward. I walked down and admitted a very sweet old woman with hair frosted electric blue. She was hemorrhaging into her bowel. The smell was terrible. She was quite embarrassed. She sat on a bedpan while we talked, and she interrupted my interview now and then with bursts of diarrhea and clots. She should have gone to the intensive care unit, but all the beds there were full, so I got her. I put lines into the spidery veins of her arms, transfused her, ordered all the tests that the resident had recommended to me, and sat down behind the ward clerk's desk to read about her problem. The head nurse interrupted me.

"Here," she said to me, "there's somebody I want you to see."

"What's wrong?" I asked.

"You're the doctor," she said. "You figure it out. This guy just doesn't look right. While you do that, I'll get your new patient settled in for you."

In a private room at the end of the long hall was a man alone. He was one of Harry's players, a "faggot," Harry had called him, and a shooter. He'd been in and out of intensive care with some obscure pulmonary infection, another complication of AIDS.

I went into the room. The man was sitting up in bed, leaning against the wall. He looked about my age and was even thinner. His hair was brush cut. His skin was pale and sweaty. His pajama top was open and wet. The bones of his arms and chest showed up starkly in the poor light. His mustache was ragged, and his beard was growing out in patches, like a new cancer. He did not look up when I came in.

"Hello," I said, trying hard to hide my fear of his sexuality and his disease.

He cocked an eye at me. The sweat in his hair shone under the one working fluorescent bulb.

"What the fuck do you want?" he asked. He spoke in a tired whisper that was yellow with bitterness. Through my paper isolation gown and rubber gloves, I felt his hatred touch me.

"The nurse wanted me to see you," I said.

"Fuck her," he said. His voice was flat and dull. He closed his eyes. He put his arms around his shoulders.

"What's wrong?" I asked, squatting by his bed rail.

His eyes opened slowly, as if looking at me exhausted him. The eyes were sunken and sallow, but steady, and over their depths I saw my own reflection dancing.

"I feel like shit," he said. "I'm sick, and I want to be alone."

"Sick how?" I persisted.

"Fuck off and leave me alone," he said, and his eyes closed down again.

He shivered. I put a hand on him. He was cold and wet, like a drowned fish.

"Don't touch me," he said, but I left my hand where it was. "Take your hand off me," he threatened, "or I'll give you my disease."

I took my hand away, feeling his sweat through the glove. He grinned at me malevolently. Then I touched him again.

"No," I said. "Tell me what's wrong."

He swallowed. The Adam's apple bounced in his thin throat. "I'm just sick," he said.

"That's all?"

"And... Oh, Jesus," he gasped. He retched once, then again, and then he fell forward over his own legs. He threw up blood, dark purple, the color of the shrouds put up during Holy Week, with clots in it that quivered like gelatin. The blood soaked into the sheets. It splattered on my pants and streaked the floor. It spilled onto my shoes.

He lay pitched forward like that, retching and coughing and sniffling, while I stared at him, frozen. After a moment he straightened up and fell back. He swallowed twice, panting, exhausted. Blood hung at the corner of his mouth and ran over the short hairs on his chin. It colored the back of his pale arm when he wiped his lips.

"Oh, God," he gasped. "Oh, God. Oh, God. Oh, shit."

I called in the nurses. While I was starting lines, the man threw up again. His blood was everywhere. It spilled out where I placed the intravenous needles until we had the tourniquets off and the fluids hung and running. It ran over my fingers, and somehow it wound up on my cheek. I drew blood for lab tests and cultures, and I ran into the resident in the doorway when I headed out toward the nursing station with the tubes.

The resident looked at me, at the welter of nurses' whites over the bed, at the guy passed out on the bloody sheets. He took it all in—the mumbling, the cursing, the confusion, the smell—and he shook his head. He started asking questions, and he started giving orders. First, though, he spoke to me.

"Your laxative must have been a little strong," he said.

"No," I said. "This is another guy, with AIDS."

He ran his eyes over my bloody clothes. "What's wrong with him?"

"I don't know. He wasn't feeling well. The nurses called me in to see him. I'd just started talking with him. He said he was sick."

"He was right."

"Then he started barfing blood all over me."

The resident patted me on the shoulder. "Cool down," he said. "It looks like you've done all right. The guy's still breathing, isn't he?"

"Yes."

"Well, good, That's a start. What have you done for him so far?"

I went over it for him while he went over the patient. He interrupted me now and again, to ask the nurses things.

The man was rasping, coughing to clear the blood from his throat. He lay still, save for the glare of resentment that he threw at us as we moved above him. While we talked, he vomited once more. A nurse caught the clots in a plastic basin. Our charge nurse, standing by his shoulder, checked his blood pressure again.

"It's dropping out," she told us. She was very matter-of-fact.

The man's eyes fluttered, turning up inside his head. Behind the limp lids and dark lashes, the whites of his eyes stared at us, blank and dead as plaster.

"He needs a bed in the unit," the resident said.

"But there aren't any," I told him. "They turned away my first admission just a couple of hours ago."

"She wasn't this sick," he said. "We'll find somebody we can throw out. It's easy to do. But we'll need blood to get him there. I'll get the bed, if you'll get four units for us."

"Sure," I said. "Can do."

There was one old woman in the blood bank that night. She was smoking a cigarette and watching a tiny portable television set. She didn't look away from the screen when I spoke to her.

"It'll take over an hour to cross-match that much blood," she said. She stubbed out her cigarette and started leafing through the requisitions I'd brought her.

"But I need some blood now," I said.

"You can't get it now," she said, intent on the television.

"What about type-specific blood? Can you release two units of that?"

"Do you know his blood type?"

"No."

"Then you can't have type-specific blood," she said.

She sat down and folded her hands. We stared at each other awhile.

"Damn it," I said, "you know his blood type. He was transfused last week. You have to have his type on file somewhere."

She sighed and scratched her head. "It's not that easy," she said. "Look: how long have you been here?"

"All day."

"That's just what I thought. Another one of those one-day wonders. God, I hate July. You kids don't realize yet that your patients can die from blood that isn't fully cross-matched."

"But he's dying right now, for Christ's sake."

"Don't curse at me."

"I'm sorry. But my patient is bleeding to death while we're here arguing."

"Hey, kid, listen: don't get excited. You'll last longer that way, believe me. Do you have release forms for type-specific blood?"

"No."

"Then I can't give you any."

I took a long breath. My fists closed. I wanted to sit down. I wanted to rest. Christ, the job was hard enough without this. This wasn't supposed to happen. I leaned over the counter. I kept my voice very calm.

"You listen," I said to the tech. "I will tell you this once. You will give me the release forms, and I will fill them out. You will look up this man's blood type while I do that, and you will give me two units of blood for this man when I have finished. You will do this because if you don't, I will call up your supervisor at home and wake her up. I will write you up for the chief pathologist and carry my complaint to his office person-ally. You will do this, because if you don't, this man will die, and I will report you to my chief resident and my attending and my chairman. I will light your ass on fire and hang it so high that this whole city will think that there's a new sun in the sky. Do you understand?"

She did the necessary and gave me the blood.

"There's no need to be hostile," she said in a surly voice. "I'm just trying to protect patients from gung ho kids like you. I mean, he could get hepatitis from this. He could get AIDS."

"He'd already got both," I told her.

"What?" she said. Quickly she put down the tubes of blood I'd given her. "You mean this stuff's infectious?"

"Read the fine print on your requisitions," I told her.

"How am I supposed to handle this?" she asked.

"That," I said, "is your problem."

Then I was humping the cold plastic packs of blood up back stairs and down dark halls.

They had the guy on a gurney when I got back. His big

lines were in. He had a catheter draining urine from under the sheets. I gave the blood to the nurses.

"Quick work," said the resident. "I wasn't sure you'd make it back in time."

"I live to please," I said.

They hung the first unit there in the hallway. The guy was trying to sit up, stoned by shock. A nurse with a hand on his chest whispered in his ear, and he lay still.

After they all had gone, the ward was quiet again, save for now and again a cough, a whimper, mumbles in an old man's sleep, the ticking of a metered intravenous drip, and the slosh of the housekeeping woman's mop in the empty room at the end of the hall. Then my beeper fired again, and I wandered off trying to remember where the telephones were.

When Harry came in that next morning, I was leaning over the bar of the nursing station with my face on my arms. I had pulled off my bloody new shoes and wore only paper shoe covers from the operating suite over my stained socks. The blood on my trouser cuffs had dried and darkened; there had been no time to clean it off. My shirt was wrinkled. I was buzzed on sleeplessness and the traumas of the night and the hits of coffee I'd done at three and five and seven to stay alive.

"Hey, baby," said Harry, "what truck hit you last night?"

"No truck," I said. "Just three admissions, a transfer out of the unit, and your man with AIDS."

"Yeah," Harry said. "I heard about that. Strong work there, dude. Got that faggot off the service fast. Shit, what trash. I couldn't even bring myself to look at him yesterday."

"I noticed that there wasn't a note from you on his chart. And his counts—didn't you notice that his hemoglobin was down two grams in three days?"

"Come on, man: you know yesterday was too crazy to have gone leafing through all that paper."

"Shit," I said, turning away.

"What?" he asked, following me down the hall to where our new resident was waiting to round with us. "You would have played it differently?"

"I don't know." I shrugged. "I'd at least have known something was wrong with him."

"Wrong with him? Hell, he's going to die. That's what's wrong with him."

"But he didn't have to try to do it on my shift."

"Better yours than mine, boyo."

"In your ear," I said.

Harry slapped me on the back. "Lighten up, man," he said. "It won't happen again."

The resident was balancing three cups of coffee in his hands, and he gave us each one. His coat was new white and stiff with sizing.

"Nobody died last night," he said to me.

"No," I admitted.

"That says good things about you. Cream and sugar?"

"No," I said. "I'm an intern. Everything's black to me."

The resident smiled and handed me a cup.

"I'm an intern, too," said Harry, "but I'll take everything you'll give me."

"I'll bet you will," said the resident, and we went off down the ward, discussing case histories outside closed doors, stepping in to thump chests, press bellies, hold hands, or just say hello. I took notes on three-by-five cards, planning out the day. Then the resident went off to conference with the chairman. He took Harry with him as far as the elevators, yelling at him quietly for not knowing his patients and their illnesses. When he had gone, Harry went off for doughnuts. I took the medical students around the ward again, changing intravenous catheters, writing notes, drawing blood.

It was a short day after that: rounds with the chief resident, lunch, radiology review, patient care. I spent half the afternoon with a diabetic whose blood sugar level bounced from near zero to off the scale. Each time I drew his blood to see where the insulin had brought him, he cursed me. They were flat curses, whispered at the window, just loud enough for me to hear. I tried not to hear them, so I could force myself to come back and stick another needle into him each time he needed it.

A gray woman hiding behind rouge lay on fluffed pillows in a private room. She was very wealthy: she had a private nurse, embroidered pajamas, and a room so full of flowers that it stank like a florist shop. Her nurse called me in. The patient had just come out of the coronary care unit the day before. She had a touch of chest pain again. I did a cardiogram and called the resident. We rushed her back to the unit. As the orderly wheeled her away, she lay on her gurney, panting with pain like a sick dog.

Writing orders, checking labs, scrawling notes: I kept busy. At the end of the day I looked for Harry. He was in the chart room, looking at a chest film on the view box.

"Look's like she's in heart failure," I said.

"Yeah? I was thinking that."

"Good thought. Tried any diuretic on her?"

"You know, I was about to. I was waiting for this, though. It just came up."

"If you wait too long, she'll drown," I warned him.

"I'll get to it. I thought you'd gone home."

"You know I can't go home until I sign out my players to you."

"Yeah, I know. I thought you'd forgotten."

I didn't answer that. We went over the list of my patients: names, ages, their diagnoses, their lab numbers, their allergies.

"Watch out for this one," I warned him. I circled the name.

"Who?"

"An old woman who came in last night. The gastroenterologists have searched her from the mouth down and from the anus up, and they still haven't found where she bled from. She worries me, though."

"Why?"

"Maybe because she's too nice to last. I don't know. I just worry."

"You worry too much," Harry said. "I'll watch out for her."

"Thanks," I said. Then I left him and his ward.

Outside, the city smelled of heat, hot tar, and hot engines:

July. The dusk was red in the west, full of dust and the murmur of traffic. I went home, to unopened moving cartons and the beer in the refrigerator. I dumped my bloody clothes into a bathtub of cold water and stood by the front window of my apartment, watching couples walk downtown and feeling lonesome. Supper was canned and cold and only half-finished before I fell asleep.

In the morning I went looking for Harry. He was still in the chart room. He looked ravaged. His face was dark with stubble and fatigue.

"How are my players?" I asked him.

He looked up warily. His eyes were charged with perplexity and fear. All the jauntiness had been burned out of them.

"I got five admissions," he said. He looked down at a chart blankly, sulking.

"Ouch," I said, feigning empathy but knowing that every admission he took was one I'd never have to work in. "How are my people?"

He stared down at the scribble he'd been writing. "She's dead," he said.

"What? Who?"

"Your old woman. The bleeder. She died. She deceased, boxed, kicked, snuffed, died. She died."

"How, for God's sake? She was all right when I left."

"She bled again. A lot. She bled and bled, and then she died. We tried resuscitating her, but she just bled until she died."

I had to sit down, remembering her, remembering her face, her blue hair, the politeness she'd used to hide her panic from me.

"Damn," I said. There were no other prayers to say for her.

"I got five admissions," Harry said. He held up his hand for me to count the fingers. "Five fucking admissions."

"She was too nice to last," I said.

"Can you believe it?"

"I remember," I told him, smiling to myself, "how she

refused colonoscopy until I told her how Ronald Reagan had had one. After that it was okay: she was a good Republican, she said, and willing to follow his lead."

"And that guy you sent to the unit the night before, that faggot—he died, too. He got septic again and went down for the full count."

"God damn," I said, and I couldn't forget—would never forget—the poison in his eyes as he'd glared at me before those eyes glazed over.

We sat there together a long minute, lost inside our own heads. Then the medical students came in, and then the resident. Harry put his chart away unfinished. We went into the hall to see the players again.

"It's a bitch, isn't it?" I said to Harry when we'd finished rounding and the resident was gone.

"It's not that," Harry said. "It's unfair. How can they expect us to do all this? Nobody can. It isn't fair."

"No," I said. "It's just the way it is."

"How profound," he said scornfully. "Listen: I have to get some sleep, man. Can you take my pager for a while while I crash?"

"Sure," I said, "for a little while. Five admissions is bad. Find me in an hour or so."

Harry crawled back to his call room. I went back to the routine. I answered pages for him: nursing requests for headache pills for cranky patients, lab reports, an outside call from some woman. Then I took my first hit from emergency: a college girl with a lump in her thyroid and a fever. We brought her in and cooled her off. Harry's pager called me out before we were quite done to see a patient with pneumonia who couldn't breathe. I called in the resident. We gave her some oxygen and changed her antibiotics to kill the bug growing in the cultures Harry had never checked. I went back to my admission, polishing up her paperwork.

Then everything went down. A transfer from the coronary care unit that Harry had picked up the day before, a fifty-year-old father of four, died. We called the resuscitation team, and it

seemed that half the hospital ran into his room, as if it were a
subway car at rush hour. We shocked the man until I thought we'd
burn the hair off his chest, but he was dead, and despite all we
tried he stayed that way. The crowd filtered away.

Harry's pager went off at my hip. It was the resident, at the
nursing station.

"Where the hell is he?" he was yelling.

"I don't know," I said. "He was going to rack out for an
hour. I didn't know he was going into hibernation."

"Well," said the resident, "find him. Now. And if you
can't find him, since you agreed to carry his beeper, I want you
to fill out the death note, the death certificate, and the autopsy
permit, after you notify the attending and call the family."

But before I could even look up the dead guy's chart, Gina
took me by the elbow. She was charge nurse that day.

"I wanted you to know," she said, "that Mrs. Praczyk's
temperature is back up to a hundred and three and that she's
having chills. Dr. Wilkerson told us this morning to give her
some Tylenol, and that brought her fever down for a while, but
now she's febrile again, and she's not looking well at all."

We went to see Mrs. Praczyk. She looked more than
unwell: she looked terrible. She was withered and old, with the
limp gray hair that neglected women grow in cheap nursing
homes. She lay on her side, curled up on herself, shivering in
the July heat. Then the shivering stopped. She unfolded. Sweat
beaded up on her face, over the veins and wrinkles and dark
spots of age. It collected in the deep hollows above her collar-
bones. She didn't answer when Gina shouted her name in her
ear, but when I rapped her right kidney, she screamed for Jesus.

I held her down while the nurses pulled up her gown. They
spread her thighs and ran a catheter into her bladder. Her urine
was full of pus, and it stank like a kenneled dog.

Again, there were no beds free in the intensive care unit, so
we snaked in big intravenous lines there on the ward. I drew
her blood and ran her cultures to the lab while the fluids and
antibiotics poured onto her fever.

Like a bonfire in a rainstorm, the fever died down and

smoldered. Mrs. Praczyk's blood pressure, flattened by the endotoxin in her blood, pushed up toward normal. It was almost there when Harry strolled by. He had on a big grin, but when he saw us working on his patient, he slid it into his pocket.

"She doesn't look well," he said to us.

"No shit," said the resident. "She looked damn near dead, thanks to you."

The rest of us stood in the hallway, waiting for orders, while the two of them yelled at each other over the delirious woman's body. Gina and I went out.

"It's amazing," she said, shaking her head, "what a little authority does to some people. From the way he's raking Harry over the coals, you'd never guess that he was killing old women on the same ward in the same way this time last year."

We all went back to work once the fireworks were over. When I signed out to the cross-cover resident at half-past seven, Harry was still going.

"You heading home soon?" I asked him.

He put down his chart. "Sure," he said. "I'm all in. It's late. Let's get out of here. Let's get a drink. I need one worse than you could know."

"Thanks," I said, "but I need something to eat."

"Good idea. We'll order up a pitcher and a couple of burgers. The nurses say there's a decent grill down the street. We'll eat. We'll get shit-faced, and we'll curse this damned place together. We'll have a hell of a time."

"Harry," I said, "I can't do that. I'm on call tomorrow. I've got to fix something to eat, and then I've got to get some sleep."

Harry looked at me for a moment as though I were an extraterrestrial. Then his face went hard.

"All right," he said. "Fuck you." His voice was bitter. He pushed his charts off the workbench and onto the floor. Random pages spilled out. He stared at the mess. "Fuck this job. Fuck this place."

He went into the locker room and came out with his

knapsack. People were staring at him. I got up and took him by
the arm.

"Harry," I said, trying to keep my voice low, "you can't
just walk out, not like this. You've got to sign out your
patients. What if something happens tonight? Ron doesn't know
any of your players."

"Fuck Ron," said Harry. "Besides, they've all got to die
sometime."

"But not tonight. Give the poor bastard a break. It's his
first night on call."

"Shit," said Harry, but he sat down. We racked up the
spilled charts together. While I called Ron, Harry tore a blank
page out of a chart and started scrawling names in his doctor's
handwriting. When he was through, I walked him to the street.

It wasn't that I ever particularly liked the guy. After only
two days I'd lost any respect I'd ever had for him in medical
school. But I knew that if I didn't pick up after Harry, if I didn't
help him out, he might not make it through the year. In that
case all the interns would be left one man down. Our hours
would get longer, and the call schedule would tighten. More
than that, though, Harry scared me. He could be me; I could be
him. We were all untested, all on the edge, and we never
knew—really knew, inside—that we could never fall off. Harry
was tottering, and by helping him go on, I kept myself from
crashing.

I left him at the front door of the hospital and walked
outside. Already outside was a foreign country, full of noise and
motion, of people intent on money and love, on traffic and
trivia, on all manner of things save death. On the street men
called up to dark women lounging on stoops or leaning out of
windows and waiting for the right look, the right word, to
come down. There were kids in the streets and weedy lots
paved with bits of brick and broken asphalt between the tene-
ments. On the littered courts near the projects, the boys, naked
to the waist and shining, shot hoops under the streetlights.

At home I locked the door on all that. I threw my whites
against the bedroom wall and went out to run. In the night's

new darkness, I ran down to the river. The black water sucked
at the bridge piers and the garbage. I ran past other runners, as
warily silent as they. I ran on and on, breathing in the exhala-
tions of the city.

My days and nights went on like that, tangled up in the
lives of people dead, or dying, or trying to die, or perhaps only
faking. Life became a series of admissions, like mileposts along a
highway, overtaken in a rush, resolved briefly into individuals,
then left behind as each patient was discharged home or transferred to the units or sent to the morgue. Here and there, like
splashes of light and landscape glimpsed through windows in a
tunnel wall, was the life outside.

We interns gathered in bars to escape the faces in the steel
hospital beds. Harry scouted the bars out for us. He was the first
into the one that became our favorite. He went there one night
with a nurse he'd picked up in the emergency room, and later
on he invited me. It was a nurses' bar, where they went from
the wards to ease the transition back to reality with cheap
drinks. It was not very much fun to watch, but some of the
women were put together quite well, and a guy never knew
what he might end up taking home. When I went in for the first
time, I was out of place and far behind the rest of them. Harry
had left the ward two hours before, trailing after the women
freed up by the three-thirty shift change. I'd stayed on, making
sure all our players were tucked in as well as I knew how before
I changed out of my whites and into my jeans in the public
bathroom off the hospital's main lobby.

The summer sweat on my back chilled and dried when I
came in off the street. Harry was at a table against the far wall,
and not alone. He waved to me.

"Hello there, old man," he said. "Save anybody since I've
been gone?"

"No," I told him.

Harry filled up the pause in conversation with a flash of his
hand. He was trashed.

"'Course not," he said. "Can't save anybody. Not a one.
Nobody can. I learned that my first night on call. It's all the will

of God." He winked at the woman he was drinking with. "He still tries to save them, though." He shook his head and nodded toward me. "Don't you?" he asked. When I didn't answer, he turned back to the woman. "This guy's a great saver," he said. "A great intern. A giant. A genius. Another young Osler in the making, right here in this dumpy little burg."

"Shut up, Harry," I said, still standing.

"Oh, my. Now I've made him mad. But it's true. Christ, you've saved my ass often enough. 'Harry, watch out for this. Harry, don't forget to order that.' Answering impossible questions for me on rounds. Guy's a great saver."

He winked at the woman again. She sat there, behind a polite smile, running a finger over the beads of water on her highball glass. Her smile was makeup, like the lipstick, the blusher, the eye shadow. She hung it on her face to deflect us while she concentrated on important things, like her drink, and it was all she left behind to entertain Harry while she let her mind drift off to some place on the far side of the moon.

"Introduce us, Harry," I said. "The lady doesn't want to hear about work."

Harry stood up and did what I'd asked him to do, apologizing profusely, like a drunk. I watched her come back from wherever she'd been to focus briefly on me. The lines of her smile tightened for a moment. She gave me her hand. We said hello.

She had gray eyes and Celtic red hair that she wore long. Her mouth was small, but the lips were full, and when she let go of my hand, she pressed a strand of that hair against those lips, playing with it, playing with me. I didn't rise to the invitation, and besides, it was only a reflex for her, conditioned flirtation. When Harry started chattering again, his words slurred and garbled, she dropped her hands back around her glass, and the woman behind the eyes fell far away again.

"Harry's very generous," I told her.

"Yes," she said. "He's buying my drinks."

"He just gets this way sometimes," I said.

"I like him this way," she said, shrugging.

"I like you both, too," said Harry. "Here: sit down and join us." He pulled me into a chair. "This," he told the woman, "is my man. They probably would have fired me already if it weren't for him."

"No," she said in a tone of voice that said she knew that he was probably right but knew as well that he was picking up the check.

"Well," Harry told her, "he certainly keeps me from being beaten as often as I ought to be."

"But I would have thought you're the kind of man who finds excitement in a little beating," she said to him.

"Only if it's mutual," he said with a leer.

I let that line of conversation go by.

"It's sweet of you to look after him," she said, to let me know she didn't give a damn.

"He exaggerates," I said.

I went up to the bar and ordered nachos and beer for my dinner. For once Harry was right: it was a depressing place. There were too many women looking for too few men, and Harry had the best-looking one all to himself. There were knots of women around tables and at the bar, with interns and residents here and there among them. A few I knew from work. White pants, black beepers, and the driven way they poured stories about other men's mistakes into women's ears distinguished the rest from the civilians.

A ball game played on the big screen above the jukebox, and I joined some of the guys who sat apart from the women to watch it, more enthralled by the classic choreography of the diamond than by the mating dances going on around us.

When I went back to the bar for a refill, Karen was there, drinking alone. Being an intern, too, she had on a white skirt. We struck up a conversation. She introduced me to the gang from her unit at the end of the bar. She looked out of place, a woman doctor in a nurses' bar.

Harry and his nurse got up from their private table. He went to the jukebox and threw in quarters. They danced through the random rhythms of the songs. She danced with her head hanging back, staring at the old pressed-tin ceiling tiles while her long hair shivered and Harry bounced around her. Somebody asked me up, and we joined them. Then there were people all over the open space between the tables and the bar, going at it hard, bumping each other, spilling beer on the sticky floor. There were two women dancing with me, three with Harry. A couple of the guys got up to join in, but most only stood at the bar, chewing on their beer glasses and looking at our exuberance with disapproval.

Then I was dancing with Harry's nurse. She was moving in little half-circles, wholly self-absorbed. She was staring at the door, at the front windows, at anything but me. So I slammed down on my knees between her feet. It hurt, but it got her attention. I got up, and we started moving together. I was dancing faster and faster, pressing against her, pressing her to come alive. She did. We opened a space for ourselves among the sweating young bodies with the flutter of our white shoes on the dirty floor.

When she was out of breath Harry cut in, and I went back to the bar. I stood watching them.

"Come sit with us," she said when the floor got too crowded and they both were spent. She clung tightly to my arm and put her lips too close to my ear for me to refuse, so I filled a last glass, and we waded through the mob to their table. She started talking about herself, flushed with liquor and dance. Her name, she reminded me, was Michelle Corrigan—Micki, after her father. She'd been born in the city, and she liked it.

"Why do you do it?" she asked me, changing the topic and the tempo of our talk.

"Do what?" I said, fanned by her change-up.

"Work in that fucking place." She gestured across the street, to where the shadows of the hospital were creeping toward us as the sun went down.

"I don't know," I said.

She grinned and took a pull at her drink. "You're a liar," she said.

"He loves it," Harry said.

"No," I told them, "I hate it."

"You really are a liar," she said.

I sat back in my chair and scowled at her. I put my feet up on the fourth chair at the table and tipped my chair back. She looked at the stained pink laces, and she knew what they'd been dyed with. She stared into my face smugly.

"You," I said, "are a bitch."

She knocked down the last of her drink and smiled at me through the bottom of the glass. She ran her tongue around its rim, then put it down.

"You're right about me," she said, "but I'm right about you, too."

"He does it because he cares," said Harry. "He's one of those caring physicians." The sneer in his voice jangled in the air more jarringly than the ice cubes in her empty highball glass.

"Shut up, Harry," I said. "You're drunk."

"Do you?" she asked.

"Do I what?"

"Do you care?"

"I suppose."

"Such conviction," said Harry. "But it's true. He does. I told you that he was a saver."

"Do you save them?" she asked.

"No," I told her. "If I wanted to save them, I couldn't. If I could, I don't think the really sick ones would want it."

"Then why do it?" she asked.

"It's personal."

"Tell us," said Harry. "We're all friends here."

"Fuck you," I said. I looked back at Michelle. She was drunk, too, but even drunk, she was sober. "It pisses me off," I told her. "Death pisses me off."

"Eloquently phrased," Harry said. "But I don't see it. Death's one of my best friends. Pals since childhood, you know."

"Pals to the grave," she added.

"Sure," he said, uncertainly.

She turned on him.

"It pisses me off, too," she said.

"Well," he said, "excuse me. But it seems that death covers our paychecks. If it weren't for death, we'd be out of a job."

"Harry," she said, "you're morbid."

"I certainly am. That's why I'm in this business." He reached into the pocket of his white pants. He pulled out a packet of rolling papers and a plastic bag half-full of dried weed. "But let's change the subject. Anyone care for some?"

"My God," she said. "Harry, put that away."

But he kept right on rolling his joint there on the bar table.

"It's very good shit," he said to us. "And there's more than half left—plenty for the three of us."

"Thanks," I said, "but I've got to go."

"Oh, no," he said. "It was just getting fun."

"I'm sorry," I said. I stood up.

"So am I," Micki said to me.

Harry ignored me. I stood there until he was done, until he'd licked the paper down and wiped the seeds and bits of stem onto the floor.

"I'll see you tomorrow," I told him.

"Here," he said, "we're leaving, too."

He crammed the plastic bag back into his pocket, and the two of them got up. We waded through the crowd to the door. A softball team had come in while we talked. Most of the nurses and residents had gone home. All the rest were paired off or drunk. We elbowed past them all, calling out and waving to the few we knew.

On the sidewalk, next to him, she looked fragile and small. He stood with an arm around her body, with his fingers fanned out on her hip. I smiled at them and shook her hand. She told me that we'd have to get together soon, and I couldn't disagree.

"See you at eight," I said to Harry.

"Maybe," he said. He grinned, teasing me.

He handed her a pack of matches, and she lit the joint for him. She took it from his lips and offered it to me. I declined. We said good-bye again, once or twice. Then they went off together.

Under the clouds, after the bar lights and the drinks and the music and the sound of voices, the quiet July darkness in my room was like tar, thick and gloomy. Later, rains came and cleared the air. I lay in bed listening to fading thunder and then to the plashing, gentle as kisses, of roof drops on the concrete outside my window.

In the morning the sky was clean, a brutal blue. Harry came in late again. A little before nine we tagged along behind the resident to open rounds. Harry whispered in my ear.

"Have a good time last night?" he asked.

"Sure," I said, sick of his grin. "It was great. You?"

"Baby," he said, turning his eyes to the ceiling, "she ain't much to talk to, but when the lights go down—"

"Harry," the resident interrupted, "would you care to tell me what you're grinning about?"

"No," he said.

"Then can you tell me how Mrs. Carranzada is this morning?"

"I haven't heard anything about her," he said, "so I guess she's doing just fine."

It went on like that for weeks. We all tried to help Harry along. He didn't give a damn.

One day, a little after noon, we were in a patient's room. He was dead. We were trying to bring him back. It wasn't working. Harry got off the man's chest and went over to the resident directing the show.

"Call it off," he said, "before the nurses send his tray back to the kitchen. I missed breakfast, and I'm starving."

All the interns in the room broke up laughing. We kept on for a few more minutes. In the end all we could save was Harry's lunch.

In the long run there was no saving Harry. In the long run Harry didn't want to be saved. I knew that from the day I walked in on him one afternoon. He was in the bathroom. The door was locked, but the latch hadn't caught. When I pressed the handle, the door swung open. Harry was leaning over the sink with his forehead against the mirror. He'd seen me come in. His sleeve was rolled up, his tourniquet on. His syringe was on the floor, dropped in his panic.

"For God's sake," he whispered, "close the door."

He sat on the toilet seat and picked up the syringe. "Baby, baby," he said, "don't scare me like that."

I stood against the closed door with my arms folded.

"Man," I said to him, "you are crazy. You can't do that shit on duty."

He uncapped the syringe and drove the needle into his arm. He pushed down the plunger, shivered, and sighed. Then he stood up and put a hand on my shoulder. He was leaning hard on me.

"But they're killing me," he said. "I can't take it."

"You have to take it," I told him. "They're killing all of us. That doesn't mean you have to be dead."

"I have to. I am. I'm dead. I'm way past you now."

"No."

"Shit. What do you know? All you need is a cup of coffee, and you're wired for the day. I can't keep up with you unless I'm coked. If it were any one of the other guys, I might have made it, but nobody can keep up with a hotshot doc like you. I died trying. You started strong, and you keep getting better. I look like an idiot next to you."

"You're not trying. And you're not an idiot. Remember: there's people depending on you."

He leaned over the sink, staring into the mirror, looking for something that wasn't there.

"I never asked anybody to depend on me," he said.

"But they do."

He smiled at his reflection, then turned and smiled at me.

"That's their mistake," he said. He slapped me on the shoulder. "Come on—let's get out of here before people start to think we're getting it on."

But he put his hand on mine before I could turn the door handle. "You won't tell anybody about this?" he asked.

"I won't have to," I told him.

"We'll see," he said.

That week the chairman called Harry into the main office for his second warning.

On Friday I signed out to Harry. Then I called the night resident and went over all my sick players with him, just to be safe. By then we were all doing that. And the nurses had instructions to check all orders with the residents when he gave them. We tried to hide that from him, but he knew. And still he didn't seem to care.

The bar across the street that evening was crazy with women. Micki was sitting alone at a table by the window. Her hair was pinned up. Instead of makeup she wore a bruise under one eye. She was watching the traffic pass. I sat down at her table and did the same for a while.

"How are you?" I asked.

"Fuck off," she said. She did not turn her head.

"Sure," I said.

I got up and went to the bar. I sat down there and looked at her, looking back quickly enough to see her staring at me before she glanced away. I joined in the flirting and tried to forget her, except that whenever I turned her way, I saw her watching me.

After a long time she came up and asked me to dance. The first numbers were fast, mad things. She held her liquor well, but she danced in a tight, controlled way that gave away how much liquor she'd had. She let her hair down after the first song and splashed it all over her body.

The music slowed. Lovers got up from dim tables. Micki stood still, with empty hands open toward me, waiting for me to take her in my arms while couples kissed and spun around us. I looked at her stupidly.

"Would you like another drink?" I asked.

"I'd rather dance with you," she said.

"Oh," I said.

"You look disappointed. I thought we were having fun."

"Sure. We were. I was, anyway."

She put her arms around me. We moved awkwardly awhile.

"Why?" she asked.

"This isn't going anywhere," I told her. "You know that."

"You're being loyal to Harry," she said.

"Why not? He's my partner."

"He isn't worth it."

"You believe that? I thought you loved him."

"Loved him? I partied with him. I slept with him. Love is shit. I learned that from him. I got this shiner from him. Did you think I walked into a door?"

"I try not to think," I said.

She laughed a little and held me close. Her body was warm and soft and damp from the dancing. She led, with her bruised cheek on my chest.

"Relax," she said, but I couldn't do it.

She shook her head and laughed again. It was a short, pained laugh, bitter with incredulity.

"The crazy bastard," she went on, remembering. "You know, I did tell him that I loved him. He knocked me out of the bed."

"Nice," I said.

"I had to throw him out."

"Obviously."

"I tried calling him at home. He wasn't there, or more likely he just wouldn't answer. I was stoned enough to fall asleep eventually, but I woke up before morning. I tried calling again, but it was no good. I went by to see him on the way to work, but he wasn't there."

"He came in to rounds this morning, on time for once. He didn't say anything about it."

"He may not even remember," she said. "He was blind at the time."

"He's on call tonight."

"I don't see how he keeps it up."

"He doesn't. I'm carrying two-thirds of the service. They've assigned us an extra medical student. The chairman's given him a final warning."

"No."

"Again. It's his third."

She laughed again, rubbed her face against my neck, and pulled me to her.

"Talk to him for me," she said. "Tell him that I'm looking for him."

"I thought he wasn't worth it."

"He can't help himself. I can't either. Promise me?"

"Sure."

The music quit. I relaxed, knowing at least what she wanted from me. She took my hand, and we went back to her table. All around I saw the ward gossips' eyes follow us.

"You know," she said, tracing out the veins on the back of my hand with the tip of her finger, "you look a lot like him."

"People say that," I said. "It isn't true."

"It is," she said, "but at the same time, you're not like him, really."

"Is that a compliment?"

"Yes. You listen. I appreciate that."

"I'm a doctor. I listen to people's stories for a living."

She let go of my hand. "You don't have to be that way," she said. "I'm trying to be nice to you."

"Don't be," I said. "I'll talk to Harry. You don't have to seduce me to make sure I keep my promise."

She swung around in her seat sullenly, her face to the window.

"You want another drink?" I asked her.

"Please," she said.

When I came back she'd put her face back together, had rubbed the despair out of her eyes.

"Let's change the subject," I said.

"To what?" she asked.

I shrugged. "I'm the listener," I reminded her.

"All right," she said, and so she told me about her father, and I listened. "He's an ex," she told me. "Ex-marine, ex-cop, ex-husband."

"Ex-father?"

"No," she explained: he was a good father, like he'd been a good Democrat and now had become a good Catholic. "He's

tired," she went on, "that's all. He's been tired for a long time."
He lived on the first floor of the family duplex, smoking
cigarettes and watching ball games day after day. He lived on
his pension. The second floor of the house had been his since his
brother-in-law died, and he fixed the plumbing for the renters
upstairs when the pipes choked on their paper diapers. He ran
errands for the ward boss. He spent his evenings at the Knights
of Columbus, or in the corner bar.

"I go by to see him every couple of weeks," Micki said, "to
change his sheets, to vacuum the rugs, to scrub down his
kitchen. We sit over beers, and he tells me stories about grandparents and cousins, about losers and heroes, about Irishmen."

"And your mother?"

"She left him when I was four."

"I'm sorry."

"That's the one thing he doesn't tell stories about: his
marriage. There isn't a picture of her in the place. I know: I've
looked everywhere for one, cleaning. He must have burned
them, like she burned him."

The conversation faded out, like the light outside. We sat
silently, watching the traffic signals change through the window. I looked at my watch.

"I have to go," I said.

"But it's early yet."

"Not for me. I was on call last night."

"I didn't realize. I'm sorry."

"That's all right. I've had a good time."

"Me, too. Can I drop you somewhere?"

"No. My car's in the hospital garage. I'll be fine."

"All right. And thanks for helping me."

"I'll talk to Harry," I said. "I'm not sure I'll be helping
you."

She stood up to kiss me good-bye. Walking through the
echoing garage, listening to the sweet songs on the radio as I
drove home, I felt the ghost of that kiss on my lips. I was still
thinking of it—and damning myself for a fool—when I fell

asleep, buzzed on the amplifiers' afterburn in my ears and the taste of regret in my mouth.

After rounds I bought Harry doughnuts and coffee. We sat together in the cafeteria, and I listened to him curse his patients and his luck.

"I ran into Micki," I broke in.

He tipped back his chair, trying not to sneer. "And how is she?" he asked.

"She's all right, considering somebody beat her up the other night."

He laughed. "God," he said, "I was really messed up that night, even for me. But she asked for it."

"She said to tell you that she's looking for you."

"I'll bet she is. She can look for a long time before she finds me. She's got the look in her eyes now. It isn't just for fun anymore, not for that little piece. She's got her claws out, and she wants to get her hooks in."

"It's not like that, Harry. I think she loves you."

"Exactly, boyo," he said, "and I've got no use for a woman like that. She's looking for commitments, and I haven't got any to give—to her or any bitch."

"You're a jerk, Harry."

"No. I just know myself. And I can read her like an open book: she's looking for a husband."

"You've got to be kidding. Not her."

"Sure she is. She's a woman, isn't she?"

"Yeah, but Harry—"

"Tell her the party's over. I don't make commitments. And I don't hang around women who want them."

"Man, you're crazy."

"You're damned right I am. It's the only way to be." He stood up. "Hell, you'll see I'm right. If you don't believe me, marry her yourself. She'll say yes the first time you ask. Damned if she won't."

He strode away. I never told her what he'd said. She never asked.

There was only one week left until the first rotation ended.

All through August we'd watched Harry come apart. We kept him working, the resident and I, so we wouldn't have to carry all his load. We almost made it.

I came up from lunch early one afternoon, and the nurses told me that Harry was in the chairman's office again.

"It wasn't so bad," the chief resident told us later, "that he left the line open. Sure, he should have known better than to give potassium like that. But I've done the same thing, or nearly, and almost killed people. If any of us says he hasn't, he's lying. Giving wrong meds in wrong doses by the wrong routes: it's part of learning. You feel bad about it, and you swear never to do wrong again. But to defend it the way Harry did, to say that the poor sick old bastard was dying anyway—well, even if that was true, I couldn't let it pass. I had to call him in."

But the chairman still didn't fire Harry, just gave him one more final warning. By then, for Harry, it had become a game. Every day he was pushing harder, mocking the rules old men had made for doctors in training, daring the boss to throw him out. One day he didn't come in until noon. We canceled rounds that morning, and I took over all Harry's players, which pushed me to twenty-eight. When Harry showed up, he was drunk. One of the attendings hustled him off the ward, away from patients and their families. When the chairman got back from his businessman's lunch with the medical school dean, Harry was fired.

To hear the secretaries tell it later, Harry went out fighting. He lunged across the desk and swung at the chairman, broke a lamp, and started knocking framed diplomas off the wall. He earned himself an honor escort and was paraded out the front door of the hospital between blue uniforms.

Without him to help me, the rest of that week was like combat. The resident and I took our first incoming from the emergency room that morning, and the admissions office shelled us mercilessly and daily until the weekend. I ran down the halls with my head down. There were patients crashing all over the ward. There was never any time for us to dig in and organize: we patched up the sick, and we wrote off the dead. I quit wearing a tie I went scuttling from room to room in a two-day beard and a bloody scrub shirt, drinking coffee from a pint mug and catching naps on the morgue gurney behind the public toilet.

Somehow we stayed alive—most of us. None of the deaths were surprises: lung cancer, metastatic breast cancer, pneumonia in an eighty-four-year-old paralytic, bedsores burrowing through the backside of a demented nursing home derelict. But they all died slowly, so that they stank before they died. They all died afraid of dying, unless they recognized death no better than they recognized the children and grandchildren who held their hands and whispered of their grief and their love and their pain to heedless ears. The deaths were all wasted, empty of dignity, of meaning, of hope. They left me with nothing but the taste of crematory ash in my mouth and an abiding anger in my soul.

Before Harry left, I'd started dating. She was a nurse on our ward, blond, a little plump, very sweet. Twice we went out to pizza halls, drank beer, and talked of home. She was from western Massachusetts, from a mill-town family, but born after the mills had moved to Taiwan. She had a wild kid sister and parents who served their union and the Sacred Heart Society with equal faith, and she told me stories about them all.

It fell apart once Harry was gone. We sat on her sofa one night when her roommate was gone. She kissed me eagerly, with promises on her lips, and I kissed back, until I remembered things I hadn't done for the sick on my ward. As her mouth and her hands worked, my eyes closed. I saw the faces of my dying patients, the lines of bone under taut skin, the spotted hands, the white bellies. I smelled their smells, of shit and unguents, of gangrene and old urine, until I had to go outside to breathe. In the doorway, I kissed her good-bye.

Later, at home, I sat in the dark with another beer, listening as the voices of couples fighting mixed with the melodies of love songs sifting through the box elder leaves of the brownstone courtyard. It was easy to make excuses: she saw how hard I was working. After a while she stopped asking me out. We were always very cordial to each other afterward, but the hurt in her eyes damned me every time we passed in the halls.

I put her out of my thoughts. I was learning to be efficient.

The first ward rotation ended. I left the people I'd known for eight weeks during my baptism of fire. I went on to the unit.

On that first morning in intensive care, we walked around, the departing night crew, the new resident, and two green interns. It was a different world, a world of machines. Their sounds filled the rooms: the metronome beat of cardiac monitors, the susurration of respirators, the electric whine of portable X-ray cameras driven from bed to bed, the stammer of pagers. All the rooms were clean, the wounds all covered, the patients all silent. Most of the sick we met that morning lived in the limbo of coma; the rest gnawed respirator tubes and spoke only with their eyes. There were no raised voices in the unit. We in white who fluttered round the sick were too busy for such trivialities as conversation. There was talk in the chart room, and here and there among the beds when we conferred, but our words were hushed by the monotones of the machines and the immanence of death.

Michelle was in the next-to-last room. She had brushed her red hair up. It was set off very well by a wine-colored scrub suit under a long white coat. When she saw me she turned away, and when we came to her patient she did not speak to me. We finished rounds and went on to the X-ray board. At midmorning, though, I went looking for her.

"How's your life?" I asked her.

"Fine," she said. She was untangling tubing. She did not look up.

"That's good," I said. "Seen Harry lately?"

"Off and on," she said. She walked around the bed, straightening sheets for an old woman with Raggedy Ann hair gone gray.

"You don't want to talk to me, do you?" I asked.

"No," she said. "Did you want to talk to me?"

We stared at each other down a long pause.

"No," I said. "I was just making conversation."

"You must have better things than that to do your first day here," she told me. "Is this your patient?"

"No," I said, looking through my list. "She's Carrie's."

"And where's Carrie?"

"I don't know. Around. Why?"

"She needs to be around here. This girl's got a temp."

"Yeah? How high?"

"Hundred point nine."

"That's not a fever, though."

"No? Tell me, doc: what are you brilliant young scientists calling a fever these days?"

"A temperature isn't considered actionable until it hits a hundred one."

"Is that so? Well, somebody had better act on this fever. This woman's tachycardiac, and her heart won't race for long. She's outbreathing her ventilator, and that's not just because she's scared." Michelle pulled down the woman's cover sheet. "You see this line?" she asked, pointing to the big central cath that ran into the woman's groin. "It's eight days old. It's been begging to get changed since it was put in. I've been begging to get it changed for days, ever since the site started turning red. The last team procrastinated so that they could sleep, so that heroes like you could have the benefit of the educational experience. Now it's infected. My girl's septic, and she'd going to die real soon unless somebody changes her lines and starts running antibiotics through them."

"I'll tell the resident," I promised, and I left them. I could feel the eyes of the two women—patient and nurse—follow me as I walked away.

I told the resident, but before she could do anything we were paged to the emergency room to admit a homosexual with fever, a new recruit to the AIDS epidemic. We went through the routine, handling him with rubber gloves. We cultured every space we could put a needle into, trying to catch the germs that made him sweat. The resident was called back upstairs for some emergency; I finished alone. The man was thirty-two. He worked on the fourteenth floor of one of the state office towers downtown. He was sweating and hyperventilating—more from fear than from disease, I thought, until I saw his chest films. His lungs were full of trash. I called the pulmonary specialists down to see him, and they signed him up for bronchoscopy.

I went upstairs on the elevator with him. He lay on the gurney with his hands folded stiffly. His lover rode with us, and on the way up he leaned over the rail and took my patient's hands in both of his. He pressed his face to them. His tears moistened their fingers. Then the elevator stopped. The doors opened. We pushed the gurney down the hall together. Outside the bronchoscopy suite, they kissed each other good-bye. I went in with my patient alone. The other man stayed outside, weeping silently for the two of them.

On the way back onto the unit, I walked by Michelle's room. It was empty. She was gone. I did some useless things for a while. When my new patient came back two hours later, he had a hole in one lung from the biopsy; the surgeons had been working on him. We put him in Michelle's room. I found her there.

"What happened to your girl?" I asked.

Michelle hit me with a look full of fire and acid. She crossed her arms and stood in the doorway while the orderlies rolled the new guy in.

"Died," she said.

"No."

"Hell, yes. I told you she was going to."

"Jesus. I'm sorry. I did pass the message on, you know."

She smiled wryly and shrugged. "It's not your fault," she said. "But a lot of good you passing my messages on has done me lately."

She grinned, and I smiled a little, trying to figure out what she thought of me. We set up our patient: orders, drugs, lines. That afternoon his lungs failed. We intubated his trachea and started him on a respirator. He would stay on it thirty-seven days.

I strolled around to study my players: a fat woman with bedsores so deep that changing her dressing took thirteen yards of two-inch gauze pack, a shriveled smoker with dead lungs who lay inert all day while his respirator did his breathing for him, an alcoholic with cirrhosis who'd hemorrhaged the night before and who tried to bite his nurse whenever she reached over to comb his hair. There was one kid my brother's age, just out of high school; he lay in a coma with leukemia, hepatitis, failing kidneys, and a mother who cried at his bedside all the time.

It was like that in the unit. So many of the patients were young, for only the old have earned the right to die. The young die, too, of course, but when they first try, they are caught, then pounded and shocked back into a semblance of living. They are rolled into the unit, there either to recuperate or decompose until doctors and family despair and turn off the machines.

Still, with those machines came an illusion of control. By each bed as I rounded that first day, nurses filled tables with numbers: lab results, vital signs, culture reports. We monitored the flow and oxygenation of blood, the production of urine, the input and composition of gas in the respirator tubing. We walked through the rooms titrating oxygen and fluids, potassium, sodium, chloride, calcium, magnesium, and phosphorus, along with albumin, red blood cells, and platelets. We added and took away antibiotics, diuretics, bronchodilators, analgesics. We listened to chests and bellies, touching gingerly bodies that could not respond.

After hours I went looking for Michelle. There was no one I knew at our usual bar, only a couple of touch football teams celebrating—victory or loss, I couldn't tell. There was a dance hall uptown she'd said she hopped at sometimes, but she wasn't there. I thought to wait for her, but the beer in the place was overpriced and warm, and the lean boys in black jeans and the college girls with their been-there eyes stared at me until I knew just how old twenty-six can be, and I had to leave.

At home I played rock music too loud while I ate refrozen pizza. I played the music until the ceiling tiles shook and my tiredness hit me like a wrecking ball. I fell asleep trying not to listen to the girl next door break her bed with the boy upstairs.

I met Michelle the next day, over lunch. It had been a long morning. An old toddler with heart failure had remembered to take his pills too well: he'd finished a full bottle in three days. He was still convulsing when his daughter found him. It took us hours to quiet him down. When we were through his numbers were on their way toward normal, but his brain was like an ice-cream cone dropped on a hot sidewalk and forgotten.

Michelle was sitting by the window, looking out at the dumpsters and the laundry and the coal bins for the heating plant behind the hospital.

"May I join you?" I asked her.

She said nothing, but with her foot she pushed a chair toward me. I sat down and started working on my tray.

"You're not talking much today," I said.

She put down her fork. "What's it to you?" she asked.

"To me? Nothing."

"Liar," she said.

I chewed on that awhile. We watched men in blue shirts unload blue shirts from the back of a truck.

"I'm sorry I got mad at you yesterday," she said. "But I'd been working with that woman for most of the eighteen days she was in that unit. I'd started to get attached to her. It wasn't your fault."

"I'm sorry she died," I said. She nodded in polite gratitude. "I went looking for you last night," I told her.

One eyebrow went up. "Not very successfully," she told me.

"You weren't around."

"I was with a guy."

"Oh. A new guy?"

"No. We go back pretty far."

"That's nice. Serious?"

"You could say that."

She seemed to lose interest in talking. I worked on some macaroni and cheese. She watched me eat. I tried not to look at her staring. I went on to a hamburger. The ketchup dripped out the back and onto my leg. She laughed.

"Were you thinking about cutting into his time?" she asked.

"No," I said. "Nothing like that. I was just making talk."

"Bullshit. You were making time."

"No."

"Don't lie to me. I've been around a little. I can read a man's face. What do you take me for, anyway—a virgin?"

I stumbled around, trying to think of the proper answer to that question. "I wouldn't know," I said at last.

Her grin was ready to burst; she was playing with me. "I think we should go out," she said.

"No," I said, choking.

"Sure. We could have a good time. We should do something together."

"That's all right."

"You don't like me."

"I didn't say that."

"But that's what you're thinking."

"No."

"Then let's do something. Tomorrow night."

"I'm on call tonight. I'll be dead."

"I know how to keep guys like you alive," she said almost deadpan. "Come on—you're just making excuses. You don't like me at all. You think I'm too forward."

"No. It's not that at all. What about your guy? The serious one?"

"Oh," she said, "he's very open-minded. He's willing to share."

"I see."

"It's a date, then. Tomorrow night."

"But where will we go?"

"I'll take care of that."

"Shit," I said.

"See you upstairs," she said, standing.

"Yeah, I guess so."

"No enthusiasm," she chided. "You have to have enthusiasm. You really shouldn't treat a girl any other way."

"No," I said.

"Cheer up," she said. She pecked me on the cheek. "It won't be so bad."

That night was bad, though. At eight we took a transfer from the surgeons—a fifty-year-old plumber whose hemorrhoids they'd just taken off the week before. Now he was feverish and groggy, and they dumped him on me to figure out why. He was a puzzle until his nurse and I turned him onto his side. His scrotum was a tense blue black, and the skin came off on the sheets. We called the surgeons back to take a look. They put their intern up against the wall for not bothering to look before. Then they took the patient to the operating room and cut off his gangrenous scrotum, burying his testicles in pockets inside his thighs. I went by later and took a look; they did a very neat job.

After that we were called out to the floors to pick up a girl with ascending paralysis. When we got to her she was numb below the neck, and she couldn't breathe. We stuffed a tube into her trachea and took her to the unit. She was perfectly conscious through the whole thing. We told her the French eponym for her disease, told her it was self-limited, and told her that she'd probably be back to her old self in three to six months. We parked her in a corner of the unit where the machines could breathe for her until then.

Somebody died on the cardiac unit, and we spent an hour over her until somebody woke her cardiologist and he called us off. We ran to resuscitate a woman on my old ward. There were high-fives and handshakes from all my old friends on the night nursing crew. The patient's heart was trying to play dead when we got there, but after we hit her with the defibrillator a few times, it gave up and started beating again. The residents assigned her to the intern from the heart unit, and we left him there, cursing us, as he started to write up her history for the chart. Toward dawn we were called upstairs to a rehabilitation ward to resuscitate a legless diabetic whom the nurses found cold on their morning rounds. We worked him very briefly, as a sop to attendings and malpractice lawyers. Then we went off to catch what sleep we could before the day crew came on.

In between all that I wandered the unit, calling up the resident now and then with new numbers and new ideas, playing with dials, falling asleep on a countertop.

After rounds I went down for breakfast. I sat at the end of a table full of interns eating Danish and gabbing.

"So," said one, "this incontinent old fart calls in his nurse. 'Nurse,' he says, 'I'm going.' So she puts him on a bedpan and goes out. He calls her back. 'Are you finished?' she says. He just grabs her arm. 'Nurse, I'm going,' he tells her. She looks in the pan. 'No,' she says, 'you're not.' He shakes her arm. 'Yes, nurse,' he says. 'I'm going. I'm going.' She looks again: nothing. Then the old guy falls back in the bed. He's gone. Dead and gone. He really had been going all along. No, man, I swear to God it's true."

Everybody laughed but me. It had happened on my ward to one of Harry's patients. The poor nurse had been devastated. I got up and finished my pastry on the stairs, its sweetness bitter in my mouth.

At six Michelle came to hurry me along. I was almost through with charting. She sat and talked with the ward secretary about how tough their jobs were, then changed to bitching about docs they'd both dated.

"Here," Micki said to me as we went down the broad steps in front of the hospital, "put this in your pack." She gave me a paper bag with a pint flask inside, and I stuffed it into my knapsack with unread journals and yesterday's underwear.

"Where are we going?" I asked her.

"First," she said, "I want you to meet my favorite guy, like I told you. Then we'll get something to eat. You hungry?"

"I need another cup of coffee," I said. "I'm not sure I'm up for this."

She took my arm in the crook of hers and ran me down the sidewalk. "Poor baby," she said, laughing at me.

She took me across the street, over grass killed by the

September frost, through half-empty parking lots, and into the Veterans' Hospital. We took an elevator to the fourth floor. We went down a long hall littered with old men in wheelchairs. Sitting on the edge of an old steel bed in a room with five other men was her father. There was football on the television, replays playing in slow motion to nobody. The room smelled of burned-out cigarettes, drugstore cologne, and well-dressed wounds. When we came in, the storytelling stopped and the old men watched the young woman walk across the floor with her red hair flaming for them.

Her old man got up when she came in.

"Well," he said, "look what the cat dragged in."

She turned her face up to him and kissed his cheek. "Hello, old man," she said.

He grinned and held her and patted her back. Like the rest of them, he wore uniform pajamas with an oversize robe and green foam-rubber slippers. His thin red hair was combed back and slicked down. His skin was thickened by too much sun. His fingers were stained with tobacco. At the open throat of his blouse was the tip of the red, angry scar that marked a fresh chest wound.

Michelle introduced me. I shook his hand; it was all bone. Then I stood against the wall and gazed at the two of them, father and daughter, talking about relatives outside and their lives inside, while the others watched the three of us.

"And how are you really, Dad?" she asked. Her voice turned soft and whispery after the bantering.

"Oh, well enough, kid. Well enough. The nurses here have tried to put the moves on me—you know how nurses are—but I kept them off."

"Watch out for those nurses," she said, glancing at me.

"Yeah, I've managed to fight them off, by and large."

"Oh, so it's by and large, is it?"

"Well, now," he said, "it wouldn't do to make the nurses angry, would it? After all, they do run the place."

"That's true, Dad. You know that's true. Are you having any pain?"

"None to speak of They give me pills enough for that."

"That's good. And you get enough to eat?"

"There's plenty of food, but none of it fit to eat. You know I ain't got any appetite anymore, anyway."

"But, Dad. You've got to eat."

"Sure. When I get home, then I'll eat. We'll have dinner together. Ain't that right?" he asked me.

"Sure," I said.

"He don't talk much, do he?" Mike said to his daughter.

"Not like you, Dad."

"A quiet man, without the gift of gab," he said, eyeing me. "And yet at least he's got a good Irish name. Not like that Orange bastard you ran around with last summer."

"Who, Harry?"

"Yes, Harry. Harry. Christ, Jesus, and Mary: Harry. What kind of a name is that for an Irishman, I ask you?" He was asking me.

"Good enough to please the queen," I said.

"Damned right," he said, "and no woman else. You stick to the real Irish," he told his daughter. "And quit running with those dagos and Jews and Polacks and spics, too."

She was silent a minute or two.

"Here," she said, getting up from his side and stepping over to where I was. "Let's have it."

I pulled out the flask for her, and she slipped it into a drawer that held two white handkerchiefs, a Social Security envelope, and an open bag of imitation butterscotch candy. There was an empty liquor bottle there, too, and Michelle passed it to me.

"Can't leave this out on the ward, can we?" she asked me.

"Hell," said Mick, "we just walk them past the elevators to the other ward, where they keep the vegetables, and we dump them in the lounge there. Don't anybody there know where they come from."

"Dammit, Mick," one of the guys in the room said, "you shouldn't ought to let her bring that stuff in here."

"Shut up, Hubert," another told him. "You're just pissed

'cause your kid don't never come up here to see you, much less bring you booze. She ashamed of you, Hubert?"

"That ain't it," Hubert said. "It just ain't right, having hooch in the hospital."

"This ain't hooch," said Mick, pulling out the bottle to study the label.

"And this ain't no hospital, Hubert," another threw in. "It's a goddamn nuthouse, and you being here proves it. Leave Mick alone."

"You do share it, don't you, Dad?" Micki asked.

"Sure I do, girl," Mick told her. "Everybody gets his licks."

"That's right, Micki," one man said. "Everybody here as wants, gets."

"It still ain't right," grumbled Hubert. "Ask the doc. He'll tell you: it ain't right."

"All right," said Michelle to me. "You're the doc. Is it all right?"

"It's your liver," I told Mick.

"But is it right?" Hubert pressed.

"Sure it is. And you know why?"

"Why?"

"Because," I told them all, "if I tell you anything different, Mick's kid here'll kick my ass. That's why."

"Shit," said Hubert while the others laughed at him.

"Listen, Hubert," said Mick, "you're so holy, you should have been a priest. How in hell did you ever get into the army?"

"I was drafted. You don't think I'd volunteer to live with a bunch of assholes like you guys, do you?"

They started hooting him. Then a nurse came in. We slammed Mick's drawer shut. She pushed a wheelchair over to Hubert.

"It's time for your radiation treatments," she said.

Hubert got into the chair meekly, and she pushed him away. Micki said a few words to the old man. She gave him his mail—mostly bills—with love from the family and another kiss. We all shook hands around the ward.

"Hey, doc," one man said to me, "you watch out for that girl. If she's half as crazy as her old man, she'll have you so you don't know up from down in no time."

"Hell," I said to him, "if that's all I got to worry about, I'm home free. I haven't known that for years."

They all waved good-bye. They were a very happy crew.

"That's a cancer ward, isn't it?" I asked Michelle as we went out through the lobby, past the bored guard under Mr. Bush's picture.

"Yes," she said.

The night was blue-black and twinkling with cold. There was ice on the sidewalks. We walked downtown to a restaurant she knew.

"What's he in with?" I asked Michelle.

"He's got a squamous cancer in his right lung."

"Did they get it all?"

"What?"

"Somebody put a hell of a mark on him. I presume it was the chest surgeons."

"Yeah," she said. "No, they didn't get it. When they opened him up, there were mets to the trachea and across to the left side. They took one look and closed him."

"Damn."

"He's refused the radiation treatments and the chemotherapy."

"No. That's not so smart."

"It is for him. You're thinking like a doctor, saying that. You see, he had a friend die of the same thing—not the same, of course; they're never the same—and he took the radiation, and he died from that before he could die from the cancer."

"But that's an exception to the rule."

"For him," she explained, "there aren't any rules, and there aren't any exceptions. There's just his friend, who's dead."

She took my arm and put it around her shoulders. We walked in silence down the cold streets until she found the restaurant.

"You're really not hungry?" she asked.

"I'll eat something," I said. "Right now I'm too tired to even work up an appetite."

We went in. The place had cinder-block walls, painted blue, with a deep maroon carpet and weak lighting. The tête-à-tête tables were full of young lawyers and bureaucrats in pastel shirts, eating salad with sorority grads. Here and there were women together, serious women, without men.

I looked all over the menu for a good steak, but the only ones they had came from a tuna. Michelle ordered one, and it was fine, if you liked tuna.

"How's your meal?" she asked.

"It's fine. Very artfully done."

"You don't like it," she said.

"That's not true. I love vermicelli, and the sauce is intriguing. I'm mainly just tired, is all."

"Here, have some more coffee."

She flagged down a waitress. The coffee was black and strong and scalding, but it wasn't working anymore. The conversation went to hell.

"You want to go, don't you?" Michelle asked.

"Hm? Oh, no. We'll stay as long as you like."

A guy with a ring in one ear and sunglasses on a cord around his neck came over to our table. He and Micki talked about the band he worked in, about club gigs and guitar men. I listened to them talk while I spaced out, drowning in the undertone of hushed voices all lost in the big room.

Then she was introducing me. We shook hands.

"You an intern?" he asked.

"Yeah," I said, smiling like an idiot, no good for anything more profound.

"Tough job, I hear."

"It's a job."

"But the hours, and the things you guys have to put up with—you must all be crazy."

I looked him over. I had been thinking the same about his work.

"It helps to be a little crazy, I guess."

"I could never do it."

"It gets routine after a while."

"You guys," he told Michelle and me, "are sick." Then he rubbed her shoulder. "I'll see you later," he said. "I got to go."

"From high school," she said with an explanatory wave of the hand after he had gone.

Then the check was paid. We walked past guys in tight pants and girls in pink skirts with lots of thigh shown off well by lace stockings. They all sat in pairs along the bar, legs swinging idly, ready to entangle. We went back to the hospital, and I was in her car. The engine was ticking over softly, and she was talking to me.

"Care for a drink?" she asked.

"That's all right," I said, apologizing. "I know I'm not much for company tonight."

She leaned across the seat and kissed me. "You're being very sweet," she said. "You're trying hard. I like that."

"Thanks," I said.

The lights of the oncoming cars hurt my eyes. I let them close.

She parked outside her place. Half-naked trees shaded us from the corner light. Her apartment was upstairs, off a second-story landing that had one dim lamp with a torn shade, an oval stained-glass window, and a smell of mothballs. While she went into the kitchen to fix our drinks, I settled back on the sofa. I was dizzy from the day and the night and the day after and now tonight. I felt myself deflating on the pillows like a punctured blowup punching doll. I listened. From the back of the apartment came kitchen sounds, nice, homey sounds: ice in glasses, the refrigerator door, a woman singing.

Michelle woke me with her hand on my shoulder. She was sitting on the edge of the sofa, one arm over me. She had on her white uniform, and her hair was pinned up.

"I have to go to work," she said. "I hope you slept well."

I lurched up, pressing into her. There was gray light in the window. The air smelled of coffee and, so close to her, of woman's soap.

"There's fresh coffee on in the kitchen," she said, "and I set out towels for you in the bathroom."

Her voice was gentle, like her fingers brushing the hair out of my eyes. I swung myself past her and stood, dropping her afghan on the carpet. I rubbed the unwashed stubble of two days' beard on my face.

"What is it?" she asked, her voice concerned, a little confused.

"I have to go, too," I said.

"But it's only six-thirty. I thought your rounds didn't start until eight."

"That's right," I said, "but I still have to go."

"Why? You can stay here. It's no problem. I'll leave you a key, and you can bring it in with you. It's not a far walk."

"You don't understand," I said. "It's not that. I can't stay here."

"But why?"

"Christ. Why? Because I'm a fool. God, I'm so embarrassed. Some date, wasn't I? I looked worse than your sickest patient. I couldn't hold up my end of a light conversation. I fell asleep in your living room. I'm really sorry. I feel like a jerk."

"Don't," she said. "I'm not sorry. I had a good time."

"Don't bullshit me."

"Excuse me. I'm not bullshitting you."

"Don't start that. I may be a damn fool, but I'm not that blind. You don't bring a guy home just so you can drape a blanket over his face while you sip his drink alone in the kitchen."

"But you looked so tired. I couldn't wake you."

"I looked like hell. You were very kind, but you see why I have to go."

She sighed and stood up. "All right, you dumb bastard," she said. "Suit yourself: be a fool. You weren't before, but you're being one now."

She went into the kitchen. I heard her putting dishes in the sink. She went into the bedroom and came out in a long coat. I was standing at the window, looking out on the street. There were snowflakes in the air.

"I thought you were leaving," she said.

"I am," I said.

"Well, then get the hell out."

She watched me with her arms folded while I picked my coat out of the closet, caught my knapsack off the back of a chair, and left. She locked the door when I closed it.

The hall was cold, and the street was colder. Dirty puddles scummed with ice were dusty with snow. The sky was gray and aloof. Snowflakes blew about aimlessly. They blew against my face, melted, and ran down my cheeks. In the wind my eyes burned.

I drew a week's vacation, and I wasted it at home. I watched television with my mother, drank beer with my father. I went to church with the two of them and smiled politely while they showed off the young doctor to all their friends. I went off alone, running down side streets under gray skies. I drove out into the country, where the cornstalks were yellow and the trees were bare, and I walked with my kid brother's dog over the dead leaves. I read pop magazines and pulp novels. I covered myself with the ephemeralities of ordinary life to hide from myself the marks—not scars: too fresh for that—the dead had left on me. The anodynes failed, and I went back to the city. The dead were dead, and I was not. For that, there was no excuse or explanation, and work was the only penance I could offer for the sin of being a survivor.

My work I wrapped around myself. It was a cloak that shut out fantasies, memories, dreams, and shame. Under its mantle there were no abstractions anymore, no love, no tenderness, no compassion. There were only bodies, digits on lab sheets, the slickness of fresh X-ray film, the smell of adhesive tape and soap and blood, the sounds of bowels and breathing and heartbeats in the earplugs of a stethoscope, and the endless whisper of the respirators in the unit, like the distant, ceaseless sound of surf in a storm.

I learned about the unit, where diseases moved faster than the lab techs, and despite my inexperience I had to guess at diagnoses. Still ignorant, I treated what I saw with what I knew, and I prayed—prayed that in the blur of saving and dying, I recognized my mistakes before they were fatal, knew fatal mistakes before they were repeated, and saw repeated mistakes before I got caught.

I quit drinking, except alone, and then only in the dark, at home in the cold, listening to mice chase each other through the brownstone's walls while the north wind wrestled with the trees beyond my black windowpanes.

I heard that Michelle still went out nights, but I did not try to find her. I heard that she was still as wild as ever, that she was seeing other interns: Ira, David, Paul, even Rick, the bozo who'd transferred from some Caribbean medical school to fill Harry's place. I hoped she had better times than she'd had with me. Carrie ribbed me about Michelle as we waited for the residents to start rounds one morning.

"You know," she said, "for a time there I thought you two were really going to be an item."

"You thought wrong," I said, "again." I threw a chart in the rack, picked up another, and kept on writing. She didn't take the hint.

"Don't get defensive," she said. "It was obvious."

"I am not defensive," I said. "And it certainly was not obvious."

"Sure it was. She was sweet on you, too."

"Bullshit."

"No. It was true."

"Then she must just have gotten smart. And she didn't take very long to get over it, did she?"

"Ooh, you're horrible. So sensitive, too."

It was too ridiculous. I got up and went out of the room. Carrie's laughter followed me down the hall. I played with X rays until the residents and the students all came together.

That day Michelle and I worked on a fat, dropsical woman with a weak heart and sick lungs. Almost a month ago she'd caught a cold. It turned to pneumonia, and she'd been intubated. We extubated her a little before lunch. I went by to see her at the end of my day. She was breathing on her own, but not very confidently.

Michelle had gone home long before. We had said little to each other all day, and that of no significance, a few formal words that screened my pride and my heart. I leafed through her notes in the bedside chart. Reading the careful female script, I could see the pen; seeing the pen, I knew the fingers. I felt them reach for me.

I shook myself back into the present. The woman's lungs sounded clearly through the stethoscope. All her numbers were in order. She looked up at me mutely, through the frightened eyes of a hurt animal. I touched her arm. She winced at the sudden pressure on the venipuncture bruises.

"You're doing well," I told her. "You're fine."

Her facial muscles twisted—a grimace or a smile, I couldn't tell.

Later that week I was on call. I worked through the round of admissions and crises, praying for them all to die so that I could rest. As I ran from room to room, the work became a wave that crested and broke and bore me away, drowning. It ebbed a little before dawn, and we were all still alive, my patients and me. I found myself in the nurses' lounge sipping bitter coffee brewed the day before.

Michelle found me there. I dropped my eyes when she came through the door, and she walked past me without speaking. I was still sitting there, watching the coffee cool, when she came out of the locker room.

"How are you?" she ventured.

"Great," I said. "I'm great. How about you?"

"Fine. You look tired. Bad night?"

"Just the usual."

"Is our patient still alive?"

"They're still alive, damn them."

"I see."

"How's your old man?"

"The same. He's home now. I see him almost every day. He's hurting, but he's still toughing it out."

"Still refusing the radiation?"

"Oh, yes."

"Crazy old bastard. You've got to admire a guy like that."

"I do," she said. Then her face brightened. "I saw your old friend Harry the other day."

"Yeah? Speaking of crazy bastards, how's Harry doing?"

"He's worse than ever, now that he doesn't have anything to keep him occupied. He says hello."

"Hello, Harry, you son of a bitch."

"He's going to put himself under," she said, "if he doesn't lay off a little. I spent four hours with him last night, for old times, and I'm still high."

I threw away the coffee and got up. The stuff tasted terrible anyway.

"Some guys'll do you that way," I told her. I started to go out.

"You know," she said to my back, "I was trying to be nice and talk to you. I'm trying to be your friend. You don't have to be an asshole."

I paused a moment, then kept walking. She followed me. I stopped and turned to her, and she walked into me. I looked down into her eyes, mad as hell.

"About that," I told her, "you are dead wrong."

On Friday Carrie and Michelle were working with a very sick woman. The patient was in coma, had been for weeks, as different organ systems failed. At midmorning she finally died.

I ran across the ward to her when her monitor alarms went off, dodging frightened visitors who froze in the center of the hall and blocked my way. Michelle had her mouth on the woman's cracked lips, blowing air in while Carrie rode the patient's chest, pumping. I strapped on the leads of the cardiac monitor while the other doctors straggled in, breathing hard. Somebody put the paddles in my hands. I looked to the resident, who glanced at the monitor, then nodded. I waited until the others were clear of the body, then put the paddles to the woman's chest and shocked her. She leapt in the bed and lay still, pulseless. We turned up the juice and zapped her again.

Then Carrie went back to cardiac massage. Somebody got a tube down the woman's throat, and we gave her raw oxygen. We gave her adrenalin, fluids, drugs. I shocked her again.

A rhythm showed on the monitor. It was weak, grew stronger, faded, and disappeared. I shocked her once more, but the rhythm wouldn't come back. We pumped on, pushing ever more powerful drugs into her sclerotic veins. The rhythm came back again, only to fade away once more like ripples disappearing on the sea. I got up on the bed and took my turn at pumping. I kept going a long time before the resident told us all to stop.

We stood around the monitor, watching the straight, flat line trace out on the paper.

"She's dead," I said.

"Be patient," said the resident, and as we watched, the needle jumped and was still, throbbed twice and was still again, fired once more and caught rhythm.

So we all went back to it. The backboard that supported us cut into my shins as I knelt by her chest, pumping. I looked up. Michelle was watching me. She looked away when I caught her eye. She focused on the intravenous tubing, injecting meds when the resident called for them. There were empty syringes with their long needles broken off all over the medicine cart beside her.

"Are you getting tired?" someone asked me.

"No," I said, grunting with the effort of resuscitation, "just pissed off."

"What is it?" asked the resident.

"She's dead, damn it," I told him.

"But she's still got a rhythm," he answered.

"Show me," I said.

I counted, and at five I jumped down. Another intern was up and pumping before I could get to the monitor.

"This isn't a rhythm," I said. "This is garbage."

"As long as she's got it," he said, "I can't stop."

After a few minutes the throbbing needle steadied, and the line it drew grew straight again. There was one last quiver, then nothing.

"All right," said the resident, "let's call it."

We all stood down. Micki and I glanced at each other across the corpse. Micki smiled at me, tentatively. I frowned, rolled my eyes, and shook my head. We all started to leave.

"Wait," said the resident, "she's coming back."

I looked at the woman. She was just as dead as before, but the needle was dancing again.

"Check her pulse," the resident instructed.

I felt at her neck for the carotid. "No pulse," I said.

"Then let's start again," he told us.

"Shit," I said, loud enough for him to hear. I got back on the bed. My shoulders ached. My fingers were cramping.

After ten minutes we stopped again.

"We've lost it," the resident announced.

I got off the bed and went back to the monitor. The tracing was dead flat. I unplugged the monitor from the wall, and the tracing stopped altogether. I went over to the body and pulled the wires from the electrodes on her legs and arms.

"What are you doing?" the resident asked me.

"She's dead," I told him. "I'm cleaning up."

"But her rhythm might come back."

"She'd still be just as dead."

"But you can't just disconnect her like that."

"I just did," I said, coiling her wires around my fist.

"That's totally inappropriate," he said. "Give me those wires."

I gave him the wires. He plugged the monitor back into the wall. When he went to put the leads back on the patient, I unplugged the machine. When he went back to plug in the monitor again, I pulled off all the leads and pulled the sheets up to the patient's chin.

"I can't believe you just did that," he said.

"Believe it," I said.

No one else said anything.

"Do you have any idea what kind of trouble this could get you into?" he asked me.

"Look," I said, "if it makes you feel better, go ahead and

fire me. I really don't care anymore. If you want to take care of all my patients alone, go ahead and fire me. If you want to stay up all night working on these people, then fire me. Is that what you want?"

"You bastard," he said.

"Then get off my case," I told him.

I went for the door.

"I can't believe anyone would do this," he said again.

I whipped around in the doorway. "Here," I said to him, "believe this."

I went up to the dead woman and took her by the shoulder. She had no flesh there, only bone. I shook her. She bounced around on the bed. She was already cold.

"Hey," I shouted into her ear. "Are you dead? We have to know. Are you really, really dead? Tell us the truth, or we'll put the paddles to you again."

I put my ear to her lips. I listened to the infinite silence inside the toothless mouth. A sound came up to me like the sound of the ocean inside a shell. I straightened.

"She says she's dead," I told them all. My voice was tired, my anger spent. "She says to fuck off and leave her alone. Are you satisfied?"

"You're crazy," the resident said to me, amazed.

"I guess maybe that's true," I said. "But it's the only way to be around here."

"Where are you going?" he asked.

"To call her daughter," I said over my shoulder. Then I stopped and turned to him. I felt beaten. I felt like a fool, again. My voice was chastened. "I'm going to fill out her papers. Then I'm going to try to save the poor bastard in the next room, and the guy across the hall, and the woman at the end of the unit. Do you want to help? Or are you going to stand here all day and play with a corpse?"

I went on down the hall and back to work. Eventually they all joined me.

The daughter couldn't decide for or against autopsy for her mother when I popped the question to her. I gave her the line we had all been taught to throw in order to get the bodies to the morgue. I explained how autopsy would help us to know what had happened, how that knowledge could be used to benefit others in similar situations of great need. I pitched it beautifully, but it was all wasted. She didn't hear me. She could only hear herself crying, and she went on for a very long time.

Later, Michelle came up to me. The unit was quieter, and I was catching up on my charting.

"Hello," she said.

"What is it?" I asked her.

"Well," she began, "everybody's been saying—"

"I don't care what everybody's been saying."

"Shit," she said. Then she tried again. "Look, I just wanted you to know that we all feel you did the right thing, pulling that woman's monitor leads."

"I didn't do it because it was right. I did it because I was enormously pissed off at this place and what it does to people. I did it because I had other things to do. And I don't care how all of you feel about it."

She stood there a moment, grinding her toe into the linoleum, watching it work, and shaking her head. She looked up and caught me staring at her.

"You don't have to act like this," she said. "Not with me."

"I'm not acting," I said. "It comes naturally."

"That's not true."

"Isn't it? How would you know? And why should I care?"

"I'm your friend, damn it."

"Are you?"

She pursed her lips and turned her back on me. "I wish you'd stop," she whispered. "I wish you'd just stop this."

"Stop what?"

"Stop these games."

She turned back and faced me. Her chin came up, and her voice rose. "God," she went on, "I wish you'd stop acting like you have no feelings, like you're some kind of doctoring machine."

"Oh, do you?"

"Yes."

"You'd rather I walked around crying and hysterical when these people die? Or maybe you think we'd all be better off if I just didn't give a damn about any of these people, if I went home early and came in late and slept when I was tired and went home when I was completely disgusted with the whole thing, like most of the other interns? Or maybe you want me to just flame out, like your pal Harry? That was certainly pretty to watch, wasn't it?"

"No," she said.

"No what?"

"No, it wasn't pretty. No, I don't want you to be like that. I just don't like seeing you hurt. I've been watching you these last few weeks, and I can see how this job is hurting you."

"I volunteered." I shrugged. "Besides, what is it to you?"

Then Carrie came into the chart room, looking for the coffee urn. Michelle went out.

"Damn you," she said to me.

Leaving, she splashed me with her eyes. The look was acid; I burned all day.

Of course, I paid for pulling off the old woman's leads. My service went from eight players to fifteen. Every day there were more admissions, and I was assigned two for each one that Carrie got. We took them from the emergency room, from the doctors' offices, from the wards. We ran to resuscitations, lugging defibrillators and shaking pens and loose change from our pockets in our hurry. When we succeeded in our resuscitations, we cursed ourselves, knowing that the patients, having survived death, now required new tubes, new lines, new numbers, new orders, and new notes in thick charts in order to stay alive another hour, another year. I worked like I had the week when Harry left, except that the patients all were deathly ill. Still, these were the last weeks of the rotation. The days went by quickly, like the last miles of a marathon.

At midweek I got a page from the chairman's office. He wanted to chat. He wanted to review my progress to date. His secretary was very cordial. I had other things on my mind, but she would not be put off. We made a date.

Thursday, after morning rounds, I sat in the chairman's waiting room, looking at my hands and at the photographs of the secretary's kids and the framed prints of Renoir girls and the carpet pile, worrying about my people on the unit and waiting for the man to catch up with his appointment book.

The room was quiet. There were no sounds of respirators, no alarms, no shouting, no tears. It was all quite serene, and it had nothing to do with me.

The secretary showed me in. I sat with my legs crossed in a deep blue armchair. The room smelled of pipe smoke and textbooks.

"How are you?" the man asked after the handshake.

"Great," I said, settling back in the chair. "Everything's going really well."

"Is it?" he asked, sounding bemused. "That's good. I don't hear that often from interns. I'm glad to hear it from you. You're in the intensive care unit now, aren't you?"

He had a manila folder open in his lap with my name on the tab. While we talked he thumbed through the pages.

"Yes, sir," I said.

"Enjoying it?"

"Oh, very much. And learning quite a lot, too. It's like you told us back in July, that first day: we're living on the exponential slope of the learning curve."

"Yes. It gets a little steep at times, though, doesn't it?"

"It's never dull."

"Exactly. Getting along well with the other interns?"

"I'd say so. Although, of course, the job doesn't leave a lot of time for socializing."

"That's true. Made any close friends?"

"Not really. As I said, there isn't much time for getting close. We hang out together, if that's what you mean."

"Sure. You're not married, are you?"

"No."

"Have a girl?"

"Nothing serious."

"Any hobbies?"

"I like running. I go camping when I can. When I was a kid, I had a stamp collection."

"Did you? I went in for coins myself. They were real silver then. It's getting a little cold for camping these days, isn't it?"

"Yes, sir."

"Getting a little cold even for running, now that we're starting to get snow now and then."

"Yes, sir."

"Then what do you do with your free time now?"

"Well, sir, frankly there isn't much free time just now. Fortunately, I find the work very fulfilling."

"That's good. That's very good." He held up my folder. "Your resident and faculty evaluations from your first rotation were quite laudatory, you know."

"Thank you. No, I didn't know that."

"Still, I get the impression from talking to your colleagues that you are a very hard-driving individual."

"I don't like seeing people die. I try to work hard to keep that from happening."

"That's good. That's very praiseworthy. Still, it always happens in the end, doesn't it? I also get the impression that you are a difficult person to get close to."

"Some people have that opinion. I'm not a glad-hander."

"Yes," he said dryly, "I can see that." He took a long breath and turned a few pages in my folder. "You worked with Harry Wilkerson on your first rotation, didn't you?"

"Yes."

"How did his leaving affect you?"

"I carried his caseload for a while. It wasn't fun."

"But I mean emotionally."

"I thought it was overdue. I was relieved."

"You knew he had an alcohol problem?"

"That was certainly the rumor."

"Drugs, too?"

"Possibly. I didn't know him well. As you said, I'm a tough guy to get close to. Harry and I were never close."

"You have no such problems."

"Oh, no, sir."

"I'm glad. You see, I worry about you. Yours is a very stressful job, and you seem to be very good at it."

"Thank you."

"But the stress has a way of coming to the surface. It requires release."

"I'll keep that in mind."

"I'm sure you will. You see, some people can handle that stress better than others. Dr. Wilkerson couldn't handle it at all. Still, we all have our limits. Even you."

"Of course."

"And you know what your limits are?"

"Yes, sir."

"And you know to come to me if you should feel that you're pressing those limits?"

"Yes, sir."

"Fine. I just wanted to hear that from you." He closed my file and dropped it on his desk, closed. "I want you to know that my door is always open to you. I'm here to talk with you, if things get too rough, if you ever need a friend."

"I'll keep that in mind, sir."

We stood up. We shook hands. My palm was sweaty and cold. In the hall I leaned against the pastel wall. Feeling strangled by the man's politeness and hypocrisy, I shed my tie. I balled it up in my breast pocket to get it out of my way. Then I went back to work.

There were two new admissions waiting for me. One was a simple case: an asthmatic cardsharp who'd stayed too long in a smoke-filled room. The other was a young guy, very young. He'd picked up a girl in a bar, and from her he'd picked up a case of crabs. The feel of lice crawling made him crazy. He washed three times a day with a pediculocide meant to be used weekly. Even when the bugs were all dead, he could feel them moving over his body. At night he woke, and they were crawling over his belly and his genitals, up over his chest, into his ears and nose, filling his mouth. He absorbed the ointment through the scratch marks on his skin. By the time he came to see us, his liver was poisoned and his bone marrow was dying. There were streaks of old blood around his nostrils and over the excoriations the jaundice drove him to scratch deeper every day. We tied his hands to the bed rails, transfused him, gave him platelets and antibiotics, worked on him hard, but he still died quickly, as the young ones do.

That evening, working on my third admission, I watched Michelle go out. She had on a blue scrub suit, but she covered it with a black wool coat. She kept her hair tucked away under the collar. Her broad-brimmed hat hid her eyes from me when I waved good-bye.

The third patient had arthritis. His limbs were stiff from joint disease and old strokes. He had pneumonia, the old man's friend, but his attending wouldn't let the two of them get familiar. The family didn't realize that the old guy was dying; they'd watched him fading for so many years that the last step didn't register as final. The old man died anyway, in the end, without the consent of his doctor or his children. In fact, he died three times that week. Twice we brought him back, each time more heavily bruised, more heavily medicated. The third time, though, he beat everything we threw at him and got away.

I went down to the cafeteria just before eight, filled my tray, and had just enough time to sit before my pager went off. I ran upstairs, trying not to aspirate my first mouthful of meat loaf. By the time the crisis had passed—I've forgotten now what it was—the cafeteria had closed. I had pale coffee for dinner and gnawed my hunger until morning.

The emergency room called. It was Ira, one of Michelle's new friends.

"Listen, guy," he said, "I hate to do this to you, but Harry Wilkerson's down here."

"So?"

"So we're admitting him to you."

"Harry? What the hell happened?"

"He tried to kill himself. He got drunk and tried to crawl into some bushes in Washington Park around dark. Luckily for him, he passed out before he got in too deep, or he'd never have been found. It's going to freeze tonight, hard, and in a few hours he'd have been dead. The cops brought him in. He's hypothermic and in coma. Can you work him up down here?"

"Sure," I said.

I left instructions on two of my problem players with their nurses and went downstairs. Harry was in a private room, away from the noise of the emergency ward. He wore a white gown under a white sheet, and he was as calm and still as snow. His face was bloodless, and his hands on the sheets were pale and cold. His half-lidded eyes glistened, all white. He was as white as his sheet, white as a scar, white as death. He was angel white.

Ira stood at the head of the gurney, playing with tubes. Harry wore a big-bore tube down one nostril, with another tube in his mouth. He had an intravenous drip running into one arm and a bladder catheter draining out from under his sheets. He had a temperature probe in his rectum and three blankets on his chest. I worked him over quickly. Ira went outside to take care of the papers. When I was done, I sat down beside him.

"How's it been down here?" I asked him.

"It's a zoo," he said. "It's a mess. It's started snowing outside like you wouldn't believe."

"I wouldn't know," I said. "I haven't been outside since dawn."

"I haven't either, but when you go out into the lobby and the doors open for another case to roll in, you can see it falling outside. The surgery boys are already catching hell from the trauma cases the ambulance jockeys are carting in—people who've been putting off putting on their snow tires. If Harry hadn't been found when he was, this would have dusted him over. He wouldn't have turned up until spring."

"How cold was he?"

"Ninety-one point two when the paramedics first checked."

"He was always a pretty cool guy."

"He'll get over it, the shit. I mean, it's not like I don't have enough to do tonight without having to warm up a drunk intern."

"I hear you. You think he did it on purpose?"

"Probably. Word is that his medical license had been revoked, pending completion of an alcohol rehab course. He was thrown out of the course last week, since he'd never been to a single class, and they made his revocation permanent today."

"Damn."

"Nick got into the chairman's office and looked up his mother's number down on the Island, just to let her know. Turns out he brought down his bankbooks and the title to his car in a box of med school memorabilia last weekend. Told her it was for safekeeping."

"The stupid son of a bitch."

"Well, it's not like we haven't all thought of doing the same thing, when the shit really starts to go down around this place."

"I suppose," I said. We sat and thought about that for too long. I stood up to go.

"Hey," said Ira, "I hope I don't have to call you down again soon."

"Not as much as I do," I said. He grinned in sympathy. "Still, it's only until the weekend."

"Yeah," he said without enthusiasm. "Then I'm out of here and into the coronary care unit. Is that as bad as they say?"

"It's bad," I said. "I'm not sure it's that bad. I'm not sure anything's that bad."

"Where do you go next?"

"Across the street."

"The old V.A. Looking forward to it?"

"Sure."

"You're crazy."

"You're right. Listen: you seeing much of Micki Corrigan these days?"

"That piece? No. I tried calling her off and on for a week or so. They say she's hot stuff, but the bitch is never home. I gave up on that. You know how it is. Even interns get the message after a while."

"I've been there," I said, wondering if I'd ever get the message myself.

"Sure you have." He clapped me on the back. "If I ever learn to round my patients as fast as that woman gets around the residents, I'll be in clover."

"Where'd you hear that line?"

"From everywhere, man. From her. She told me she's been out with half our damn class this fall, and none of the guys have lasted more than a week."

"Harry did."

Ira tipped back his chair and laughed. He shook his head. "I'll be damned," he said. "Still and all, though, they do make quite a pair, don't they? I mean, they both seem to love the fast lane."

"Or used to, anyway."

"Yeah, but I'm sure for Harry it's just a temporary setback."

"I'll try to make sure of that," I said.

"You did your first rotation with him, didn't you?"

"Yeah. I was his teammate until they fired him. I inherited his service."

"Shit," said Ira.

"That's what I said at the time, and what I did, too. Still, we all survived."

"We did. I wouldn't repeat those two months for love or money, though."

"Same here. I got old on that ward too fast."

An orderly wheeled Harry out of his room. I went out into the halls. The echoes of our footsteps were the only sounds, and they reverberated with the memories of Harry and me in the heat of the summer. The rattle of elevator doors jolted me back to the present: Harry and I were together again, and he had hurt me one more time.

For an hour I stood over him, washing his stomach and rectum with warm salt water to bring up his temperature. I thought of the sick jokes he would have made if he'd been doing the same job for me. He'd have been flirting with the nurses, telling them that I deserved what had happened to me, telling them that I was wasting his time. But the nurses had better things to do than flirt with me, so I wasted my time alone with Harry.

He warmed up slowly. His drug screen came back from the toxicology lab looking like a ledger of illegal substances. There were trace amounts of PCP and marijuana, a little heroin (or maybe it was morphine; even after he'd gone, Harry sometimes could get one of the nurses on the general medicine wards to palm some of that for him). He had enough cocaine aboard to restock a Colombian freighter, and his alcohol level was high enough to have killed me.

Harry wasn't going to die, though. When that was certain, I left him for the ones who might.

On one of the wards a nurse got behind in dispensing meds. She forgot one of the old women on her list. When the night crew went in just after four to rectify the error, she was dead. We were called up to resuscitate her. We worked on her very briefly. When we left, the medical students were practicing intubation. They wrestled her tongue off the back of her throat again and again, driving an endotracheal tube between her vocal cords until rigor mortis began and they got bored.

By the time I got back, it was morning. Harry had started to wake. He was groggy and tossing, like a man trying to shake himself out of a nightmare.

Michelle had come in. She was across the room, working on another patient. She had on a short white dress and a lab coat. Her hair was pulled up into two braids, coiled tightly above her ears. I watched her hands untangle the skein of tubing over her patient's head. Her hips curved out as she leaned over the bed.

Harry distracted us both. He pulled himself off his mattress and sat up. His hands clenched the bed rails and rattled them in their sockets. Then he fell back on his damp pillow. Michelle went to his side, gesticulating, cursing him gently.

He lay still. His eyes were full of her. Slowly, with ultimate deliberation, his hand went to the respirator tube taped to his face. He pulled at the tube, the tape contorting his face, tearing away, hanging free as the tube came away out of his throat, slick and shiny with mucus and saliva. He looked like a snake swallower reversing his trick.

Michelle tried to stop him, so with his free hand he hit her. He hit her across the face, on the arms, over her breasts. Then he pulled out the lines threaded into his veins. Blood ran out and mixed with the fluids that spilled from the disconnected tubing and over the sheets. He slapped Michelle with his bloody hands, spattering her uniform, her skin, her eyes.

She stepped back, her face twisted up with surprise, dismay, disgust. Harry's hands went under the sheets. They came out holding his bladder catheter, its securing balloon still inflated. She fumbled at his hands as he swung the catheter at her, whipped her face, sprayed urine across her shoulders.

Then I was on him. I jackknifed over the bed rail and threw myself over him. I held his shoulders and pinned him to the mattress. He strained to sit up. I looked into his face and saw all my hatred mirrored back at me. In my nostrils his breath smelled as sour as old sins. My cheek touched his—both unshaven—and his skin rasped on mine. His curses were in my mouth. He bucked under me, panting and moaning as he fought to rise, fought to break away. Our chests filled together, sucking in the same air as we wrestled. I crushed him under me, full of all the anger and envy he had ever made me feel.

Then he shuddered, surrendered, and lay still.

"You," he whispered.

"Yes," I hissed. I tried again to see myself in the black centers of his eyes, but he had closed them against me. The sockets were rimmed with blue and cut with the gray lines of his great fatigue.

"You saved my ass again," he said.

"No," I lied.

"Damn you," he said. "I never asked for you. I never asked to be saved—not now, not then, not by them, and not by you. You knew it, too, but you kept on, damn you." He paused for a breath. "Such a waste of time."

"No," I said.

"Goddamn you," he cried. He threw his head back, and the tears ran down. From the hot center of all his angry hatred—of himself, of me, of life—he screamed his curses. He howled at all of us, again and again, his broken voice full of pain and despair, until somebody hit him with enough tranquilizer to drop him back into coma.

I stepped back from him. Across his bed stood Michelle. Her arms drooped at her sides. Her cheeks were streaked with blood, like tears wiped away in haste. Her eyes were gravid with pain, and they asked for me. I wanted to reach out to her, to comfort her, but instead I stepped back into the crowd around the bed, back to the shelter of my work.

Michelle stepped around the bed to follow me, but there was work for her to do, too. When I looked back from the doorway, she was helping another nurse slip canvas cuffs around Harry's wrists and ankles. They tied him to the bed frame.

"How is he?" the resident asked me a short time after.

We were loitering behind the nurses' station, waiting for the attending to show up for rounds. The coffee was bitter. I stood by the pot, shucking packets of sugar and artificial cream into my cup to cut the taste.

"His numbers are all back to normal," I told him.

"Then get him out of my unit," he said.

"He's still pretty sick. You want him to go to one of our wards or to psychiatry?"

"To one of our wards. Psych won't touch him."

"But he tried to kill himself. He needs to be committed for therapy."

"You can't prove that, and if you can't prove it, you can't lock him up. His insurance has lapsed, so he can't commit himself voluntarily. Besides," he added, grinning, "if we don't get him back on the street where he can get a drink, he'll get DTs."

"Christ," I said, "you're even more cynical than I am."

"Give yourself time," he said. "You're coming along nicely."

So we sent Harry to the wards. As soon as he could stand, he walked away.

In his place we put a woman who'd tried to kill herself with her father's insulin. The ambulance boys had found the empty vial, and they'd filled her veins with sugar. They saved her life, after a fashion By the end of the week, when I left the unit for the V.A., she too had gone out to the wards She sat in a padded high chair and babbled to the nurses in her own language like a fourteen-month-old child, when she wasn't gnawing the sleeves of her cotton gown. She was a very pretty young woman.

It was midafternoon on the last day of that rotation. Michelle and I were sitting over the remnants of lunch. The cafeteria line was closed. We were alone in the big room.

"You know they took Harry's license away," I mentioned to her.

"Yes," she said. "He told me. He called me and told me, a few hours before the cops found him. He was already too drunk to talk straight."

"I didn't realize..." I began, but she shrugged me off.

"He wanted to see me," she went on. "He wanted us to go away somewhere together—Mozambique, Montevideo, someplace crazy. I told him no, of course. He told me he loved only me, that he'd kill himself if he couldn't have me. I still said no. I was tired of his games. He told me about his license being taken away. I told him it was his own fault. He started to cry. When he started cursing me, I hung up."

She threw her fork onto a plate of chicken and peas. She put her forehead against her folded hands. She sat with her head bowed. There was nothing I could say. Finally she looked up.

"I'm surprised he didn't call you," she said.

"I was here," I told her.

"Still, I'm surprised. He thought—he thinks—a lot of you, in his own fucked-up, jealous way. The way you two used to meet at the bar, the way you used to stand up to his joshing, the way you used to cover for his mistakes; he thought you were his friend."

"We were just using each other," I said.

"He didn't see it that way," she said, and the narrow look on her face told me she knew I didn't, either.

I stood up and looked out the window. The slush was melting on the sill. The wet snow falling stained the trees black.

"Then he was stupid," I said.

"Damn you," she said after a moment. "Sit down."

I sat.

"Damn you for a fool," she went on, "don't be like that. We were both his friends, once, and he hurt us both. Admit it. Why can't you show any emotion? Why do you have to play the iron intern all the time? My God, when are you going to start acting like a human being?"

"When I start being treated like one," I said. She was getting on my nerves. Part of me wanted to believe that she wasn't playing with me, but I was too exhausted to find out.

"You're so full of shit," she said. "You have to let yourself feel things."

"I don't have time," I broke in. "In an intern's schedule, there's no time set out for feeling things, just like there's no time for eating or sleeping. Any time I take out for that detracts from patient care, and in a madhouse like this, anything that detracts from patient care gets people killed."

"But you still take time to eat and sleep."

"You have to feed the machine to keep it running, but you don't have to let it feel. Feelings get in the way of efficiency."

"But you have to show your feelings, or you'll break down."

"Not me," I insisted. "Feelings just get in my way."

"Just like friends."

"Sure."

"You didn't used to think that way."

"I used to be young and stupid."

"And now?"

I put my feet up on the table and thought about that. There was a point to all this, and I knew that I should figure it out, but I was too tired to try. I knew, too, that she was right, but I still couldn't see that I could do anything about it. I rubbed my eyes, but I still couldn't see through the fatigue.

"Now I'm old and stupid," I said.

We stared at each other for the longest time, me grinning like an idiot, Micki just shaking her head.

"I guess you are," she said at last, and then she walked away.

I sat alone and watched her leave, then turned away and watched the eaves drip, too tired to sleep, too sleepy to call her back to me.

After work I went out looking for someone. None of the people Harry and I used to laugh with were in the bar across the street. I wandered down the avenue, stepping into narrow bars full of smoke and men. I drank neat whiskey out of shot glasses. The wind blew out of the west, out of the darkness that overwhelmed rows of streetlights. Walking up to a corner, I saw a young woman in a long quilted coat leaning against a lamppost. Her breath congealed in the cold and vanished in the wind. A dirty car pulled up, and a man with red hair spoke to her through the window. She smiled when the car came alongside, ignoring the slush it threw up onto her boots. She kissed the man through the open window, got in through the open door. The car waddled away through the melting snow. The naked trees shivered in the cold.

At home I ate canned ravioli with a bottle of California red. I read a journal. When the journal was done and the can empty, I sat at my desk, drinking the cheap wine until I spilled the last glass into my lap. I turned off all the lights. I fell asleep in a dirty bed with the wine still wet and chill across my thighs.

At the V.A. I inherited a list of disasters, but by midweek I had all but the worst one of them on the mend. He had lymphoma. The chemotherapy we began my first day on the ward had overwhelmed the soft tumors in his neck and his groin and under his arms. The cancer died, and its cells, breaking down, poured their toxins into his blood. He went in and out of shock, delirious, faltering, but never sick enough to transfer to the intensive care unit and out of my hair. He was a handful, and what with the new routine to learn, the new schedule of rounds to pick up, and all the other sick to care for, he kept me in the house until almost ten every evening.

In the lobby one night, as I went out, was a family weeping. They had kept watch for days over one of the other intern's patients. Now the man had died. Having given them the news, his doctors had just left the family and gone back to the ward to take care of the living.

There were six in the family. Three young men stood apart. One sat over an ashtray, filling the dead man's absence with smoke. Two others stood at the doors, their backs to each other, looking out in opposite directions. On the vinyl sofa, a woman sat with her arms around the grieving wife, rocking her. The old lady sobbed out loud, but the young one cried silently, the tears sheeting across her face.

On the floor, oblivious and ignored, a toddler in a blue snowsuit knelt with a toy truck, talking to himself, gurgling and giggling as he pushed the toy across the dirty carpet.

He pushed it across the room, to where a woman lay against the wall, slumped down on the arm of another sofa, asleep. She was wrapped in a coat, and she slept with her legs curled beneath herself. Her feet, in gray socks worn thin at the heels, stuck out from under the hem of her coat. Her boots lay on the floor. The kid drove his truck around them and back to where the other women nursed their grief.

The sleeping woman lay with her hair coiled in a knot on the top of her head. In her sleep the pins had come loose, and the tail of her braid drooped across her shoulder.

I knew the color of her hair, I knew the line of her body under the rumpled coat, I knew the set of her face: I knew Michelle at once.

At first, when I sat beside her, she didn't move. Then, slowly, she came to life. She looked up at me. She put her arms around my waist and her head on my lap.

"How did you know I was waiting for you?" she asked.

"Guess I'm just too smart for my own good," I said. "You know how doctors are."

"Hush," she said.

I gazed down at her face. That night it was an old face. The skin was too tight over the cheekbones. There were wrinkles around the corners of her eyes and at the angles of her mouth. Her brilliant hair was dull in the bad light, flecked with gray and tangled. The flesh beneath her closed eyes was dusky and sagged. Her lips, without lipstick, were chapped.

"It's Mick, isn't it?" I asked her, and from the way her hands tightened against the small of my back, I knew that was why she was there. She nodded after a while.

"You should have paged me," I told her. She sat up to speak at last.

"I was sure you'd gone home," she said.

"I'm not that smart. You know that," I said, and she smiled, finally. "What is it? How is he?"

"He died early this evening," she told me, knowing I'd known without asking. "God, I'm so tired."

"I'm so sorry," I told her, knowing that people who meant nothing to her had been saying that to her for hours. "What can I do?"

"Nothing," she said, and my heart sank. "There's nothing left to do. He arranged most of it weeks ago, when he got home from the hospital. The other things—the autopsy permit, the collection of personal effects, the calls to all the relatives—I've already taken care of."

"I see," I said.

"I just need..." she began.

"Yes?"

"I don't know. I just...it's so hard to say this, to know how to say this to you. You're such a hard bastard, you know." She stopped. I put an arm around her shoulders. "I just could use a friend right now, is all."

"And you think I'm one?" I asked.

"I don't know, God damn it. Are you?"

I looked into her face, there so close to mine, so full of hurt and exhaustion and willing vulnerability, that for once I couldn't lie to her.

"Yes," I said. "I hope so."

"What time is it?" she asked.

"It's half-past ten."

"God," she said, "it feels like it ought to be tomorrow."

"You really don't have anything else to do?" I asked.

"No," she said.

"Then let's get out of here."

Michelle pulled on her boots. She picked up the paper bag that had stood beside them. We walked into the entryway. The air was riven with cold. She put up the hood of her coat. Then she took my hand.

"Where should we go?" she asked.

"Far, far away," I told her.

We stepped off the curb and into the night. In my car we drove north through the city, past dark neon signs and black store windows, past still houses and empty side streets. We drove to the interstate, where the trucks groan past endlessly and the lights never dim.

We took a booth at an all-night cafe. Outside, headlights flashed by, illuminating the road to Buffalo and Boston. The grumble of diesel engines and the whine of shifting gears sang the dissonant chorus of the road beyond the broad glass windows.

The one waitress in the place sat on a bar stool by the cash register, reading a tabloid. Two men in tight jeans sat apart, sipping coffee while their cigarettes burned the minutes away. A lone woman in a corner booth hummed along with the country music station overhead. The waitress folded her paper when we sat down. She pushed herself heavily to her feet.

"Sure you don't want anything to eat, honey?" she asked Michelle.

"No," Micki said. "Thanks. Tea is fine." She smiled for us. "I'm not hungry. Tired is all."

I held Michelle's hand, and when the waitress was gone, I asked her: "How long were you up with him?"

"Since midmorning yesterday," she said. "He had a room to himself. His nurses got me a reclining chair out of the lounge, and I slept for a few hours last night. They admitted him Tuesday, you know, when he started spiking a fever. He'd developed pneumonia where the tumor blocked a bronchus.

They dragged it out a little with antibiotics. Still, in the end, he got his way."

She looked to me. I tried to think of pleasant things to say. But it was no different from the way it was on the wards, no different having known Mick, no different knowing her: after death, words are puny. I put my fork down, trying to look respectful while she told the story. I knew I should feel sympathy, but I felt nothing, just tired and stupid.

She waved her hand at me, annoyed. "No," she said. "Eat."

"I'm sorry," I said. "I didn't want you to think I wasn't listening."

"You don't have to listen. I know you're exhausted. You just need to be.

"He died late in the afternoon," she went on, staring out through the frosty windowpanes at the play of traffic on the highway. "I sat with him, with the door closed. His breathing spaced out gradually—you know how it ends. I started out holding his hand. It was so cold that I dropped it and sat by the door. Every few minutes he'd sigh. The scars on his chest would go up and down. Then he'd lie quiet. I'd think he was gone, and then he'd sigh again. Finally, I realized that he wasn't going to sigh anymore. I went out and got his nurse. She called up the intern, who did the rites with his stethoscope and went to fill out the papers. I went down and signed things in the business office. By the time I got upstairs again, the nurses had him all laid out.

"I went in and looked at him. I felt like I was supposed to do something—to kiss him or cry over him or cross myself and say a Hail Mary for him. But he was too dead for any of that, so I went downstairs. I called the family. They were all relieved. I called the funeral home, and we finalized all the arrangements.

"Then there was nothing else to do. I sat there in the lobby by myself, watching the cop at the front desk stare at me and trying to think of somebody I could find to talk to. And damn it, there wasn't anybody."

"Except me," I said.

"I thought about trying to call you. I didn't think you'd come. When I woke up and saw you there, I didn't think I could ask you. I wasn't sure I know you well enough to trust you. It's just that all the people I do know—well, I knew they'd all say no."

"So you took a gamble on me."

"You are a strange bastard," she said.

"I'll accept that as a compliment."

"Quit grinning. We're supposed to be grieving here."

"I'm sorry," I said, and immediately stopped smiling. She took my hand.

"No," she said. "I didn't mean that. Go ahead and smile. I like it."

So, being both exhausted, we sat and smiled at each other for the longest time, like teenagers, holding hands. We talked about foolish things, morbid things, about dead people we had known, about family, about work, about what we'd wanted to be, growing up, and where we found ourselves. It was all empty talk, but it filled up our time, and it seemed to make us happy.

The waitress was very nice about refilling our cups, but after a long while even she grew tired of us. We were well into morning when we finally went out.

We drove back toward the city. She put her hand on my shoulder as I held the wheel. She put her arm around my neck. She kissed my cheek.

"Take me home," she said dreamily.

I held her on the landing as she fumbled in her purse for the key to her apartment. The heat of her body felt very good through her clothes. I kissed her once inside the door. It lasted a very long time.

She hung up our coats. I took her into the bedroom. We lay together on the bed, kissing. I opened her blouse.

"Here," I said to her, "turn over."

She purred as I rubbed the skin and the long muscles of her back. My fingers went up and down, from the taut muscles of her neck down the supple curve of her spine to the bony prominences of her pelvic bones above the belt line of her jeans.

I kept on until I was sure she was asleep. When I took off her shoes, she never moved. I covered her with the blanket at the foot of the bed and turned out the light.

I went home alone, letting the door lock behind me. I was too tired to sleep, still wired from all the cups of coffee I'd had listening to Michelle talk to me. I went outside and walked. The air was crisp, but not bitter cold, the way the weather gets during a November thaw. I walked through Washington Park, feeling good the way you feel at Lent, having sacrificed something for a good reason, but knowing very well that it will be there to go back to later. I walked for a long time under the bare trees, listening to the stillness of the night and dreaming.

In the morning Michelle called me at work.

"Why did you leave me?" she asked, hurt.

"I went for a walk. I wanted to let you sleep. You're very beautiful asleep."

She paused a moment to let that sink in. "I thought you didn't want me," she said.

"No," I said, "it isn't that. We have plenty of time. You just looked so tired. It seemed like the least I could do for you."

"I see."

"Besides, we're even now."

"So that's how it is," she said with a gentle smile in her voice.

"Yes."

"All right. Listen: I called to see what you're doing Saturday."

"Tomorrow? Nothing, after rounds. What are you planning?"

"Want to go to a funeral?"

"Sure," I said. "That'll be a hell of a date. Just right for a couple of morbid kids like us."

"I'm sorry," she said. "I shouldn't have asked."

"No," I said, "I'll be there."

She gave me directions to the church. It was called St. Patrick's, of course.

"The mass starts at ten-thirty. Can I meet you there? I've got a lot of family things to take care of beforehand."

"I'll be there," I promised her.

There was no wake, she told me later, he had not been that kind of Irish. She winked when she said that, but she'd kept the visiting hours quiet all the same. Being on call, I never saw the mourners, but I didn't have to. I knew them all right. I knew the stocky neighborhood mortician in the black suit who knew all the mourners by their first names. I knew the color of the roses and glads around the open casket, absolving by their profusion the guilt of those who never came. I knew the feel of the leisure suits and the old tweeds the men wore. I knew the shy faces of the nephews' children and the hushed voices of the husky aunts in Sunday clothes who knelt behind the daughter as she prayed, then stood behind her as she shook the hands and kissed the cheeks of mourners, whispering to her encouragement and the names of people forgotten in childhood. I knew the faraway smiles of the old women as they talked among themselves of high school beaux, and I knew the smell of cigars in the lobby that the men with slicked-down silver hair smoked while they retold stories of work and an ancient war until the man in the black suit interrupted to close down the Victorian house for the night.

I didn't have to see the church to know it, either, with its old high altar and its stained-glass windows, inscribed with the names of long-dead Irish men and women, illuminated by the November sun. I was there. I was late, caught on my way off the ward by a family from up the Hudson who arrived with a box of chocolates and interminable questions for me. I left the candy on the front seat of my car and hid in the back of the church with the old friends, clearly no relation.

Michelle was in the front pew, alone. Her back was very straight, and her red hair was covered with the kind of black lace that young women hadn't worn to mass in twenty years. Behind her were her father's sisters and brothers, then their children and grandchildren, all the Irish generations in their best clothes. The kids played in the pews with crayons or key rings; the youngest stared dumbly over his father's shoulder at the ranked faces along the aisle. There were a few distant relations in the pews behind the close family. Farther back the pews were filled with neighbors, guys from his old unit, pensioned cops, some of the girls he'd dated in high school, and the kids who used to mow his lawn.

Mick himself lay in a dark oak box between the front pews, waiting patiently while the priest went through the mass. At communion we all filed past him with heads bowed. When it was over six old men picked him up and walked him through the great front doors of the church and into the back of a hearse, cursing the weight of the box and the cold of the brass handles. I stood apart, at the foot of the church steps, until Michelle came out.

"Excuse me," she said, squeezing the hands of a square matron in black whose teenage sons standing behind her wore faces eloquent of ennui.

Micki stepped over to me. She kissed my cheek like a cousin.

"You came," she said.

"Hell of a good time," I told her, smiling just at the look of her in a black dress with the buttoned-up collar.

"Straight from work, by the look of you," she said.

She touched my unshaven face with her soft fingertips and glanced down at my creased white pants. I shrugged apologetically.

"Anyway," she said, taking my hand, "I'm glad you came."

"Wouldn't have missed it for the world."

She put her lips to my ear. "Listen, you punch-drunk old thing," she whispered, "be serious, or I'll have to beat you in front of all these people."

"I'd like that," I said.

"You're so bad," she said, laughing, "I'll bet you would."

People were staring at us, waiting to go. She led me away.

"Come on," she said, "we're going for a ride."

I stood with her a moment longer, being introduced to the family. They were all Corrigans. None of her mother's people were there, and to hell with all of them, as one of the uncles said to me. Micki pitched names past me until I felt struck out. Then she got into a black Buick with a chatty aunt. I rode in an orange Volkswagen with the college crowd, our neckties off.

Headstones the color of ice marched in rows over the hill, among overgrown yews and junipers and bare sugar maples. We drove up past the Italians and Poles and Germans to where the Irish were. The names stood out boldly on the pale granite.

They put the old man's casket into a hole in the mud. The dead grass was soggy, and we stood on a sheet of plastic while the priest said his few words. Then we all crossed ourselves once and started down the hill, leaving Mick to be tucked in forever by the young men in flannel shirts who stood by the road, leaning on their shovels and watching us.

For a respectful couple of hours we stopped at an aunt's house in the suburbs north of the city, eating soda bread with deli meat and cheese and drinking bottled beer. I drank coffee and tried to act as though I belonged there. The men took off their coats and smoked while the women talked over cups of tea and plates of butter cookies and diaper changes and the kids chased each other through the rooms or watched Saturday television.

Then Micki and I were jammed together in the back of a Subaru with a cousin who waited bar downtown, driving back to the church where our cars were parked. Her kid fell asleep on the way, crying into Micki's lap.

Finally we were alone. It was late afternoon. We sat on the couch in her living room. She lay on my lap with her back to me, with her head on my chest and my arms around her. Her arms were thrown back around my neck, and she was looking up into my eyes.

"I'd always wondered how it felt to be a survivor," she was saying.

"Did you now?"

"Sure. It says I am in yesterday morning's paper, right there in print on the obituary page: 'Survivors include his daughter, Michelle.' It was right above the line about where to send flowers."

"And how does it feel?"

"I don't know. Different. Better, when you think of how he got to be, before he died—nothing but bones and bruises. But terrible, if you remember how he used to be. Weekends in the summer, when I was a kid, we'd drive up to Lake George and watch the sailboats go by. We'd live for days on hot dogs and ice cream. Friday nights, we'd go down to the Legion Hall, and I'd sit in a tall-backed chair with a green bottle of cold Coke in my lap, listening to stories of places I'd never been while the men shot pool and drank their beers. On Sunday mornings, he liked to read the funnies for me before we dressed for church. I used to sit alone in a front pew, or maybe with Aunt Mary, if she was up and dressed in time for the nine o'clock service, while he stood in the back in his one good suit with the other ushers, leading the people in. For my confirmation, you know, he bought me white shoes."

She lifted her face. I kissed her forehead. She arched her body, bringing her mouth up to mine. In the window, red roses salvaged from the funeral home leaned against glass growing frosty with the waning of the afternoon.

She broke away from me, sat up to pull off her shoes, then curled around me with her knees drawn up and her head on my shoulder.

"I wonder if he's happier now," she said. "Happier, or just dead, I suppose. He wasn't very happy when I knew him. Not since my mother left him, anyway."

"Well," I said, "women will do you that way sometimes."

"Oh?" she said, sitting up. "Do you think so?"

"Sure. Some women, that is. Not you, of course."

"Of course," she said. She sat on my legs with her knees straddling my hips and the skirt of her black dress riding up her thighs. She took my face in her hands. She kissed me. "How could you even think that?" she asked.

"Well," I started, but then she kissed me again.

"Yes?"

"I mean, just figuratively speaking."

"That's it."

"You know, to make conversation."

"Certainly."

"I didn't mean it the way it sounded."

"Hush," she said.

The room grew dark as the autumn night closed down and the clouds closed in.

"Listen," I interrupted after a time, "I have a little problem."

"What's that?"

"I need to go out."

"Out? Why?" Her face froze.

"I need to do my laundry."

"Like hell."

"It's getting late."

"It's too late. All the Laundromats are closed."

"But you see, I'm out of underwear."

She fell back on the sofa cushions and laughed. She ran her fingers over my hair and kissed me lightly on the nose.

"You won't get away so easily this time," she said. "Just don't wear any." Her voice got husky. "I never do."

Then we were in her bedroom. Our shadows flickered on the wall as two purple candles burned on the bedside table.

"I don't mean to interrupt the passion of the moment," I began.

"You have." She sighed, sitting back.

"Sorry. I just wanted to ask you—"

"I know what you wanted to ask," she said. "We're adults. You're a doctor. I'm a nurse. There's no point pretending to be romantic. You want to know if I carry any contagious disease. The answer is no. I will not give you herpes. I do not carry AIDS, or gonorrhea, or syphilis or chlamydia or warts or anything else too nasty to touch."

"Actually... Shit, it isn't that," I said. "I just was wondering— how do I ask this?—if I need to do anything about birth control."

She bit her lip and stared at me. She looked away and shook her head. She glanced at me again, then covered her face with her hands, watching me through the fingers as they massaged the tired muscles around her eyes. After too long she smiled for me and touched my lips with her fingers. But the smile was weak and rueful as an old man's passion, and her touch reached out to me from a place I could never go.

"You're so Catholic," she said softly. She put her arms around herself and lay across the mattress, away from me. "That isn't something you need to worry about. The surgeons took care of that years ago."

She let go, and her arms fell out to her sides. I sat on the bed like a fool, one finger running up and down the crook of her arm.

"What do you mean?" I asked her.

"I mean," she said, "that it's all gone. There isn't anything there to conceive with anymore."

She opened her eyes and studied the ceiling.

"I don't know why I'm telling you this. It's nothing to you. I've never told anyone about it, not even my dad. I guess I don't need to worry about it getting back to him anymore, though, do I?"

"No," I said, "I guess you don't."

"When I was fifteen," she went on, "I had a crush on one of Mick's friends, a younger guy, married, very handsome, tough and strong and nothing like the jerks who followed me around at school. He was a gentleman, I thought—nothing like you—with money and very good clothes. But he didn't ask about contraception, and I didn't care. That was for girls who weren't in love. After the abortion, I never saw him again. I couldn't face him, and besides, I had such pains. I'd never had such terrible pains. I thought they were a normal part of an abortion—you know, a penance from God for such a mortal sin. Mick found me on the floor one afternoon. There was blood all over my clothes. By the time he got me to the hospital, I was septic. I almost died. It was the gonorrhea that did that to me. Later, the gynecologist told me that at surgery, he couldn't find anything normal. Instead of organs, I had abscesses all strung together. He took them all out. Ever since then, I've been fine. I haven't had to worry about sex at all."

"Jesus," I said.

We lay on the bed together, very far apart. She shrugged again, then sat up on one elbow. She blew me a kiss.

"I got used to it," she said. "It's just part of life. Every morning I take my womanhood from a pill bottle."

I ran a finger down her cheek, over the hollow above her collarbone, around and around the curve of her breasts and the circle of her navel and the swell of her hips.

"Well," I ventured, "it doesn't show. Even the scar is hardly there."

"I've learned to hide it," she told me.

Then she laughed. She pulled me down, stroking my face with her fingertips and with her heels the small of my back.

She woke me in the night, crying in her sleep. I lay awhile in the bad light that came in through the dark windows, watching her face contort as she mumbled words I could not understand. Then I reached out and held her. I put my body across hers again and kissed her face, her cheeks, the lids of her eyes, her mouth. She woke with a start and stared at me a moment, then buried her face in the hollow of my neck.

"Promise me," she whispered, this strong, tough woman suddenly soft and frightened in my arms. "Promise you won't hurt me, too."

I stared down at her, at those great gray Irish eyes looking back at me, trusting and questioning all at once.

"I'm just a man," I said, "but I'll try."

Holding her, I felt her body relax. She fell asleep softly, like a dove, nestled against my heart.

In the morning she was herself again. We went to my place. She stepped gingerly across the dirt that was ground into the hall carpet, and she ducked nicely under the bicycle hanging from the ceiling in the entryway. Inside, the apartment was full of light. Michelle glanced around at my mother's old kitchen table and chairs, the twin candlesticks, the desk against one wall, the bare wood floor with dust mice in all the corners, and the unmade bed in the back room. The walls under high, old ceilings were bare, save for a few posters advertising bicycle races in bright colors and a black-and-white framed photograph of a man in a high collar and a woman in a white dress.

"You don't go in for furniture much, do you?" Michelle asked me.

"What I've got does for me," I said.

"I guess so. And you're into bicycle races?"

"I used to race. There's no time anymore."

"Too cold, too. Have you ever seen the downtown criterium that they run in the spring?"

"I've never been here in the spring."

"We'll have to catch it this year," she said. Then she halted. "Or shouldn't I assume?"

"Go right ahead," I said.

She blushed a bit and tried to cover that by walking up to the old photograph. "Who are these people?"

"My mother's parents," I said. "That's their wedding picture. They met on the boat from Liverpool, and they got married that same year. She used to tell me how strange she felt in those days. She'd just cut her hair. She was trying hard to be a good American girl."

"She still looks the colleen," she said approvingly. Then she turned around to face me. "Where do you sit in this apartment of yours?"

"At the table," I said, pulling out a chair.

"No. I mean when you want to relax."

"On the bed." Her eyebrows went up. "Or on the floor. I throw a pile of pillows down."

"That's unique," she said.

"I suppose. It suits me."

"Yes," she said, and kissed me.

I started stuffing clothes into a laundry bag. She poked at the dishes by the sink.

"I thought guys got over this before they left college," she said.

"Over what?"

"Living like a bum. This is disgusting."

"I don't live here," I told her. "I live at the hospital."

"Shit. Well, listen: don't try this at my place. If you ever leave your clothes lying around my floor, I'll burn them. Then where'll you be?"

"Trapped naked in your apartment for the rest of my life."

"You'd like that, wouldn't you?"

She stood against an empty white wall with her arms folded and her head cocked at me. We watched each other for a long moment, suddenly too serious.

"Yes," I said.

Michelle grinned and grimaced and shook her head. "You're crazy," she told me. She stepped away from the wall and kissed me.

"It's the only way to stay sane. You know that. They say it on the radio all the time."

"Damn you," she said. Then she clapped her hands and danced into the center of the room. She spun around in the dust and the beam of light that struggled through the dirty window.

"Okay," she said, "this is getting to be too much fun. Let's go do something really exciting this morning."

"Like what?"

She ran up to me, pinned me against the doorway. She kissed me for the longest time, and then she broke away.

"Let's go watch your clothes spin," she said.

So we went uptown to the Laundromat and talked about empty things to pass the time. We watched the teenage mothers drop quarters into the big machines, then jive with the boys who came in off the sidewalk to see them. We got out just in time to see the congregation coming out from late mass at the cathedral, and we both waved to show that we didn't feel guilty about not going that week.

For lunch, we ate kebobs at a Lebanese restaurant where the coffee was thick and sweet and served in demitasse cups. On the street, a flower seller stood with her goods wrapped in green paper against a wind that poured out of a clear sky and tumbled down the river. I tried to buy Michelle a handful of roses.

"Please," she said, "I know you're in love, but I think I've seen enough flowers to last me out the week, after yesterday."

We walked down the street in silence. She took my arm. We walked up the avenue to where the bars were opening up for the afternoon. We drank cheap sherry and talked ourselves happy again. We walked through the park and came out at the art museum. There was a drama to the pictures there that I'd never noticed when I was sober.

We went home to her place and cooked stew for supper. She told me stories of growing up in the city while I cut up the meat and vegetables and watched her move about the kitchen. We ate a huge meal with a bottle of Beaujolais, and then we went to bed. I folded my clothes and laid them on a chair in her bedroom. She lit the candles and turned out the lights, and she made love to me, flickering above me like the candle flame. After, she nuzzled against my cheek.

"You know I love you," she said.

"Yes," I told her, shivering at the thought.

"I trust you. I haven't trusted anyone in a long time."

"That can be dangerous."

"Life is dangerous, but we're survivors, right?"

I held her to my chest. It was the only answer I could think of.

I woke before dawn and kissed her. "When do you have to go back to work?" I asked.

"At the end of the week. It's called bereavement leave."

"Well, some of us have to keep slaving away. No: don't get up. I can let myself out. You sleep. You've had a hard weekend."

"No thanks to you," she said, pulling on a robe. "I'll drive you in."

"You don't have to."

"You're damned right I don't."

She pulled up outside the hospital steps. I opened the door and sat there with one foot on the curb. I held out my hand. She just stared at it.

"What's this?"

"It's a handshake. People do it when they say good-bye."

"Don't I even get a kiss?" she asked, her voice tinged with incredulity and suspicion.

"Sure," I said. I kissed her on the cheek, then shook her hand. "It was a great weekend. I hope I helped you to feel a little better, about Mick and all. I'll be seeing you."

Her face turned as soft and warm as Irish flint, and there was blood in her eyes.

"Yeah," she said. "And I thought you were different. I thought I could believe in you."

I gave her hand a squeeze and got out of the car. Before I slammed the door on her, I stuck my head inside. "Maybe you can," I said. "One question for you, though, Michelle, before I go."

She would not turn her head to look at me. "What?" she snapped.

"I was wondering: will you be keeping your maiden name?"

At first her face was blank. Then her eyes opened very wide. Her mouth started working, but no words came. I closed the door and went back into the hospital. I could hear Harry's voice chuckling at me inside my head, and I didn't give a damn.

"God damn you," she shouted as I walked away. "Are you out of your mind?"

I turned to wave to her and nodded. She was out of the car and pounding on the roof with both her fists.

"Who the hell do you think you are?" she cried.

I pointed a finger at her. "I'm a strange, hard bastard," I told her, "and a lot more besides. I'm also the man who's coming to dinner tomorrow, and you'd better call me tonight to tell me what to bring."

"Shit," she said, but when I turned away at last to return to my sick old vets, she was still smiling at me.

fatigue

*W*hen the pains came, she fell back on the table panting. There was blood on the sheets, mucus and amniotic fluid. Her feet were in delivery stirrups, under sterile drapes that framed her perineum. When she pushed, the baby's dark hair glistened in the surgical lights, and her hemorrhoids swelled purple.

I stared at her vulva (that was what I was learning to call it), a green intern, fascinated, terrified, impotent. I forgot all the textbook precepts, all the pages of pictures, the graphs and diagrams, the statistics, the admonitions. The immediacy of this image, of birth, bleeding, and pain, washed all that away.

"You nervous?" John Pereira whispered in my ear. He was the chief resident, my mentor for the morning while the others on the obstetric team worked their way through a cesarean section in the room next door.

"What?" I asked, surprised out of my reverie. "Yes," I said, grateful for the distraction while the woman lay gasping between contractions and the baby receded up the birth canal.

"I was sure I was going to drop my first one, too," he said.

"Well," I said, "it happens, doesn't it?"

"You'll be all right," he said. "Babies have plenty of handles."

Then the woman came erect. She lifted her head off the plastic cushion. Her hands clenched her thighs. Strain contorted her face.

"Here," said John, taking my hands in his. He put my palms against the woman, against the baby's head, against the wet black hair of the mother and child.

The head lifted, emerged over the mother's slick skin. The baby's face, squat and ugly, grimaced.

"Now," John said, "hands here, turn, and gently pull. Ease downward."

We all pulled together.

"Now, push, Mama," John said, and the woman took a full breath and bore down. One of the baby's shoulders came free. The other followed. There was a gush of fluid, warm as bathwater, flecked with vernix. It ran over our hands, up our wrists and the sleeves of our gowns. It soaked through the cotton and bathed us.

The kid was in my hands. It gasped and coughed. Pereira sucked the mucus from its mouth and nose, clamped and cut the cord, and then looked at me.

"Well," he said, "you can't keep it forever."

I cradled the baby at my chest. It began to cry. It clutched at me, grabbing my wet gown in tiny handfuls. It wept angrily. It was deep pink, the color of ripe cherries' flesh, not yet the mother's deep black. It was a boy.

"Hold him up," said Pereira. "Show Mama."

Awkwardly I held up the kid.

"Did you want a boy?" Pereira asked the woman on the table.

"It don't matter none"—she sighed—"long as he's healthy." She closed her eyes, shivering.

"But you wanted a girl," he finished for her.

The woman smiled for him, opening her eyes. "It don't matter," she said. "I been knowing it a boy from how it been kicking at me. Just like a man-child, kicking all the time, not giving me no rest. I knowed it a long time now. It don't matter no more."

"But you was hoping," said John, falling into the dialect.

"Yeah," she said, "I been hoping. But that's all over now. He all right?"

"He's fine," we all said.

We gave the kid to the labor nurses, who dried and swaddled him. They handed him to the mother. His square head and flat nose were deep in the blankets.

We delivered the placenta, sewed up the tear in the birth canal with gut, cleaned off the fluid and clots and shit. The mother swung herself onto the wheeled bed, with its new clean sheets and its fresh warm blanket. Save for her soiled gown, she was naked. Her breasts, hanging down, showed through the loose fabric. Her slack, empty belly shook when she moved. We covered her and took her to the recovery room. She held the baby in her arms, talking to him, cooing and caressing him, kissing him.

"You the ugliest baby I ever done seen," she said. "You ugly like your daddy. You ugly like your brother. Ooh, and you hungry like you mama. You suck on them fingers. Yes, child, you suck on, pretty baby. We get us something to eat, soon enough; soon enough, sure."

Pereira left. It was easier after that, catching babies. At dawn I was delivering my seventh in twenty-four hours, and the novelty was gone. I was doing it alone, following the women in labor, through delivery, onto postpartum wards.

I didn't sleep. All night the nurses asked me questions I couldn't answer. I called the senior residents, who got up, gave offhand answers, explained patronizingly, and crawled back to bed. I walked in the halls or sat in the staff lounge, listening to the rhythms of the fetal monitors, to the pants and grunts and moans and screams and prayers and curses of the laboring women against the gentling voices of the nurses. It went on all the next day, until the new team came on.

I drove home. The July heat was horrible. Walking to the

parking deck, I broke a new sweat. It ran wet over the accumulated stickiness of the night's nervousness.

There was a haze over the sun, brilliant orange. The green of the live oaks shimmered through the heat and the traffic exhaust. I got lost, looking for our new apartment among the monotony of town-house rows on the burnt-grass hillside.

Katherine was inside. She had her feet on the coffee table. A gin and tonic was beading up between her ankles.

"What do you think?" she asked when I came in, after I'd given her a kiss on the cheek.

The apartment was decked out in crumpled newspaper, empty packing cases, and furniture in disarray. Unhung pictures leaned against bare walls.

"I can't think," I said. "I'm too tired."

"Tired? Poor baby." She got up and put her arms around me. Her skin was sticky, too, and she smelled of sweat and dust. "Here," she said, "drink this. It's what I needed, too."

The glass was half full of gin. The alcohol and the lime and the bitter tonic's fizz burned the dry heat off the back of my throat.

"Whoa," she said, "leave a little for your wife. Besides, you've got work to do yet."

I put down the glass. "Work?" I asked stupidly.

"Sure. We've got to put the pictures up, and the dishes. I can't do that alone."

"But I'm tired."

"Of course you're tired," she said. She stroked my hair. "You're an intern. You'll be tired all year. I'm not waiting that long to get my pictures hung." She finished the drink. "Come on, you old ball of fire."

So we spent an hour hanging pictures, moving furniture, wiring the stereo, lifting stacks of plates to high shelves.

"What's for dinner?" I asked when we were done.

"We're going out. We deserve it. You survived your first day as a doctor. We have our new home. It's time to celebrate."

"Celebrate? No. Show a little mercy. I'm dead. They killed me."

"Sure they did. That's all right. I'll resuscitate you. But first we're going out to eat. Change your clothes."

We drove downtown, to some place with seafood and fatty prime rib. She drank wine; I drank coffee. In spite of that, I still fell asleep at a traffic light on the way home. Kate woke me with a few shakes.

"We're home," she said. "Upstairs, you hero. Come on."

I remember lying on my face, half-conscious, while she pulled off my shoes and threw them into the closet. She rolled me over like a corpse, unfastened my pants, and dragged them off. I didn't resist until she started kissing me again.

"I really can't, Katie," I said, "not tonight."

"All right, dead man," she said after a moment, trying not to sound too disappointed. "What time do you have to get up?"

"What?"

"When do you have to be back at this wonderful job of yours?"

"Quarter to six," I mumbled. I turned onto my face again, hugging the pillow. "I have to be up before five."

"What? That's sick. God, that's crazy."

"I have to see all my patients before rounds."

"Crazy," she was grumbling as I fell asleep again. "Don't you dare wake me. I'll beat you. I swear to God."

The clock went off in the dark, and she never moved. A cockroach scuttled across the bathroom floor when I stumbled against the light switch. I was on my second cup of coffee before I could focus on the face in the mirror well enough to shave it.

The heat of the new day was a wall, and the pale red sun hung low upon it. I parked on the empty top deck of the parking garage and watched the mockingbirds peck in the asphalt under the trees. Inside, rounding, I woke narcotized women sleeping off labor, tore bandages from raw wounds closed with neat lines of steel staples, palpitated full and tender breasts, wrote orders for meals and prescriptions for contraceptives.

My pager went off in the middle of it all, and I changed into scrubs just in time to catch the baby that some woman I'd never met pushed into my hands. I filled out her papers, spoke to her nurses, and then went downstairs to finish the tedium of rounds.

It went on like that all day, all week, all month. The fascination of new birth faded as the bloodstains on my white shoes darkened. I came home to eat and sleep so I could go back to work and do it all over again. One weekend Kate drove us to the beach, after Saturday morning rounds. I slept in the car, fell asleep on a towel on the strand while she swam and chased the sandpipers. In the night, the skin on my back blistered. When she touched me, I cried out.

That next day I was on call again. At two in the morning a high school girl came in, laboring hard against an unripe pelvis. The nurses were great, coaching her through the waxing pains while I tried to resuscitate a seven-month gravida only hours out from cesarean section whose kidneys had died from toxemia.

Around five-thirty we took the high school kid back.

"Move on over to the delivery table," Carol told her.

"I can't," the girl said. She lay on her back until the pains came again; then she curled up on her side. "Take it," she whined. "Why can't you just take it?"

"We can't do that, child," said Carol. "You got to push it out your own self."

"No," said the girl.

"Yes," said Carol. "Now, you switch your bottom on over here."

"No. I can't. You got to take it."

In the end we had to pick her up and lift her to the delivery table. Strapped in the stirrups, iodine dripping down her thighs, she screamed on and on, cursing us brutally between breaths.

"Hush your bawling, now, child," Carol said to her. "You just hush yourself and push."

"I can't," she blubbered. "I can't."

Betsy put her head in the door. "Sandy wanted me to let you know," she said to me, "that your other patient has a headache and rising blood pressure."

I could envision the woman convulsing, or paraplegic from

a stroke, or on dialysis for life because I was stuck in the delivery room with a hysterical child in labor. I could see the recriminations, the postmortem review, the legal conferences, the extra work, but I couldn't see the answer.

"Wake one of the other residents," I said. "We'll be out when we can."

I turned to the girl. "You have to push this baby out," I told her.

"No!" she howled. "No no no," she babbled on, a long lungful of negation that rose in pitch and volume as another contraction took her.

"Yes," I said.

"Come on, baby," Carol said.

"Noooo!" She screamed.

Carol was listening to the baby through the mother's abdomen. "The heart rate's down," she said to me.

I started pounding on the girl's thigh with my fist, harder and harder, trying to reach her through the drape.

"Stop that," she said. "You hurting me." Her face turned sullen.

"Shut up," I said. "You're damned right I'm hurting you. I'm hurting you until you start pushing when Carol tells you to."

"I ain't."

I held my surgical scissors over the drapes and snapped them at her.

"You sure are. If you don't push, I'm going to have to cut you. If you don't push, I'm going to hurt you like you never knew. I'll cut you so wide, you'll never stop bleeding. I'll cut you so deep you'll never find your own hole again. I'm going to hurt you so bad you'll scream until next week, if you don't push this baby out."

"No!" she yelled.

"Then push. There's another contraction coming."

"No!"

I hit her again, on the inside of her thighs. The baby was

right there, the mother's skin stretched tight and almost breaking under the uterine pounding.

"I'm going to cut the episiotomy," I said to Carol.

"Don't cut me. Don't. Please don't cut me."

"He got to do it, baby," said Carol.

"No," the girl whimpered.

The contraction faded. The girl cried when I injected her
with the local anesthetic, but she lay still, weeping softly, when
I cut her. When the last contraction started, Carol put her arms
around the girl and sat her up.

"Now," she ordered, "you push. You hear me? You push
for all you're worth, before the doctor got to go hitting on you
again."

"No."

"You better," I said, "or I'll start hitting on you. You sure
don't want that."

"No."

"Girl," Carol said, exasperated, "you got to have this
baby."

"No I ain't."

"Oh, yes you do," I said, and with Carol holding her and
me lifting the baby's emerging head and the girl pushing a little
between her howls, we got the kid's head out. After that it was
easy, rotating the shoulders, pulling the body free. The medical
student, next to me, clamped the cord. I let her deliver the
placenta while I sat down to stop shaking.

"My God," the student said later, "that was awful."

We were sitting at the nursing desk, with blood all over our
clothes, filling the chart with dry notes about the baby's weight
and the kind of suture I'd used to sew up the wound.

I looked at the student, in her clean, starched, white student's coat. My belly muscles were still clenched with the
tension of the delivery, and I stank with the smell of the baby's
fluid, the mother's blood and urine, and my own sweat. I shook
my head and then went back to my writing.

"These fucking women," I mumbled, "I hate them. I hate
all of them."

"What?" said the student.

"Nothing," I said. "I was just kidding."

But she didn't laugh. Then it was sunrise, and we went downstairs to round again.

Kate didn't laugh either, when I told her the story.

"But that's so brutal," she said.

"There wasn't any other way."

"There's always another way."

"Not always."

"Of course there is. You were too tired to think of it."

"That's not true. I'd had two hours' sleep. I was doing good."

"Right."

"Whose side are you on anyway?"

"Yours."

"It doesn't show."

"You're just too tired to see it."

We went on like that for a while.

"What's for dinner?" I asked her.

"Don't change the subject. And there isn't anything for dinner."

"Why the hell not? What have you been doing all day?"

"I found a job."

"Shit. A job?"

"Yes, a job. Don't act so surprised. I can't stand this damned place anymore. It's blank. It's ugly. I can't just sit here all day like some kept housewife while you play doctor."

"So you got a job."

"That's right."

"Well—are you going to tell me about it?"

"It's at a bakery in the college part of town, working the morning bread shift and the retail at breakfast time."

"Oh, wonderful. You have a bachelor of science in nursing, and you're going off to bake bread?"

"Yes."

We stared at each other. She turned away first.

"I start Monday, at five o'clock."

"Five o'clock?"

"So the bread will be ready when we open at seven."

"Now, that's brutal," I said.

She went out for a pizza. I cracked open a beer and fell asleep on the couch.

"Here," she said, "eat this."

"What?"

"Eat. You have to eat. You're human, remember?"

"What? Oh, sure. Right. Thanks."

She sat on the couch next to me. While I ate she put her arms around me, put her hands around my neck, and shook me.

"You," she said. "Why do I love you, you nut?"

"I don't know," I said. I looked into her gray eyes and that crazy face she kept pushing all that red-blond hair out of. "You must be a nut, too."

"Nuts about you," she said, and she kept me up much too late that night.

That next day the labor deck was quiet. There was only one woman laboring. She was a longtime shooter, with tracks in her arms that made it impossible to start her intravenous lines until she pointed out for us the last place that still took the needle. She was a smoker, a snorter, and a part-time whore. She'd come in the night before. She'd gone on through the hours, desultorily. She went back to the delivery room cursing me for her pains.

She was a small woman, with tangled black hair and skin the gray-brown color of old wood. She had tight hips, so tight that when she pushed the baby's head into my hands, I felt the soft burst as the episiotomy tore into her rectum.

There was a loop of umbilical cord around the baby's neck that came over the head easily. The face was smeared with shit and vernix and blood. The eyes clenched and opened, blinking away the green amniotic fluid while I sucked out its mouth and nose with a long plastic tube. I turned the head to deliver the first shoulder, but the baby was stuck. The face began to turn purple.

While I pulled, the nurses unstrapped the woman's legs

from the stirrups and flexed them up toward her chest, and the student with us fell across the woman's belly, pressing the baby down and out. The woman screamed. The nurses yelled at each other until one went out for help.

Pereira came in. He never stopped to scrub, nor even paused to put on gloves. He later explained to me maneuvers too complex to remember, rotating the baby this way and back, delivering one arm, then the other, with one hand buried halfway to the elbow in the woman's body.

When the kid was out, bucking and crying under the warming lights, Pereira went out. He washed his hands and came back in, gowned and gloved. Together we sewed up the woman's lacerations. Pereira talked calmly about needle placement, suture selection, the pathophysiology of dystocia.

My hands shook from the adrenaline. Pereira held apart the bleeding, torn tissues. We had the anus closed, and I was working on the vagina when he dropped his end of the suture. He swore gently and held up his left hand, with the fingers spread.

"You got me," he said, picking at the glove where the puncture was, where his blood spread as a thin red film under the latex. Then he shook his hand a few times, and we went back to work.

"I'm sorry," I said.

"Forget it," he told me, shrugging. "Just screen her for syph and AIDS and hepatitis before she goes home."

"Sure. I'm really sorry."

"Don't be. I do it to myself all the time. It comes with the job. Just close the wound, and let's get the hell out of here."

And that's what we did. We forgot about it all, until months later.

On Sunday morning, after another night of call, after rounds, after circumcisions and discharge orders and enough coffee to get me to the car without falling on the sidewalk, I came home. Kate was standing in the window. She had her hair brushed back, and she wore a fresh white dress, a cotton one, soft and ironed smooth. She came to the door to meet me, kissed me quickly, and took my arm.

"We're late," she said. "Hurry and change your clothes."

"Late for what?" I asked.

"For church, silly. It's Sunday. You missed mass last week because you were on call. You've got no excuse this time."

"The hell I don't. I'm exhausted."

"You can sleep afterward."

"I'm going to sleep now, standing up."

"No. Come on. You have to go."

"Why?"

"Because it's a law of the church."

I fell on the couch and covered my face with a pillow. I peeked over the edge. She was scowling at me.

"The hell with the church," I said. "Pray for me."

"I will not. You're going to hell."

"I can't," I said. "I have to be on call again tomorrow."

She slammed the door.

The electric clock sat in the darkness, crying. I reached for it, only fumbling it to the floor. My head felt feverish from fatigue, my eyes unfocusable. I picked up the clock. Kate was already up, dressing.

"It's four o'clock in the morning," I said, blinded by her light.

"I know," she said. "Remember? I start work today."

"Sure. Right."

I listened to her play with faucets and cereal bowls while I tried halfheartedly to fall asleep again.

" 'Bye," she said, too cheerily.

I pulled the sheets over my head in answer.

"See you tomorrow night," she said.

"Great," I said. "Have a nice time. I'll be home as early as possible."

"And as late as usual, I'm sure."

"Yeah."

Then the front door closed. I lay alone, listening to the air conditioner whisper in my ear.

It rained that week. Later, a mist rose off the black streets. It hung in the atmosphere, a haze that softened the streetlights' glare. The air was heavy with water and heat, and sweat stuck my shirt to my skin.

Inside the bakery was my wife. She sat at a pine table, drinking coffee. At other tables, other women sat, silent and solitary, with hair limp in the heat and straggling in their faces. They all wore loose skirts, sun-faded, with shirts cut for men's chests. Two men bent over a backgammon board, engrossed. In one corner a couple whispered, pausing now and then to chew the ice in empty glasses of tea.

"Take off your tie," Katie told me, and when I did we went behind the counter. She introduced me. The bakers wore aprons and bandannas. They were all young and smiled easily. We stood around the cooling racks, the ovens, and the cutting tables, breathing in the smell of pastry and yeast.

"What can I get for you?" Kate asked me on our way back to her table.

"Nothing," I said, nervous out of my element, out of the hospital. "Thanks."

"But it's my treat."

I sat playing with the flickering candle stub between us, avoiding her eyes.

"All right. A cup of coffee, then."

The coffee was sweet and blond, smoother than the roach killer we brewed in the ward kitchen. I sat with my shoulders hunched over the mug. Sipping it scalded my tongue. I broke a new sweat.

"What is it?" Kate asked.

"Nothing."

"Yes," she said. "Look at me."

I looked at her. Her eyes reflected the candle flame.

"I don't belong here," I said.

"Of course you do. You're my husband."

"This is where you learned to wear that damn fool bandanna, isn't it?"

Self-consciously her hand went to the gaudy cloth across

her forehead. It showed sharply scarlet against her new suntan and her bleaching hair.

"It is a little foolish, I suppose. Like a uniform for people who won't wear uniforms."

"That's it. And I don't have one."

"We could get you one."

"It wouldn't fit. What kind of people are these, anyway? Freaks? Communists?"

"Some of them," she said. "Anarchists, socialists, Democrats."

"Faggots?"

"No. Some are gay."

"You look like a damned hippie."

"I am a damned hippie. I used to dress like this all the time."

"No. When?"

"Ages ago. During a former life."

"I guess so. Before you met me, anyway."

"Oh, yes. Ages and ages ago. Before you. Before I got old."

"You aren't old."

"That's relative. I'm old here."

"No."

"Look around."

I looked around.

"What are you staring at?" she asked.

John Pereira was sitting at a table across the room. He was screened from us by the broad leaves of a potted shrub. The leaves shadowed his journal as he sat alone, reading.

"He's my chief resident," I said.

"The guy with the wonderful outrageous tie?"

"Yeah."

"Well, you have to introduce me."

He smiled as he stood. Kate held out her hand. He took it in both of his.

I introduced them.

"Charmed," he said, and she, bashful for once, said nothing. We brought our mugs to his table. He held the journal in his lap while we talked.

"I love your tie," Katie said.

He fingered the free ends, loose Italian silk. "Thanks," he said. "My sister got it for me last year, on a trip to the old country."

"What old country?" she asked him.

"Portugal," he said. He spoke the word with an accent, with clean consonants and sharp syllables. "My people are all old New Englanders, fishing people, boat people since Cabot."

"Who?" I asked.

"A local character, from south of the border, from a long time ago." His accent was gone now, and he was smiling at my ignorance.

"And what brings you to this hole?" said Kate.

He shrugged, glanced down at the journal upside down across his thighs. When he smiled again, it was a wan smile, not pretty at all.

"Lost, I guess," he told her. "You?"

"Oh," she said. "I just follow around behind the wonder child here."

His face darkened, focusing on me. "You're very lucky," he said.

He looked back at her, frowning slightly, until she dropped her eyes like a genuflection.

"I appreciate that," I said.

His lips pursed the way the vets' did in the V.A. Hospital at my medical school when I told them that I understood how bad combat must have been.

"No," he said, "you only understand when you've lost one."

She blushed at that. He looked only at her face, but she colored for him as though his eyes had worked her up and down the way mine loved to, the way other men's did.

"I think I'll pass on that one," I said.

He looked at me sharply, as if noticing me for the first time.

"Yes," he said. "Good idea."

He picked the journal up out of his lap and set it on the table, open. Kate stood. She stepped behind me, positioning me between him and herself. She put her elbows on my shoulders and went on talking with him.

"He doesn't need anybody to leave him," she said. "He does all right without that."

"He's a good learner," Pereira said.

"And I hear that you're a good teacher," she answered him.

He smoothed down the pages of his journal and tipped back his chair. "That just shows how much he still has to learn," he said.

He started reading his journal. I knew I should get up. I wanted to turn the table over on him. I did neither, only sat while Kate's fingers worked the muscles in the nape of my neck.

When he saw that we weren't taking his hint and leaving, Pereira looked up from the pages and thumbed through them a moment.

"Tell me," he said, looking past me, "what do you do while your husband's away working for me?"

"I work here," she said.

He blinked at that one. "No lie?" he asked us.

"No," I said, breaking back in, sitting up straighter, "and I don't know why, either. She could make much better money back on the wards."

"As what?"

"Nursing," she said. "I got tired of changing sheets and cleaning old men's behinds. Then, too, I've never lived this far south. I wanted to meet the people."

"How noble," he said.

"No," she answered, "but it's better than sitting home watching the soaps all day, like the other wives." She paused. "And you? Why doctoring? I suppose that's your way of being noble."

He drank down the dregs of his coffee and glanced at her

over the rim of his cup. "Noble, hell," he said. "I became a gynecologist because I like to cut women."

Katie started laughing into her fist as he stood.

"I have to get home," he explained to her. "I have to catch some sleep so I can watch over this youngster tomorrow."

They shook hands for a while.

"We'll have to get together again," he said.

"I think we will," she answered him.

"You don't have to sound so sure of that," I told her after he had gone.

"Oh, for God's sake," she said, turning from her reverie back to me, "don't be such a husband."

"But I am a husband. I'm your husband."

She scowled at me, then shook her head. "Just shut up, then. You know, you can be so obtuse sometimes."

We drank the rest of our coffee in silence. When hers was gone, long after mine was finished, she got up and kissed my forehead. "Come on, baby," she said. "Let me take you home."

The leaves on the dogwood trees curled in the August heat. In the torpid air the humidity was viscous and suffocating as hot oil. In the heat even the wind wilted, and all the world was still, save for the insects droning tirelessly in the treetops and the diesels moaning along distant highways.

At night the delivery room was cool and ordered. We brought the women back and delivered them and let them sleep off their labors in the quiet of the recovery room at the far end of the hall. Outside that door, the ward was full of the metronomic rhythms of the fetal heart monitors and the cries of the laboring mothers and the low, gentling voices of their nurses.

On duty that night, we were in the back with a girl, Jason, the second-year resident, and I. The girl was lost among us strangers, our surgical gowns to her like sorcerers' suits. She was docile and fat, and she had no idea what was happening to her. She had smiled when we told her the baby was coming, and she thrashed at us under her pains. When I examined her cervix, she lay with her knees slack and her cow brown eyes very wide, the way she must have looked conceiving the kid.

The social worker said it was the stepfather's baby; the sister named their brother. The patient had no idea.

Now we had her in stirrups, draped. When we told her to push, she sat up and grunted. Then she fell back, confused by the yelling and the incessant pain.

"I got to go bafroom," she said to Lydia, her nurse.

"No, child," Lydia told her. "That ain't your bowels moving. That's your baby's head. You got to push it on out for us."

"Baby head?" she asked us, perplexed.

"Yes, child. That's your baby coming on down."

"My baby?" she moaned, and the moan peaked into a wail of negation as her contraction started again. "No!"

She howled and flailed at us, crying, denying, lost in a bad dream.

Jason went to put forceps on the baby. The girl was calm enough while he snaked a catheter into her bladder, but when he put his hand into the birth canal, feeling for the lie of the skull, the position of the bones and sutures and fontanels, she screamed in protest and pulled her hips off the table. She pulled her feet out of the stirrups and cocked back one knee. She kicked Jason in the chest with one broad, dark bare foot. He tumbled back, over the instrument tray, breaking the glass cabinet along one wall.

Pereira came through the double doors of the delivery room. He stood over Jason, grinning.

"What the hell are you doing on the floor, doc?" he asked.

Jason got up slowly and explained our problem a little sheepishly. I stood against the wall, trying to be inconspicuous.

"Well, doc," Pereira said, "if that's how it is, then gas her."

So one of the nurses went out to page the anesthesiologist. That was when the baby's heartbeat went to nothing. Pereira slung on a pair of gloves. He stood over her naked, bucking buttocks with one hand inside her until he got in a nerve block. Then he put the forceps on, riding between her tossing hips like a rodeo man until he pulled the purple baby from between the great thighs. I stood by him and cut the cord while the baby curled up and coughed and, finally, cried.

"How can you stand it?" Kate asked when I told her the story. We were in bed. She lay across my chest, her chin on my shoulder.

"Stand what?"

"Experiences like that. That's horrible."

"Happens all the time. I don't let it get to me."

"You don't feel anything? You don't hurt for them?"

"I hurt enough for myself. Getting up from a sound sleep at three in the morning: that hurts. I'm too tired to hurt for them."

"No," she said.

"Sure. They hurt me. I hurt them. Nothing's for free."

She got out of the bed. She stood by the window, her arms folded over her breasts, silhouetted in streetlight.

"That's sick," she said. She didn't turn around.

"No," I told her. "It's just real."

The artificial light coming through the window broke up in her hair, diffracted in it, diffused through it into the room. It quivered as she clutched herself more tightly.

"What is it?" I said.

"The moon's full," she said after a moment. "It's beautiful."

"A full moon?"

"Yes. There's a halo around it, from the haze outside, yellow and green and blue."

"They must be going crazy on the labor deck tonight, then. A full moon always brings the babies down."

She stamped a foot and turned on me. She stood with arms akimbo, her lithe, lean lines hard against the window light. Her face was dark in shadow.

"Don't you think about anything but work?" she asked. Her voice was bitter cold in the heat of the evening. She stood solitary in the darkness, naked, beautiful, and angry. I knew that she was waiting for me to answer, to apologize. Instead I turned my face to the pillow. It was soft, cool, silent, accepting.

Kate sighed and walked to the bed. She sat next to me and put a hand on my bare shoulder. I brought a hand up to hers. I stroked it. My fingertips ran over the skin. She shifted her hip on the mattress, and I felt her smoothness against the small of my back.

"What is it?" she whispered. Her breath caressed my ear, wafting through the fog of my fatigue.

"You have great veins," I said. "I could get a needle into you anytime."

It was a joke. I turned to embrace her in play, but she was too fast. The bedroom door slammed, then bounced open. Through it, after a moment, came the blue glow of the television and the false sound of fake laughter almost loud enough to drown the sound of her crying. Like a lullaby, the rhythm of her sobs lulled me to sleep.

When I awoke she had the beside lamp burning. She was drinking from a full tumbler. In her lap she had a paperback novel open.

"What time is it?" I asked.

"Almost two," she said, not looking off the page.

"You're still up?"

"Couldn't sleep."

"What are you drinking?"

"Gin and tonic."

"Can I have some?"

She handed me the glass.

"Jesus," I said. "How much gin did you put in this?"

"Enough to put me down for a couple of hours."

"What's the matter?"

She looked at me at last. "You're a jerk," she said simply. "I don't want to talk to you."

"I'm not a jerk. I'm an intern."

"Not all interns are like you."

"Sure. We're all the same. Nobody can get away from it."

"I'll bet John Pereira isn't like you."

"No. He's older. What are you reading?"

"Chekhov. Go to sleep."

"Isn't he one of those Russkie dissidents?"

She smiled, just a little.

"Yes. A dissident. Now go back to sleep."

I turned onto my belly and nuzzled the pillow. "You shouldn't read that radical stuff," I told her. "Why don't those guys quit stirring up trouble and do something productive with their lives, like learning a trade?"

She laughed and put down the book. She ran her fingers through my hair and patted my head. "He had a trade," she said.

"Yeah? Nothing respectable, I'd guess."

"No," she said. "Nothing respectable. Now go to sleep."

I fell asleep, dreaming of snow.

At the end of August the heat broke. It was time for all of us to move to other rotations, other responsibilities. Pereira invited all of us—the whole obstetrics team, spouses, and a few nurses—to his house for a feed.

The house was nondescript and small. The white paint was cracking off the clapboards, and in the square brick porch pillars the mortar was crumbling. The porch swing creaked, and the honeysuckle, unpruned, sprouted at wild angles above the windows like uncombed hair before the eyes of a forlorn child.

Inside, though, the house was light, cool, and spare. The wood floors wore no carpet, and all the furniture was worn and comfortable. There were books everywhere—paperbacks with bent spines, open journals, obese medical texts.

We arrived on time and so were early. John was in the kitchen. He stood over a pot of spaghetti sauce that spattered red the white enamel stove and the bright yellow wall. The room smelled of onions and oregano and steam, softened by the smell of cut grass that came in through windows open to the fenced backyard.

John put down his wooden spoon to shake my hand. "Here," he said, waving at the room. "Come on in. You're the first ones here. The rest are all late. It'll be just like morning rounds, never a one of you ready on time. Sit anywhere. How are you?"

We told him that we were fine. The kitchen table that we three sat around had flour in the cracks between its leaves. John, in jeans and a bib apron over a bare and hairy chest, had his feet up on it.

"And you," Katie asked him, "how've you been yourself?"

"Well. Still working at the bakery?"

"Yes," she said. "Up too early and getting fat from it." She prodded her belly with the point of a finger.

"And now her pinko friends have her taking dance lessons, if you can believe it," I said.

"I believe it," he told me. "You're not pregnant?"

"No," she said, coloring a little. Then she looked at me. "My friends aren't pink. They're all honestly red, thank you."

"You like dancing?" he asked. She nodded modestly.

"Not that she needs lessons," I said. "You should see her on the dance floor. She can outclass me any day."

"I'll have to see it sometime," he said.

She smiled for him, then gestured at me. "I'm trying to keep from getting old and fat and bored waiting for this old man to get home," she said.

"Ah," he said, "now that's a way you'll never be." Then he looked out the window, where the ivy grew up the back of the house. "But the job is hard on the wives. It certainly is."

His voice trailed away, and I remembered stories I'd heard about a wife and a bloody divorce.

Kate got up, to break the stillness. She went to the window. "Look," she said. "It's a hummingbird."

Pereira stood up. They stood at the window together, leaning forward, almost touching in the little window frame, intent on the blur of color in the bushes below.

"Tell me, John," I said, and he turned, and the little bird spooked and was gone. "Have you got any beer in the house?"

"Christ," he said, "I'm sorry. Sure. Let me get you one."

He cracked open a can for me. Then the other residents began to show up. I sat at the table and shook hands with the husbands of the women residents. Not doctors, they were tanned, bearded, muscled. They wore old chronometers, safari shorts, running shoes, styled hair. We tipped beers to each other, talking of pennant races, mutual funds, and the idiosyncracies of our wives.

John served the spaghetti onto platters. Kate grated parmesan cheese onto a wooden board and passed the salad around the table, as though she were the woman of the house. It was a good sauce, lively and full of wine, the kind my mother used to bring home from the restaurants downtown when I was a kid.

We talked about work as we ate. Like all residents, we couldn't leave it. That was rude to the spouses, who drank beer or Burgundy quite patiently. We talked about the job endlessly, tirelessly, bitching about the hours, about the interminable conferences, about patients, nurses, faculty, other residents. John kept still. Like the complaining, the drinking went on and on. After a long time somebody got up and turned on a Braves game. Kate started on the dishes. I picked up my seventh beer and went out.

In the other room I listened to the conversation wander around the usual subjects, the words filtered through alcohol and fatigue, faded and unintelligible. On the black-and-white television screen, the ball players were far away, minute giants, heroes at a distance, filling bases at random, struck out by pitches too fast to see. Long balls flew impossible distances, lost among the reaching hands of a measureless crowd.

When I woke, the others were gone. The television was black. The only sounds were the cicadas in the treetops and the voices of Katie and Pereira, sitting together under the warm kitchen lights. The dishes were stacked on the long sideboard. The table was scrubbed, the cloth folded and set away. Their voices were low and soft, harmonizing. They talked of seascapes and summertime.

I stood up. My head was light as beer foam but still too heavy to carry. I rested it against the doorway. Kate looked up and noticed me.

"Did you have a nice nap?" she asked, smiling.

"Wonderful," I said, grinning back, stupid with sleep.

"Sweet dreams?"

"No," I said.

"Not bad dreams?"

"No. No dreams. I was there, then—piff—I was dead."

"You're lucky," said John.

"I used to have great dreams," I told them, remembering. "In color. In them, I could run forever. I could fly. That was ... was a long time ago. Then ... then I ..."

"Became an intern," said Pereira.

"Yeah," I said, "something like that."

"I think it's time for one intern to go home," said Kate.

"What?" I said.

"She says it's time to head for home, big guy," he told me, "time to hit a cold shower."

"What?"

"I'm sorry," said Kate. "He's drunk."

"That's okay," I told her. "It's not your fault."

"He's not bad," John said. "He passed out before the serious drinking started."

"I'm drunk," I told them. "I'm punch drunk. I've been hit too many times. I'm wasted. They've wasted me."

I started wandering around the kitchen again, looking into covered pots, opening cabinets aimlessly.

They led me outside. I didn't see any point in resisting. They had me outnumbered. Kate had an arm around me. She was soft and smelled nice. We went down the steps slowly. The air was hot and full of the green smell of summer.

"Put him to bed," John said. "We've got to start hitting him some more in the morning."

"I'll take care of him," she said. "He'll be all right."

"Sure. He's just tired. Thanks for coming out. I enjoyed talking with you very much."

"We'll do it again soon, I'm sure."

"Of course," he said. Then he turned to me. "How about you, man? Did you have a good time?"

"Great time," I said. "Wonderful. Fantastic. Marvelous. Better than my wedding night. But who won the ball game?"

"I don't know. The Braves, maybe."

"Maybe. They were great, weren't they?"

"Very. They were magnificent," Kate said.

"They were unbelievable," Pereira told me.

"I saw you wink at her," I said. "I'm not as drunk as you think."

"Ah," he said. "You've caught me."

They laughed at me together. I didn't give a damn. Eventually Kate drove away. We stopped just across the railroad tracks so I could throw up in the weeds.

"Did I embarrass you?" I asked her.

"No," she said. "You were wonderful, fantastic, marvelous. Much better than my wedding night."

"I feel like shit," I said.

"You should," she said.

That Monday I started in the clinic. It was a different routine, less pressured than the delivery suite. It was oriented to the remitting cycles of women's bleeding, to the waxing and waning of pain, to the classification and correction of itch and discharge. A medical student followed me from room to room, asking questions of the women, repeating exams after me.

"Does this hurt?" I asked one woman, with one hand on her belly and one in her vagina. She looked at me impassively.

"No," she said.

"This?"

"No."

"How about here?"

"Motherfucker," she said, pushing up from the table. She sat half-erect on her elbows, half-naked in a bloody gown. Her eyes cursed me long after her lips were silent.

We gave them antibiotics, narcotics, hormones. We sent them up to the cutting tables in the operating suites with uncontrolled hemorrhages, incomplete miscarriages, abscesses, tubal pregnancies. One night, covering the emergency room, I sat on a high stool between a high school girl's legs. The blood ran in clean maroon lines over her buttocks and the white exam paper and the gray steel table. The medical student with me watched in awe as I pulled clots from the girl's vagina.

"Here," I said to him. "Sit here and tell me what you see."

"What is it?" he asked. His eyes were eager. He was a sharp, short-haired guy, chatty and hungry to impress.

"Just tell me what you see," I told him.

He cleared the open speculum and adjusted the lamp above his shoulder. Then his straight spine went limp.

"Shit," he said.

"What is it?" I asked again.

"Feet?" His voice had a nice tremble to it.

"Good guess," I said. "You want to deliver it?"

"No," he said, very quickly.

"What feet?" asked the girl, starting to sit up. "Whose feet you talking about?"

There were not only feet between the speculum's jaws, but legs and hips and the supple line of a dead baby's spine snaking into the girl's cervix. The toes were tiny, the soles flat and unlined. The muscles of the legs were soft. The skin was purple black, the color of old blood. I pulled the fetus free with a small pair of forceps.

"I'm sorry, ma'am," I said to the girl. "It looks like you're having a miscarriage."

"You mean I be pregnant?"

"Here, now," said the nurse, "don't sit up like that while the doctor's working."

The head of the fetus caught, then pulled free. It was a girl.

"No," I said. "The baby's out. You're not pregnant anymore."

"Oh, Jesus," our patient said. She dropped her head against the vinyl tabletop, flexing her toes in the stirrups. "Oh, Jesus Lord," she said.

The cord broke, of course; she was only four months along. With the baby out, the bleeding slowed. We sent her upstairs to the operating room. A senior resident stationed there sucked out the afterbirth. After that she was fine.

At conference the next morning, John brought pastry. He gave me a couple of doughnuts.

"I stopped by the bakery," he said. "Had a cup of coffee. Your wife was there, behind the counter."

"Was she? Not in among the ovens this morning?"

"Not this morning. She sent you these, said to say she's thinking of you."

"Thanks. Tell her I think of her, too, sometimes. Not times like last night, though."

"Bad?"

"It was terrible. Women hurting and bleeding. Women hurting and not bleeding when they're supposed to. Some of them bleeding and not hurting. A few not hurting or bleeding, just lonely, in for a tune-up before the weekend."

He laughed. "You'll get used to it."

Then the lights went down and the slide show started. I stayed awake through the doughnuts and a pint plastic cup of sweet coffee. Then I slumped down in the chair and fell asleep. I woke up clapping when the lights went on, agreeing with the others that it had been a most valuable lecture. Then I went to clinic.

An old woman was there, waiting for me. Her daughter stood behind her, answering my questions. The woman herself was quiet, embarrassed by my questions and by the time that she had to take to understand them. She was white and bent and frail, the kind of faded belle who sits behind gawky crape myrtles and a dusty yard, rocking away her last days on the warped porch boards. Only last week, the daughter said, she'd noticed that the old woman was having trouble walking. It seemed there was a mass from the female region that pained her.

We put the old lady in stirrups. She had trouble bending her hips and knees, but we helped her, and she was too ashamed to complain about her pain. I stood outside while the nurses draped her.

It was a classic case, I pointed out to the student. There was no mass, only the vagina turned inside out and hanging down over her anus. The ulcer came from it rubbing against her underclothes. The smell came from the ulcer.

"How many babies did you have, ma'am?" I asked her.

"Seven," she said after taking a moment to count. When

she spoke she lifted her head off the table, and the whole thing came out farther. "They was six boys, one girl."

"That was me," said the daughter. She was sitting at the other end of the table and couldn't see what we were pushing around. "I'm the onliest girl."

"And how much did the biggest one weigh?"

"The biggest? That must have been Eustace. He was birthed at nine pounds and seven ounces. Died in Korea in nineteen and fifty-three."

I had the woman sit up. I explained to the two of them how childbirth stretches and menopause weakens the pelvic supports.

"And so the female organs come down like that," I said. "Tell me: do you have to push all this back up inside to pass your bowels?"

The old one looked at the daughter guiltily, like a child caught in a fib. Then she looked back at me.

"Yes, sir," she admitted.

"Why, now, Mama," the daughter said, "you never told me that.

"And how long have you had this problem?" I asked.

She glanced at the daughter again.

"A year or two?" I said.

"Maybe."

"Maybe more?"

She nodded.

"Mama," said the daughter. "Why ain't you told none of us? We could have brought you in ages ago to get fixed up."

The old woman just shrugged. "Didn't want to trouble y'all none," she said. "I reckoned it was all just part of the change."

"Or else you thought it was cancer, and didn't want to know. That it?"

She nodded again.

"It's not cancer," I said.

Her stoicism relaxed visibly. She nodded once more and bit her lip. Her eyes teared up.

I called in one of the chief residents, and she set the woman up for surgery. We had the surgery team come down to examine her, along with a couple of stray students and one of the new obstetrics residents. It was a classic case.

"That must hurt like a son of a bitch," the obstetrics clinic intern said to me. "Man, you better be damn glad you ain't a woman."

"Yessir," I said to him. "Yessir, I surely am."

In the clinic, when Kate came by a few weeks later, there were women everywhere. They were all over the waiting room, in the halls outside with their arms around their lovers, on gurneys waiting to go upstairs, lined up at the registration windows with their Medicaid cards in their hands, chasing babies in and out of the bathrooms. Other babies sat on the floor neglected, too young to run, crying in wet diapers.

Kate stood out from the other women like a camellia blossom in brown leaves. Her hair hung free. She had on an old white dress shirt of mine, and the tawny color of her skin glowed through its worn weave. She kissed me, and all my patients smiled.

"Hello," she said, and then, leaning back, her hands on my shoulders, "I have a surprise for you."

"What?"

"Silly. If I told you, it wouldn't be a surprise."

"Then when do I find out?"

"Soon," she said, kissing me again. "Are you busy?"

"Look around," I told her.

She did, and laughed with me.

"Can you get free for lunch?"

"When?"

"Now. I have to be back at work before one."

"I can try."

"You don't sound very hopeful."

"Look around again," I said. "This isn't a clinic; it's a fucking circus, with all these damn women here."

She put a finger on my lips. "Don't," she said. "I'll wait."

It was like shooting clay pigeons. The nurses set the patients up, and I blew them away: a few questions, terse answers cut off in midsentence, a quick exam, a prescription. Even so we ran late most days, and the women sat waiting for hours.

"Can't you get free?" Katie asked again, later. "I have to go back to work soon."

"I can't leave here. We're overbooked, and I'm five behind for the morning, with the afternoon patients already starting to show up."

"Did you have lunch?"

"No."

"Aren't you going to?"

I looked at the stack of charts, at the bodies waiting, at my watch. "I guess not," I said.

"What about your surprise?"

"Tell me now."

She frowned and looked over her shoulder. "I can't. Not here. Come outside with me. Just to the parking lot. I'll tell you there."

"I can't leave."

"Please, honey. For me."

"I can't," I said, getting annoyed. "That's all. I can't leave my patients."

Her eyes clouded, and she held me close in valediction. She pressed that sad face against my shoulder, and when she turned it up she was smiling again.

"Remember," she said, "I love you. I hate your job and what it's making of you and of us. But I still love you."

Then she kissed me one more time and went out. She stopped in the doorway, turned, waved, smiled, and was gone.

Mary, the head nurse, came over. "Congratulations," she said.

"Thanks," I said without thinking, all my thoughts just gone out the door with Katie.

"How does it feel to be pregnant?"

"What?"

"Oh, Lord. Don't tell me she didn't tell you."

"Tell me what?"

"Oh, dear God," she said, putting a hand over her face and peeking at me through the fingers. "She really didn't tell you?"

"She's pregnant?"

"Didn't you know why she came here today?"

"No. I thought she came to visit."

"You didn't notice the needle mark where the blood was drawn?"

"No."

"I can't believe this. You seriously mean she didn't let you know?"

"She tried, I guess. I guess I was too busy to listen. The blood test was really positive?"

"My God. You men: bastards, all of you."

I sat down. "Shit," I said.

"I think you should give the poor girl a call, at least," said Mary.

"She's working."

"Then call her at work."

"She's not there yet."

I sat against the wall. The noise in the room faded in and out. Mary walked away. Others came over to shake my hand. I smiled for them. After a while I got up and went into a room.

"Hello," I said.

"How you doing, doc?" the woman on the table asked.

"Fine," I said. "I'm doing fine."

"You sure? You look a little peaked to me, doctor."

I sat down by the table and rubbed my face. "I just found out I'm pregnant," I said.

"No," she said. When I nodded, she broke out laughing. "Doctor, that just beat anything I ever hear. You pregnant. Lord. And I thought I was in trouble."

In the evening, with the dusk coming on, the cool air blew in through the window, carrying with it the susurration of distant highways. I sat over a mug of coffee, trying to wake up, watching Kate set the table. Her face was backlit by the kitchen lights. She moved smoothly, gently, arranging tablecloths and silverware on the small table.

"I still don't understand why," I said.

"Are you happy?" she asked.

"Yes."

"Well, I knew you would be. I knew that your mother would be, too."

We laughed at that. "I knew that if I asked you, if we planned it, you'd be in a panic for weeks and weeks, anticipating. I didn't want that."

"I wouldn't panic."

"You certainly would. You're panicked now."

"No."

"We'll see," she said. She finished with the table and stood by me. "Here," she said, touching me, "push back your chair." She sat in my lap.

"You're sure it's all right?" she whispered.

"Yes."

"I was getting so lonely, is all. You know, you're never home."

"I'm home now."

"You know what I'm mean."

"I'm sorry."

"No, don't be. I knew what I was walking into last spring. Those wedding presents didn't come for free. I knew that."

"Right."

She hopped up sprightly. "Are you ready for supper?" she asked.

"Sure."

"It's not much, just another chicken, a few vegetables, some wine."

"You aren't drinking wine, are you?"

"A little. We're celebrating."

"But you're pregnant. You can't do that."

She stood in the kitchen door, one hand on her hip, one finger pointed at my eye. "Why the hell can't I?" she asked.

"Because it's bad for the baby: alcohol, caffeine, all those things. You should be staying away from them."

She turned her back on me. "Bullshit," she said. Then she came out with the chicken. "Here: chew on this awhile."

She came back with a bottle of California white and poured two glasses.

"You really shouldn't," I said.

"Cheers," was all she said in answer. "You see: I told you that you'd be in a panic as soon as you found out." She took a long sip. "I'm not going to be one of those upwardly mobile madonnas who worries all the time. We're going to have a baby, and we'll kiss it when it's good and spank it when it's bad, and if we're lucky, it'll grow up to be a staid old brick like you instead of a terror like me."

"You still shouldn't drink."

"Oh, for God's sake. Eat your dinner and go to bed. Stop being such a wienie."

The rest of the meal was quiet.

"Do you want a boy or a girl?" I asked. We were in the kitchen, washing dishes.

"I don't want to know," she said. "I don't want to think about it. I don't want to make any plans. I've heard too many of your horror stories."

"But you'll be fine."

"Hush," she said, putting a finger on my nose. "Don't put the jinx on me."

"I see. Who's in a panic now?"

"Oh, just shut up," she said, "before I have to have another glass of wine."

On Friday night, coming out of the clinic late, I met her at the bakery. She had her bandannas on, a red one around her forehead and under her hair, with a pair of purple ones belted at the waist. Her loose blouse was sky blue. When she stood up to wave as I came through the door, she was like a flag in the wind.

"Hello," she said brightly. "Come sit with me."

We sat at a corner table. Across the room a young woman was tuning her guitar, waiting for the evening crowd.

"Try this," said Kate. "It's what I'm drinking now."

"What is it?"

"It's herbal tea. Rose hips, mint, lemon grass. Good stuff."

"It's terrible."

"Yes. It tastes like virtue. But I have to drink something to keep away from nasty old coffee."

"You're too good." I said, and I kissed her.

We sat by the window and watched the people going by. A boy swept past on a bicycle, a rose in his teeth. Two women in electric colors, acrylic faces, and reflective sunglasses sat on a bench with their arms around each other. A woman in a gray flannel suit and white running shoes pushed her baby stroller around the street corner. Behind us the guitar started playing softly and began building.

"You look good tonight," I said.

"Thanks," Katie said. "Mostly I'm just tired. When I finish here, I go home and sleep until you call. Some mornings I feel sick, but not as much as I thought I would."

"Are you putting on weight?"

"No. Should I be?"

"Not yet. Give it another month or two."

"I really don't feel different, only very tired."

"Give yourself time. You'll feel different soon enough."

"Great. You know, I wrote to your mother today. She sent us a present as soon as you told her the news."

"What is it?"

"You'll see. Something typical."

"What? Tell me."

"It's foolish, really. A champagne cooler. Just right for the young professionals on the conception of their first child. She must have read about it in the Neiman Marcus catalog."

"It's just like her."

"Pisses me off, though."

"She was only trying to be nice."

"Oh, I'm sure. But you see, I can't use it now. I have to look at it every day for the next seven and a half months and remember I can't use it."

"You're being very good."

"You're goddamned right I am. I'd kill for a bottle of champagne these days."

"You've done wonderfully so far."

"I'm doing terribly," she said. She pushed her tea away, so hard that it spilled. The pink pool ran into my lap.

"Let's go home," I said. "I'll fix you some warm milk to help you sleep."

"Warm milk? I need a double vodka." She sighed and slumped down in her chair. "I'm just tired," she said. "Already, I'm just so tired."

"We're all tired," I told her. "We'll just go home."

She put an arm around my shoulders walking to the car. She leaned on it, a dead weight.

One Sunday I slept late. When I got up Kate was in the bathroom, kneeling by the toilet bowl.

"What are you doing?" I asked her.

"I'm throwing up, like a proper pregnant lady," she said. "What did you think I was doing? Getting a drink, maybe?"

"No."

"Well, then. Quit watching. Go fix yourself some breakfast or something."

"Are you really sick?"

"No, baby. I'm fine. Really. I throw up once in the morning, and I'm fine all day.'

"Is there anything I can do?"

"You? Sure. You can join me. We'll make it a family affair. We'll throw up together." She sank back on her heels. "No," —she sighed—"there's nothing you can do. Go make yourself some breakfast."

"Don't you want anything?"

"For breakfast? Do I look hungry?"

"No."

"You're right, doc. Good diagnosis. I'm not. You go ahead. I'll be along."

For church she put on her makeup. Watching the women walk back from communion, I knew she outshone the best of them, my wife.

She called me at the hospital. We had just finished sign-out rounds. The day teams were pulling out, and those of us on call were digging in. On the labor deck we were reviewing the inpatients, organizing before the next round of incoming arrived.

I took the page, an outside call. I expected some lost, incoherent woman with a month of pain asking for a pass out of work or a brassy girl asking for tips on technique. Instead it was Katie. She was crying, and not quietly. She was choking on her tears, sniffling, breaking away into inconsolability and wandering back. She was weeping, and across the wire I could feel her body rock. She was bleeding, she said, bleeding a lot, and the pain was growing. She was hemorrhaging, on and on, soaking towels.

"Can you walk?" I asked her.

"Walk? Yes."

"Then call the neighbors, or a cab. Somebody. I'll meet you in emergency."

"You'll be there? You're not busy?"

"I'll be there. I'll see you when you come. John, too. I'll talk to him and see if he'll come with me."

"Johnny's there?"

"He's here tonight on call. We'll take care of you."

"The baby, too?"

"We'll see about the baby."

"You think I'll lose her?"

"We'll have to see."

"But maybe I will?"

"Maybe. Maybe not. Should I call a cab for you?"

"A cab? No. No. I'll drive."

"You can't drive. Let me call for you."

"I'll be all right. It just hurts sometimes."

The crying was calmer now, the gasps, the wrenching great gulps of breath quieted, controlled.

"I'll see you soon," she said, still sniffling a little. "I love you."

"Damn it, Kate," I said, "get a cab. Don't be a fool."

Then she hung up the phone.

"Shit," I said.

"What is it?" Pereira asked.

He was behind me, leafing through a chart, looking for nothing.

"Katie," I said. "She's aborting."

I watched it all, just watched, impotent. Now and then I held her, held her hands, kissed her, kissed her face, her palms, her neck, cradled her, rocked her. Mostly, though, I just watched. I watched the blood being drawn, watched the intravenous fluids being started. I watched John sit between her blood-slick thighs, watched the torn, ragged bits of placenta drop on the steel tray, watched her body twist and rise off the table with the agony of his examination. I watched the march to the elevators and followed her gurney down the long, bare halls. I watched the clock outside the operating room, then sat to watch her breathe, small and limp in crumpled white sheets, behind a plastic mask in the recovery room.

She woke up coughing, sat up, fell back. She looked into the brightness around her, big-eyed, unseeing, and then fell asleep again. Like a child, she curled up on her side, nestling against herself. I touched her hand, caressed it. She opened her eyes.

"Are you mad at me?" she asked.

"No. Hush."

"I had to drive. There wasn't anybody else."

"Hush, baby."

"I didn't have any cash for a cab."

"Shush. It's all right."

"I wasn't sure you'd be there. You're gone so much, you know."

"I was there."

"I know. I was so scared, though, darling, so scared."

She reached for me. I put my arms around her, gently, afraid to crush her fragile toughness.

"Aren't you mad at me?"

"Nobody's mad at you, baby," I said.

She slipped back into sleep. Then she moved, a softness under the stiff sheets. She squeezed my fingers.

"Do something for me?" she asked.

"Anything for you."

"Recite some poetry for me, like you used to do in the old days."

I said nothing, so she went on.

"Don't you remember? That winter, when I had the flu, and you kept me still with poetry. You lit candles, on the windowsill and in those mismatched saucers we'd picked up at a secondhand shop. You told me poems until I fell asleep every night."

"But that was ages ago," I objected. "I don't remember any poetry."

She curled tighter, kissed my fingers. "Don't sigh so deeply," she said, almost smiling. "Any kid could tell you: you could lose your breath that way."

"But we're not kids anymore, Katie."

"Do you remember the snow that winter, the big flakes spattering on the windowpanes and the dead leaves in the yard and you reciting poetry to me?"

"And you sick as a dog."

"But happy," she said as she nuzzled into the harsh linen, the plastic pillow.

John came over from the Dictaphone. He leaned over the bed rail. The lines where the cap and mask had been were dark in the olive skin of his face.

"Is she asleep?" he asked me.

"Morphine dreaming," I said.

Her eyes opened. "No," she said. "These dreams were real."

"I hope not," he said.

"Sure they are. Johnny?"

"Yes?"

"Tell us a poem."

"What, now?"

"Yes. Now. We can't remember any. We're too old."

"Then I'm ancient. I only remember pieces of poems I used to know, little fragments, memories of days when I wasn't a doctor." He paused. "I know that winter death has never tried the earth, but it has failed. And I shall see the snow all go downhill in water of a slender April that flashed tall through last year's withered break and dead weeds like a disappearing snake. There's more, but I've forgotten it. I'm sorry."

But she—she was smiling to herself, eyes closed tight. "And nothing will be left," she said, "white but here a birch, and there a clump of houses, with a church."

"That's it," said John.

"Damn sentimental Yankee," she said to him. Then her smile wilted. "But he was wrong, wasn't he? The snow outlasted him. The snows outlast all of us, don't they?"

"Katie," I broke in. "Stop. You were doing so well."

"Oh," she said, "I'm doing pretty well, considering. It's just a little setback, after all, this miscarriage. And there isn't anything to be done about it anyway, is there?"

Then she crumpled. Her face drew up, her tears blossoming. She bit her lip, trying to fight away her grief and failing.

"I'm sorry," she said, trying to choke back her sobs. "I only wish to God it didn't have to hurt so much."

We gave her something for her pain, but it didn't touch what was hurting her. Later, asleep under the morphine again, she lay quiet. She had a private room with big windows opening out to the trees before the hospital. I sat and watched her face in the stray light from the hall. Her hair fell across her face. It was past midnight when my pager called me away. I left her alone with her dreams, going back to the dim wards where silent nurses made their rounds among women wakeful with exhaustion.

In the fall we went north to New York. We stayed upstate, with Katie's people, in the lake country. At night we slept together in an upstairs room of the old family house, with one tall window open and the quilts deep and soft and warm over us, listening to the trees in the yard while the last leaves rustled in the west wind. We ate beef and apple pie, and in the evenings

I watched the news with her old man, drinking his bourbon and agreeing with his union politics. Days we spent on the road, visiting the friends of her youth or walking across wet black fields lashed by the early snow that came slanting into our faces, watching the last geese glean broken cobs from cutover cornrows. We worked our way through the wine country, past square Italianate farmhouses built of fieldstone and brick and past the forty-acre vineyards that sloped down toward the frost-broken lakeshore road by the flatness of broad waters, drinking white wine from green glass bottles until the low sun set.

Back on the job, I started my surgical apprenticeship in earnest. Rising at five to be in the big house by six, I woke women confused by pain in order to finish rounds by seven so that I could make the operating room by half-past, learning the art of the healing slash.

Just before Christmas John Pereira got sick. He had been away, rotated out to the community hospital. Katie had seen him, she'd told me, weekends at the bakery or at the jazz joints downtown where she spent the nights I spent on call. He was looking very well, she said, negotiating for a partnership in western Massachusetts, in the mountains, in an old mill town on a river we'd once tripped through on our way to or from Boston in days long gone, where little houses on steep streets trailed off into second-growth woods.

He came into the emergency room one night and was admitted. I went to see him the next afternoon. He was in an isolation bed on the internal medicine ward. He smiled when I came in, a pale smile like the rim of winter sun that was setting outside his window. Under the fluorescent room lights, the jaundice made him look tanned, but the pigment was in his eyes, too, and in the palms of his hands. He wore hospital pajamas too loose for his frame, and I could see that he was as embarrassed by them as he was by his illness.

"They were such typical internists," he said. "They asked all sorts of questions: was I exposed at work to hepatic toxins or uncooked seafood; had I traveled recently; did I abuse intravenous drugs? No more than most doctors, I told them. They didn't like that: too flip for a sick man. Had I engaged in homosexual relations? None that I was sober enough to remember afterward, I said, and that pissed them off, too. I told them that I had hepatitis from an accidental wound sustained during surgery, that I needed admission for intravenous hydration until I could quit puking. I told them I needed narcs to ease the pain under my ribs, and they decided then that I was a shooter in for free hits of Demerol—as if I couldn't get those anytime."

He sighed deeply, then caught himself, his left hand clutching his right side. "Damn," he said. "It's right here. Put your hand here."

I put my hand on his belly, on the yellow skin where he had pulled up the blouse of his pajamas. The muscles tightened against the pain my touch brought him, but beneath them I could feel the firm, smooth liver, the rounded edge a handsbreadth below his ribs.

"Shit," he said. "And they do that twice a day. Then they bring the medical students in to feel it, too."

"They wanted to know last night," he went on bitterly, "if I drank to excess. What's excess? More than you? More than your Baptist grandmother? Sure, but never enough, and certainly never enough to do this. They got exasperated. So did I. They went on with the medical history. It was too much. I was too tired. It had been all I could do to walk in from the parking lot: I had to sit down in the gravel once just to let the nausea and the fatigue pass. They wanted to know what my grandparents had died from, what I smoked, if I'd been transfused, all the bullshit. I cut them off. I threw them out. They threatened me with discharge. I told them that if they tried, my chairman would call their chairman. They knew what that meant. They desisted."

He closed his eyes. The overhead pager outside gabbled on. Footsteps came and went on by. Johnny smoothed his pajamas and the cotton blanket with one hand, watching the little motions his fingers made.

"How is Kate?" he asked when he tired of that. He didn't wait for an answer. "I had thought she might stop by. I tried to call, but you both seemed to be out this morning, or maybe the phone was out of the wall."

"We were out," I said. "She's the same, always bitching about this or that, about work, about me, talking about going back to school, getting into teaching or nursing administration, all of it vague. She wants to move. She hated the heat last summer, and now she hates the mud. She's longing for snow."

"Yes," he said to the ceiling. "It's hard on the women. It certainly is hard on the women."

He tried to squeeze off a smile for me. He didn't do it very well.

"And a baby?" he asked. "Are you two still working hard on that?"

"I don't know. I'm never home, and when I am, I'm exhausted. She won't talk to me about that, except to say 'Not now' and change the subject, barking at me for leaving my clothes on the floor or forgetting to take out the garbage. If I press her on it, she walks away. I don't ask anymore."

We sat in silence awhile, looking at each other with nothing to say. Then he looked away to the stormy seascape hanging on the wall.

"Well," he said, "they're throwing me out tomorrow."

"That's a good sign."

"Yeah. I can keep soup down about half the time now."

"Great."

"Fucking marvelous, isn't it?"

"I don't suppose they have any idea when you'll be back to work. You know that the other chiefs are all livid, knowing that they'll have to cover your call while you're out."

He shook his head. "Soon, I hope," he said. "Not soon enough to satisfy them, of course. I can't go back until I clear the virus. I'm very infectious, you know."

I hadn't thought of that, but he gestured to the cubicle that hid the toilet and shower. On the door was a red sign, spelling out instructions for the proper handling of all his wastes, blood specimens, and soiled linen.

Finally the silences between our sentences grew too long to listen to. I stood and gave him my hand. He shook it briefly.

"Well," I told him, "we're all rooting for you."

"Oh, I know. Even the chairman sent flowers." He leaned over to the nightstand and picked up a card from among the flower arrangements. 'Best wishes for a speedy recovery,' it says. I'll bet he wishes for that. He can't spare any residents these days."

Eventually I left him.

"Tell Kate to come by and see me," he said as I went out.

"Sure," I said. "Look for her."

But I'd been on call the night before, and exhaustion racked me like a fever. I ate a cold supper while leafing through an outdated journal. Kate asked about my day and my night.

"Same old thing," I mumbled, trying to forget.

"That's all?" she asked. "Nothing interesting? Nothing remarkable?"

"No," I told her. "Nothing."

"There must have been something. A doctor's life can't be all that dull."

"No."

"Look at me. God. I'm talking to you, damn it."

I looked up at her.

"Talk to me. Please. I'm your wife. You're supposed to talk to me."

"All right. But nothing happened worth telling about. It was all just the same old shit. Trash on the wards, trash in the emergency room. Nothing new."

I went back to eating. She talked to me while I faked interest randomly. She told me what was playing in the theaters, whom she'd seen at the bakery and in the headlines. She told me the news from Soweto and Salvador. She told me about a protest rally she'd been to—for or against what or whom I never quite caught.

"I'd really like you to come with me to the next one," she said. "It's this Saturday. You're not on call."

"What?"

She jumped up and started walking around the room, gesticulating, shouting.

"For God's sake. Don't you listen to me at all anymore?"

"Yeah," I said. "I listen. And no: I don't want to go."

"Why not?"

"Because I'm tired," I told her, too tired to keep the exasperation out of my voice. "On Saturday, I'll still be tired. I don't want to go to meetings with your freaky friends and hear people yell and bitch. I hear that all the time at work. I want to sit at home and listen to the quiet. I want to go to sleep and not give a damn."

"Please go," she said. "It's important to me."

"No."

"Shit."

"And don't call me to bail you out when you get arrested."

I was wiping the meat juice off the plate with a piece of bakery bread when she came back into the room.

"Are you finished?" she asked.

"Yeah."

"Then put your damn dishes in the sink. You never put them away. You never wash them anymore. What's happening to you?"

"I told you. I'm tired."

"Well, I'm tired, too," she said, following me into the dim kitchen with its counters strewn with dirty dishes, stained with spilled soup, scattered over with beef bones, bread crumbs, and cheese crumbs. "I'm tired of living in this hole. I'm tired of this place, this fucking town. I hate the weather. I hate the people. I hate the food. I hate everything about this shitty little burg." She paused for breath. "God, I hate it," she said.

Then she paused. I was leaning against the kitchen door with my hands in the pockets of my wrinkled whites. It was time for an embrace, an apology, some dramatic gesture. She looked at me, waiting for it, hoping for it, maybe. But I was too tired, really too tired, too drained, too spent, too beaten, to rise to her passion.

"Why don't you just say it?" I asked her.

"Say what, for God's sake?"

"That you hate me, too."

She snorted, shook her head, ran a hand through her hair. She turned her back to me and folded her arms.

"You're so pitiful," she said. "Just go to bed. Please. Just leave me alone."

I did. I woke in the night. Her pillow was empty. I got up, groggy, feeling for the bathroom door in the darkness. She was on the sofa, asleep. Her arms were around a cushion. She didn't wake when I whispered her name.

That next night I was asleep early again. I woke when the telephone rang. Katie answered on the kitchen line. I crashed back to the mattress, sticky with a sweat that came more from work and worry over patients whose ills I didn't understand than from the heat of the waning Indian summer outside.

She came in shouting, pulling the bedclothes off me and slapping me. Like her hands, the light hit me in the face, too harsh, too sudden to endure without flinching.

"You asshole," she was screaming. "Get up. Get up, you son of a bitch. Get up, you shit. I'm talking to you."

She pulled me up. I sat on the edge of the bed, squinting at her in my underwear.

"What is it?" I asked, trying to fend off her hands. "What?"

"Why didn't you tell me he was in the hospital, you little fuck? Didn't he ask you to tell me? Jesus Christ. Didn't you think I had a right to know? Goddamn you, you shit, don't you ever think about me? He had to call himself, sick as he is. Why? Why didn't you tell me?"

"I forgot," I said.

"You never even thought about it."

"I did."

"Liar. You never think about anybody but yourself."

"That's not true."

She was pulling on her shoes. Then she stood up. Her face was livid with disgust.

"Just stop it," she said. "Just shut up. I'm sick of hearing you."

She went to the door.

"Where are you going?" I asked her.

"I'm going to see him. I haven't seen him in almost two weeks. I thought he was busy, but he was sick. I need to talk to him. He wants to talk to me."

"What time is it?"

"It's quarter past ten. Why?"

"Just asking."

She went out. I lay on the bed, listening to the car pull away. She had left on all the lights in the apartment. I got up and wandered around the empty rooms, hitting switches. In the dark, I tripped on the bed. I fell into it, feeling nothing at all.

In the morning the clock radio woke me. The schooled voices of public broadcasting kept me company over a bowl of wet cornflakes.

On the way to the hospital, through the darkness, all the cars I passed looked like hers. As they went by I wrenched myself around in my seat, straining to search for her face in every window. But in all those cars were strangers, and I tried not to cry in the empty elevator that took me to the waking wards.

It was late the next evening when I came home. I dropped my things by the door: a jacket soaked in the rain, a knapsack full of damp papers, used underwear, and an unread magazine. Katherine was in the kitchen. I sat at the table, slumped into a chair, and said hello. She had an apron on, and she was slicing onions.

"How was your night?" she asked.

"Same," I said.

I watched her fingers work the onion and the knife. They held the bulb against the board, split it, turned it, sliced it. The blade came down on the wood solidly, smoothly, methodically. It came down again, again. It brushed against a knuckle, drawing blood.

"Goddamn it," she said. She put the bleeding finger in her mouth, and only then did she look up at me. She put down the knife.

I stared at her, as hard as I could. I looked into her eyes, afraid that if I looked away, I'd never see them again. We watched each other across the close, domestic space of kitchen, doorway, and dining room. Then her lips pursed, paled, narrowed. Her head fell, and she leaned forward over the bloodstained board with all her weight heavy on her one good hand.

"How was your night?" I asked.

"What?" she said.

Her head snapped up. The corners of her mouth drew down. The little lines around her eyes twisted. "Nothing happened," she said.

"You're a liar," I said. I spoke from the strength of my fatigue, feeling nothing at all.

"No, really. I want you to know that."

She stood straighter, making an effort to compose her face. She brushed a wisp of hair out of one tearing eye with the back of her forearm. "I needed to tell you that," she said. "It's important to me for you to know."

I stood in front of her. I pushed my chair under the table. "Too fucking bad," I said.

Then I went to the bedroom and locked the door. She tried to open it. She called my name. I fled into sleep, the intern's refuge. In the night I heard the front door slam. I heard her engine start, then fade into the sound of raindrops outside the window.

But in the morning, going out, I saw her curled up on the sofa under a torn blanket. She was still as death, save for the eyes that followed me as I moved to the door.

"Bye," I said softly, tentatively.

She said nothing. Her eyes were full—of reproach, regret, resignation, or rejection. I couldn't see which, in the darkness, so I closed the door.

Pulling out of the parking lot, I thought I glimpsed her in the front windows, silhouetted against the bathroom light I'd left on. But perhaps it was only the reflection of my own headlights on the glass. I waved anyway, knowing she'd never see.

At work I told everyone that I was only tired. It was winter, and by then all of us were in a black mood. We were working too much, forgetting small things often, big things now and then. Betsy didn't check a pregnancy test on a bleeding forty-three-year-old before she took her to the operating room, and she ended up aborting her by accident. Rick walked into the wrong room one night and gave a postpartum woman chemotherapy. I was the same way. In the operating room my mind drifted homeward. I saw Katie smiling, sleeping, saw her doing other things— our things—with other people. Surgeons, testy, snapped me back into their world, yelling at me to cut a suture, shift a retractor, tie down a knot. Later, on the ward, X rays went unread, lab numbers uncharted, students' notes unchecked. On afternoon rounds I forgot patients' names, forgot why they'd been admitted, had to be prompted by other residents.

When it was over for the day, I sat in the wardroom, alone, afraid to go home, afraid she'd be there, more afraid she'd be gone.

One of the senior residents came in. "You know," she said, "it doesn't help to feel sorry for yourself."

"What?" I said.

"I know how tired you are. We've all been through it. We've all survived. You'll survive, too."

"Yeah. But sometimes it seems like it'll never end."

"It ends. You die or you graduate, and nobody dies."

"I suppose."

"Believe me: it's true. But listen, guy: you've got to get with the program. The operating room starts late because you aren't there on time. Just now, we should have finished by four, and here it is past six, all because you went through rounds without a clue to what you were doing. We've all noticed it. Even the chairman's noticed it. It's time to get back on the team."

"Yeah, I guess."

"Don't guess. It's time."

"Okay."

"That's the way to be. And don't be late to rounds tomorrow."

"No," I said.

She stood up. She had on a huge smile. It was all over her face, like a cancer, eating into her skull.

"You'll make it," she said. "You'll be fine. You'll see."

"Right. I'll be great."

"That's it."

She pumped my hand for a while. "And listen," she added, "don't forget: we're all your friends here, in case there's something we can do or there's something you need to talk about."

"I'll remember that," I said.

"No problem, then," she said, leaving me alone again. "See you at six-thirty."

"Right."

"Sharp."

"Six-thirty sharp," I told her numbly.

"Attaboy."

She went out, and the emptiness of the big house seemed to fall all over me. For the longest time I couldn't get up. There seemed to be nowhere to go.

And of course Katherine wasn't home. I had expected it, had known it, had known where she would be. The apartment was dark. I looked for a note to confirm what I knew, but there wasn't even that. I scrambled a couple of eggs for supper, pushed them around a plate, and scraped them into the garbage. I washed the dirty dishes from the night before. I read through fragments of last Sunday's paper. I turned the radio on and off. I went outside and leaned over the railing. The street was empty, the parking lot quiet. Among the repeating ranks of the town houses, here and there a lamp burned behind a shaded window. The undertone of traffic far away came to me from behind a low hill, as monotonously ever changing as the sound of falling water. A train whistled for all the crossings, its note rising up and fading out. The siren call of an ambulance ran shrilling through the neighborhoods. I went inside, drank a beer, and went to bed. Katie's quilts wrapped themselves around me. I fell asleep with the lights on and a country singer's voice moaning in my ear.

In the morning Kate was home again. She was asleep, a book of poems open on the floor beside her. Frost looked at me from the jacket. Her head had fallen back against the arm of the sofa, exposing lines of her throat above the hair that curled beneath it.

I went to the bathroom, shaved, bathed, dressed. When I came out she was awake. She lay stretched out on the cushions. Her face was older. In the weak light the wrinkles around her eyes and at the corners of her mouth stood out. The skin beneath the eyes sagged. She drew her knees up against her chest and wrapped her arms around them.

"Good morning," I said.

She focused on me, frowning. Silent, she watched me cross the room into the kitchen.

"How are you?" I asked.

She stared at me for the longest time, as though she were trying to remember my name. She fell back onto the cushions and covered her face with her hands—not to cry, not to hide, only to shut out the light a moment longer.

"He's gone," she said from behind the mask of her fingers.

"Is he?" I said, not needing to ask who. "Where's he gone to?"

She sat up, stood, started pacing across the far half of the room. "Back to Massachusetts. I took him to the airport last night."

"That was nice of you."

I went back into the kitchen and started playing with something on the stove. She followed, leaning on the door.

"Do you know why he left?" she asked me.

"I couldn't imagine," I said, "and I don't think I care."

"For you," she went on, ignoring my answer. "He said he was doing it for you. Can you believe it?"

"No," I said.

"I couldn't either."

I turned and looked at her. I pointed my spatula at her. I started to ask, then had to turn away.

"Why didn't you go with him?" I asked, trying to focus on the sausage spattering around in my skillet, trying not to pay attention to her at all, trying not to think about the way she looked or the way she was looking at me.

"He wouldn't let me," she said.

She said that with only the briefest hesitation, quite frankly, the way she might have told me that dinner would be late or my mother had called, the way she might have told me any annoying bit of bad news she'd run across. And after she'd told me, there was nothing to say, except good-bye.

"You have to go to work?" she asked me.

"I'm on call. Again."

"You'll call me tonight?"

"Why, for God's sake?"

"Because I asked you to," she said.

We both waited a very long time for me to answer. In the end, though, her reason was still enough for me.

"All right," I promised, "I'll call."

She kissed me on the cheek, for old times' sake. Then I took up my knapsack with its journals and books, unread letters, unpaid bills, and peanut-butter sandwiches, and I left her there.

Of course, there was never time to call her. We were in the operating room all day. Between cases I sat in the chart room sucking coffee out of stained styrene cups to stay awake. Then the surgeon's mask would go back up. I'd scrub and stand by the operating table, holding retractors until my hands cramped. After that there were patients to see, notes to write. Someone stumbled into the emergency room with blood soaking through her clothes, and I went back under the operating room lights with the night call team. There were fevers to look into, calls about chest pain and dyspnea. I fell asleep over a page of orders, but my beeper woke me, crying insistently.

I called the number. It was Kate. There was music behind

her voice, and it mixed with other voices. She was shouting into the telephone.

"Did you try to call?" she asked.

"No," I said, too tired to work up an excuse.

"I knew you wouldn't," she said. "But that's okay. I'm not home."

"Where are you? It sounds like a madhouse."

"I'm at Sensations, dancing. Been here for hours."

"That meat shop? For hours?"

"Oh, hush," she scolded. "Don't be so Victorian. It's fun. I couldn't just sit around the apartment by myself tonight, thinking and thinking. Besides, I've met some very nice people: Steven and Frank and—say hello, Frank."

There was a pause. Then a man's voice came over the telephone.

"Hello," he said, obviously drunk.

"Put Katie back on," I said.

"Who?"

"My wife."

"Your what?"

Then there was more shouting, and finally Katie again.

"We've been having a great time dancing," she said.

"And drinking, too." I said.

"Oh, pooh," she answered. "Stop being such a prude. You know, you're always such a prude. Drinking helps keep my mind off my mind. And anyway: how are all your women?"

"They're all fine," I said. "They're alive, anyway."

"Poor them. I hope you're keeping them happy, all your ladies."

"Sure. Everybody's happy here. That's why we're in the hospital."

"Good. That's really good. We're all happy here, too."

"I'm happy for you."

"That's right. We're all happy about each other's happiness. We're all so happy I can't stand it. Here, Frank, be a dear and get me another one of these. Will you be home tomorrow?"

"Are you talking to me?"

"Of course. Who else would I be talking to?"

"Frank. Or Steven. I don't know."

"They're off getting the next round. They're both very drunk, you know."

"No, but I can guess," I said.

"I'll bet you can. Will you be home tomorrow? I asked you that, didn't I?"

"Yes. And yes, I'll be home."

"So we can go out together then. We need a date."

"Katherine. I have to sleep sometime."

"You can sleep later. You can sleep next year, when the new interns come. We'll be together all the time, like when we were first dating, when I used to take you around to all the good places in New York."

My pager went off again. It was the number to the emergency room.

"Next year," I said, "everything will be great."

Katherine talked on and on, about the band and the clothes that the bartender wore, the colored lights, the taste of her new drink.

"I have to go," I said.

"Oh, you. You're always all work and no play. You're such a dull boy sometimes. Most times."

"Right. I still have to go."

"Oh, all right. Tomorrow?"

"Tomorrow."

"Great. A hot date. It's about time. Say 'I love you, Katherine.'"

"I love you, Katherine."

"That's it. You don't have to mean it. Just say it again, one more time."

"I love you, Katherine."

"Bye-bye, baby," she said. "I love me, too, just as much."

"Take a taxi home," I told her, but the line was already dead.

I called the emergency room next. The triage nurse had a

visitor for me: a nineteen-year-old girl in pain after having gone two months without contraception or menses.

The halls were still, all the way to emergency, save for the sound of elevator bells and the murmurs of night shift nurses in screened-off rooms. The stillness was intimate, embracing, like a cloister. It was good for thinking—about all the possible problems my new girl might have, about journal abstracts I'd read, about the color of spring back home. All kinds of thoughts came to me, but behind and beneath every one of them was Katherine, my stranger; her crazy voice inside my head went speeding away.

The madness in the emergency was a familiar relief, a welcome distraction. A drunk with vomit on his beard lay mumbling to himself under a torn sheet on a gurney in the hall. Tubes of blood were strewn about the countertops. Harried nurses shouted at doctors and cops and patients. Clipboards sat about bearing scrawled sentences abandoned in midsentence.

My patient was sitting on an exam table between steel stirrups. She wore a faded hospital gown, open at the back. She was studying the dirt between her bare toes. She watched her feet swing forward and back while we talked.

"Well," I said, sitting down and starting to write, "I hear you've been hurting."

When the questions were answered, the exam done, the labs back, an hour later she proved to be neither pregnant or—as best I could tell—in any pain. She was constipated to the eyes, but that was all. She got an enema and a clinic appointment, some hormones to make her bleed, and a free pack of birth control pills. She went home smiling, after I asked her to wash her feet.

I went up to the labor deck, where the nurses kept a pot of coffee hot all night. I had a cup to put myself to sleep. A couple of medical students were watching a late movie outside the call rooms. I took an empty bed by the bathroom and fell asleep on top of the sheets. The roar of toilets woke me. I got up and went downstairs to round again, shaking awake sleeping women, frightened women, women lost, or narcotized, or only bored.

When I came home Kate lashed her arms around me and gave me a wet kiss. We had another glass of wine, and then she shut me in the bathroom until I'd washed the night off my skin. We ate downtown in a noisy place with peeling paint and roaches, where undergraduates in T-shirts ate three-dollar pizzas and drank Budweiser and threw up among the dead weeds in the alley. Then we went to the bakery to say hello to Katie's pals and listen to an old man with a twelve-string sing train songs while I tried to slurp down enough espresso to stay awake.

The dance hall was on the first floor of a new hotel. We were dressed wrong, but business was slow, or maybe the bouncer just liked the way that Kate smiled for him. He had on a pinstripe suit without a shirt, a bow tie, and basketball shoes with the toes cut out so his bare feet showed. He gave Kate back her smile and waved us in.

Above the dance floor was a shining globe that spattered light all over us. The floor was empty. Around it, knots of people at tiny tables yelled at each other, took drinks from waitresses in low-cut leotards, flicked cigarette ash onto the deep blue carpet. There was no band, only a guy in dark glasses at a sound booth by the bar. We took a table off the main floor, under a poster of a woman's torso dressed only in tire tracks. A waitress jiggled by. Kate asked her for an amaretto sour.

"I'll have a Genessee," I said.

"A what?" she said. She put her pencil in her mouth and sucked on it.

"It's a beer," I said.

She moved her pencil in and out between her lips, then shook her head. "Whatever it is," she said, "we don't have it."

I asked for something Canadian. She switched off to the bar, in her too tight skirt.

"What are you watching?" Kate asked playfully.

"I was just thinking," I said, "that with clothes that tight, she'll get a vaginal infection."

"Silly boy," said Kate, giggling a little. "With clothes that tight, she can get anything she wants."

"I guess so," I said.

"You've never been here before, have you?"

"No," I said.

"What do you think?"

"It's a real class place."

"Oh, come on. It isn't that bad. It can be fun."

"I'm sure."

"You'll get used to it."

"Eventually."

"Johnny said to tell you he's sorry," she said, and she said it without turning to look at me, without even a flicker of change in her voice.

"Great," I said.

"No. He really was."

"I am, too."

"Are you?"

"And he looked pretty damn sorry the last time I saw him, there in that hospital bed."

She sat back and finally looked me in the face. "Don't be that way," she said in a tired voice.

"Me? You brought him up."

"Then forget it. We were doing so well."

"Right. We were fantastic."

The waitress came up with the drinks. Kate went through hers as though it were lemonade. I sipped my beer, looking around at the people at the other tables, the square men in white shirts and full mustaches, the plump blondes with pastel eyelids and hard perms.

"Here," said Kate, "the hell with them. The hell with all of them."

She got up and threw back the ice melt in the bottom of her glass. She took me by the arm and pulled me onto the dance floor.

Dancing, she was all languor. She danced with her eyes closed, with her hair over her face, with her skirt swinging at her legs. She danced with her hands clasped over her head, with her head back, with her lips just open, smiling to herself. She turned in small circles, tracing arabesques with her toes. I slowed to keep pace with her, trying to follow her twirling under the flogging of the music.

When the music changed, we sat down. Other people got up to take our places. Soon the floor was crowded. Kate finished my beer. Then she got up again and went into the crowd. I tried to tag behind her, knocked someone's linen sport coat off a chair, apologized twice, and lost her among the bodies. The music was crazy and fast, and all over the floor people were moving madly. I walked among them, lost, dodging hips and elbows, looking for her.

She was in a corner, away from the people and the lights, watching her own feet move to the music. I tried to follow her moves, too awkwardly. She held out her hands to me. I took them, and she fell against me. We staggered back, up against a wall. She sagged against me. We stood there a moment, swaying, my arms around her, the sweat of her back on my palms, her breasts pressed against my chest, rising and falling as we breathed.

"What about John?" I asked her.

"What?" she said.

"What about John?"

She led me out onto the dance floor again, shaking her head. We danced slowly, marking time with our feet while I waited for her to answer.

"You're such a kid," she said. "You know that? You take things so seriously. You make me feel young again, just like he made me feel so old. You don't understand that, do you?"

"No."

"I didn't think so. Anyway, he's gone now. The hell with him, I say."

"Right," I said after a pause. "The hell with him."

We tried to go on, but my legs were too stiff. I was exhausted, and my concentration was gone. She gave up. She turned her face up and kissed me. Her mouth tasted of almonds and alcohol, open fully and pressing hard into mine.

"Take me home," she whispered, and though I couldn't hear her above the music, I understood. We went out through the couples in red and black and hard colors, moving against each other. In the car she put her head on my shoulder and her hand in my lap.

"You know," I said, "you really should put your seat belt on."

She didn't pay any attention to me.

The apartment was dark. I turned on the lights.

"No," she said, striking the switch. She took my hand. I walked behind her to the bedroom. She turned down the sheets and kissed me. She unbuttoned my shirt and undressed me. In the darkness that came in through the bedroom window, I watched her undress, too. She did it slowly, watching me watching her.

Then she pressed me back against the mattress. My eyes closed, and I lay still as death while she caressed me. Her lips were on my ear, on the curve of my neck, on my shoulder. Her mouth caressed my nipples and played in the spiral of hair about my navel. Her fingers massaged my crotch, and her tongue tickled my penis, teasing me to life. I kissed her in the crook of her elbow as she spread herself above me, her long hair spilling down. Her skin was salty from the dancing. She drew me inside her body, and her slickness ran down between my legs. I moved with her, touching her tenderly out of habit and instinct. We went on and on for ages, fucking each other. After she came, she lay with her head on my chest, her breathing quick but quieting.

"Tell me," I said.

"Yes," she whispered in the throaty voice I'd once loved so much.

"Was that me? Or was it Johnny?"

Her smile dissolved as she pushed herself up and back. Her brows came together in a look of incredulity and hurt. She rolled away. For a moment she sat at the foot of the bed, frozen. Her skin was cold white in the darkness. I put my hand against the long muscles of her spine. Saying nothing, she got up and went into the bathroom. She stayed there a very long time. When she got back into bed, she woke me.

She sat across me, straddling me. She put my hands on her breasts, and she kissed my eyes, first one, then the other.

"Does it really matter?" she said.

I lay still, feeling her move against me. "No," I said, "I suppose not."

She leaned down and kissed my mouth. "That's right," she said. "It doesn't matter at all."

After that, things were fine. The winter passed to spring after just one snow. The days got longer, and sometimes when I got home the sunlight had not yet faded into full blackness. We sat at home, watching marital comedies on television. My rotations at the hospital changed, then changed again. I began to learn what I had to know to keep my patients alive.

One night, that first month after Pereira had gone, I came home tired. Katie was sitting in the front room. She was reading the morning newspaper. She was wearing one of my shirts and nothing else. She drank three glasses of wine while I ate dinner. Later we sat on the sofa together. We talked about our work. She put down her glass when we started petting.

"Why," I asked her, "do you have to be drunk before you can make love with me?"

She never missed a stroke, never even slowed down. "Honey," she said, "don't ask me questions you don't want to know the answers to."

I didn't see John Pereira again until June. I heard rumors about him: that he was in Boston, that he was back in town but too sick to work, that he had gone again, no one knew where. Katie said she'd heard he was doing better, that he hoped to get back to work soon. When I asked her how she knew, she only shrugged and said, "Everybody knows." I dropped it.

After the first weeks the other residents quit feeling sorry for Pereira. They were resentful of the way his work devolved onto them. And that work, our work, went on and on: the endless nights, the blood on the floor, the screams in the delivery rooms. It all went on and on.

We went looking for a party one night, Katie and I, for old times' sake, and we found Pereira. It was the weekend, and I had both days off. We were sitting at a table against the wall. It was June, and the candle flame between us trembled in the air-conditioning. We'd come in while the band was tuning up, and now they were warming to their music and breaking into a sweat. The vocalist kept calling people to the dance floor, but nobody was drunk enough to go. I was drinking beer, and Kate—nine weeks and four days pregnant—was drinking nothing at all.

Pereira came in with a blonde in a backless white bodysuit and a red skirt. Her long hair was loose, and it ran all over her deep tan. She had one arm around John's waist, one hand in his pocket. She was leaning on him hard, and he looked none the worse for it.

His collar was undone, his tie untied. The part in his hair he'd left at some bar on the way to the dance hall. He put out his cigarette at a table far from ours, and they ordered drinks. They were strawberry daiquiris, and they came in pint glasses with the sweat of the place beading up on them.

I took Katie's hand. "Look," I said, pointing them out to her. "Who's that with John Pereira?"

She hadn't seen the two of them come in, but she took it very well.

"I have no idea," she said. She picked at a scar in our table's finish. "She's rather nice looking, isn't she?"

"I wouldn't know," I said. "I'm married."

"Don't be a jerk," she said. "Go say hello to him."

"All right. Let's."

"No," she said. "You go. I'm not feeling very good."

"I'll bet you're not. It's an odd time for morning sickness."

"It's not morning sickness," she said. "Now get off my case and go say hello to him. He's a friend of yours." She turned around in the chair and started waving at one of the bar girls.

"Like hell," I said. "He's more your friend than mine." But all she had to say to me she said quite well with the back she kept turned to me. "All right," I said. "I'm going. Don't leave without me."

She turned back, all false smiles. "I'll be there in a minute," she promised.

Pereira's woman sat with her chair turned around, holding it tight between her knees and propping her elbow on its back. John had his chair tipped back and his feet up on her chair seat, between her thighs. He sat up when I came by.

"Johnny," I said, holding my hand out for him. "Long time no see. How the hell are you?"

He stood to shake my hand, and she followed him. We stood around the table for a long, awkward moment after the usual pleasantries, beaming at each other with nothing at all to say. Johnny saved us.

"Here, Celine," he said to the woman. "Sit a bit while I get this old bastard a drink."

We went up to the bar.

"So," I asked, "how are you, really?"

"Rested," he said, "after all these years. You?"

"The same, man. The same. The year's almost over. They took the new interns around on Wednesday."

"That's right. The new year starts this week. You know, you lose track fast once you're out of it. It's fucking wonderful, I can tell you."

"When are you coming back?"

That question touched him. I leaned against the bar and watched him deflate. He folded his hands and studied them. Then he turned to me, and his voice was cold sober.

"I'm not coming back."

"What do you mean? You've got to come back. You've got six months to make up."

"I know that," he said. "I've had some bad news, though. I broke it to the chairman just a few weeks ago."

"What news?"

"I'm a chronic carrier. I'm still contagious."

"No."

"Yeah. I look pretty good. I feel great—although, sure, maybe I get tired a little quicker than I used to. But I feel good. Still, in my veins, the virus flows. I'm an epidemic with legs."

"No. Johnny that's terrible "

"That's just what the chairman told me. 'John,' he said, 'that's terrible. We'd love to have you back. The profession needs men like you. But you can't operate if you're still infectious, and I can't take you back if you can't operate.'"

"Damn."

"Well, he's right, of course. Wouldn't want to make those fine women we care for sick, would I? A slip of the scalpel, a needle through a glove, and it'd be another life ruined."

"But that's so awful. What'll you do?"

"Do?" He laughed, gesturing all around the bar. "I'll do this. It's great fun here. Everybody in this place is so friendly. Celine, over there, is very friendly. We pass the time together."

"But what about a job?"

"Hell," he said, "I don't know. I'll find something. There's got to be a market someplace for used gynecologists. I think I'll recycle myself as a shrink, specializing in hysterical women. I could be a radiologist, too, and spend my life shooting X rays at people. Then, too, I always liked pathology, and I can't infect a corpse."

"Christ," I said. "I'm sorry."

"Don't be. Hell, I never liked what I was doing, anyway. I'll find something else. I've already sent out letters, you know. But nobody interviews until fall. Chairmen all over are waiting now to see how the new kids shake out, so there aren't any openings now, not that are worth a damn. By winter, though, I'll have a place. I'll be an intern again, somewhere."

He shrugged and smiled for me. He looked at Celine, and for a moment his smile was real. He lifted his glass to her.

"Cheers," he said. "Until then, I'll keep myself occupied."

I raised my glass to him. "Say, though," I said, "you shouldn't be drinking. What about your liver?"

"Have to keep occupied," he said, wiping the foam off his face.

"And what about Celine? Does she know you're infectious?"

"Have to keep occupied," he said again, winking this time. "Seriously, though, it's okay. She's got herpes. We're even."

He knocked down the last of his beer and ordered two more for us.

"Katie's here," I said.

He put down the cigarette he was lighting and looked over to our table. "Yes," he said after he'd lit the cigarette and taken the first long draw. "I saw her when we came in. Saw both of you. Excuse the smoke. Didn't want to come over, did she? Feeling shy?"

"She's pregnant. She's not feeling well."

Pereira turned and frowned at her. She raised my empty beer mug to him. He saluted her with three fingers, like a Boy Scout.

"Doesn't show," he said. "How far along?"

"Nine weeks."

"Congratulations. Who's her obstetrician?"

"Honniker."

Pereira choked on his beer. "No," he said. "That hack? How'd she end up with him?"

"I sent her. He's been very good to me this year."

"Oh, well, I'm sure she'll be fine. Sure she will. She's a tough woman."

"I hope so. This time."

"She'll be fine. She's a wonderful woman."

There was a long pause. We sat and played with our drinks.

"Listen," Pereira said softly, without meeting my glare, "I've wanted to tell you for a long time. There was nothing between us, except friendship." He smiled to himself. "Could have been," he said, then went on, wiping the smile away. "Wasn't, though. Wasn't ever. Nothing."

"That's what she told me."

His face brightened. "Did she? She's telling you the truth, you know."

"I think you're both lying."

"Do you? That's unfortunate."

"I really don't give a damn."

"That's probably even more unfortunate. For her. She's a wonderful woman."

"Yes, I know. You said that before."

"It's true," he said, then: "Here, let's go see Celine. I forgot all about her."

"He's going to be a daddy," Pereira said to Celine with his arm around my shoulders. She got up and threw her arms around me.

"That's great," she said. She had nice breasts, and she knew how to wear them. "When are you due?"

"Oh," I said, "next year."

She let go of me, dropped me just like that. She put her hands on her hips and glowered at Johnny. "He's an obstetrician," she said, "and all he knows is next year?"

"Celine's a pediatrician," Pereira explained to me. "She started residency the same year I did. She's in practice on the hill now, working at County Hospital."

"I used to have to take care of all this fool's mistakes," she said, "after they were born."

"She can tell some great dead baby jokes," Pereira told me.

"I can imagine," I said, and then, to her, trying to get sober fast: "Katie's due the first of February."

"That's nice," said Celine. "I'm happy for the both of you. Is she here with you tonight?"

"Yeah," I said, "she's here. She's not really feeling up to snuff, though."

Kate waved at us again. She was working on another beer. Pereira stood to give her a theatrical bow.

"She's fine," said Celine. "Ask her to come over. We'll make it a party."

"She's really not up for it," I said.

"Shit," she said. "Ask her. Or do you want me to?"

She walked over to our table and sat down. She and Kate started talking animatedly.

"Why didn't you tell me that she was a doc, for God's sake?" I asked John.

"Didn't seem important," he said.

"I'd have tried to act a little more professionally. Christ, I thought she was just a bimbo you'd found someplace. You made me look like a damn fool."

He smiled. "Man," he said, "you looked like that from the minute you dropped your eyeballs down the front of her dress, and knowing her business wouldn't have changed that a bit."

The girls came back together.

"You didn't tell me that she worked at the bakery," Celine said. "We've met there many times. I didn't recognize her in these clothes until I got to your table."

"But she doesn't work there now," I said.

"Yes. I know. She told me she's gone back to nursing."

"Really?" asked John.

"Better money," Kate said.

"Shitty job, though," said Celine.

"I know, but there's a kid coming now," Kate said. "And how are you, John?"

"Fantastic," he said.

"Liar," she said.

"Katie," he said, shaking his head, "you always see through me. I see you've gotten yourself knocked up again."

"The wages of sin," she said.

"I thought it was the wages of marriage," he said.

"Same difference," she said.

They stood about, staring at each other like a couple of teenagers. I sat down. Celine took my arm and pulled me back up.

"Here," she said, "let's dance."

So we went off to the dance floor. The band was licking along nicely, and the floor was crowded. Celine had some good moves. Katie and Pereira went by us, cheek to cheek. After a couple of tunes we swapped partners.

"I thought you weren't feeling well," I said to Kate.

"I can't hear you," she shouted.

"I said I thought you were ill."

She rolled her eyes. "I finished your beer," she said. "Then I finished one of my own. That helped. That helped a lot." She kissed me, grinning.

"You shouldn't do that," I said.

"What, kiss you?"

"No. You know."

"What?"

"You shouldn't be drinking. You're pregnant."

She turned around and danced with her back to me, rubbing her shoulders across my chest. She wasn't showing at all yet, and she still looked very good. Not like Celine, but very good.

When the music paused, we all sat down. We talked awhile about things of no importance. Then the music was too loud to do any talking. Kate got up again with Pereira, and I danced with Celine. She danced with her chest out, shivering with the music, her eyes half-lidded. The music slowed. The lights went lower.

"I have to pee," she said to me.

While he danced with my wife, I sat at Johnny's table and drank tequila, tasting the worm. Kate had her arms around his neck and her face turned up to his. Even in the bad light I could see that they were talking, but all that I could hear was the vocalist onstage whining about the death of love.

Celine came back. She smiled at me once, then concentrated all her attention on her drink until some friends of hers came up to chat. I sat apart, with my arms folded and my glass empty, until the set ended and Kate and Johnny got off the floor.

"We have to go now," I said to them. "I'm on call Monday. I've got to get some sleep."

"On call?" said John. "Jesus, I'm sorry. I wasn't thinking. And here it is, almost midnight."

"He can sleep in tomorrow," said Kate. "We can stay a little longer. We're having a good time."

"We are not," I said. "We're going home."

"Oh, for Christ's sake," said Kate.

I stood up. Everyone else followed.

"We'll have to get together again sometime," Celine said to Katie.

"We certainly will," I said, cutting off the conversation. Then there were handshakes and kisses all around.

"We'll be going soon, too," said Celine. "John gets tired early."

"That must be tough for you," I said.

They all let that slide. We went out. Kate got in the driver's seat. I leaned in the window.

"Here," I said, "you can't drive. If there was an accident, the steering wheel might hit you in the belly."

"But I'm not drunk, so if I drive, there won't be any accident."

"I'm not drunk," I said.

"Just shut up and get in the car."

"I'm driving. And I'm not drunk."

"Stop shouting, for God's sake. You certainly are."

"I certainly am not. And I'm not shouting. Now get out of the car."

"I won't. You're drunk. You've been a jerk all evening. You're thoroughly wasted. You've totally embarrassed me tonight, between your peevish, jealous moping and your leering at Celine."

"I've embarrassed you? You're one to talk, the way you've spent the whole night throwing yourself at that washed-up old lush."

The car door opened. It hit me in the groin hard, so that when she jumped out and slapped me, I went down on the gravel.

"Get in the car," she hissed. "Get in this car right now. And if you ever, ever say one more cross word against John Pereira, I will kill you on the spot. I swear to God I will."

I looked up and rubbed my stinging face. I thought that she was going to kick me, from the look of raw hatred on her face. Instead she just got back in the car. The engine started.

"Hurry up," she barked at me. "Get in the car, you goddamn little...little husband."

I got up. All around the parking lot people were staring at us. I staggered into the car, and we drove away.

All the way home we said nothing to each other. We undressed in silence and got in bed without a word. But in the morning, when I woke, she had my breakfast ready. She served it to me in bed, and I knew that she had been right, months ago. Nothing mattered, and everything was going to be just fine.

casualties

For us, in that year, leukemia was a sign of election: only the good died so young.

The dead had many faces, and as interns we knew them all. Most were the old faces of men and women grown weary of life's game. Under our care they died by degrees: hearts slowed, kidneys shriveled, bits of brain faded away like lost memories. Diabetes, arthritis, cancer, stroke: we saw death as it came, fought it as best we could, and then left to let the nurses pull a sheet over what remained.

Some of the dead wore other faces, though—young faces, faces not yet marked by the waste of years. Those were leukemics' faces. In that year of our internship, even when we had become intimate with death, when we knew the dead better than we knew parents, brothers, sisters, lovers—even then leukemia remained for us a world apart.

We watched our leukemics die, mocking them with futile ministrations. They awed us with the foolish nobility of each new breath, the wonderful tedium of eating and sleeping, brushing teeth, opening cards, bathing, combing hair. A precious, fragile finitude glowed though skin porcelain pale, shattering shields of cynicism we held before our eyes to hide our mortality from ourselves. The desperate hope, the hopeless courage—or perhaps only the ignorance of death—that we nourished in them humbled us: how might we answer, dying young? We begged the question, burying it with work. We blurred its sharpness behind microscope slides, concentrating our lives on a different focal plane. We trivialized the question with the minutiae of our days, the sediment of urine, the sound of a breath, the color of a stool. We sustained our leukemics with chemotherapy and antibiotics, with lies and other men's blood. We denied our own impotence until they died—of course, they all died—and we could forget them.

That year we came to know the dead too well, and yet there were good times, too. At night, off call, we'd put the textbooks and journals on the shelf. We'd go downtown with the nurses and drink and play loud music from old jukeboxes made of steel and glass and neon light. We'd dance fast in a close space, kicking up our heels to make room for ourselves in the hot, jumping crowd. We'd pile into a couple of cars, herding close to feel one another's warmth as we drove down to the river, where we'd sit by a bonfire, shoulders touching, on the cool grass. We'd build fires in rusted barbecues by the riverbank, watching waves lift and break and melt away among the pilings of the railway bridge. On weekends we'd lie in the park by the hospital with a couple of six-packs in the cooler and music on the radio, under verdigris Victorian statues and rustling trees and the false warm sun of autumn. One nurse, telling me the story of her workday, started to cry. Driving back to the hospital, I kissed the tears in her hair, on her red lips.

That year I lived alone. After a night on call, I'd go home and read about disease over ice cream and beer until I fell asleep in an unmade bed. I kept a journal. I browsed the used bookstores near the public library, reading lines no one remembers. I loved the smell of old paper and the perfume of the old woman whose rheumatic hands caressed my books while wrapping them, then made change from an empty box of Garcia y Vegas.

All of us were tired all the time that year. Internship was

combat, and we never came off the front line. Leon fell asleep
interviewing a patient. Janet passed out standing up against a
wall outside a patient's room while the chairman described the
detailed diagnostic tests for diseases we'd never seen. Chris slept
through all the operator's pages in the intensive care unit one
night until the nurses had the hospital police break into his call
room and shake him back to life. I never did that. But when I
walked up to the wards by the back stairs, nausea started with
the first flight. I walked into strangers in the hall, too slow to
move away. Food was tasteless, sleep black, flat, and shorn of
dreams.

"I understand," I told her. She was my patient, another
leukemic. We said that to all of them when they told us how
afraid they were of dying.

Like a cat, she narrowed her eyes and drew back her
shoulders. The movement pulled forward the heavy catheter
between her breasts. It hung there like a flaccid worm, like a
long white leech, feeding on her. It ran into her heart; we used it
to deliver chemotherapy too toxic for mere veins.

"Bullshit," she spat at me. "You don't understand. You
can't. You never will."

I stood by her bed, frozen by her fierceness.

"You can't understand," she said, leaning forward in fury.
"You never knew me outside this fucking hospital. Before I
came here, my sisters and I ran the only women's shelter in
Greene County. You didn't know that did you? You probably
don't even know where Greene County is. You can't understand what that meant to me. We loved each other, my sisters
and me. I had two daughters there, both just teenagers, both
just learning what it means to be women, and we loved each
other, too."

She stopped to scratch the dermatitis on her hands. Her
eyes dropped. Her voice fell.

"You can't understand what it's like to be here, to be
locked up to rot so far from the mountains. You can't understand what it's like to see the resentment in my friends' eyes

because they have to do my work for me now. You can't understand what it's like to know that to your own children you're some kind of monster, bald, sick, bleeding, dying. You can't understand what it's like to live in a place like this, too full of kindness and pity, but empty of love. All you care about are my numbers—my fever, my stools, my blood counts. You can't understand what it's like to sit here alone after the man tells you that your bones are full of cancer and the last, most experimental treatment has failed. You can't understand," she said, her voice decomposing into sobs. "Dear God, you can't."

She was crying. The blue bandanna she wore to cover her scalp sat askew. She had one hand over her face. It was an old woman's hand, spotted and ugly, though she was barely forty. I looked at her. She was ugly. She knew that I saw her that way, and she hated me for that.

I looked away, to the snapshots by the bed, to the child's woolen Eye of God hanging in the window, to the empty teacup, to the thread of smoke rising out of her full ashtray. The tears ran over her lips, dripped off her chin, onto her quilted robe. She wiped her nose with the back of her hand and looked up at me.

"We used to touch each other," she said. "No one touches me anymore. My children, my friends—they're afraid of me. In three months, no one's hugged me," she whispered to herself. "No one."

She sagged on the bed, crying again uncontrollably, inconsolably. The tears deflated her. She sat limp, racked, broken. The bandanna came away. The smooth, veined scalp showed the lines of her skull. I sat on the bed beside her and put a hand on her shoulder. She curled into my lap and I rocked her in my arms.

After a time she sat up. "I'm better now," she said. "I didn't mean to bitch at you like that."

I stood in the middle of her room, hugging my clipboard to assuage my own loneliness. I shrugged.

"It wasn't anything you did," she said.

"You were right," I said. "We don't have anything left to offer you."

She took my hand and squeezed it. "That's not entirely true," she said.

I stepped outside. The hard fluorescent light blinded me. The noise of telephones, overhead pages, and people shouting broke against my head.

"There you are," said Rosalie, the ward's head nurse. "I've been looking for you. There's somebody I want you to take a look at."

The woman in the room, the woman I'd held, was sent home in the morning. Some of the nurses went to her funeral, later that year. I was on call; I had no time to grieve.

We were dancing, my red-lipped nurse and I. The floor was empty, and the lights, red and purple and yellow and blue, spun around us. They glowed in her hair. We danced away our fatigue. We stomped out our memories of bleeding and pain under the electric rhythms of the music.

Later, on the street, the snow fell. It covered the dirt, the garbage in the gutters. It softened the shapes of buildings and of people walking away. It cast halos around streetlights. It fell on her hair, melting. I touched the drops. She took my hand and led me on and on.

Under the heel of my hand, her breastbone rose and fell. Up and down, I counted the cadence of chest massage. For half an hour we had pressed her resuscitation. Now all her ribs were broken. Her sternum floated free, grating on the ends of broken bones. We all studied her monitor and watched the fluttering of her heart. The electric wave spiked up, jagged, and we put the paddles to her. The current ripped through her body. She arched and lifted and flopped like a gaffed fish pitched across a pier. After a while her heart's fluttering stopped. We quit with the paddles and went back to our routines.

Every death diminishes me. Oh, God, how small I have become.

*   *   *

Over Christmas I went home for three days. My parents were full of questions. I gave them the answers that made them happy. I told them that I ate well, slept all the time, and went to church every Sunday. My father cooked steaks. My mother made ravioli. At midnight mass I put five dollars in the collection basket. My mother held my hand. I watched them try to hide the hurt in their faces as they came back from communion while I sat in the pew. I went out before the closing benediction to breathe in the clean frost and listen to the small-town traffic putter through the darkness.

At the train station it was like returning to the front, only no one cried. With my duffel over one shoulder, I held them, my mother first. We said the usual things, unable to say the things we meant to tell each other, feeling them too deeply for words.

I watched them through the window as the train pulled out. He kept one arm around her as they stood in the snow on the platform and waved.

The train pulled away, through a factory town the color of brick and rust and new snow. The square white Yankee houses wore Christmas lights and icicles. We moved into the woodlands along the river. I fell asleep counting telephone poles, the stolid crucifixes that marked off the miles back to the city. The dirty window glass cooled my hectic cheek.

At first the symptoms were easy to deny. We all were always exhausted. We came to work in the dark and left after dusk. We were all depressed. We were sick of the monotony of death. The flu went around; nobody had had the time to stand in line for shots. Janet called out sick, and there were only two of us to cover the wards that night. I couldn't focus. I dropped charts, tubes of blood, dirty needles. Between admissions, between calls about patients with fever, patients with dyspnea, with chest pain, nausea, and loneliness, I leaned against the walls, resting my head against the institutional paint and plaster, praying for death. My guts were clenched, and there was fire in my blood. The world whirled, as if to throw me off. I cursed God and went back to work.

Later, Rosalie woke me. I sat up, wiped the saliva from the corner of my mouth, and stared down at the illegible scribblings in the chart I'd fallen asleep on. The hall clock was closing on seven, and the new March sun played in the thawing air behind the window grime. I tried to stand, but my fatigue hit me in the chest, and I fell back. I reread the notes on the page before me, signed them, and racked the chart.

In the night, in the call room, the rigors had awoken me again. I had lain on the steel bed, shaking myself to sleep. Now the fever had broken. There was sweat in my armpits, over my chest, down my back, and all over my face. The new light made my eyes ache.

I pushed myself up, leaning hard on the desk. I turned to the door, and I took a couple of steps, aiming for the hall, but as I stepped through the doorway, it moved left. It hit my shoulder. The shock slammed into my brain. I reached for a chair, but it jumped on me. I wrestled with it as we clattered to the floor together. Nurses, clerks, and orderlies watched us tip and go over.

My hands slid out across the linoleum. I lay on my belly. Nobody moved. It felt good to be lying there, because I knew what was wrong with me. There was only the little matter of pinning a name on it. I knew that I was going to get a rest now. I was out of the battle. The dead would keep dying, and doctors were going to keep fighting to stop them, but I would not be with them anymore.

The room was suddenly cold again. The sweat chilled on me, and the shaking started again. By then people were all around me, shouting out my name. I lay on the floor, jerking around with my chills, scaring everyone and not caring at all.

Rosalie's hand was on my forehead, her fingers in my hair. She brushed the hair off my face.

"It's okay," she said softly. "It's okay."

She was lying, but that was all right, because we both knew it. And I was grateful for the lie, and for Rosalie, the woman

with the boxer's face and the shoulders that were broad enough
for the kid nurses to cry on when their patients died.

"It's okay," she lied. "It's going to be all right."

I tried to get up, but before I could get off my knees,
somebody turned off the sun, and I pitched over. The gritty
floor tiles were cool on my skin, soothing and welcome like the
feel of the canvas on your face as the referee finishes the count
and you know you don't have to get up and face the punches
anymore. I lay on my knees, curled around myself. Rosalie
cradled me, crying out for a doctor.

They put me on a gurney and drew a white sheet over me.
Rosalie tucked a blanket under my chin. I lay on my side and
watched the ceiling tiles go by.

"But who's going to round on his patients?" someone said
to no one in particular. We didn't wait for the answer. The
fluorescent lights glared down at me. We swerved into an open
elevator. The doors rattled shut, and the world dropped away.

A woman's hands were washing the vomit off my face, off
my lips. Her cloth was wet and rough and warm, her fingers
smooth and gentle. "Lift your head," she said, and the head
lifted. She changed the pillowcase, held a cup of water to my
mouth. Out of gratitude I fell asleep.

The intern came in.

"Hi there, kid," he said. "What the hell happened—you
been into some bad drugs, or what?"

"Go fuck yourself," I said.

"What'd I say?" he said, laughing at his own joke. "I'm just
trying to be humorous."

"Go fuck yourself."

"Okay, fine. You have a classic case of acute, severe humor
deficit. It's an occupational disease. But it doesn't get you into
the emergency room."

"No."

"So what the hell happened? I heard you fell."

He took the cap off his pen with his teeth and started
scrawling across his clipboard. I looked at him. He looked

pitiful, with the ink stains on his breast pocket, the wrinkles in his jacket, the wrinkles around his eyes. I turned onto my back and watched a bad light bulb flicker.

"I went to ground," I told him. "That's all. I went to ground, just like some piece of nursing home shit. And you know what?"

"What?"

I struggled up onto one elbow, grinning. "It felt good. It felt very, very good."

I fell back. He didn't say anything.

"Does that scare you?" I whispered.

"No," he said, but his eyes told the truth. "Let's just get the history, okay?"

We got the history. It didn't seem to make him any happier. He flashed a light into the darkness inside my head. He thumped my chest, listened to my heart and lungs, fingered my belly, hammered my knees. When he was done, I put my face in my pillow.

"You don't look so good," he said.

"Man," I said, "tell me something I don't know."

He took my blood and my sputum. A nurse gave me a plastic jug for urine. There was not much in it when she took it away, and what was there didn't smell very nice, but she seemed grateful for it. They put a catheter in my arm and poured sugar and salt water into me. They rolled me away and took mug shots of my chest, full face and profile.

I lay a long time in the soft light outside the radiology suite. My friend Sarah, a nurse, walking by, stopped and put a hand on my shoulder. The sheet was wet with sweat. She pulled it off my shoulder, to see the line running into my arm. There was horror in her voice when she mumbled my name.

"Hi," I said, trying to play cheerful. "How's things?"

"What happened to you?" she asked. Her eyes were wide, full of perplexity and pain.

"Well, you see, I just had some X rays taken. I think they've forgotten me here."

"But what's the matter with you?"

"I've been sweating," I said, holding up my arm, "and the adhesive tape here seems to be coming loose where this catheter's stuck into me. Do you have any tape on you?"

"But what's wrong with you?" Her voice was rising.

"Well," I ventured, frozen in my rambling, suddenly confused. "Well, I guess I really don't know."

I let the arm drop and stared at her. Then I looked away. I started puttering around with the little catheter dressing, trying to stick it to my skin again.

She pulled a roll of tape out of one pocket. "Here," she said, turning professional, "leave that alone."

Her wise fingers put the dressing together again. "Your IV bag's empty, too," she said. "Did you know that?"

"No," I admitted.

"How long have you been out here?"

"I don't know. I think I fell asleep. They were going to take me back to Emergency."

"Here," she commanded. "You just wait here."

"I'm not going anywhere," I said, but she was gone. She came back with other people.

"I don't know," one of them was saying querulously. "We called for a messenger to take him back almost an hour ago. Listen. No. Lady, just listen. We don't do transport."

She wasn't listening. She was cursing them all, telling them what she hoped would happen to their parents and children if they ever got sick. Other voices came. Sarah was slapping the wall with her hand and shouting. The others' voices turned soothing. The shouting quit. Overhead, the straight, square lines of the ceiling tiles went wavy. Then they began to flick past as we rolled down the hall. It was like going home again.

Janet's hand woke me. We were back in my room in Emergency. She was leaning over the bed rail with her hand on my shoulder. The strength in her fingers strengthening me, I uncurled. She was frowning, her chapped lips pursed.

"Hello," she said.

"Hi," I answered her. The silence was bad. "You don't look very glad to see me."

She smiled, or half her face did. One corner of her mouth curved up. The angle of one eye crinkled.

"I'm glad," she said. "What's up, doc?"

"You really want to know?"

"Yes. They called me down to admit you."

I let that sink in awhile. I had hoped they'd be sending me home.

"So," I said. "It's like that. All right. Help me."

My fingers stumbled over my shoelaces. Together we pulled off the shoes and peeled away the socks.

"Jesus," Janet said.

The feet were the color of drowned fish. Bits of cotton lint clung to the toes, to the cracked skin that wore the imprint of the fabric of the socks. A mild case of athlete's foot had blossomed, after too many nights on call and too many nights at home falling asleep too tired to unlace the shoes. The skin was pink and peeling. Crusted yellow ulcers trailed streaks of red over the macerated flesh. The feet were cold. I waved a broken toenail for Janet and hid them under the blanket.

"Why didn't you show that to anyone before?" she asked.

"I wanted to see if they were good enough to figure it out themselves," I said.

"You goddamn fool," she said.

Her face was full of anger, and her black hair fell over her hot cheeks. She turned away, looked around, took a long breath. Then she turned back to face me.

"Did you know you were coming in?" she asked.

"No, but I thought I might."

"I drew your admission."

"You said that. At least I'm a little lucky."

She didn't smile. "Don't ever try to hide anything like that from me," she said.

"No. You'd find out anyway."

There was another pause.

"I have to examine you," she said.

"Of course."

"Could you put a gown on?" She pulled one from a cabinet over the sink. "I'll be back in a minute," she said. She stopped at the door with one hand on the knob. After a long time she turned around. "Did anybody show you your counts?" she asked.

"No," I said, suddenly afraid.

She took the lab slip from her clipboard and handed it to me. All the parameters of the cellular fraction of my blood were there. The numbers, by themselves, looked quite innocuous. I looked at them stupidly, as though the printing might change if I looked long enough. There was a catch in my throat that tasted of panic. I listened to the adrenaline running around in my head.

"That's not very good," I said.

"No," she said. "I'm sorry. God, I'm so sorry."

I smiled for her. It was the hardest thing I'd ever done. "Don't be," I said. "Hell, it isn't your fault."

For the longest time after she had gone, I just lay on the gurney, listening to my heart beat on unperturbed, as though it might go on forever. There was nothing to say, and no one to say it to. My head wouldn't clear. The light in the room was too bright. All the objects around me stood out, unreal, too real, too permanent, when I was suddenly so transitory.

Panic—panic chased through my mind. To fight it down, I tried to sit up. It was a very simple procedure, and it took me a very long time. Then I undressed. It was easy, as long as I took my time. The tie was already off, the dress shirt put away. I pulled my undershirt over my head. It did not smell nice at all. I put on the gown, fastening all the snaps carefully. Then I took off the trousers, the white uniform of my internship. I smoothed away the creases, folding the clothes carefully. I lay with the trousers in my arms, like a widow with her wedding dress.

D'Andrea came in while Janet was doing her exams. He was the chief of hematology. He was stiff, very thorough, very good, very much of the old school. His veiled eyes were set in the kind of blond, aristocratic north Italian face my Sicilian grandfather used to warn me about. Still, I liked him, because he knew his job. Once, when we had spent weeks together in the fall beating his leukemics into remission, he had put his arm over my shoulder and told me that I showed promise. It was as close to a compliment as he ever came.

"How do you feel?" he asked. He came straight up to the bed. He held out his hand. I took it and shook it. He didn't let go.

"Me?" I said. "I'm great."

"You look great," he said.

"I guess I've fooled everybody, then."

I looked at Janet, but she was sitting by the door with her face in my papers, keeping out of it.

"How long have you been sick?" he asked.

"About twenty-six years," I said.

"Don't be a wiseass," he said.

"Six weeks," I said, "about. Maybe a little more."

"Why didn't you see a doctor?"

"I saw doctors every day. They were all busy. I was busy. Every time I thought about getting free and stepping out to sit two hours in some doc's waiting room, people I was caring for would try to die, and there was never anybody around to stop them but me."

He gave my hand a squeeze. "I guess you've got time now," he said.

"I guess."

He put down my hand and held the stretcher rail. He looked down a moment, as though he were praying. Then he looked at Janet.

"What will we do with him?" he asked her.

She shrugged. She was keeping well out of it.

"Look," said D'Andrea, "you don't have to act tough."

"I'm not acting." I said.

"Shit," he said.

Then he switched into the vernacular, and we talked for a time about symptoms. He listened to my chest with his stethoscope. He pushed on my liver and spleen, which hurt like hell. He looked at my feet. After that we talked about chemotherapy, about the choice of antibiotics, the placement of permanent intravenous catheters, about experimental drugs, vaccines, study protocols. He spoke enthusiastically about articles in arcane journals. Eventually I got so tired that I quit listening. When he was through, I agreed to everything.

"One thing, though," I said.

"What's that?" he asked. He stood there, loose and relaxed, enjoying the work he did so well. He stood with his hands deep in the pockets of his long coat, feet solidly planted and square in shiny black shoes.

"When I die," I said, "don't resuscitate me."

"Don't be morbid," he said after his surprise had passed.

"No," I said, "I'm not morbid. But I'm not stupid either. I'm no sucker. I'll sign on for the duration of your protocol. I know what that means. I've lived it every day with my patients: the hair falling out, the nausea, the oral sores, the diarrhea, the bleeding, the serial infections. Now I get to live it for myself, for six months maybe, maybe a year, maybe two. But when I'm dead, I'm dead. That's all."

He rubbed his forehead, thinking. I watched the well-washed fingers working against the lines cut into his skin by years of responsibility and fatigue. I saw the sculpted hand, with the cheap wedding band poor young doctors buy above the heavy gold watch. I didn't give a damn what he decided. I was just a piece of meat in the grinder now, and there was nothing I could do to change my future.

He put the hand down. "All right," he sighed.

We looked at each other for a long time. Then he shook my hand once more, said a few encouraging words, and turned away. He motioned to Janet. They went out together.

That evening, on the cancer ward, in a new bed, I watched the colors change on the old brick outside my window, the yellow changing to red to purple as the sun went down. Then there were only lights in the windows, shadows of movement passing before them, and the black blank spaces in between.

The room was private and peaceful. There were no ghosts. The dead had been washed away with hypochlorite and phenol. Still, I couldn't sleep. Instead I drifted off into hallucinations of normalcy.

The nurses woke me. Every four hours, on their rounds, they ran through their routine: temperature, pulse, blood pressure, respirations. In the time between, they woke me to change bags of antibiotics, bags of saline, bags of blood. They emptied the blue plastic urinal that hung from the bed rail by my face.

In the night, out of the darkness, my nurses spoke to me. Over the long weeks, the short months of my internship, we had cried, fought, bitched, struggled, laughed, suffered, and worked together. Now they all were hushed. "How are you?" they said, and I told them: "Linda"—or Meghan, Carol, Diane, Pamela, and all the rest of them—"I'm fine, really I am. And you? The kids? The old man?" "All well, all well," they said. Everyone was doing great, and the heart's thoughts went unspoken, save by their hands, by the cloth for my hot forehead, by the fingers left longer than necessary on my arm, and by the break in their voices that cried out the pain that they felt, feeling mine.

Not that it hurt, though. It was all like driving headlong into a wall: the first thing you notice is the sudden quiet and the change in speed. There is always time later for the pain. Sure, my muscles ached, my head throbbed, my back cramped. The intravenous tubing tangled in the sheets and pulled on the bandages. But there was no pain, really. Really. I kept telling myself that.

Above my head, the black blood dripped, a silent metronome. One by one the moments fell away. Before the bag was empty I was asleep again.

Very late that night, Janet came in. I woke with the turn of the doorknob.

"Are you awake?" she said.

"No," I lied.

"I'm sorry," she said. She backed up through the wedge of light that came in from the hall. "I'll come back tomorrow."

"No," I said, "I haven't slept this much in months. Besides, it must be tomorrow by now, anyway."

She came in, pulling the door shut silently.

"What is it?"

"Nothing serious. I just wanted to see how you are."

"Uh," I said, "I'm just ripping."

"I'm sorry," she said. She bit her lip and turned her face from me. "It's a stupid question."

"No. What do we tell our students? There are no stupid questions, only stupid answers. Fuck it. I'm all right. Don't worry about me. How are you?"

"Me? I'm great. Don't I look great?"

"Sure you do. All interns look great. What time is it?"

"It's quarter past one."

"And you're not in the rack yet?"

"No. I've got a few midnight labs to check."

"Well, then: the hell with me. Beat it."

"There's nothing I can do for you?"

"You've done it. All the times this year when you've covered for me, when you listened to me curse and complain, you were there. Now you've written all the right orders. You and D'Andrea have put a good plan into motion. You know there's nothing else you can do."

She stood up. She stood with her feet together, holding herself tight in her arms. I saw that she was crying.

I held one hand out to her. The cath tubing lifted with it, tenting the sheets. She spun toward me and took my hand in both of hers. We watched each other without speaking. The streetlight, pale and soft, lit half her face, a single tear's track, half her wan smile, leaving the rest of her in darkness.

"Dry up," I said. "You'll trash your makeup."

She sniffled and laughed. She sighed. She threw back her head and shook the hair off her face. "Damn you," she said, smiling.

"That's the attitude," I told her. "Don't get emotional over your patients. We've been over that before. The hell with patients, I say; they're not worth your tears. They burn you out and don't even say good-bye."

She stared at me a little too fondly. She was sniffling.

"Blow your nose," I said. "You're being gross."

She laughed again and wiped her nose on the sleeve of her

white jacket, trying to be unobtrusive. I had to smile, in spite of myself.

"All right," I said. "By the way, how's Nick?"

"He's doing fine. He's busy with the restaurant and the kid."

"Say hello for me."

"I will. Next time I see them. Maybe next week."

"The joys of married life."

"Gotta love it."

She opened the door.

"Do me a favor?" I said.

"Sure," she said.

"Leave the nightlight on."

She nodded. She left it on and closed the door.

In the darkness I floated, limp as seaweed. I rose and fell on waves of fever and fatigue. I listened to the night lapping at the edges of consciousness and ebbed away into endless eddies of sleep.

Before dawn the phlebotomist came. She was very good: a tight tourniquet, a quick lance, and all the glass tubes with their rubber stoppers in pretty colors filled. It almost didn't hurt at all.

Breakfast came. I pushed it around the plate. Then, for fun, I watched the frost melt off the windowpane.

Janet, on rounds, stepped into the room. Her clothes were rumpled; her makeup was shot.

"Bad night?" I asked.

"Same old stuff," she said. "There was an arrest in the intensive care unit. I drew three admissions. McChesney down the hall has pneumonia."

"You had three admissions, plus me?"

She hesitated. "Yeah," she said, "plus you."

"I'm sorry," I said.

"Don't be," she said.

"I'm better," I told her to answer the question in her eyes. "I still feel like somebody tried to kick my balls out my ears, but the rigors are gone, and I feel a little stronger."

"That's good," she said.

Hastings, the senior resident, came in. "Physician," he said, "heal thyself."

"Fuck you," I told him.

"That's the spirit," he said. "You're looking better."

"Thanks."

"You looked pretty damn bad yesterday."

I sat up for them. They asked the appropriate questions. They percussed, auscultated, palpated. The feet looked better.

"We'll check your cultures today," Hastings said. They started out.

"Wait a minute," I said.

"Yes?" said Hastings.

"Where's my medical student?"

"You're not serious," he said.

"Sure I am. I'm a very serious patient."

"We'll put you on the serious list," he said. "You want a medical student? For everything?"

"Sure," I said, "inside the rules: lines, bloods, the usual taps."

"Marrow taps?"

I thought about that for awhile.

"What the hell," I said. "Marrows, chest taps, cisternal punctures—the works."

"All right," Hastings said. "You're crazy."

Then he went out. Janet just stood there, shaking her head.

"So," I said, "I'm sick in more ways than you'll ever know.

"Some of us know," she said sadly, and then she went out, too.

My mother was at home. Though I wasn't there, I could see her. She was sitting in the kitchen alone, now that my old man had been packed off for the day. She sat watching the chickadees at the feeder outside the window and drinking instant coffee. She was wearing the quilted robe that I had bought for her when I was waiting tables in college. She turned off the talk show when she heard my voice on the telephone.

"Hi, Ma," I said.

"Hey," she said, "it's you." Her voice was full of glad consternation. "How are you?"

"I'm in the hospital."

"Oh, that's good. How's work?"

"I'm not working. I'm in the hospital, in bed. I got sick yesterday."

"No. Baby. Oh, my God. Sick? You got sick? Sick with what?"

"They think I have leukemia, Ma."

There it was, straight out front. It was easy to say. I'm fine; it's just a touch of leukemia, thanks.

"Leukemia? Oh, my God, my God. Leukemia." And then the question: "Isn't that cancer?"

"Yeah, Ma, it is. They're not sure yet. They still have some tests to run."

"No. Baby. Baby. Cancer. No."

"Yeah, Ma. They think they can treat it, though."

"They can? They can treat it?"

"Maybe. Sometimes."

"Maybe sometimes? Baby, is that all you can tell your mother? Maybe sometimes? That doesn't sound too good. Only sometimes?"

"Most times," I said, and the lie came easily.

"Thank God. But cancer? That's so bad. I don't know what to say. I mean, when you were home, you looked so thin. I knew you weren't taking care of yourself. But you said it was just work, being tired. I told you, you should eat, you should rest, and you didn't listen. And now this."

"Yeah, Ma, I guess that's how it is. Now I get to rest."

"Don't make fun of your mother. Don't make jokes. This is serious. How can I tell your father?"

"I'll tell him, Ma."

"He's at work, you know."

"Yeah, Ma, I know. Bring him out here. I'll tell him."

"I'll bring him out. He was going down to the Legion post

tonight to meet some of the guys for bowling, but I'll bring him out."

"Ma. Christ, let the guy go bowling. I'll keep."

"Baby. Don't say that. Don't even joke about that. Go bowling, my God. I'll bring him out. Don't worry. And Vic, too. And Lisa, I'll call her. And Theresa, and Domenic. I'll bring them all out."

"No, Ma. Jesus. Don't bring all them. Lisa's way the hell up at St. Lawrence. She's got classes. Terry and Dom's got families. Just you and the old man—and Vic, too, if he wants to come."

"No, baby. We're your family. I'll bring everybody out. They'll be glad to come."

"Forget it. Tell them I'm too tired, if you got to call them all. I mean, I really ain't going anywhere. Tell them I'm beat, and I know they're all thinking of me. Tonight, just make it you and the old man and Vittorio."

"You sure? You really tired?"

"Yeah, some. But I'm doing better."

"I don't know about Vic. He don't do nothing I tell him anymore."

"Yeah? And I'll bet he's still running with that Filipina girl, too."

"Oh, my God, don't even talk to me about her. Why can't he find some nice Italian girl?"

"There hasn't been one of those available since you got married, Ma. You never did like those colored folks much, did you?"

"It's not that. Just let them keep to their own kind, that's all."

"She's really all right, Ma. She'll give you a fine Italian grandson one day."

"Stop. My God, stop. No more joking."

"All right. No more joking. I'll try to forget I'm sick some other way."

We listened to each other trying to think of something to say.

"I got to go, Ma," I said. "Somebody just came in."

"Okay, then. I won't keep you. You be good."

"I will. I can't be much else, stuck here in bed."

"It must be so hard on you. You always was my good boy."

"Sure I was, Ma."

"I'll see you tonight. We'll leave right after dinner."

"Okay."

"You getting enough to eat? I'll bring you something."

"No, Ma. I get plenty."

"But it's that hospital food. That's not fit for an animal. I'll bring something you like. I'll start it right away."

"You don't have to, Ma."

"Sure I do. I'm your mother."

We left it at that and said good-bye. She went back to the television and the chickadees. I wondered what she was thinking. There was no payoff in my doing that, so I quit. Instead I watched the bedsheets gather dust. Thinking of home, of snow on the lawn and the garden, of the smell of sugar cookies baking and the smell of the garlic sausage in the red sauce on the back of the stove, thinking of the sound of my mother's voice amid all that, at home, I fell asleep.

"Hi," he said.

I was awake, sitting with the head of the bed cranked up, watching rock music videos with the sound off. Timid as it was, his voice broke starkly against the sickroom silence. He stood with his face just inside the half-open door. On his face he wore a hopeful, doubtful look, like a kicked puppy.

"Come in," I said, and he did, hands in pockets.

"I'm Jason," he said. "Levin," he added. "I'm your medical student."

"I'd never have guessed," I said, holding out my hand to him.

He wore a short white jacket with the sizing still stiff in it, with his tie too neat, a waif with a cowlick and scratched glasses. We shook hands.

"How are you?" I asked.

"Oh," he said, ambushed by the question. "I'm okay, I guess. How are you?"

He had read my chart already, so he knew the answer to his question before the words were out. He bit his words off short and looked down at his shoes.

"I'm fine," I said. "How the hell else would I be?"

"That's nice," he said.

"Yeah," I said, "isn't it. Here: sit down."

He sat. I led him through the formalities. He was from down on the Island. His father was an orthodontist. He loved our city; it was so unaffected, after New York.

"You need to take my history and do my exam, right?" I asked him.

"I guess," he said.

"You know," I told him.

"Yeah."

"Then let's go."

He pushed his glasses up to the bridge of his nose. He was so earnest, so careful, so awkward. I remembered.

He went through all the questions. I helped out a little when he forgot the sequence of the litany. I pulled up my gown for the exam.

"Can you feel the spleen?" I quizzed.

"I think so," he answered.

"That means no, doesn't it?"

He did a little bobbing and weaving, then said: "Well, yeah."

"I know the code. It's all right to tell me you don't know. I don't grade you."

I took his hand, held the fingers under my ribs. Two weeks before, I'd first felt it there, growing.

"Here," I told him. I took a deep breath, and we felt the soft organ bump his fingers. His eyes got suddenly bright. It didn't hurt much.

"Yes," he said. "Right there. I feel it. Neat."

I put his hand away, sick with pain. "Sure," I said. "Neat. Christ."

The deflation was instant.

"I'm sorry," he said.

"Don't be an idiot," I told him. "You're going to be a doctor soon. It'll be your job to hurt people."

He thought about that a moment. Then we finished the exam. He ran his hands over my skin, touching, tapping, pressing. The flesh shivered under his fingers, tense and pale in the cold room. It rolled and rose and lay flaccid. I closed my eyes to the violation of it all.

"Thanks," he said after.

I turned on the television again, with the sound up this time.

"You did fine," I said. "Now get lost."

He left grinning, very proud of himself. He would never forget. None of the good ones ever could.

I sat up quickly with the rap at the door, rubbing my eyes. Oh no, I said, no, I wasn't sleeping. Just taking it easy. Sure, they said, we understand. We just wanted to stop by, to say hello, to wish you luck, to see how you are. Oh, I told them, I'm fine, fine, only tired.

All afternoon people in white coats filed through. For them there were no visiting hours. They had only to knock and enter—or else they just walked in. I was not very good theater, but I seemed to hold them fascinated. There was no drama for any of us, no suspense, only a minor question of the timing of the ending. It was like watching a character out of Poe, only I was no fiction; I was too real.

We just wanted to bring you these cards, these flowers, they'd say. Oh, I'd answer, they're lovely, thanks—sure, put them there by the cabinet, on the windowsill, with the others. You shouldn't have, though. Ah, but it's the least we can do for a colleague, a friend, a classmate, you.

Thanks so much for coming, I'd say when the crippled conversation died. Give my best to all the nurses we used to know on the rotation we shared, to all the patients we shared still undischarged after all these weeks, to the ward clerks, to the orderlies. Do you ever see So-and-so? Neither do I. Come again sometime, anytime. It was so nice of all of you to stop by, so nice, so nice.

And then again, sleep. Then the knock, the door unlatched. I'd sit up quickly, reaching behind myself for the smile that had somehow fallen away.

In the afternoon they came for the marrow biopsy, to confirm the diagnosis we all knew. We filled out the papers, the consent, the lab forms. After that came the needles. I turned onto my belly and put my face in my arms. I held myself very still, hiding my fear far from my face. The anesthetic burned. There was heavy pressure at the hip, and Janet was saying with Jason the reassuring things doctors say to calm themselves, hoping the patients think the words are for them.

The biopsy needle bit bone.

The pain was a point, and the point was far away. I soared high above it, swirling and spinning. The pain lifted and licked at me as the needle twisted into the marrow, and I rode it, galloping. I embraced it, and we dove together into the abyss. Then there was only nausea and a taste of acid and all the old fatigue.

"There," Jason said. "Finished."

There was a moment's pause, and D'Andrea spoke.

"He's got a good core," he said.

I turned over and rested on the leaking hole in my bone. I looked at Jason, at the apology in his eyes and the proud smile on his lips. I had to smile back at him.

"You did great," I said. "I barely felt it."

We laughed together, and our lie was whole again.

Mama brought macaroons. She brought butter cookies dusted with nutmeat and powdered sugar. She brought little sugared wafers laced with anise and dotted in the center with jam. Like everyone else, she hung in the doorway at first, unsure of the etiquette.

"Come on in, Ma," I said. "Don't you know it's rude to stand in the hall like that?"

"Oh, baby," she said, and she came up to the bed in a rush. She put the tin with the cookies on the bedside table. She threw her arms around me, and I embraced the smell of bath powder and laundry soap. She was crying.

There was Vic, in the doorway, and the old man behind him. Father and son, they stood: Vic with his hair slicked down and brushed back, his hands in the pockets of his old army coat, leaning against the lintel; and in the hall, the old man, his hair shorter but slicked back, too, gone gray, gone altogether at the temples. The old man stood awkwardly beside his big son.

I rocked my mother's head on my shoulder and stroked her old woman's hair. "Shit, Ma," I said, "he skipped bowling. You must have told him I was sick or something."

"Shut up, you," she whispered. "No jokes. This time is serious."

"I guess so," I said. "I haven't seen you look this way since the night Terry told you she was pregnant."

Vic snorted. I winked at him, trying to keep a little humor alive in the room; it was a tough resuscitation.

They all settled into the tiny room, Ma sitting on the edge of the bed and holding my hands, Papa in the only chair, Vittorio propped against the dressing table.

"So," I said to them, "how is everybody? I haven't seen anybody since Christmas."

"Good," said Mama. "We're all good. How are you?"

"I'm better, Ma, much better. I had a bad fever when I first came in, but that's gone now."

They all nodded. We all sat and tried not to look uncomfortable. The pain in their faces made me want to cry. Then Ma opened her box.

"Here," she said to me, "I brought these for you. Your favorites."

I took the box. While I was opening it, she started bawling. It was better that way than having to wait. We watched her cry. After a while she quit.

"I was just thinking," she said, "about when you were little. You ate a whole box of these, not even a crumb left. I had to spank you. You looked so sorry, then."

"I wasn't sorry, Ma," I told her. "I was sick."

She had to laugh at that. We passed the cookies around. We said the correct things, but none of them were right. We talked about the weather, of course. It seemed the spring would never come. We talked about the relatives, about the old man's job, Vic's job, the latest news in the little town we came from. At eight Vanessa came in with a thermometer.

"Have a cookie," I said.

"On my diet? Be real."

She didn't need any diet, and Vic's eyes were all over her uniform.

"Sure," I told her. "Take one."

She looked at me archly. "All right," she said. "You forced me. But if I die of a heart attack, it'll be on your conscience."

"So kill me," I said.

It was the wrong thing to say. Everybody fidgeted. Then I did the introductions, to change the subject again.

Vanessa said hello to the folks. She said hello to Vic. She liked what she saw, and their staring lightened the mood in the room awhile. She said nice things, and we were happy again. Then she went out.

Papa stood up. "We got to go soon," he said.

"Joseph," Mama objected.

"No," I told her, "he's right. Visiting hours are almost over. Nobody will say anything if you stay, because of me, but we shouldn't bend the rules until we have to."

"You're right," Mama sighed. "I don't want to be no trouble. I'm just being your mama. You know?"

"Yeah, Ma, I know. Papa?"

"Yeah?"

"I need a favor."

"Sure. What kind of favor?"

"I need a place to go when I get out of here. I'll get out.

Almost everybody does. It'll take time, though, and I won't be in very good shape then."

"You'll come home," said Mama. "Don't even think like you have to ask."

"That's right," Papa said. "Listen to your mother. That's no favor. That's what the family's for."

"I need somebody to close the apartment," I went on, "to bring all the stuff home, to call the landlord and close out the lease."

Papa looked at Vic.

"Sure, kid." Vic shrugged.

"We'll take care of it," Papa said. "Don't even think about it. You just get well."

"Thanks, Papa," I said.

He came over to the bed. Mama put an arm around his waist. He put his hand on my shoulder.

"You just get well," he went on. "Anything you need, all you got to do is ask us. You just work on getting out of here."

"I'll try, Papa," I promised.

"Good," he said.

They put their coats on.

"Vic?" I said.

"Yeah?"

I started rummaging around in the drawer of the bedside table for my key ring.

"Listen," I said, "my car's in the garage. It ain't doing anybody any good there. While I'm here, the oil's going to sludge and the battery'll run down. I want you to take it. Connie can drive it. I'll give Ma the name of the guy who holds the insurance on it. We'll work it out."

Connie was the Filipina, Vic's woman. Ma's face pursed up when I said her name, but she kept her peace. Vic smiled.

"We'll work it out," he said.

I gave him the directions and the keys. We shook hands. Ma kissed me again as the others went out, on the forehead.

"Have you talked to the chaplain?" she asked me.

"Ma," I said, "I got nothing to say to him." Her face

clouded over. "All right," I said then, "I'll talk to him. For your sake."

She smiled. Papa stood in the doorway, impatient, shaking his head.

"I'll talk to Father Antonelli," she said. "He'll get in touch with your chaplain."

"That'll be great, Ma," I told her.

Then more handshakes, more kisses, more promises, more lies. Then they were gone.

I lay a long time on the bed, thinking about them, about being a kid, about where we'd traveled together, about things we'd said to each other or never said. The thoughts went faster and faster.

I pushed a button by the bed rail. A light went on.

"Yes?" said the light.

"Ramona," I said, "I think I'm going to need something to help me sleep tonight."

"Sure, honey," the light said. "I'll tell your nurse."

"You want a cookie, Ramona?" I asked, but the light had gone out.

That weekend was quiet. The rush and hustle slowed. The halls grew still. Nurses stopped to chat, but the one I was looking for all through those days, the woman with the sad eyes and the red lips, my friend, never came. I never knew if that was because she cared too much or not at all.

Vic came, and Connie, too. He wheeled me down to the lobby. They talked about their plans to move: maybe to Atlanta, maybe to the coast, where her people were. It was tough staying around, with all the good jobs taken or just gone. When they had money they'd go—in six months, a year, eighteen months at the outside. They were certain of it.

I wished them luck. It was a dead town. The mills had all moved to Taiwan. The only people still living in it were either too old or too broke to leave. I'd left. A lot of good leaving had done for me.

We three sat by the big glass lobby doors and watched people come in for the afternoon shift change: nurses in bright quilted coats and knitted scarves over white uniforms, hospital cops in blue and black, tired young mop jockeys in brown uniforms and long hair. We sat by a radiator, near a window, and talked while the night snuggled up to us.

They went back to their little town, and I went upstairs. In the dark, alone, the quiet pressed upon me. Through the open door I listened for sounds: hoarse whispers in the hall; a radio in the room next door; instrument carts rattling by; and the tired, bored, ceaseless cough of a bronchial cancer patient. I fell asleep listening to him hacking, hacking, hopelessly hacking.

The morning sun burned bright yellow on the snowy windowsill. Through the glass the hard blue sky hung empty and dull behind the warm red bricks of the hospital. I sat in bed and listened to the winter wind whistling in the casements.

The chaplain was a young man. He wore black, save for his collar. He had the dark face of the paisano, with black hair and thick black sideburns. He sat at my bedside, very straight in the single chair. In his hands he held the communion box, and his fingers wandered over the black velvet as we talked.

"Father Antonelli asked me to visit you," he said after the usual pleasantries.

"Yes," I said. "My mother called him."

"That was thoughtful of her."

"She's good that way."

"Would you like to take communion today?" he asked, opening his sacramental box.

"No," I said.

"Oh," he said. "I thought—"

"My mother called, Father. I didn't. I don't take communion anymore, but I'm afraid my mother doesn't acknowledge that. I haven't taken communion for years."

He put the box on the bedside stand. "Why not? If you don't mind telling me."

"I've broken too many of your rules, Father. I'm out of your club."

"I see. Then would you like to make confession?"

"I can't."

"Sure you can."

"No," I said. "I'm not sorry. I'm no theologian—the only reason I used to go for religious education was because that was where the girls were—but as I remember, you have to be sorry for your sins before you can confess them. Isn't that so?"

He nodded glumly. The conversation stalled. It nosed over into a steep dive. We sat and waited for the crash.

The hell with it, I thought. Still, I'd promised Mama. And it wasn't the poor guy's fault. It was his church that made the rules. He just worked there.

"It's not that they aren't good rules," I told him. "And I'm sure I'd be a much happier person if I'd kept them. But I didn't. And I'm not sorry. So you see, I can't confess."

"Would you like to talk about it?" he asked me.

I shrugged and stared over his head to where all my cards were hung. A little lie had made him feel better. I got him back into his role as counselor. It was like listening to the detached professional questioning on a psychiatry teaching tape in medical school. But I had nothing better to do, and there was nowhere to go, so I told him a story.

"It was ages ago, Father, two or three years back. We were in love, and full of dreams. We dreamed about places we could go, things we could change." I smiled to myself, remembering. "We broke all your rules."

"I see," said the priest, and the memory was broken.

"No, Father," I said. "You can't. Or maybe you can. I don't know. We were both in medical school. We spent our free evenings at a volunteer clinic downtown. We worked with the garbage of the streets—drunks and bag ladies, pushers and shooters and whores, kids swollen up by pregnancy and similar venereal diseases, women cut up by their men, old diabetics with their legs cut off, hypertensives out of control. We worked without enough drugs, without enough suture, without enough heat, without enough gowns. We worked with no quiet, no privacy. And we loved it."

"I'm sure," he said, and I wished he hadn't.

"Anyway," I said, "I'm sorry, but I'm not sorry."

"And what happened?"

"She had to move. She was that kind. I had to stay. I don't know where she went. Nicaragua, maybe, or Ethiopia, or Thailand. Or maybe she just moved across the river. I don't know."

"She must have hurt you," he said.

"We hurt each other. That's what love is all about, Father."

We sat in the harsh sunshine, feeling the room grow warmer. He was out of questions, and I was out of story, so I played it just like in the textbooks.

"Where are you from, Father?" I asked him.

"From Amsterdam," he said. He smiled, picking up on the role change and going along.

"How'd you end up here?"

"The year I finished at the seminary, the bishop came to speak. I listened to him talk about parishes in the inner city. He made the work sound like what I went into the church to do. When I was ordained, that was where I went; it's easy to get a place where only fools rush in. I worked with the same people you did, trying to soften the harshness in their lives."

"You can get old fast that way," I said.

"They do take a lot from you," he admitted.

"And they give back damn little." He frowned at that. "Don't get pious on me, Father: they don't."

"They help you to learn about yourself."

"And are you pleased with what you've learned?"

"Are you?"

"Christ, Father. You should try out for the Jesuits. I'm only trying to make conversation."

"I'm sorry. I don't know the answer."

"I don't believe that, either, but we'll let it go. Why did you leave, if it was so educational?"

"The old bishop died. The new one closed the parish. The church was always empty, except for the old people, and they all passed away. There was no one to pay the bills."

"Holy Mother Church," I said. "Nice."

"No," he said, "but it was necessary."

"You don't believe that."

He thought about that awhile, then stood up in answer. "You're sure you don't want to make confession?" he asked.

"Maybe some other time," I said.

We left it at that. He went off to minister to the faithful.

Before noon the sun shifted. The room cooled quickly. I wrapped myself in cotton blankets and watched television doctors save their patients from inevitable death until they put me to sleep.

Then it was Sunday evening.

"Ma," I said, "if I ate all this, I'd die for sure. I can't eat all this."

She sat beside me in her best brown wool suit. When I said that, her lower lip started to curl out, like a hurt little girl's. I took her hand.

"Shit, Ma," I told her. "I don't mean that I don't like it. I just haven't got much appetite."

"But you're so thin. You got to eat."

I chewed up another cookie. It was the least I could do for her. But the lasagna I couldn't touch.

"I cry for you," she said.

"Ma," I said.

"You got to try."

"I'll try, Ma. Papa, did you bring the stuff?"

"Yeah, we got it. Me and Vic hauled all your junk out of that dump." He made a face. "Jesus, it was filthy. Didn't you ever clean it?"

"Sure. Every couple of months."

"Christ," he said. "Your mother spent all day yesterday cleaning it."

"The dishes," she said. "My God."

"I did those every couple of months, too," I said. "I was working all the time. It was just a bachelor flop."

"A bachelor flop," said Mama. "I guess so. A nice girl would never go there."

"Mama," I said, "you know I never associate with nice girls."

I looked at Vic. He was keeping quiet, enjoying the whole thing. It took the heat off him for a while.

"Anyway," the old man said, "here's those notebooks you wanted."

He reached into the grocery bag that the food had come from. Off the bottom he handed me the copybooks. There were five of them: two of journals, two of stories, one blank.

"What the hell do you write in those things, anyway?" Papa asked.

"Not much," I said. "Stories I've heard. Things I've seen here and there. Places I've been."

"You still doing that?" Mama asked. "I thought you quit after high school."

"I did. When I became a doctor, I started again. I've heard so many stories I couldn't bear to lose."

The books were dog-eared, smudged with graphite, coffee-stained. I leafed through the pages.

"What kind of stories do you write?" Mama wanted to know.

"Crazy ones," I said. I sat up and leaned toward her. "Romantic ones." I grinned at her. "I write them to seduce women with."

"No," she said.

"Yeah," I told her, deadpan. "I turn down the lights. The room gets quiet and dark. I read her a story. Then I hop her."

"No," said Mama. "My God. Did I raise you like that?"

"Ma," I said, "I guess you must have."

When they had gone I took out the copybooks. I opened one, read a few pages, skipped around. They still brought out the same memories, the same feelings, still recalled the smell of the same places, the color of leaves, the color of voices. There was so much unwritten.

On the next afternoon the pathology report on the marrow biopsy came down. D'Andrea strolled by to talk about it. There were no surprises.

"Do you want to see the slides?" he asked.

"I'll pass," I told him.

"They're classic."

"Thanks," I said. "Save them for the residents still in the business. I pass."

We talked about my case. The sepsis had resolved. The fever was gone. All the numbers looked promising. Clearly it was time to initiate chemotherapy. Of course, it would be difficult. The antibiotics would continue for two weeks, and that would complicate matters. Certainly I knew what to anticipate. But we all had the highest expectations. In the end things would turn out well. My skepticism was known, but results were improving constantly. We all had the highest hopes.

A nurse came by with the papers. I had already been randomized on the chemotherapy protocol. The therapy would be quite aggressive. She was quite enthusiastic about it all.

Jason came in to start a fresh intravenous catheter.

"How are you at this?" I asked him.

His eager smile faded. "I'm okay," he said.

"Have you ever done one?"

"Yes."

"How many?"

He looked at his feet. "One," he said.

"Jesus," I said.

He stood there, trying to think of an answer to that.

"Well," I said, "I guess it's time to learn."

I took off my robe. He put on the tourniquet. The veins corded up, soft, curving, warm.

"Put the needle in here," I said.

"Here?"

"Yeah. No. Christ, don't hold it like that. Here, no: put your fingers like this. Yeah. That's better."

"All right," he said. "You'll feel the needle next."

"Yes," I said. He was certainly right about that. I watched him sweat. "Look," I said, "you've got to push it in. I'm not geriatric yet, and neither are you. Push it through the skin. . . . That's it. Deeper. . . . There you go. Feel it give? See the blood come back? Now: thread the catheter in. Quick, quick. . . . No.

Now plug in your line. Quick, before you get blood all over the floor. . . . Christ, man, the nurses are going to kill you."

He taped the cath in place nicely; somebody had taught him to do that much quite well. But there was blood all over his fingers and all over the bedsheets and the floor. Still, it was in.

"Now do you see how it's done?" I asked him.

He nodded, grinning like a medical student again.

In the morning, ages before dawn, a woman in a blue scrub suit woke me. She shaved my chest and left me alone with my skin on fire. I sat in the dark, sinking in and out of the shallows of sleep. I rode to the operating room through the hospital's waking hustle.

Good-bye, everyone said. Good-bye. Good-bye.

In the operating room a very nice anesthesiology resident pumped me full of Valium and narcs. I watched the surgeons burrow the big-bore catheter under my skin and into my veins. It was a very dull show. I took a nap.

When I woke the catheter was dangling from a nest of gauze. My shoulder was throbbing and my throat was dry. The world wore the elegant colors of morphine. I understood very clearly that this was all happening to someone else.

"How are you?" the recovery room asked.

It was a marvelously considerate thing for a woman to ask. And she was so beautiful. Oh, she was gorgeous. I watched her play with my dressings, leaning over my bed.

"Oh," I said, "I'm fine."

When she smiled I was happy again. Then she turned away, and the pretty colors ebbed away. The pain began to rise. It rose higher and higher. I lifted a hand.

"Excuse me," I said, but no one came. "Excuse me. Excuse me."

I tried to sit up. Then the nurse came back. She touched my shoulder.

"What is it?" she said. "You know you can't get up."

"It hurts a little," I told her.

She hit me with more morphine. After a while my world was beautiful again.

Janet came after the surgeons had peeled off the dressing in the morning, after my blood had been drawn for the day, after the team had rounded and D'Andrea had dropped by, after the breakfast tray was gone and I'd had a chance to wash my face and read and even write a little. She came in with gloves and three syringes. All the syringes were full. They came in a plastic bag with bright orange warning labels.

"Ready?" she asked.

"Are you serious?" I said. "Nobody's ever ready for this shit."

She cleaned my new catheter. She slipped a new steel needle into the plastic cap. She hung a bag of saline from a pole and the headboard. Into the tubing she pushed the chemotherapy.

We called it the Red Death, for its color—like cherry cola—and for what it did to people. It trickled into the intravenous tubing, swirling out of a tiny needle and turning the saline in the plastic line hot pink. It swirled into my chest, feeling like an almost forgotten heartache.

Janet watched my face. I kept it flat, so she wouldn't see, and after a moment the pain eased.

"Don't bite off your tongue," I warned her.

She looked up from the syringe she was fixed on, startled out of her concentration. When she worked, the tip of her tongue came out over her lower lip. She pulled it back into her smile. We laughed.

"Does it hurt much?" she asked.

"A little," I said.

I faked a smile. She faked believing it.

"I don't like to hurt you," she said.

"Like hell," I said. "You're a doctor. You live to hurt people. I know your type."

"You should."

"Oh," I said, "I'm a real bastard."

"You like to think that, don't you?"

"Yes."

"You shouldn't."

"No?"

"No. You're really just an asshole."

"Yeah? And you . . ."

We traded insults for a while. She was pretty good at it.

"You," I said, "are an intern."

Her laughter quit, and her smile went off into the next room. "You've got me there," she said.

We sat in the sickroom silence, holding on to the memory of laughter as a talisman against our pain.

After the chemo came the waiting. We all waited: me and Janet, D'Andrea, Hastings, Jason, all the nurses. Vic and the old man waited in the evenings. Mama waited constantly, from the hour the place opened for visitors in the morning until the loudspeaker outside the room told her to go home. The young priest came to offer me the solace of a religion I did not believe. Clocks and calendars lost their significance. Time's punctuation became more concrete. Drops from a bag of saline broke the day into tiny pieces, and they flowed into me. I marked time by the ineluctable round of nurses checking vital signs, by the daily routine of work rounds and venipuncture, by the hanging of bags of antibiotics and chemotherapy, by the tedium of meals.

At first I slept a lot, watching the big flakes of a late snow lash at the double windowpanes until I slid into their white seduction. Then I learned about the nights, their blackness dense with loneliness and fear. After that, until the fevers came again, I tried to spend my days awake, walking or sitting in the hall, or sitting in the lobby by my wheeled IV pole next to the tall windows and a hot radiator. I sat and watched the living bodies pass, watching the cut and color of their clothes, the patterns of lines on their faces and the shadows of street dirt and snowmelt on shoes and skirts and the cuffs of white trousers. I watched the faces, all different, all alive. I sat against the wall, as if behind glass, watching real lives go by, feeling tired and small and distant. I sat in my blue robe with a notebook on my knees and my feet up on the bright newsmagazines, with a pencil in my hand. The paragraphs flowed. Mama read a Gothic novel.

By the weekend the waiting was over. My blood counts fell to nothing. My appetite trickled away into viscid diarrhea and a constant nausea tinged with bile. D'Andrea locked me in my room to protect me from the infections of a living world. My meals were sterile. Mama had to wear a mask to kiss me. I was an old man suddenly, and the short struggle from bed to bathroom and back grew Sisyphean. Sitting up exhausted me, and the pauses in Mama's monologues expanded until they enveloped our evenings, and there was nothing left for her to say except the whispered round of her rosary. Her words wrapped round me. Her voice caressed me. Swaddled in the simple serenity of her faith, I slept at last.

Then the fevers resumed. There was a pain under my ribs, teeth-chattering chills. Again I went drifting off on a hectic sea, bobbing on waves of dim delirium and dreaming of home.

Janet broke in on those dreams, questioning, prodding, tapping. Vicky came in, in her fine white nurse's uniform, with plastic cups for sputum and urine that Janet fed to microscopes and labs. Jason drew blood from the catheter in my chest and from the used bruise in the crook of my elbow where my veins still ran. Slumped in a wheelchair, tangled in tubing, with Vicky pushing, I was trundled down to radiology for chest X rays.

"May I see the films?" I asked when we were through.

The technician scowled, but Vicky shrugged off his objection.

"He'll read them better than you will," she told him.

So the tech put the two films on a viewbox for us. There was nothing much to see, just a little white haze low down in the tangle of bones, the tracery of vessels, and the long arc of the big central line.

In the elevator, down the dark, still corridors, we were both quiet, both thinking too fast for words.

"It doesn't look so bad," Vicky said finally.

"No," I said, sounding even gloomier than I felt, "just bad enough."

Back in my room I lay with my face to the wall. The rigors came on again. I curled around myself, shivering. Janet touched my shoulder.

"It's pneumonia," she said.

"I know," I said. "We looked at the films."

"I've talked to D'Andrea. We'll get new antibiotics started right away."

"Thanks."

"You'll feel better."

She stood there a moment, waiting for me to turn to face her. But I was comfortable looking at the wall. I kept my back to her. I was afraid. There were things she was better off not seeing, and I felt better not showing off my terror.

"Is there anything I can do?" she asked.

"Sure," I said.

"What?" she asked hopefully, eagerly.

"Get the hell out of my room and go to sleep," I told her.

She whispered my name and touched me. I turned against her hand quickly, and the pain in my chest swelled and burst and ran all over me as I sat up. I pinned her wrist under my fingers

"Don't touch me," I said. "You did good, but now your job's done. You found the problem, you found the treatment, and now you go to sleep. You can't help me from here."

"Not any?" she asked.

I fell back on the pillow, onto the damp, sick-smelling sheets. "Janet," I said, "all you can do from here is hurt yourself." I looked up into the pain in her eyes. "You can't help me. There are things you can't change, that you can't touch, that you can't understand. I get to wrestle with them alone. You have to detach and let me do that."

"I'm sorry," she said.

"So am I," I said, and I thought that was the end of it. I closed my eyes. But she didn't go.

"Shit," I said. "Don't cry. It makes you look worse than I do, and that's pretty damn bad. You did good. Really you did. I'm proud of you."

"Thanks," she said, sniffling.

"I promise: if I need you, I'll call right away. Direct. You'll hear my voice coming out of your beeper."

"Okay," she said. She smiled, finally.

"Now, for God's sake, get some sleep."

I put out my hand. She squeezed it hard enough to hurt. Then she left me alone. I turned back to the wall and filled my mind with the sound of my breathing. It's steady, soothing rhythm drowned death's patient pacing outside my door.

In the morning I was brave again.

For days the fever thrashed and fought against the drugs. Eventually it died. I sat around and watched it go. There was nothing I could do. Janet and Hastings and D'Andrea made all the decisions. I took the drugs, accepted the transfusions. Eventually my blood counts struggled back to normal.

It took a long time. It took so long that the residents changed to new rotations. Janet moved across the street, to the Veterans Administration Hospital; Howie, an intern I didn't know, took her place. Mama went home for a rest and came back only on weekends. Papa didn't come at all anymore.

The next marrow biopsy showed no malignant cells.

"That's an excellent prognostic sign," D'Andrea told me.

I sat with my legs curled up under me. I had on a striped robe that Janet had lifted for me from a linen closet over at the V.A. My hands were deep in its pockets. With a red bandanna over my bald head, I looked like the derelict vets who lived in the television rooms of the crowded wards, waiting for discharge papers that never came, looking lost. Only I wasn't lost yet.

"Don't bullshit me," I said. "We both know it's still there. The leukemia's not dead. It's just hiding. Give it time, and it'll be everywhere. We both know that."

D'Andrea sighed and sat down. He was looking old. I could empathize. You take care of people for a while, and they get under your skin. You string them along for weeks and months at a time, and they die on you anyway. They die in waves, just when you think you're winning. The staff tried to keep it from me, but of course I could hear the voices of the resuscitation teams in the night, see the lights outside my room. I knew what they meant: in the last few days D'Andrea had hit a big wave.

Now he just folded his hands and looked at them. "You don't have to be so hard on yourself," he said.

"No?"

"No. You can hope. It's not as bad as you make it out to be."

"How would you know how bad it is?" I asked him.

"Don't pull that."

"Then don't lie to me."

We paused, squaring off, thinking. I didn't want to think. That I could leave to other people.

D'Andrea started talking again, about percentages, about consolidation, adjuvants, regimens, drug combinations, marrow transplants, complications. We skipped over the complications; we both knew them too well. It was all quite amicable. Talking facts, we were both quite congenial.

Mama brought the whole family in to get tested for the marrow donation. She brought in cousins from Buffalo, an aunt from Queens, an uncle from God knew where. If D'Andrea had let her, she'd have pulled Grandma out of the home to get tested. It was no good, though. Nobody matched.

"It happens, Ma," I said.

"But why?" she asked me.

She was crying. I couldn't stop her. I was too tired to try. I just lay on the pillows and listened to her go on.

"How the hell should I know?" I said. "Maybe I'm the milkman's kid. Maybe you brought the wrong baby home from the hospital twenty-six years ago."

That shut her up. Her eyes got huge. She leaned into my face, took hold of my hands insistently.

"No," she said. "That never happens. That couldn't happen. They took footprints."

I tried to smile. "Shit, Ma, I know that. I was just joking."

She flopped back in the chair, almost reassured. "I just don't understand," she sighed.

"I don't either, Ma," I said, knowing that there were no explanations for death. "You'll have to ask your priest. He's supposed to have those kinds of answers."

The second time around, the chemo was worse. I threw up

when Howie brought the drugs into the room I threw up again
when he pushed them. I threw up when lunch came, and
dinner, and breakfast. I called D'Andrea in.

"Get me some THC," I said.

"I can't get that," he said. "Try the other stuff we've
ordered for you. It works better in blinded trials."

"Your stuff's worthless," I said. "And why can't you get
THC? It's on the street. Why can't you get it?"

"The pharmacy won't carry it. It's political."

So I had Vic bring me some. He rolled the joints himself,
his special present. I sat by the open windows and blew smoke
into the early spring air. It worked very nicely.

Soon, though, I was too weak to smoke. I was too weak to
write, too weak to eat, too weak to sit up. The diarrhea turned
bloody. I was too weak to walk to the bathroom. The nurses
tired of my bedpan calls quickly.

In the night I coughed. Little jets of green stool leaked into
my pajamas. I lay in my own shit and cried, cursing my life.

I slept with the fluorescent lights on my face. I fell asleep
dreaming of death, of some medical student's hands on my
chest, pumping, of the great needles piercing me, neck and
groin; of the noise; of the pain as the cardioversion paddles lifted
me off the bed in a last, long spasm, depositing me in stillness
for the nurses' final cleansing. I dreamed of bleeding, of vomiting
clots onto the pillow, of the darkness embracing me on sheets
slick with blood as the smell of clotted feces suffocated me. I
cried out. No one came. Again and again during those nights, I
died. No one noticed.

In the mornings a false spring sun poured through the
window. It spilled through the dirty glass, shimmered in the
dust motes that hung in the sickroom air, and shattered on the pale
yellow walls. Spent, inert, I passed my days watching the light's
color change, grow stronger, fade, fade away, and die.

The fevers came back. Fungus grew in the tubes of blood
that the students collected. The antifungal drugs gave me the
shakes, turned my guts out. The transfusions started again, red

cells and platelets. There were pills to take every hour. None of them were worth a damn.

Then I was back under the cold lights of the operating room. My central catheter, infected, was cut out. The interns and students started peripheral catheters again, into my arms, the backs of my hands, my feet. The intravenous solutions, the narcotics, all corroded my veins, sclerosing them into hard, red, tender cords that throbbed, oozing blood.

Every day again, Mama came. It was as in days long forgotten. She fed me, turned me in the bed, pulled my pajamas on and off. She carried my bedpan. Over my head she hung Grandpa's rosary, with its beads of mahogany and ebony, stained by the sweat of the dead man's fingers. At night it hung from my IV pole like a benediction.

Looking in the mirror, I could see why Papa stayed away. I tried not to look, and when I looked I tried not to see. The Italian cheekbones were too sharp now, the olive skin too sallow. The thin blue veins of my scalp drained the color from my face. The lips were pale, chapped, furrowed, old. Only the eyes held their living hue, a deep earth brown. At their centers, inside each iris as I gazed into the mirror, staring out at me, was the reflection of myself suspended in the emptiness of my pupils.

Janet came to visit. She looked beaten, as lined and tired as her white uniform. We laughed at stories we knew or had heard about the mad vets she was working with, about smuggling booze and stealing cigarettes, about death from DTs and cirrhosis and lung cancer and heart failure and all the other things that killed men. While I talked she fell asleep in the chair. She didn't hear my last story. She sat with her head on her shoulder, tipped back, with her mouth open and her hair straggling across her face. I watched her breathe, watched her chest rise and fall. She started to snore. It was a wonderful sound. It was peaceful. It was alive. I let it blow the loneliness away. But after an hour I pushed the call button. One of the night nurses came in and helped Janet into her coat. Janet held my hand. I gave it a squeeze, playing brave. I never saw her again. It was just as well, for her.

"So," the priest said, "I hear from your doctors that you're going home this week."

"God willing," I said.

He smiled tolerantly. "No," he said. "I'm sure you'll go. You look well. You're doing much better than any of the other people on this ward."

"That's not saying much," I pointed out.

He was right, though, this priest. I was doing better. The bone marrow was still clean—no cancer cells, and not much of anything else, either. The latest biopsy looked like the morning after nuclear war. Still, I was walking again. I was spending time in the lobby, and sometimes I even walked out to the street. I could shower without the spray knocking me to my knees. I had shaved off the stray coarse hairs on my face that had survived the chemotherapy, although the only razor the nurses could find for me was a surgical prep shaver, about as humane as tearing the hair out by its roots. I was eating again, too. Mama was happy. She had fixed up my old room at their house. It was going to be just like the old days there.

"I won't believe it, Father," I said, "until my feet hit the street."

"You'll make it," the priest said. "Have some confidence in yourself."

"Shit, Father. Look around. Look around, and then tell me about confidence."

"You'll go home."

"No, Father," I said to him. "There's no going home from the cancer ward. It goes with you. There's too much death here. It clings to you like a burr under your shirt. It gets under your skin. It gets into your blood, into your bones. It was like that when I was the doctor, and I know it'll stay that way now that I'm a patient. You can't get away from it."

"Sure you can. In a few days, you'll be home. Things will be different. You'll see."

"Different? Maybe. But still the same. I'll still be bald as a baby rat and twice as ugly. Every time I look in the mirror, every time my mother cries, with every bruise and every cough and every ache, I'll remember that I belong here. I belong here. I don't belong out there. Out there is for people who are gong to live."

The priest got up. He put his communion box on the dresser. He put his hands on the windowsill and stared out at the Sunday morning traffic working to and fro under the stoplight.

"Is it really so bad?" he asked.

"No," I said. I was gong to say that it was worse, but seeing his earnest young face under the dark hair, I held back. "It's not so bad. I was just feeling sorry for myself, is all."

"Really?" he asked. "Because it gets to me, this place, this damned hospital."

"But look at the numbers, Father. Most people here go home."

"But so many don't," he said. "So many. I tell them to hope, and then they die."

"Don't worry about them," I said. "God will take care of them."

"Will he?" said the priest. "You don't really believe that."

"Sure."

"No. You're laughing at me."

"That's not true, Father. You have to have some kind of faith to survive around here."

"Perhaps. But it's hard for faith itself to survive. I tell people that death has meaning, but then I see them die, and sometimes I just cannot believe anymore. Death is so . . . what is the word? Not horrible. It was that, when I first came, but now it's just wasteful. It's not noble, only stupid."

"Well, I guess everybody has doubts. Look at Saint What's-his-name—he had doubts, didn't he? And he was a saint."

"Augustine? I suppose. But I feel like such a fraud. I tell the families that God cares, but the suffering seems so random. I read my Bible—I read to them from my Bible, and the words seem so false, so divorced from what I'm seeing."

"But it makes them feel better, doesn't it?"

"Yes. I wonder, though: can they see the doubt in me?"

He stood up and started pacing around the room. He started waving his hands around, just like an Italian, as he spoke.

"This morning," he said, "I was called into the intensive care unit. A man was dying. A young man. He had asked for me. He had requested the anointing of the sick. When I got there, he was unconscious. They were working on him, the doctors and nurses. He came around soon after I got there. The others left us alone. The man started mumbling to me. He wanted to touch me, to hold my hand. He was a homosexual. He had AIDS, and he was dying. And he wanted to hold my hand. I was so repelled. He was so thin. The spit had dried in his beard. He smelled terrible. His hands were soft and white, with thick hair black against the skin."

He stopped and stared at his own pale hands. "I made myself touch him," he went on. "I hated him for making me do that, and I hated myself for feeling that way. I mean, I'm the priest. I bring God's forgiveness to everyone. But this man was so repulsive. . . . He tried to make confession. He forgot all the forms. He started blurting out his sins, begging for absolution. He told me all the details, all the acts, the times, the places. He went on and on, naming dozens of men. It was terrible. He passed out again, whispering as he slipped away. I said the words over him, touched him with the oil. Then I called the doctors. They went back to work on him. I went away wondering what penance I could assign to him if he lived."

He was standing at the window again, looking for something. Then he turned to me. Hell, I didn't have it.

"You did the right thing, Father," I said, to take up the silence.

"But I didn't want to. I should have wanted to."

"Fuck it," I said. "You're human. If you were divine, they'd have kicked you up to the Vatican by now."

"Perhaps," he said gloomily.

"Or else they'd have crucified you."

He laughed at that, finally. It was about time. I was supposed to be the lugubrious one.

"I guess you're right," he said. He didn't sound convinced.

"Of course I'm right. I learned that my first month here. I had such great hopes, you know. I thought I could do so much, save so many lives. But I ran into my own limitations that first month and settled down to doing the best I knew how. And then, of course, I got sick."

"You would have been a wonderful doctor," he told me.

"Whatever." I shrugged. "Who knows? God, maybe. Anyway, you did the right thing. Ask the guy in the unit you were just telling me about. He'd tell you the same."

"I can't do that," said the priest. "He's dead."

That killed our little conversation. He came to my bedside and shook my hand. "I'm glad you're going home," he said.

"Thanks. It'll be wonderful, I know. I shouldn't be a pessimist."

"You'll be fine. I'll pray for you. I'll miss these talks we've had."

"So will I," I said, although most of the time he'd done all the talking while I'd concentrated on breathing and staying awake and not throwing up.

"Say hello to your mother for me," he said.

"I will. She thinks the world of you."

"She's very special."

"We all like her."

It went on like that a long time. Finally he went out. I took a nap to keep from thinking. Then I went out into the hall, doing laps—to the nursing station and back—to pass the time until Mama came.

Mama's daffodils blossomed bright yellow before a dirty crust of melting snow under the north eaves. Tongues of grass, brilliant green, licked up through the dead thatch on the lawn. I plucked a blade, sucked it, crushed it in my teeth, tasting spring.

I leaned on the doorpost at the top of the front stoop with

the wind on my face. I let my head drop back. Overhead, full, fat cumulus clouds floated in an immense blue sky.

"Well, Mama," I said, "I'm home."

She hugged me. "That's right," she said. "You're home. We'll take care of you now. You won't miss the hospital."

"No, Mama," I told her, "I'll never miss that damned place."

We went inside. Out of breath, I had to sit down; I was not ready for stairs just yet. Mama carried in the one bag of things that had made that hospital room mine: my pajamas, the robe that Janet had stolen, a torn Turner print, another by Sisley, a stack of get well cards bound together with a worn rubber band, a tape player and a few cassettes, a crayon drawing by Terry's oldest kid.

At the kitchen table, with all the old scratches and rings, we drank tea from Mama's wedding china, the two unbroken cups she got out only for special times.

"Yeah, Ma," I answered her, "I am pretty tired. It feels great to be in real clothes again, though."

"You look fine," she said. She gave my hand a squeeze. "You look real good."

I ran my hand over my scalp, feeling the scattered ends of short new hairs. "Shit," I said. "I must look like a runaway from a concentration camp."

"No," she told me. "You look like the kids who hang out downtown Saturday nights with chains on. They wear their hair like that."

We laughed. She was so happy.

"You want something to eat?" she asked. "Let me fix you something."

"I'm fine, Ma. I was wondering how long you'd take to ask that, though."

"Hush. It's time to put some meat on your bones. No more of that hospital food. What do you want? Let your old mama fix you something."

"No, Ma. Really."

"Sure. We got prosciutto, some provolone, some good bread. I'll make you a sandwich."

"Ma, I'm not hungry. I'll be fine until dinner."

"But you're so thin. Now that you're better, you have to start eating again."

She was hurt. I didn't have the heart to explain the difference between remission and cure in leukemia. Instead I got up and kissed her on the part in her hair.

"I'll be okay, Ma. I just need some sleep, is all. I'll eat later."

I went back into the back room, the one that looked out on the garden. Last year's squash and tomato vines lay shriveled on the ready black earth. Across the Albaneses' yard, I could see the church steeple and the water tower by the factory. Nothing had changed. I fell on the mattress and watched the willow wands outside the window swaying in the spring breeze, back and forth.

"For God's sake," Mama was shouting, "put that dirty thing out. It's bad enough you smoke it around me. But he's home now. You want to make him sick?"

"It's a little late for that," Papa said.

I got up exhausted by sleep, and shambled into the kitchen, trying to wipe the fatigue off my face. I stood in the doorway. They looked like guilty children, caught fighting again.

"He's right, Mama," I said. "Let him smoke the damned cigar."

Mama tore off her apron and ran up the front stairs. Papa slouched at the table, his feet on a chair in unlaced black shoes. His left hand played with the stump of a smudged-out cigar. He looked at me. He looked at the doorway that Mama had stormed through. Then he looked at his cigar.

"Shit," he said. He flicked the cigar onto a dirty plate.

I pulled two brown bottles out of the refrigerator and popped the caps.

"Hey," Papa said, "you supposed to be drinking that?"

I looked at the label, shrugged, and grinned at him. "What the hell," I said.

He studied the bubbles rising behind the dark glasses. Then he raised his bottle to me. "Yeah," he said. "What the hell."

We drank together until my bottle was half-gone. The world turned gentle under the alcohol. Papa talked about the gossip around the plant, the union hall, the Legion post. Mama came back in, not saying anything, and went back to fixing dinner. Papa went on about how hard it was to fix up the summer place in the Adirondacks now that all his kids were gone. He told me about a letter from his brother in California with news of all my cousins there. Finally Mama gave up her silence and broke in with stories about her grandchildren, her mother, and the new deacon. I took it all in. It was good to be home again and back in the family.

To celebrate, we had steak and potatoes. The meat was overdone. I left the wine untasted and skipped the dessert.

"I'm sorry," I told Mama. "I'm still kind of tired, I guess."

She smiled. The effort she made to hide her disappointment only underscored it.

"You ate pretty good," she said. "You had a long day. You look tired. Why don't you go on back to bed?"

"I think I'll do that," I said.

"Papa and I'll take care of the dishes," she said.

Papa nodded, and I stood up. But before I could get out of the room, Vic burst in. He came all in a rush, thumping up the stoop and slamming the front door. He had on black jeans, and he was showing off his broad shoulders in a tight pullover sweater. He whirled Mama around and kissed her on the forehead. He waved to Papa. He stood in front of me and held out his hand.

"So," he said, as I took his hand, "Baldy's back. How are you, Slim?"

I laughed, feeling his strong grip testing mine, the way it had done since we were kids. "Pretty good, guy," I said. "I'm doing good."

"Like hell," he said, patting my cheek. He glanced at the folks with a grin that was half chuckle, half wink.

"You missed supper, Vittorio," Papa said, "if that's why you come by. Where the hell you been?"

Vic ignored him. He looked instead to the doorway. We all looked. Connie was there, slight and shy, hanging back from people she didn't know, except to know they resented her. Mama froze. Papa ignored her, pushing potato crumbs around the cold gravy on his plate.

"Christ," he said, shaking his head.

Vic kept on smiling. He had on the kind of smile a guy wears before he spits in your eye or pisses on your shoes. It was the kind of smile I used to wear a lot, before I got sick.

"Shut up, Papa," I said. "Show a little class."

He hated me for that. Well, the hell with him. The hell with all of them and all their feuds and hatreds. I didn't have time for that anymore. I pulled out a chair for Connie.

"Come on in," I said to her. "Sit down."

She looked at Vic.

"No," he said. "We got places to go. There's people we're supposed to meet tonight downtown. We just wanted to welcome home old skinhead here."

"Vittorio," Mama scolded, "don't you ever talk about your brother like that in this house."

"Hush, Ma," I told her, putting a hand on her shoulder. "He means it right."

Eventually I got them all into the living room. We talked about Connie's new job typing copy into video terminals at the paper.

"I go to full-time in June," she said, "when classes finish."

Papa was still playing with his dead cigar. Mama sat quietly and tried to look polite.

"That's a pretty good job," I said into the silence. "How'd you get it?" Nobody but me looked very interested in the topic, but Connie answered anyway.

"Through the placement office at the community college. They do pretty good for us About two-thirds of the people in my class have jobs lined up already."

"There ain't many jobs like that anymore in this town," Papa said.

"That's true," I said. I was trying to be pleasant. It was uphill work.

"When you going to get a real job like that, Vittorio?" Papa asked.

Vic pulled out a crushed Marlboro pack, lit one, waved out the match, and spilled smoke all over the ceiling. "I got a real job," he said.

"Huh," said Mama. "Washing dishes."

"Why don't you let me get you a job at the plant?" Papa said. "I could get you in easy."

Vic gestured around the room with his cigarette. "And live like this?"

After that, of course, they couldn't stay. Mama and Papa looked black. Connie looked terrible. Vic got up and crushed out his cigarette into a souvenir ashtray from Atlantic City. Connie got up with him, and I followed. We three went into the hall.

"It was great seeing you again, little brother," Vic said. He thumped me square between the shoulders. "You really are looking better."

"Yeah," I said as we shook hands again. "It was good to see you two." I kissed Connie on the cheek.

"We'll have to do something together," she said. "Go down to the speedway, maybe, or go uptown dancing."

"Sure," said Vic. "I could find you a date. It'd be just like old times."

"Yeah," I said, "just like old times."

They went out. I sat in silence with the old people, listening to the muttering of Vic's Camaro as it pulled down the street. Papa turned on the television.

"You want some coffee?" Mama asked me.

I stood up. "No thanks, Ma," I said. "Remember: I was just heading to bed."

We all said good night.

"It's great to be home again," I told them. I think they believed me.

I kissed Mama one more time. Then I went into the back room. The window was dark, speckled with light filtered through the branches of trees. I pulled down the yellowed shade and curled up in my clothes on the bed. It felt unnatural, sleeping on a bed without a plastic pad, in a room without a call bell. It was too quiet to sleep. Then Mama came into the kitchen and put on the coffee. I fell asleep listening to the sigh of the gas jet and the sputtering of the percolating pot.

Around midnight I woke in a sweat. The house was still as death. I sat up, lost and confused. It took time to realize that the nurses wouldn't be rounding anymore.

The furnace coughed and rattled. I undressed and got between the sheets. The blankets fit me nicely. I slept for a long time.

Papa woke me with his coughing. I listened to him through the wall. He spat into the sink and finished shaving. I listened to the water run in the kitchen, to the dishes clink, to the television news drone, to the old linoleum tiles creak, to hushed voices speaking words too soft to understand. Then the front door closed. Papa gunned his engine, just the way Vic always did, and he was gone.

I got out of bed and let up the shade. The springtime light spilled all over me.

I spent those days killing time. I sat by the tall windows in the big brick library. The high ceilings, the smell of old bindings, the rustle of newspapers read by old men in drab coats, the smell of steam heat, the clatter of radiators, all had the reassuring solidity of old memories. The spring rain beaded up on the leaded windowpanes. I sat in a sprung leather armchair galloping through *Paterson* and Chekhov: doctors' stories.

The rain beaded up, too, on the tall bakery windows. It was a warm rain, sour on the lips. Fog rose off the melting snowbanks in the shadow of the courthouse. Miles of low clouds, pale gray, hung in the quiet sky. They dripped on the dark blossoms of red maples in the square. I sipped sweet black coffee at a knotty pine table. My words in the notebooks ran on and on. The hours sifted away.

On sunny days I drove to the high school to watch the teams play: lacrosse and baseball, track and field. It was like traveling back in time to my youth, only there was no place for me.

Each Thursday came the long trips to the hematology clinic. We left before Papa went off to work, driving through good kite winds with the new grass rippling in the median of the Thruway. We drove some days through heavy windshield-wiper weather. We parked in a big garage on my old staff pass. We waited for hours in a big room full of very sick people. Mama sat knitting. I swung my heels on a cold exam table, half-naked and alone, with a bandage on the crook of my elbow where the phlebotomist had done her work. D'Andrea and his resident always wandered in late, detained by crises on the wards.

We joked about serious things, spoke seriously about trivia. My mother was fine, I told him. No one had seen Janet lately, he said, but they all heard she was well. The weather was certainly miserable; still, summer always came. The list of new interns was out, and they seemed quite promising; of course, they were nothing like the ones in the current year. All the numbers were essentially normal, by the way, D'Andrea would add as an afterthought, leafing through my chart.

"For now," I said one afternoon.

D'Andrea slapped me on the back. The bare skin stung. "Come on," he said. "Don't always look on the dark side. You've got to have some hope, man. I've told you that all along."

I looked at Chip, the resident that month. His eyes flicked away to D'Andrea, to a pastel print on the wall, to the door. I knew the feeling he had, of eavesdropping, of voyeurism.

"No," I said.

"No what?" D'Andrea asked.

"No, I don't have to have hope."

"Don't say that."

"You know it's true. I have to stay alive to make your chemotherapy protocol look good. I have to take care of myself, have to take my medicine, report all fevers, keep my feet dry, and drink lots of chicken soup. I have to keep myself from thinking, so I don't go crazy. But hope is one thing I don't have to do."

"But come on," D'Andrea said. His hand went up on my shoulder. I scowled at the hand, and he took it away.

"But nothing," I said. "I'm going to die, and I'm going to die soon. No: don't try to tell me otherwise. You know I'm right, and you know and I know that nobody dies well. Dying is ugly. It hurts and it smells bad. I'm sure as hell not ready for it, but I'm trying to do it as gracefully as I know how. Still, I'm damned if I'm going to lie to myself about it."

Then I looked away from him. "Come on, Chip," I said, "listen to my chest and let my mother go home."

"Damn it," said D'Andrea, "you don't have to be such a bastard."

"Sure I do," I said, grinning at him. "I'm Italian. It's in the blood."

On the way out of the clinic, I met old friends. They were all glad to see me, and we had much to talk about. But they had to get back to work, and we had to get home. Someday, we agreed, we'd get together.

Every week it was like that: blood tests, exams, a little pep talk. D'Andrea let us slip to twice monthly, then brought us back to weekly. But not to worry, D'Andrea said: he just liked to be careful. I acted nonchalant. Mama cried.

The spring matured into summer. Buds burst into leaves that stretched and spread like waking children. The blossoms whitened the orchards and fell to earth like scented snow. Every hillside sugar bush briefly sprouted spiles and silver pails, and then the trees slowly healed their round, drilled holes. In the woods spring flowers blossomed, only to die as the forest canopy closed. The air filled with sound: insects and songbirds, water running through the gullies and gutters, guttural thunderstorms, and the noise of hot kids in big cars racing along the edge of the world.

One afternoon we all climbed into the Camaro, Vic and Connie and me. We sat in a row across the front seat. Connie had her forearms on the dashboard, and she stared at the sun as we drove south, across the Mohawk River bridge, away from stores with plywood windows, away from the soot-black but smokeless factories.

We drove out of the city into another country, a free and green country full of life, where farm roads wandered into the dairyland. We followed old roads between tumbledown walls of gray fieldstone and green moss, where the water sprang from the earth in rusty pipes and gurgled into the valley. Holsteins lounged in mud by battered barns painted white and red and peeling in the sun. Calves nuzzled in the grass, bucking and bolting. Manure spreaders tossed shit across high hay meadows. We walked along a dirt road, Vic and Connie holding hands. We slipped in the muck of tractor tracks, jumping from stone to stone across swollen streams. We climbed a pasture sodden with summer rain, churned to paste by cloven feet and late frosts.

We climbed on and on, too high for me. I sat to rest. They went on together. As I watched them walk away, his arm went up around her shoulders.

I sat on a torn wire fence. The sun was warm above the trees. It massaged my temples, caressed my face. Slowly my pulse relaxed, my breath came back.

I went on alone. The road curved west, into a wood. The light filtered down through living leaves, dappling the dead ones that lay all across the forest floor. I broke a branch from a fallen tree, and the dead wood was my strong staff as I walked along. There was a remembered rhythm to the walk, and it was good to feel it again, until my fatigue forced itself on me once more.

The road pitched up. We stood together again on the ridgeline. Beyond us, across the pasture and all down the far slope, the trees huddled together against the wind. Below us, barges pushed up the brown ribbon of the Mohawk, and the tractor-trailers traced their way along the highway's narrow track. In the distance, among the clouds on the horizon, the purple mountains stood in ranks. In between, the white of steeples and concrete towers stood out among gray tar-paper roofs that squatted on the floodplain and the hills. Connie and I stood in the mud. Vic, above us, hugged the highest limbs of a maple that stood alone on the hillcrest. He rode the wind, like the hawks we watched floating among the thermals.

Walking down, we didn't talk much. My feet were wet and cold. We wore the earth on our trouser cuffs. We sat close in the car with the heater on. We stopped in a bar. Connie and Vic drank beer; I sipped coffee, shivering.

That night I slept at Connie's place. Vic was living there full-time. His things from home sat in boxes on the landing outside her apartment door. I fell asleep on the floor while we watched television, sprawled out on a secondhand rug with a pillow under my head. I woke in the night with a blanket around me. Vic and Connie had gone out. I called Mama, who was still up, worrying about me, just like old times. I made a sandwich and ate most of it. Then I passed out on the sofa. I never heard them come in.

I started spending nights there. I could ignore my parents' futile fighting that way. Some days I dropped Connie at work and drove my old car into the mountains, parking alone in hemlock groves and listening to the rivers pass me by.

I stopped to see Mama every day. It was a quick walk from Connie's, though Mama didn't know how close their two homes were. Mama told me all her troubles: with Vic and Grandma, with Papa and the other kids. She never mentioned the troubles I gave her. I fed her platitudes; I had nothing else to give.

The hospital and the insurance company sent me letters. The two almost balanced. The digits on the bills and invoices were too many to comprehend. I kept them all in a bundle, wrapped up with a rubber band, unopened after the first one came. I would leave the settlement to my heirs and assigns. Except that I had nothing to assign, and there would be no heirs.

In the gray and black light before dawn, when darkness distorts distances and the figures of furniture and factory blocks fade into fluid illusions, I woke on Connie's sofa. My mouth was full of the taste of harsh homegrown and red wine from the old country. My clothes were soaked with the slick, hot sweat of a breaking fever. Outside, a night freight, westbound, ran dopplering down the backyard tracks, and the house shook to the clanking, squealing, rhythmic syncopation of the rails. I turned my face to the worn cushions, waking now and again to see the street-side sycamore's tracery, the worn-out patterns in the rug, and the hard lines of the walls sharpen in the waxing sunlight. When it was full day, I went out.

An old Lebanese ran a newsstand on the corner. I bought a morning paper and sat on his front step to leaf through the front section. When I got back, Connie was up. Vic was in the bathroom shaving. The coffee was hot. She cooked breakfast: eggs and cheese, oatmeal with currants and cream, small luxuries. We climbed through a dormer window and ate on the roof. The black roofing paper was already warm in the morning sun. We sweetened our coffee with the smell of summertime.

They left me alone. I walked to the market to shop for supper: we were eating well while my savings lasted. Later I sat in the park and watched the squirrels chase each other. After school the kids did the same. We threw a Frisbee around until the clouds closed in.

The night sweats kept on. My thermometer hung at a hundred point five.

I went to see Mama. She was out. I let myself in with the key she kept under the back doormat.

I called D'Andrea. He was out of his office. I left a message and waited for hours until he called back. We chatted briefly. Finally I came to the point.

"How soon can you get here?" he asked.

"I don't know," I said. "This afternoon, probably, but late."

"I'll let the clinic know."

"What do you think it is?" I asked him.

"You know better than to ask me to make diagnoses over the telephone."

"I think it's just recurrent tumor. I don't feel infected."

"We'll see," he said.

He was not a very cheerful guy. Still, his was not that kind of job. It didn't pay enough to buy cheerfulness. They didn't print enough money to buy that. D'Andrea was paid to do his job well, and that was how he did it. I tried to reassure myself, remembering that.

Mama came home. She had been shopping. I was waiting on the porch. I helped her carry in her bags.

"What a surprise," she said. "How are you feeling today?"

I couldn't meet her eyes. "Not so hot," I said.

"What do you mean, not so hot?"

"That's what I mean."

"Are you sick? It that it? You got a cold? You know, there's a bad bug going around. All of Terry's kids got it last week."

"I don't think it's a bug, Ma,"

She had been unpacking and shelving groceries with frantic motion. Now she stopped and stared into my face.

"What do you think it is?" she asked.

I looked back at her face, watched it come apart in front of me. There was nothing I could do to help her.

"I don't know, Ma," I said. I started putting away the things she still had out, to avoid melodrama. "I need to get back to Albany. I talked to Dr. D'Andrea. He wants me to see him today."

Mama just sat there and cried. There was nothing at all I could do to stop her. I put my arms around her, but that just made her cry harder. I stared past her, out the screen door, out the windows. I looked all around the place, storing up memories.

Mama let go. I went to the front door and leaned against it, staring out at nothing, at everything. Mama blew her nose.

"I guess we'd better go," she said.

"I guess we'd better."

"Just let me write a note for your father."

"All right."

"Will they keep you? Do you need to bring anything?"

"I don't know, Ma," I said. "The things I might need I never unpacked. I hated them too much. I'll be all right."

"Oh, God," Mama said, "and what will your father eat? Nothing's ready. I haven't had time to cook anything."

"Leave him a can opener, Ma," I said. "He's a big guy. He'll manage."

Eventually we left. She packed some things for each of us, wrote Papa a note, and set food out on the table. She checked all the burners on the stove and the lights in all the rooms, as though we were leaving forever.

I should have been more helpful. I should have been ready. I had been waiting for months for this to happen. Still, the statistics said I had more time. But cancer doesn't read the journals, and leukemia never went to medical school. There were so many things I hadn't had time for, though. Still, there was no sense being a jerk about it. There was never enough time. Or rather there was always time, and one always wasted it. I sat in the front seat of the car and tried to act pleasant, but Mama wasn't buying any of it. She asked me the hard questions all the way into the city.

Of course, D'Andrea put me back in the big house. I went to the same ward, just a different room, a different view. The residents were different, and the new class of interns were barely back on their feet after the shock of July. I didn't know their names. I tried some small talk with the guy assigned to me, but he was too busy. He had never known me before, and to him I was just another sick cancer patient. I stripped, and he went to work.

The nurses were all the same, though. They were very cordial, very nice. They acted as though they were glad to see me. In their eyes, though, they looked as happy about the whole thing as I was.

The goddamned patients were still the same. That was bad. They smelled the same. The look on the faces of the family members hovering over them was the same. There were new ones, but they looked like the old ones; we were all interchangeable.

The intern poked into everything when he did my exam. He was very thorough. He cultured everything: lots of blood and every bodily fluid I could produce for him. I couldn't cough up anything, and that annoyed him terribly.

We went through the same motions we had done months before. We shot the same X rays, the same nuclear scans, the same daily exams. I spent hours under huge, silent white body scanners that frisked me for abscesses and found nothing. Alone in huge rooms, I listened to electric motors talk to me. I lounged in bed, festooned with tubing. The new marrow biopsy came back studded with tumor: malignant islands in a cellular sea. Having been right about that didn't make the news go down any more easily, though. I had been wrong about not having an infection, for something was growing in the bottles of my blood that sat in incubators in the microbiology lab. It was a very unusual bug. At first the experts thought it was contamination, that the intern hadn't washed his hands well enough before sticking me. But it grew in all the samples. D'Andrea started antibiotics. They didn't help. The fever went higher every day.

Five days passed. I sat in long lines outside radiology waiting rooms. Silent senility lay strapped to gurneys all around me. Old men slept beside me, slumped over the arms of their wheelchairs. One woke, pulled up his gown, and scratched his scrotum, staring at me staring at him. Kyphotic old women called out for absent children and bedpans, getting neither.

At night I listened to the teleprinter down the hall rattle on. Scuffed slippers shuffled by my door. I hated the old patients with their relentless cancers, because they reminded me of death. To avoid them, I slept, and I met them in my dreams.

I started coughing again: the air in the little room was close and choking, always too cold or too hot. I felt fine, only tired. I quit going out onto the ward. There was no point, and I knew none of the doctors there anymore. Mama came, but she tired me. I had nothing to say to her now. Papa came, always complaining. I had to throw him out. Vic and Connie came. We had nothing in common. I told him to get a job.

The priest came.

"How the hell you been, priest?" I asked him.

"I'm well," he said. "And you?"

He was a big joker, that priest.

"Me? I'm great. I'm pretty fucking wonderful."

"It's good to see you again," he said.

"Father," I told him, "I appreciate the sentiment. But with no disrespect meant toward you, I'd just as soon never have seen your dago ass again."

"I can see how you might feel that way," he said, the bastard.

He asked me about the family. What was there to say? To tell him all the pathology would take too long. I told him the family was great.

We sat through a long silence. The priest's fingers drummed on his communion box.

"For God's sake," I said, "will you quit that?"

He quit. "You seem upset," he said.

"Me? Why should I be upset?"

"Because you're sick. Many of my sick patients are upset."

"Are they?"

I tried to load that with sarcasm. I was sick of sickness and sick people. They held no interest for me. The priest kept on, though.

"Yes," he said, deadpan. "It must be hard to face, I'm sure, especially when you're young. I'm sure it must be frightening."

"I'm sure, too," I said.

"You told me once before that you had faith," he said.

"I was lying."

"No. I could tell. In your own way, you did. You still do, though your illness makes you angry. I like that about you."

"Spare me," I said.

"You really are angry, aren't you? I understand. In your place, I don't know what I'd do."

"You'd be sick, like me."

He smiled. I wanted to slug him. I wanted to throw him out. But he was entertaining, in his way. I let him go on.

"This hospital," he said, "is enough to shake anyone's faith. It shook mine, and I'm well."

"None of us is well," I interjected. He ignored me.

"It's hard to believe, seeing what goes on, that there's meaning to this, that God cares."

"He doesn't care. He's laughing at us."

"But," the priest went on, "once the people understand that he does care, once they come to see their lives in the continuity of life and God's plan, they find their illnesses easier to accept."

"I don't have any problem with accepting," I said. 'I'm going to die like a firefly in God's jar. I accept that. That's cool by me. Maybe I should look forward to it more."

The priest just smiled, unbelieving. It was a beatific smile. He should have had it framed and hung up in a church.

"You," I said, "are a patronizing bastard, and God's an asshole."

I turned my back to him and pulled the sheets over my head. He gave up trying to strengthen my faith and talked for a while about his home. That was easier to listen to. I dropped the sheets back down. When he left we shook hands.

After he was gone I thought about him. Hell, he was a decent guy. He had tried hard. I thought I'd do him a favor. I had one of the nurses call him back the next day.

"You wanted to see me?" he asked.

"Yeah," I said. "I want to make confession and take communion."

His face lit up. At least somebody would get something out of my sickness. He would tell people about me for the rest of the month, at least, long after others in the hospital had forgotten me.

"I'm sorry," I said. "I've forgotten the forms."

He put his hand on mine. "I'll help you," he said.

We got through the formalities. He was radiant. I fed him a list of good sins. I gave him enough of the details to hold his interest. It was easy; I didn't have to make up any of it.

"And you're sorry now?" he asked.

"Yes," I said, and it was true. I was sorry nothing had ever come of it.

"What do you think would be a good penance?" he asked me.

"I could go on living," I said.

He didn't find that funny. He gave me lots of prayers to say. I told him I didn't remember how. He left me a missal with all the words printed out.

I sat back, after the pep talk was over, after the priest had gone. I read through the prayers. They were good prayers. They reminded me of my grandmother. And see where they had brought her. Well, she had liked them. I said a few for her. I said them over and over. There was a nice rhythm to them. When that got dull, I said some for my mother and father, for Connie and Vic. I said some for everybody in the family that I could remember. God knew they all needed prayers. I fell asleep before I got around to saying any for me.

The fevers were relentless. Nobody seemed to know what the hell was going on. The doctors' visits were perfunctory. There was nothing new for them to tell me—nothing good, anyway—and they were tired of my questions.

A new student came. He was a sweet kid, a twerp. He was very shy. I didn't have time for it.

"How do people think I'm doing?" I asked him after we'd traded formalities.

He frowned, unsure of how to phrase himself.

"It's that bad?" I said. "You're afraid to tell me?"

"No," he said. He fumbled with his tongue a moment. After a time he got it untied. "They say you're about the same," he told me.

"Well," I said, "that's not very good, is it?"

"I don't know," he said.

"You don't know? Listen: medical students never know much, but you ought to know the obvious. Have you read about my disease?"

"Yes."

"And can you tell me the prognosis of victims of acute

myelogenous leukemia who've failed primary chemotherapy and whose secondary treatment is deferred because of sepsis?"

"It's not very good," he said. It took him quite a long time to say it.

"Actually," I told him, "it's terrible. They all die."

He looked most uncomfortable. I liked that. It made me feel useful. It was what he paid fifteen thousand a year to feel.

"Now," I said, "tell me what they really say about me."

He looked around the room, at the ruined sheets, at the window, at his hands, at me. But there was nothing to do except answer the question.

"They say we have to wait and see where your fever's coming from."

"I see," I said. He was sweating. I took a long breath. "Listen," I went on, "you need to learn some medical jargon. Have you learned much yet?"

"No," he said, looking glum.

"You should," I told him. "It's important. It trivializes the unbearable aspects of your job. It trivializes your patients. It provides you with euphemisms that help you to put aside the thought of dying before it can touch you. Doesn't that sound useful?"

"No," he said.

"Well, it is. Now, let me tell you what my colleagues say about me in the jargon of medicine."

We looked at each other's eyes. His were a pale blue-gray pastel, like his tie. They were steadier now; he didn't try to like me anymore.

"I'm circling the drain," I said to him. "That's an expressive metaphor, a nice concrete image, with just the right sense of inevitability, and it leaves an accurate impression of how long and painful the last sucking swirl can be. They say that about me, don't they?"

"Yes," he said hesitantly.

"They say that I'm going to get the big biopsy this time, that I'll earn a celestial discharge, right?"

"Sometimes."

I sat back on the rumpled pillows and tried to rub away the insomnia behind my eyes. I was surprised to find out how much the truth still could hurt me.

"All right," I said, "that's our lesson for today. Now listen to my chest and get lost. Please."

He did as he was told. He said nothing more, but his eyes were eloquent: he hated me.

That afternoon D'Andrea dropped by.

"It's this way," he said. "Your last chest films show fluid on your left lung. I think it's your fever source."

"You think it's pus?"

"Yes."

"Can you tap it?"

"I think so."

"Christ. You inspire such confidence."

"You asked for it straight," he said.

"We haven't had much luck with anything else so far," I said with a shrug.

"Sure we have," he told me. "If we hadn't, you wouldn't have made it even this far."

I looked at my arms, at the bruises from the needles. "What about my low platelet count?" I asked. "You don't think I'll bleed?"

"We'll have to transfuse you," he said. It was his turn to shrug.

"I don't have much choice, do I?"

"No," he said.

"I could die from this needle."

"You could die from undiagnosed sepsis."

"I could die, or I could die."

"Yeah."

"Nice choice."

"In the end, that's what it comes down to for everybody."

"You're such a philosopher."

"Look," he said, "you're Italian, aren't you?"

"No. Sicilian."

"Even worse. Well, dago boy, I hear from your student

that you like it brutal. That's how I'm giving it to you. Don't you like it?"

We glared at each other, bristling like street dogs. I got tired first.

"I like it fine," I said. "I'll quit feeling sorry for myself. Go ahead: stick me."

"All right," he said.

He got up to go out. I stopped him.

"There was a reason I did that to the medical student," I said.

"Yeah?" he asked, thoroughly skeptical.

"I'm not going home this time, whatever you say. I'm not even going to make it to the end of this rotation. He'll have to watch. It won't be nice. But he hates me now. When I go out, however I go, he won't give a damn. I didn't want that on my conscience."

D'Andrea went out, shaking his head.

While the yellow platelets in their plastic packs dripped into me, I ran through the prayers again. They weren't helping.

I was coughing. I could bring nothing up, and nothing they gave me could make me stop. And each cough hurt like an evisceration.

The intern came in. We went over the papers that listed the name of the procedure, the indication, all the possible complications. I signed it: I accept, it said, the risks of pain, bleeding, infection, pulmonary puncture and collapse, and death.

"So, man," I asked him, "how big is this fluid pocket we're going after?"

"Big enough."

He was very cocky. For him it was all routine.

"You've done a lot of these taps, I suppose," I said.

"Oh, yeah," he said.

"And you're good?"

He smiled and patted me on the shoulder patronizingly. "I never miss," he said.

I went cold all over.

"Knock on wood," I said. "God hears you say things like that."

But he only laughed and took the permit away. I sat alone, in a chill sweat, waiting. The platelets were in. There was no sense in procrastinating, I told myself. I was not very convincing.

Hunched over a bedside tray, rubbing at the fire in my eyes, I made myself think of Mama. In a few hours she would come back. She would force the same sad smile on those same soft lines. She would hold my hand again. She would tell me the usual things, things she had told me the day before, things like how Terry's oldest looked at his first communion, how Papa's bronchitis had flared, how the garden looked with the zucchini and the peppers fattening, the snap beans growing long. She'd tell me about how the warm wind blew in through the lace kitchen curtains in the late afternoon and about how fine it would be when we all sat around the table together again.

The intern's knock cracked open my reverie. My memories of Mama spilled from my mind.

"Are you ready?" he asked brightly.

"No," I said, "but we might as well start."

I took off my pajama top. The medical student pulled my bed away from the wall. They sat me up on the edge of the bed. I sagged over the bedside tray, resting on my pillow.

They went over my back with their fingers, tapping up and down, over skin that resonated hollow or dull, to find the fluid.

"Here?" the intern asked.

D'Andrea repeated the percussion, sounding out my sickness. "A little lower," he said. "Here." He marked the skin with the edge of his thumbnail.

They painted my back with iodine. The soft brown circles they drew with their swabs extended onto my flanks. The stain stood out starkly against my pallor. The iodine ran down my back and collected in the waistband of my pajamas. I shivered.

"Are you all right?" the intern asked.

"Yes," I said, very softly.

"Not nervous, are you?"

I sat straight and turned to him, angry at his posturing. "Should I be?" I asked him.

"No," he said. But the brashness in his voice had faded. "I suppose it's always easier from this end of the needle."

He set up his needles. I wondered if he really was nervous himself, if that was why he'd asked if I were, too. I wondered if he felt the same tension in the belly, the same heat over the face, the same sweat at the temples and under the arms, that I used to feel every time I had to put a needle into somebody. I wondered if he were cool or if his hands shook where I couldn't see. I thought about the chest taps I'd done. I wondered how they'd really felt, and I knew that I didn't want to learn. I wondered if I could still do the same clean sticks I used to do, and I knew I'd never know.

Then the needle bit me, broke skin and burned me as the anesthetic infiltrated and the nerves went dead. The needle went in low on the left side, inside the shoulder blade.

"Can you feel this?" asked the intern. He was prodding me with the point of the needle, testing the anesthesia. I knew that, because that was the way it was always done. I could feel nothing.

"No," I said.

That was the right answer, so he went on. His fingers fanned across my side. The needle went in, went in deep, and the sensation of unbearable, unnatural pressure that was almost pain radiated over my back. I had to cough, and I had to not cough. I sat very still, fighting myself silently to stay that way.

"Aspirate," said D'Andrea to his intern. His voice was calm, reassuring. "Nothing? All right, then: go deeper. . . . No: more slowly. Then back out. . . . Good. Now pass the needle again. . . . No: angle up more. More. Tip the needle up more. . . . No: up like this."

They went on and on like that. The pain began. It started as a point, a tiny seed, and it swelled, burst, and blossomed bright red and yellow across the breadth of my consciousness. It welled up, filling me; it flooded me, lapping at the borders of my being and body, rippling back in interwoven waves to fill all the lost interstices of my brain. It lifted me, whipped me spinning and sprawling into a spangled, tangled starburst of brilliant light.

"Oh, Jesus," I said.

Then I was on my back. Something was wrong. Distorted faces whirled over me. The ugly pastel walls, miles away, fell in on me and receded into infinity, oscillating wildly with the edges of my awareness.

The medical student was kneeling on the foot of the bed with my feet on his shoulders. A nurse next to us was doing a mad squeeze job, inflating, deflating, and reflating a blood pressure cuff while shaking her head. Across from her, the resident was trying to drive a big-bore catheter into my useless veins. D'Andrea was standing over me, talking too fast for me to follow.

More nurses came. The resident's needle went in; the pain was nothing. There was the burning chill of saline pouring up my arm and into my chest.

The room was full of small noises melded in a crescendo of unintelligibility: cellophane wrappers popping, cardboard tearing, the cardiac monitor beeping. Furniture scraped against the floor as people cleared a space around my bed. A cacophony of whispered shouts, all full of adrenaline, crowded the close air.

Against one wall, the intern stood alone. He looked like a man who'd been shot and was waiting to learn just how dead he really was.

After a time the noise subsided. My belly was rigid and sore. D'Andrea was standing beside me. My hand lay limp in his grip.

"I think we've lacerated your spleen," he was saying. I tried to figure out whether that was important, but the effort was beyond me. "We've got to get you to the OR. I've called MacKinnon. You like him, I know. He's on the way down from afternoon rounds with his chief resident. The blood bank is trying to get us red cells and platelets. We'll get enough cross-matched to float you out of this. But you have to go to surgery. Do you understand me?"

"Yes," I said, "and thank you." But of course the words

didn't come. I tried a brave smile, but my face wouldn't move. I looked up at him as he waited for my answer. I looked at the broad, lined forehead, with the thick blond hair—usually so carefully groomed—falling all over it. I looked at his eyes, usually so gray and cool, and at the brows now drawn down over them. I looked at the crow's-feet around the eyes, lines deep and taut and angry and hurt, and at the tight, thin line of his lips. I looked into his eyes and saw his despair being born.

I felt sorry for him. I knew how he felt, knew the doctor's sense of grief and impotence and humiliation. I had felt all that once, too. I tried to speak a word of consolation, knowing the futility of words before the reality of death. I knew that he would reproach himself: in his eyes he had failed again in his fight against cancer. He had lost, again. The disease had beaten him, again. That was the way he would see it. I tried to tell him that he was wrong, that losing was nothing, because it was inevitable, that fighting was everything. He was a good fighter. He had been very good to me.

I tried to tell him that, but my mouth never moved, and besides, he had stood up and turned away. He was calling someone's name.

The room was enormous, and people came from everywhere to fill it. They all went to work on me.

But I wasn't there anymore. I watched them from a long distance, deep inside myself. The periphery of my vision constricted as they struggled. It closed down, like the diaphragm on a microscope, to a spot of white light that went gray, the gray ashimmer with scintillation. That point of light faded away as imperceptibly as a winter sunset on a western sea until, finally, there was only the comfort of blackness.

pilgrims

For twelve hundred years pilgrims have been journeying to Santiago de Compostela, that they might discover the grace of God. We traveled there to explore the wilderness of love—the same reason, after all.

From Madrid we had planned to drive straight to the coast. But like so many other things we intended, in the end we were too tired to bring it off. Our flight had been delayed in New York. We had slept poorly on the plane. We had missed our turn onto the N-6 out of the capital. And so, lost, exhausted, and confused, we stopped for the night in Zamora.

We had crossed the Sierra that afternoon, winding up and down the pass through pine-dark mountains. We had driven for hours across the yellow plains of Castile, past red poppies nodding in the wind, past little towns baked the color of old mud, past truck stops and ox carts and the lined brown men and women of the country. We drove under an immense sky of perfect blue, under a brilliant white sun whose rays poured in through the open windows of our little car. The sunshine washed over us, as if it meant to sweep away all the responsibilities and the sorrow, the sick and the dead, that we had left behind.

It was an old story. I was a doctor, Carla a nurse, and we were lovers. She spoke no Spanish, so she drove while I studied maps and road signs and vocabulary lists, trying to remember. We drove into Zamora at eight and checked into a three-star hotel. It had a fine lobby and an elegant staircase, deep carpets, and much marble, but it had no air-conditioning. By the time we checked in the only vacancy was a room with twin beds. It smelled of dust and disinfectant and other lodgers' clothes. We took it, too tired to search elsewhere.

The room looked out over a street of shops. The sidewalk below the window was crowded with people in bright colors. We showered and changed and went out among them.

We had not eaten since a late breakfast on the plane. We checked out a couple of restaurants, but they all were closed until nine. We wandered up and down cobbled streets with our arms around each other, caught up in the paseo. We went window-shopping, looking at the shoes, the baby clothes, the books, the dead fish and plates of food. A bar was open. There were kids inside, dressed up in neon colors, listening to the Doors and eating hamburgers.

"We could eat here," she suggested.

"You don't want to eat here," I told her. "It's only twenty minutes till the restaurants open. We'll make it."

"Hold me up till then," she said as she leaned on me. "I don't remember when I've ever been this hungry."

We went back to a place I had seen off the main street. We went up to the bar and asked for a table in the dining room. A waiter came up.

"The *comedor* is closed," he told me.

I looked at my watch. It was two minutes to nine.

"Don't be an asshole," I said in English.

He shrugged, not comprehending, and went over to a table to watch the end of an American cop show dubbed for Spanish TV. Carla and I stood at the edge of the barroom, our arms touching as we leaned against the wall. When the time was up and the commercials came on, the waiter came back.

"Please," he said with a grand gesture. "Pass inside."

I gave him a great smile. "Sure," I said, bowing and smiling, "and fuck you, too."

The waiter shrugged again. He seated us and gave us menus. Carla tried not to laugh.

"I was reading on the plane about the legendary courtesy of the Spanish people," she said.

"We're still in the city," I told you. "You'll see. It's not all like New York."

The dining room was paneled in oak and upholstered in red velvet. The linen was stiff with starch and very white. There were huge bouquets of flowers in cut glass vases at every table. There was no one else in the room. We ordered a bottle of Rioja to drink with my beefsteak and her pork loin. The food came on huge platters. We sopped up the gravy with the crusty bread and left nothing but the bones.

"Do you feel better?" I asked.

She filled my glass with the last of the wine, then leaned across the table and put a finger to my lips.

"You were right to wait," she said.

We took a stroll to the plaza near the cathedral. A couple stood necking in the darkness under an arch to the Fascist dead. We passed them, passed on down the street to the river overlook. Carla took me in her arms and kissed me. We went on like that for a long time. At last she broke away.

"Do you remember the way back?" she asked.

"Sure. I was a Boy Scout once."

"Take me there, then."

We moved past stuccoed buildings yellow under the street lamps, past the black grillwork, past young women in white and blue and red who ran giggling and shouting from an alleyway. An old man was sweeping the steps in front of the parador. The paseo was over. The streets were nearly empty. The cobbles were littered with dead cigarette butts and plastic popsicle wrappers. We got the key to our room from the bellhop and walked up the wide stairs, holding hands. She went into the bathroom. I opened the window and watched the last stragglers going home. After a while she opened the door and called to me.

She was standing in front of a mirror and brushing out her hair. She had on only a towel. She took my face in her hands and bussed me on the nose. "What is this?" she asked.

"It's a bidet."

"A what?"

I explained to her the uses of a bidet. She looked at me skeptically.

"They have a separate appliance for that?" she asked.

"Some people think it's uncivilized not to."

"Are we uncivilized?"

I unbuttoned my shirt and undid her towel. I held her against my skin.

"We try to be," I said.

I went to the bed away from the window and turned down the sheets. She lay back on the mattress with her arms above her head, like Goya's Maja, gazing at me while I undressed. I bent down and kissed her: her lips, the lobes of her ears, the points of her breasts, her navel, the arch of her mons. Then I moved my face back up to hers.

"Welcome to Spain," I whispered to her.

"It's wonderful to be here," she said. She smiled at last and closed her eyes as I slid inside her.

When she was asleep, I got into the empty single bed. I lay in the dark. I could not sleep. I got up and read a guidebook and a map, sitting on the toilet in the bathroom so the light would not wake her. I read until I was too tired to see. Then I turned out the light and got back into bed.

I am in the hospital, in the intensive care unit. I am at the bedside of my patient. She is a very old woman with thin hair gone yellow with age. Her arms are pudgy with edema. A respirator tube is taped to her face, and the tape warps her mouth into a grimace of the pain of unconsciousness. As I stand by, her heart stops beating. I mount up onto the edge of the bed and place my hands on her chest, bobbing up and down in an effort to resuscitate her. Her eyes are open but lifeless. They stare at me. We go on and on, until my elbows lock and my shoulders cramp. There is no one to relieve me. The woman's heart is dead, she is dead, but I cannot stop. We go on and on together. We are linked for eternity, the doctor and the corpse.

I woke alone in the narrow bed. I was wet with sweat in the stuffy room. I reached out for Carla, but she was not beside me. I sat up suddenly, confused, then saw her in the other bed. She lay with the sheet half off her naked body. The wrinkles around her eyes and her mouth and in her cheeks and around her nipples showed up cruelly in the bad light. She turned onto her side and drew up her knees, like a child. I whispered her name. She did not stir.

I went to the window. The cool night air flowed in over the sill. A drunk in dirty trousers was shambling down the sidewalk. A black-and-white dog followed with its tail between its legs. Later, two men walked up the street, dragging sacks of garbage to the corner. A truck drove up and wheezed to a stop. Empty bottles shattered as the men threw in the sacks.

After they were gone, only a stork's guttural croak sounded in the darkness. I looked out at the jumble of tiled roofs and antique chimneys below me. All I could see was the dead woman of my dream staring at me. I lay down on the bed with a pillow over my face, and still the dead eyes bored into me. I had fled from women like her to another country. My love lay sleeping in the bed beside me. And yet I could not shake the nightmare visions of death that had become more a part of me than the white coat and the stethoscope and the doctor's life that I had left behind.

In the morning the Castilian sun came blazing in through the open windows. I got up to let down the blinds. Carla was sitting up in bed, studying a map.

"Where are we going today?" she asked me.

I sat on the bed beside her. She leaned back against me and

nestled her head against my shoulder. I traced out the road with my finger.

"Where shall we stop?" she asked.

"Wherever you'd like."

"And when will we get to the coast? It's been so long since I've seen the ocean."

"Whenever you want to."

I said that, but I was distracted by my worries and the memory of my dream. I thought about how short a time two weeks can be, when there is so much to do, so much to learn, and so much of the world to see. I thought about how brief a life can be, when one has so much love to give and so few words.

She sensed my abstraction. "What is it?" she asked. "I know we didn't get a chance to talk much yesterday, but we were both tired. Aren't you having a good time?"

"Yes," I said.

"Then what's the matter?"

I shook my head.

"I love you," she ventured. "You can talk to me."

I ran a finger down her cheek, down the line of her neck and the curve of her breast, round the sudden hard rise of her nipple, along the edge of her ribs, the indentation of her flank, the swell of her hip. My fingers tickled into her hair. She turned and pushed me back on the sheet and spread herself above me. I stroked the skin between her thighs, the softness, the richness, the moisture. She pressed down against me, and I took my hands away. She kissed my eyes.

"God, how I do love you," she told me as she reached down and drew me inside the slick, hot grip of her vagina. We lifted and fell together on the narrow bed, lifted and fell, lifted and fell. I looked into her face, into her gray eyes, and all my nightmares fled away.

We did not get up until late morning. We went shopping for breakfast in the market building below main street. She walked up and down the aisles with our brown paper bags, pointing out what she wanted me to buy for her. I chatted with the matrons in the stalls as they wrapped up Carla's purchases. We bought cherries and peaches, a wheel of pale soft cheese, and a long loaf of bread. At a grocery on a side street, we bought liter bottles of mineral water and canned olives stuffed with anchovies. All the prices were marked in pesetas. The numbers were too large to take seriously. We paid in strange, heavy coins stamped with the faces of Franco and the king and in short, fat bills of many colors. It all seemed as unreal as our sudden happiness.

We drove out of Zamora and soon turned west, into the broken country that separates Galicia from the central plateau. We drove into the mountains, near the old pilgrim route to Santiago. The little car whined in low gear up the switchbacks of the potholed highway, past terraced vineyards and waterfalls and old women driving brown oxen through the streets of tiny towns where trees grew out over the roadway and the yards of houses were filled with rosebushes dotted with red, white, and pink blossoms as big as my hand. In the hills the forests began, lush forests a soothing green after the sere flatlands of Castile. The leaves on the trees were still fresh and pale with springtime, and the air turned cool as the evening came on.

We spent the night along the highway in a cheap *hostal* that looked out over a garden. A bent woman was weeding. I watched her work while Carla changed. Stooped over, the woman walked up and down the rows, smoothing down the soil around the seedlings of tomatoes and beans. Carla and I went downstairs and had a beer together.

"Do you mind the room?" I asked her. "If we had more time, I might have found a better one. I just got too tired to go on."

She ran her fingers over the back of my hand. I turned it over, and she pressed her palm into mine. "It's all right," she said. "We're both tired. God knows we've got a right to be. At least we can sleep together. As long as I have that, I don't need anything fancy."

We talked like that later, as we sat on the balcony with our backs up against the warm cement of the *hostal*'s south wall—

like two friends who meet after long separation. Our conversation was tentative, exploratory, superficial, trite. We spoke warily, lest one false word offend, leaving us alone in a foreign land, bereft of this love we had found long after we had ceased to hope for it. After a while even that sort of conversation died away. We ate bread and cheese and watched the sun go down over Portugal.

"We still haven't seen the ocean," she said when the darkness had come.

"We'll see it tomorrow."

"We never could have made it from Madrid in a day."

"We might have, if the plane had come in on time and we'd pressed hard."

"I'm glad we didn't. I'm so tired of pressing hard. I've been pressing hard for so long—two jobs, two kids, too much. I just want to rest."

"We'll rest," I promised her.

And that night she slept beautifully, with her head on my shoulder and her arm across my chest. I held her in my arms and watched her body move with her breathing, saw her smile in her sleep, felt her rustle against me as she shifted into her dreams. When I snuggled down under the quilt, away from the chill of the night that came in through the open door to the balcony, she half woke and rose above me and stared at me.

"I'm so happy," she said drowsily. She put her head down and nuzzled against my breast. "I'm so happy," she murmured, "so happy."

"Go back to sleep," I whispered. "I love you, too."

I ran my fingers through the curly mat of her hair and kissed the crown of her head. She settled against me and slept again.

I walk into a patient's room. She is asleep. I wake her. She is crabby and tired. She tells me to go away. But it is seven o'clock in the morning, and I must be in surgery in half an hour. I have her lie flat on the bed. In the harsh light from the overhead lamp, I take out the staples that hold together the skin over her healing abdominal incision. I go to apply the tape that will hold together the edges of her wound and notice a tiny gap in the flesh over her mons where the hair has been shaved away. I probe it with a finger, and it separates. I put my finger inside, and the hole grows. Suddenly the whole length of the wound breaks down. There is blood trapped under the skin, and it pours forth. The tissues part, and the bowel spills out onto her bed. Long coils of gut roll onto the sheet. One length spits over the edge and hangs in the air, the end dragging on the dirty floor. I look around for a dressing to cover the incision, but there is none. I look for saline to wash the bowel, and there is none. There are no gloves, so I take the bowel in my hands and try to hold it on the woman's belly. But it rolls away and falls off the far side of the bed. I cry for help, and no one hears me. The woman is screaming in pain. She is cursing me. She is cursing me. She is cursing me.

I woke with my fists clenched, my jaw clenched, my back arched, about to scream. Carla had her back to me. All the length of her spine, from her shoulder blades to the lift of her buttocks, lay against my skin. I eased out from under the covers and went into the bathroom to urinate. Then I went through the open door onto the balcony again. The hills above the river were black masses in the night. A rumbling sounded in the air, then grew louder, and the lights of a freight train came swirling down the valley. I shivered, naked in the cold, but I stood with my hands on the steel rail, cursing my job, cursing myself.

After a long time I went back inside. I stood at the foot of the bed and gazed at Carla, at her stillness, at her beauty, at the peacefulness of her sleep, at the curve of her body beneath the quilt, at the way her hair played out over the pillow and down across her face. I got back into the bed, being careful not to touch her, for fear the chill of my skin would wake her. Yet she stirred, backed up against me, turned over, and held me.

"Did I wake you?" she whispered, still asleep. "I'm sorry."

I was shivering under the covers. She came awake with a start.

"What is it?" she asked.

I could not speak. I shook my head and put a finger to her lips. She took it away and held it between her breasts.

"You're freezing," she said.

I could not answer her. She spread herself over me like a blanket. The heat of her body percolated down through me. She pressed her lips against mine, and she kept on until I lay still and warm, until I began to move beneath her gently, softly, smoothly, lovingly. I reached behind her and pulled the quilt over our heads. Our bed was a cave where my terrors could not find us. We made love together there, the two of us alone in a world of our own creation.

The rain came with the dawn. It drenched the woods and the streets and the long black strip of highway above the town. The sky was gray and lumpy. It lay heavily on the hilltops. We walked down the narrow streets of the town into the medieval quarter below the ruined castle, where the houses pressed together for shelter from the weather and the massy wooden doors shut out the chill. We walked holding tight to each other through a crowd of shoppers out to market with black umbrellas in their hands and baskets on their arms. We strolled about, poking among the vegetables for our breakfast, and then we were on the road again.

We drove through Tuy, where we walked up the hill to the fortress cathedral under an umbrella of our own, watching waterspouts jet out from mossy stones to fall on cobbles worn down by centuries of rain. We drove through the flat country of the Río Mino, where grapevines climbed up stakes of granite and bent women carried bundles of hay to mule-eared horses in the fields of black earth. At every stop I told her fragments of history, taught her about geography and ethnography and linguistics, and read to her from the guidebooks strewn across the backseat of the car.

We drove to the top of the mountain above A Garda. At the restaurant there we ate the *menu del día* by the great windows of the stone building as the clouds broke up and the mist blew away to show us the estuary and the islands where the river met the Atlantic. We could see the square red tile roofs of the town, the tiny specks of fishing boats on the river, a little toy boat that was a freighter beating upstream, and the long lines of whitecaps in the wind.

"Well," I said to her, "there's your ocean. You've arrived at last."

She stared out at the blue vastness that stretched to the edge of the world and did not say a word. She put down her knife and fork and watched the waves move across the water.

"God," she said, "it's so beautiful."

When we went outside, the clouds were gone. The sun had dried the rocks and warmed them. Carla lay down in a flat space, away from the wind and the schoolchildren who had come in the bus parked outside the restaurant. She threw the crook of her arm across her eyes while I paced about, looking here, looking there. When I glanced back at her, she was asleep. I sat on a stone beside her and read a Spanish guidebook that I had bought in the gift shop. She did not stir for half an hour. Then she opened her eyes and saw me watching her, and she smiled.

"I fell asleep," she said.

"I know. If I didn't know you better, I'd think you were getting old and lazy."

"No. I'm just getting old."

She stood up and stretched and winced as her muscles, sore from the rock, cramped.

"You're going to be stiff," I said.

She came over to where I was sitting. She put her hand on my thigh and her tongue in my ear. "That'll be a change," she said. "But then I suppose it must be my turn to do that."

I stood up and tried to catch her, but she ran away. I found her by the car, holding out her arms to me.

We stayed that night in Oia, at an inn on the beach. We were the only guests, and we had the whole upper floor to ourselves. We went for a walk along the coast road, past all the empty villas and the scrubby pines and the pastures hemmed in by walls of gray stone splotched with yellow and red by lichen. There were carnations and roses blooming in the yards, and sunflowers shone along the paths down to the water. The shore was all of stone, rocks weathered and broken, gray-and-black granite streaked with pink and ocher and olive.

When it grew dark we went inside and drank the wine of the country while our hostess taught us how to break up crabs and tear the leather jackets off barnacles to savor the pink meat inside. We went to bed with the window open and the moon shining in. The sound of the surf and the rhythms of our loving blended in the night, soft sighs that went on and on and on.

I am in the operating room. My patient's belly is open. The retractors are all in place. There is a crowd in the room. I am lecturing on the technique of radical hysterectomy. Suddenly I realize that I am not wearing gloves. I turn to the scrub nurse, and she is gone. I turn to the students, and they have left me. I peer over the ether screen to speak to the anesthetist, and she has disappeared. I am entirely alone with my patient. She begins to bleed. The blood fills up the wound. It overflows onto the floor. It fills the room. I cannot stop it. I have no instruments, no suture, no sponges, nothing. The blood rises above my knees. I try to run, but I cannot. My patient is dead, and still the blood rises, and still I am unable to move. There is a sea of blood in the room. It covers my face. I flail about in a scarlet void as it suffocates me.

The absolute blackness of the rural night overwhelmed me. I lay paralyzed in the bed, blind in the darkness, numb with fear. Under the heavy blanket, the sweat ran off me. My hair was soaked, and drops stood out on my face. Then I realized that I was in Spain, and Carla beside me. Slowly I relaxed. I got up and went to the window. I stood with my head on the window frame, resting my brow on clenched fists. I turned and slumped down against the foot of the bed. I wanted to cry, but no tears came. I went into the bathroom and took a drink of water, but it stank of sulfur, and I spat it into the sink. I paced about the room, unable to sleep, unable to stand still. I took a book into the bathroom and closed the door, but I could not concentrate to read. I splashed water on my eyes and crawled back under the bedclothes. Carla's arm went around me.

"I missed you," she said. "Are you all right? Tell me."

I did not know what to say. I could not turn to face her. I could only nod my head. She shifted her weight against me. I felt the caress of her breast against my back and her hand upon my heart. She kissed the nape of my neck and was asleep again.

We spent the morning on the battlements of Baiona, and we drove three times through Vigo trying to track down a shortcut I thought I'd found on the map. At last we caught the A-6 into Pontevedra. After the creeping trucks and hills and holes of the coastal highway, we made very good time, and we were happy, two Americans enjoying at last the speed of a small car on a good road.

We got lost in Pontevedra, too. We stopped at a cafe to drink espresso with milk and ask for directions to the provincial museum, which happened to be just outside the back door. We saw the Celtic gold and the Roman anchor and the potsherds and the heavy furniture and the few good paintings and the many bad ones. When we were hungry we walked down the street into the market, where we studied the piles of fish on ice, the stacks of chicken feet, the strings of dead pigeons, and the skinned heads of sheep and goats. We bought more cheese and bread and ate lunch on the square below the cathedral. Carla bought a straw hat with a wide blue band, and when she wore it in the sunshine so that the speckled shade came down over her tanned face, she was more beautiful than I had ever known her.

We pulled into Villagarcía at half-past three. The rain had returned. A cold wind blew the smell of dead fish out of the harbor and into the town. We were hungry. We wandered about under the dripping trees of the square, across an ancient bridge spanning a stagnant green river, past barred convent windows, through the mud of new construction, and back to the center of town. All the shops and restaurants were closed. At last we found a bar in a basement off an alleyway. We ate microwaved empanadas and Estrellas beer at a corner table. There were three men at the bar. Another stood at the electric slot machine on the far wall. He dropped twenty-five-peseta pieces into it and cursed his losses.

"How's the empanada?" I asked Carla.

"It tastes like shit," she said.

"Oh," I said. We ate our way through a long pause. "Is something wrong?"

She shrugged. "This isn't a bar for women," she told me.

I looked around at the men in their sweaters, at the soccer game on the television above the big mirror, at the dark paneling, at the women on the calendars, and I understood.

"We'll leave soon," I promised. "I'm sorry. I was hungry."

She shrugged again. "It's all right," she said. "I was hungry, too."

I got out a map and talked of places we might see before dark. She smiled and did not listen.

A woman in a black dress came down the steps from the street. She was fat and no longer young. Her legs were scarred with the varicosities of past pregnancies. Her eyebrows were heavy, and she had dark hair growing from her upper lip. She walked across the barroom floor to the man at the slot machine. She spoke to him in a sharp voice. He answered curtly. At first their voices were low. She kept asking him to come home. He tried to ignore her. She began to shout. He turned to her and told her to go away. She took him by the sleeve and tried to pull him toward the door. He hit her across the face. She staggered back but would not release him. He tore himself free and knocked her against a table. Chairs tumbled. She fell to the floor. There was blood on her lip and hatred in her eyes.

Carla ran out. I stayed to pay the check and count out change for the tip. The man at the slot machine turned back to his gambling. The woman lay silent on the floor, holding her head in her hands and shaking.

The rain came sheeting down. I ran through the puddles as it soaked into my clothes. Carla lay where she had fallen. She had the car door open. She had her head in her arms and her arms on the passenger seat of the car. She had her hips on the curb and her legs splayed out across the sidewalk. When I picked her up and turned her to face me, she hung dead in my arms. Her beautiful face had shattered into a thousand pieces. She was crying. She was choking on sobs that shook her like a storm wracking the sea. She was keening, and my murmurings could not stop her. I kissed her—her lips, her cheeks, the tears in her eyes, the tips of her ears, her wet hair. Suddenly she held me so tightly I could not breathe.

"Oh, God," she said, gasping as her anguish tore her. "Oh, God. Oh, God."

"I love you," I said. "Carla, I love you so."

"Hold me," she whimpered.

I could not think of anything more to say. After a time she opened her eyes. She stared at me. Then she buried her face in my neck.

"Swear to me," she said. "Swear to me that when we're married you'll never touch me like that. Swear to me you'll never hit me when you are my husband. My God, my God, my God, I would die. I would die if you ever did. I would die if I married another man who could treat me that way, the way my last husband did."

"I could never do that," I said.

She straightened and took my face between her hands. She gazed into my face as if to see into my soul.

"No," she cried, her face twisting up as the tears poured out again. Her voice rose and cracked. "Swear it to me. Swear it. Please."

"I swear," I said.

We stood in the rain by the open car. The rain beat against us. We kissed there on the street until our hearts were swept away.

In the afternoon we drove through the resort towns to the mouth of the estuary. We came to Corrubedo, a little fishing village near the end of the world. We took a room in a *hostal* just above the point. The wind picked up and blew away the rain. From our window we could see the lighthouse and the water. We drove into the village to buy water and fruit. For excitement we watched two dogs fighting over a drowned fish near the jetty. We sat in front of the harbor and ate sardines from a can with oranges and bread that we washed down with warm wine. Old men sat on the steps of the *casa do mar,* talking in low voices. Dories bobbed on the oily water. The lowering sun sparkled on the wet white walls of the houses. It was very quiet.

"What should we do?" I asked her.

She lifted her shoulders. "There's nothing to do here," she said, gazing out at the still water. "That's pretty clear."

"We can go somewhere else," I offered, though I had wanted to stay and was disappointed that the little town did not please her. "We have the whole north coast up along the Bay of Biscay still to explore."

"No," she said, turning to me and shaking her head. "There's nothing to do here, and nothing is exactly what I came here to do. You've been the one who can't sit still, the one who's always got to be on the move."

I thought about that awhile and nodded. She leaned forward and took my hand.

"What are you running away from?" she asked.

I stood suddenly as my heart jumped up. She let me go. I broke away from the question in her face. When I looked back, she was frowning.

"I wish you could tell me," she said. "It isn't me, is it?"

I took her hand and ran my lips across her fingers. "No," I said. "It isn't you. I will tell you. Before the end of the trip, I'll tell you. It's just too close to insanity for me to tell anyone about it just now."

"Even me? I'm going to be your wife, and you can't tell even me?"

"Give it time," I asked her. "Give me time. We'll get there, if you'll only give me time." She nodded, and we let the subject go.

After we had eaten we went back to our room. We walked to the lighthouse. The lighthouse keeper's wife was in the backyard, hanging up the laundry. There were dogs in the yard, cats and goats and chickens and guinea fowl. Beyond the lighthouse was the ocean. Two men in an open boat were trawling far offshore. We held hands and walked back toward the *hostal*.

Above the town stood a cemetery. The soil was too stony for graves, so the dead had been laid out in tiers above the ground, with their names and the dates of their births and deaths graven at their feet. They were ranked in very ordered columns and rows inside the high stone wall. They lay eight deep. Carla came up from the road and saw me reading the inscriptions through the grillwork of the gate. She was mesmerized. Then at last she turned away and put her arms around me. I held her fast. She nestled her face against my cheek and my hair.

"What is it?" I asked. She only shook her head. She nestled up against me, and she shivered.

"Are you cold?" I asked.

"No," she said. "I'm afraid. I'm afraid of being dead. I'm a labor nurse. I work with sick women every day. Sometimes I see their babies die. Sometimes I see them born dead. I have to watch them hold their lost dreams and try to comfort them as they grieve. I try not to think about death. But I wonder. I see something like this, so many of the dead laid out together, and I wonder, and I'm scared for myself. What will happen to me when I die? What will happen to my children?"

"They're good kids. They'll be fine."

"But I want to be with them forever."

"Maybe you will be. That's what religion is for."

"But you don't believe in religion."

I ran my fingers over her lips. "You're my religion," I told her.

I kissed her, there on the side of the road, in the shadow of the cemetery gate. There was no one to see us but a pair of donkeys in a pasture.

"Is that better?" I asked.

"Yes," she said.

"Besides," I told her with a smile, my hand smoothing down her windblown hair, "we don't need to worry about dying any time soon."

"No?"

"Remember: only the good die young."

"And we're no good?"

I shook my head. She thought awhile.

"I've tried to be good," she said bitterly. "I wanted so much to be good. Instead I've been only human."

"That's one of the things we have in common."

"Are there others?"

"We love each other."

"Yes," she said. "There's that. There will always be that."

That night we went to bed with the sound of the sea coming in through the window again. There were clouds building, and the surf was heavy. We made love on the thin mattress. She was very gentle to me. We went a long time. Afterward she lay with her arms and legs tight around me as thunderheads rumbled ashore.

"Sometimes," she said to me while raindrops spattered on the windowsill, "I feel so broken inside. Everything is smashed. And then you touch me like that. You touch me deep inside, where no one has ever reached me. You touch me where I had been hiding for so long, with all my hurt. You touch me, and you heal me. Thank you for that."

"You're welcome," I whispered.

I am standing by a bed on the labor ward, looking at a fetal monitor tracing. The woman on the bed is young and beautiful. She has long dark hair that spills over her shoulders. She is lying on her side with her hands on her belly, watching me. As I run the scroll of the tracing through my fingers, the baby's heart rate begins to fall. I stand and wait for it to rise back to normal. Instead it drops toward zero. The beeps and flashes of the monitor grow infrequent. Minutes pass. I call for help, and no one comes. I try to move the bed, but it is locked to the floor. I try to pick the woman off the bed to carry her into surgery for the cesarean section that may save her child, but she weighs more than all the world, and I am too feeble to lift her. I stand over her with my arms around her. I am gazing into her great doe-brown eyes. I see the trust in them, the depth of her faith in me, her doctor, but I am powerless to help her. Her eyes paralyze me, even as panic wells up inside me. I call

out one last time, and no voice comes from me. I stand by, frozen with
horror, as we listen to her baby die.

My pulse was racing, and my mouth was dry. The sweat
stood out on my face in the chill of the unheated room. My eyes
were open wide. My body was rigid. The evening rain had
stopped. The wind had died. Now and then a lonely car passed.
There were no other sounds, save the ceaseless, cyclic sigh of
the falling surf. The *hostal* sign had been switched off, and there
were no lights on the road. The room was black, and I could see
nothing. I lay awake in the blackness, remembering patients
who had died in my care, patients whose complications haunted
me, patients whose surgeries had salvaged lives left too crippled
to enjoy.

Carla turned over in her sleep. She looked at me.

"Did I wake you?" she asked, rising onto her elbows. "I'm
sorry. I know how tired you are. I know how hard you've been
working these last few months. I try not to wake you, but
sometimes I just can't sleep. I'm sorry if I disturb you."

I put her hand to my breast so she could feel the beat of my
heart. "You disturb me all right," I said to her.

She smiled and curled up around me. She laid her head on
my chest. "In the beginning," she told me, "when we first came
to Spain, I was so tired that I slept like the dead, and nothing
could wake me. Now, though, I lie awake till past midnight. I
see you sleeping, and you comfort me. But then I wonder what
will become of us, what will become of me. I wonder if you'll
ever open up and talk to me. I'd hoped for so much from this
trip. I'd hoped to learn who you are, to learn if we could live
together. Now I lie in bed and worry and worry. It does me no
good, but I can't help it. I'm sorry if I wake you sometimes."

I pressed her cheek against my heart. I had so much to say
to her that I could not speak.

In the morning we went into the village to buy groceries
for lunch. We met women in black scarves walking home from
market with their purchases in blue plastic bags. We wandered
along the crooked streets. We went into the village church. It

was cool inside, out of the sun. A bent woman walked up and down the pews with a feather duster as Carla knelt to pray. Then we walked among the houses. They were painted white or blue or green, some decorated with square tiles of bronze and aquamarine. They glinted in the sun. Two girls in short dresses ran past us. Carla stopped and bit her lip. She turned to me and hugged me tightly.

"You miss your kids, don't you?" I asked.

"God—so much I can't tell you."

"I'm sure your mother's spoiling them."

"Oh," she said, "I'm sure they're fine. I just miss them."

"Well, you'll be with them soon enough."

"Aren't you ever jealous of them?"

"No. I love them, too. I want to see them grow up. I want to see them happy with us."

She stopped. She pulled away. I let her go. She stared at me.

"Don't say that unless you mean it," she cautioned me.

"I mean it."

"I thought you didn't like children."

"That was before I met yours. Now I dream about the time when we might have little ones of our own."

She frowned for a minute. She walked ahead of me as we strolled down the smooth asphalt of the street for a hundred yards or so. Then she paused and took my hand again.

"You don't believe me, do you?" I asked her. In answer she pulled me around and into her arms.

"I love you so. I wish I could tell you how much. That's what I don't believe in. Nothing like you has ever happened to me, and when you tell me things like that, I die, for fear I'll lose you."

"There's no reason to die," I told her. "As long as you love me, I'll never go away from you."

Every day we went walking. We walked along the beach, holding hands, our shoes slung over our shoulders by the laces and our pant legs rolled up high. We walked in the run of the surf as it raced up the strand and chilled our feet. Little birds ran in and out of the waves. The sand was banded with the blue-black lines of broken mussel shells washed up by the tide. We walked into the dunes. The seed heads of the yellow-green beach grass waved fretfully all around us. The ocean hissed on the rocks of the point. We sat in the lee behind the dunes and read, facing each other, only our sandy bare toes touching.

We walked to the headland north of the lighthouse. The fields that our path ran through were blocked off into little polygons by granite walls splotched with yellow lichen and green moss. There were haystacks and piles of orange kelp in the yards of farmhouses that we passed. In the black loam of backyard gardens grew turnip greens and kale, beans lashed to tripods of sticks, the spiky leaves of onions, radishes, tomatoes, peas, and corn. Sheep huddled against the wind on the hills, looking forlorn after a shearing. A young cowherd sat reading atop a boulder while her horse and cattle grazed. She did not notice us, and we passed on without speaking.

We walked up through the dense low nettles that grew above the beach to where the thick green grass and the morning glories grew among the rocks. We walked up into the heather, through the stunted purple thistles, stumpy gray-green weeds, and brittle little bushes dense with pink-and-yellow flowers. We crossed over the hills to the mountain above the town. We walked up through a forest of eucalyptus and pine, the needles soft, the brown fallen leaves crisp underfoot. The sun was strong, but under the trees the air was cool and perfumed with the scent of the forest. The weight of the knapsack with the bottle of water and the bread and the jar of olives and the soft yellow cheese in white paper and the pair of sweatshirts felt good against my shoulders. We came out onto a crown of rock at the summit. We stood looking out to sea, our hair whipped back, our clothes pressed against our bodies as the sweat of the climb dried suddenly in the stiff wind. We stood close together, sheltering each other from the cold.

"What do you see?" she asked.

"If I look hard," I said, "I think I can see New York."

"Can you?"

"Sure. There's the statue in the harbor with her torch lit, waiting for us to come home. Beyond that is the skyline, and the place where my brother works. Then there are the Catskills, and beyond them, my parents' house. If I look close, I think I can see my mother on the back porch reading a magazine."

"Do you miss your family?"

"Sometimes."

"And do you miss your home?"

I turned to her, frowning. "You're my home," I told her. "You're all the home I'll ever need."

At the *hostal,* we were hungry every night, and we ate our way through the menu. We had sole fried with lemon. We had sea bass and hake poached in wine. We had mussels four inches long stewed in tomato sauce. We had crabs in many sizes that we cracked open with pincers. We had scallops in sherry, clams and cockles in their own juice, prawns and *langostinos* in melted butter. We drank it all down with cold pale Vina Costeira, and we went to sleep every night in each other's arms, tired and satisfied and learning to be happy.

I am in a hospital room. On the bed is a cancer patient. She is my patient. I have done her surgery only a few days before. I have told her that she may be cured. She smiles to see me. It is time to remove the dressing from her wound. She steels herself as I peel back the adhesive tape from her skin. As the dressing comes away, a stench comes up from the incision that drives me back. I force myself to lift the bandage. There are maggots in the wound. They are alive, and they quiver in the fluorescent light. The smell is so strong that I vomit on the floor. The stink fills my nose. It fills all my senses. I touch the wound. My finger sinks into the putrescence, and I cannot withdraw. My hand is drawn into the squishy pulp. My arm follows. I feel my whole body being sucked into the purple flesh and the squirming worms. The woman's eyes meet mine. She is screaming. I am screaming.

I woke up sick. My throat was filled with acid. I went into the bathroom. I threw up into the toilet. I told myself that the problem was only bad seafood and too much wine, but I knew that I was lying. I washed my mouth out with water from the bottle of *agua mineral* that Carla used to brush her teeth.

Sitting in an armchair with open suitcases spilling dirty clothes all around me, I looked at Carla. She was smiling in her sleep. She had her hands on the pillow by her face, and she was smiling in her dreams. The tendrils of her dark blond hair curled all about her face. She lay on her side, the way she liked to sleep. One breast was half-exposed. As I watched her, she woke. She did not move, except that her eyes opened, and she smiled to see me. I got out of the chair and knelt by the bed. I put my face up to hers. She lifted her mouth to be kissed, but I would not meet her lips. Instead I ran my nose across her skin. The smell of her soap and the smell of her sweat and the scent of our love drove out the stench of my dreams. When at last I fell asleep again, I did not dream.

In the morning we left Corrubedo. We stopped at Padron, where an unkempt priest showed us the mooring stone of St. James. He told us all the legends of the saint's journey from Jerusalem to Spain, of the discovery of the body, and of the crusades against the Moors. He told us of the miracles that had befallen pilgrims in Santiago through the centuries. He told us tales of the sick who had been made well, the dumb who had found speech, the lame who had learned to walk. We listened politely, and when he paused I translated his narrations for Carla. When he found out that we were Americans, he asked us if we had ever met Fernando Lamas, his television idol. We told him we had not. He was deeply disappointed. But we bought many picture postcards from him, and he grew happy again. We left him waving from the door of the old church as our little car skipped over the hills to Santiago and the end of our pilgrimage.

We walked up the steps beside the parador and came out onto the plaza, where the facade of the cathedral leapt suddenly from the cobblestones, its baroque spires stretching up all the way to God. We looked in for a moment, wandering the apses, numbed by the vast beauty of the place. Then we went up and down the narrow streets of the old town, ringing bells at every *hostal* we could find. We found a room at last, a third-floor walk-up with a window that looked out on the park and the banks and the buses and the bustle of the new city. After we had showered, we went out to a restaurant near the university.

"Try it," I said.

"Never," she told me.

"You've never had it."

"No."

"What about all the other things you refused to consider till I got you to try them?" I asked, leaning forward. "You liked them, didn't you?"

She blushed, nodding her head, so I ordered a plate of octopus. The skin was a dark orange brown flecked with red pepper, and the meat was white and chewy. We anointed it with lemon and washed it down with a bottle of Ribeiro. We watched students from the university sitting at trestle tables along the walls, debating the merits of political candidates while we toyed with each other's hands. We were happy in the restaurant, and when we had eaten, that happiness swept us down brightly lit streets to our room. It carried us through the evening, while we played together in the big bed above the noise of the city. And it stayed with us as we fell asleep all tangled together in the lingering heat of the vanished day with a sheet and our sweat wrapped around us.

I am standing by an operating table. I have a scalpel in my hand. A woman lies before me. She is naked, and her arms are spread as for a crucifixion. Her belly is an enormous mound. She is waiting for an elective cesarean section, and I am her surgeon. I cannot see her face clearly, but she has eyes like my ex-wife's, and they gaze at me full of trust. I do not realize that she is undraped and that she has no anesthetic. I begin the operation. I cut through the layers of the abdomen. The woman watches me without moving, without pain. A fountain of amniotic fluid spews forth when I incise the womb. It flows on and on, clear water flecked white with vernix. When at last it stops, I reach into the cavity of the uterus to deliver the baby. But no fetus is there. I push my arm into the woman's body until it is buried to the elbow. The womb is wet and warm and empty. The woman stares at me in anticipation. I grope inside her to find the new life we have been hoping for, but nothing is there. Nothing is there. Nothing is there.

The noise of the traffic had grown quiet. I rolled onto my side and out of bed. I stumbled up against the wall. My legs were weak. I could not stand. I could not breathe. I knelt with my head against the wall and my hands clutching the windowsill. For the longest time I could not rise. At last I lifted my head.

Outside, the city lights burned brightly. Inside, the room was dark, and there was no sound save Carla's breathing. I let my head drop. I felt my heart beating in time with hers. At last I was able to stand. I slipped back into bed. I clung to Carla as the madness of my dreams roiled all around me. She ran her fingers through my hair and whispered of her love for me until I slid into the eddies of sleep.

In a cafe that morning we had chocolate and churros. I left her there alone to read a textbook of midwifery while I walked three blocks to a news kiosk by the park.

"Do you have the *Herald Tribune*?" I asked the vendor.

"What is that—a newspaper?"

"Yes. An American newspaper."

He laughed scornfully. He shook his head. "There are no Americans here," he told me.

I thanked him and went back to the cafe.

"No luck?" she asked.

"They don't have any American papers."

"What do you want with a newspaper? We're on vacation."

I shrugged. "I like to know what's going on."

She reached across the tiny table and took my hand. She put it to her lips. "This is what's going on," she said. "This is all the news you need to know. Why don't you sit and talk to me?"

"I talk to you all day and half the night. I thought you might want a break."

She put her book in her lap and tipped back her chair. "You talk to me about medieval history and church tradition," she said. "You talk to me about geography and geology and the migration of peoples. You talk to me about Spanish cuisine and customs and the polyglot roots of the language. You talk to me about all the places you've read about that we might see. But I didn't come here to learn about Spain. I came to learn about you and me. You tell me you want to be my husband and have children with me, but you can't seem to ever talk to me about yourself. Why is that so hard?"

I picked a guidebook out of her knapsack and looked at the pictures of Santiago landmarks. "I'm trying," was all I could offer her.

"Some days," she told me, going back to her chocolate and her book, "you're hopeless, and I wonder why I ever fell in love with you."

"Maybe because you're crazy, just like me," I ventured.

"Maybe," she said, and then at last she smiled.

All that day and the next and the next we toured churches. We studied the facade of the Obradoiro, with its elaborate spires stark against the soft and cloudy sky, its twin towers as finely worked as the silver that the old women in glasses and gray dresses sold in little shops below the Plateria portal. We inspected cornices and architraves, archivolts and friezes. We pored over guidebooks until we learned to distinguish Romanesque from Gothic from Baroque. I read to her the Spanish inscriptions on museum shelves and street signs and the Latin inscriptions on the countless tombs.

In *pastelerías* we bought lozenges of bitter chocolate and coffee, caramel and orange. In pastry shops we bought eclairs, and little glazed cakes, and cookies frosted with intricate patterns of vanilla and toffee and topped with kiwi fruit and strawberries. We ate ice-cream cones under oak trees in the park, in front of the rose garden, where old men walked with their granddaughters.

We always came back to the cathedral. We strolled about the chapels that lined the apses. Carla lit votive candles before the Virgin of Solitude. I watched her kneel to pray among the stooped Spanish women in lace veils and black dresses. I dropped twenty-five-peseta coins into offering boxes on either side of the wrought-iron grille before the statue and the altar. As we walked on, listening to the Gregorian chants playing out of loudspeakers that hung from the great granite pillars of the nave, Carla took my hand.

"What did you pray for?" she asked.

"Nothing," I said. "I haven't prayed since I was nineteen. God's never listened to me."

"Never?"

I looked at the question in her eyes. "All right," I confessed. "Once."

"Did you get what you prayed for?"

I tipped up her chin. "No. Not so much: more."

At night we left the churches, and on the creaky bed of the *hostal* I learned to thank God for the only gift he had ever given me.

I am called to see a patient in pain. It is very late, long past midnight. The hallways all are dim, and all the rooms are dark. I go up to the woman's bedside. I touch the switch, but the lights do not work. Unable to see, I ask her what is wrong. She lies in bed sobbing and will not answer. I open her chart to learn her history. All the pages are blank, and in the darkness I cannot read. I take out my stethoscope to listen to her chest, but the earpieces are gone, and I can hear nothing. I put my hands out to her so that I can examine her, understand and heal her. But her body recedes beyond my reach. Her crying grows louder. It is the inconsolable weeping of a woman with a wound that will never heal. I take her in my arms to comfort her, and her body vanishes. All that is left is the sound of her crying. That sound fills the room. It fills my mind. It fills my heart. It tears me in two. I am all alone with the sound of tears.

I stood up with a lump in my throat. I was dizzy. I stumbled to the writing table and sat alone while the walls spun around me as though I were drunk. Through the window came the sounds of traffic. I looked out. Two lovers were kissing. She was leaning against a lamppost. He had his arms inside her jacket. She stood on her toes to reach his mouth. After a very long time, they went away.

I went back to bed. Carla slept with her hand on my shoulder. I closed my eyes and listened to her breathe. I timed my breathing to hers: softly in, softly out, my love. I felt her breath on my skin, gentle, cyclic, and eternal. I shifted my body closer to hers. She curled against me. In her sleep she put a hand across my eyes. The weight of her palm lay upon my lids and smoothed away the terrors of my night.

We breakfasted on almond torte and drank *café con leche,* pouring sugar from heavy paper packets into the demitasse cups. We were walking toward the cathedral when we heard the sound of fireworks. We ran but arrived too late to see the procession. We had not known it was the Feast of Corpus Christi. The air was full of incense and burned gunpowder. The plaza was jammed with people. Behind the cathedral two men in white robes were pushing a wheeled cart covered with red-and-gold cloth and laden with flowers. On it stood a golden monstrance of seven tiers, with a hole in the center where the host had been. The two stopped on the cobbles to light cigarettes. They began handing out flowers to pretty women passing by. To Carla they gave three.

Inside the church, a mass was ending. As one set of priests walked off the main altar, a new battalion marched on. They kept the masses going in relays like that all day and into the night. We found a place in the back pews and knelt and crossed ourselves. Being both Catholic, we followed the Spanish ceremony easily enough. Being both divorced, both unmarried, and both unrepentant, we did not go to communion. Instead, when the congregation lined up to receive the body of Christ, we slipped away to the museums. We mingled with a tour group from Ireland and followed their guide, listening to his stories.

I let her go first down the cathedral steps so she would not see me slip money to the beggars who sat against the grillwork of the railings. There was a gray woman in black rags, a scabrous youth with his hair tied back and his baby daughter in his arms, a blind man with broken shoes. They held out their hands to me and murmured prayers for my soul when my coins clinked in their palms.

"So," she said when I got to the foot of the staircase, "I see you've already started trying to hide things from me."

I blushed. "You've caught me," I admitted.

She took my face in her hands. "You try to act like a hard-ass," she said. "And you're really such a softie. God knows I love you for that. I only wish you could admit the same thing to me."

"I have these dreams . . ." I began.

"Yes?" she said.

I looked up at the stained stones of the cathedral. On their weathered surfaces, on the hard features of the statues and the columns and the carven scallop shells, I read the dreams of generations of pilgrims whose feet, like mine, had worn down the ancient cobbles of the plaza. I knew the suffering that had driven them to journey to an unknown land. I felt their tears and heard their prayers for forgiveness. But my own would not come. I shook my head.

Carla bit her lip in disappointment and took my arm. She led me once around the cathedral and back inside. We walked to the sanctuary, swept along in a pilgrim crowd. We climbed the steps with them to embrace the statue of the patron saint and kneel before the golden coffin that contained his relics. Caught up in the press of the pious, I forgot that St. James was only another corpse among the many I had known. I forgot my fears. I forgot my failures. I lost myself in the ritual of veneration.

We stayed in the cathedral until after dark. Wrapped in our thoughts, we had little to say to each other. We walked back to the *hostal* in silence, undressed without speaking, and lay down in the bed without touching.

I rush into a hospital room. In my pager, a voice cries alarm. I know that there is someone dying in the room. I search about for the patient but I can find no one. There is no furniture in the room. There are no windows. There are only four flat walls painted white. They hem me in. I look for a door, but it has disappeared. I run my hands over the walls, searching for a way out, a way into the world, a way back into my life, but there is none. Then I clutch my chest as a strange pain fills it. My heart is bursting. The room begins to whirl about. It goes faster and faster. I realize that the dying one I came to save is me, and there is nothing I can do to save myself. I struggle to stand but cannot. I totter and fall. In my despair, as the room goes gray, I cry out for Carla. Her voice is above me. She is calling out to me, and her voice is all around me. She is calling my name. The sound brings tears to my eyes. I struggled to rise, and as I fall back for the last time, her hand touches me.

I woke with tears streaming down my cheeks. Carla's face was above me. Her hand was on my shoulder. Her lips were on my face, on my eyes, along my skin. She was calling my name.

"What is it?" she asked. "What's the matter, darling? Why are you crying? I'm here. You know I love you."

I closed my eyes and spoke to her. "I had a dream just now," I said, "and you were in it."

"What kind of a dream?" she asked.

"I was dying," I said, "and you saved me."

My words, held in so long, spilled out. I told her about all my nightmares and the terrors of my sleeplessness. I told her of my guilt, my doubts, and my fears, of my impotence as a doctor, and of the long years of my loneliness. Through all the explanation, she sat up in the bed with her feet curled up beneath her and her chin on her hands, studying me.

"Is it really so bad?" she asked when I had finished.

"Sometimes."

"I'm sorry."

"Don't be. It isn't your fault. It isn't anybody's fault, except mine. I chose to be a doctor. I chose to leave the town I grew up in and the people I was close to so I could live among the sick and the dying. I chose to marry a woman who could not love a man like that. I guess nobody knows how bad all that can get."

She thought awhile. "I know," she said.

"Do you?"

She nodded. She sat up a moment and looked out the window. Her gaze went off to a place much farther away than Spain. She stared into the darkness until I feared she might never return. Then she smiled and came back to me.

"Remember," she said, "that I'm a nurse. I'm a divorcée. I feel the same as you. I've failed in just the same ways. I've seen all the things that you remember. They've pushed me to the edge of madness, too, and once or twice perhaps beyond. I've been to all the places you go to in your dreams. I understand."

I sighed and looked at the ceiling. "What are we going to do?" I asked her. "Two crazy old fools like us?"

"What is there to do?" she said. "We'll survive. We have each other. We'll always have each other."

"Will we?" I asked.

"You worry too much," she said with a smile. "You need to forget your patients for a little while." She sat up above me. "They'll still be there when you go back. Just for now, I want you to forget your hurt. Forget your past. Forget your pain. Those will be there, too. Right now, I want you to dream about me. I want you to dream about this."

She put my hand to her mouth and kissed my palm. She ran her lips across my fingertips and her tongue across the pulse at the wrist. She pressed my hand against her neck. She ran it down her breast. She moved it against the smooth, flat skin of her belly. She shifted it between her legs and held it there.

"Dream about this," she said as she did all that. "And this. And this. Dream about me. Dream about the way I dream about you. Dream about our love, and make it go on forever."